BLACK HEARTED

Black Knights Inc: Reloaded

JULIE ANN WALKER

To Amanda Carlson.
Best friend. Fellow writer. Tireless cheerleader.
Thank you for always having my back, calling me on my bull crap, and
keeping me laughing. Life is better with you in it.

The greatest threat to our planet is the belief that someone else will save it.

—Robert Swan

PROLOGUE

Red Delilah's Biker Bar, Chicago, Illinois

"Ya know how they say a watched pot never boils? The same is true for cell phones. Ya keep starin' at that thing and it'll never ring."

Samuel Harwood turned his phone facedown on the table. "Sorry. Just a little distracted tonight."

Which was an odd thing for a man famous for his focus to say. A man who'd become one of the deadliest Marine Raider snipers ever to graduate the program *because* he had the rare ability to concentrate on a fixed point for hours on end.

Apparently, he wasn't the only one who found his absent-mindedness unusual. Fisher, his teammate at Black Knights Inc., lifted an eyebrow. Fisher's signature Louisiana drawl sounded round and sonorous compared to the flat Midwestern accents heard around the bar. "Anything ya want to share with the group?"

"Nah." Sam shook his head. "It's nothing."

Or it'd be nothing if she'd just text me back.

"Hmm." Fisher narrowed his eyes. "That hang-dog expression says otherwise. Looks like you're sufferin' from a bad case of woe-is-mes. Careful there, brother, those can be fatal."

"Leave him alone, Fish." Eliza reached across the table to smack Fisher's arm. "Just because we live and work together doesn't mean you have the right to shove your nose in everyone's business."

"Says the woman who knows everything about everyone," Fisher countered. "I mean, ya could probably tell me what color underwear I'm wearin' and what I had for breakfast this mornin'."

"Your underwear is black because that's the only color you own. And no." She lifted a finger when Fisher opened his mouth to say something salacious. "I haven't been snooping through your dresser drawers because I have some sort of weird boxer-brief fetish. We share a laundry room, and you have a bad habit of leaving your clothes in the dryer."

"Add that to the list of transgressions ya keep against me," Fisher grinned at her. "Lazy launderer."

"As for what you had for breakfast." She ignored him as she continued. "It was biscuits and gravy. I know that because I made it. And it's not that I know everything about everyone. It's just that I have an eye for detail. Which is undoubtedly one of the reasons you all decided to hire me."

"*We*"—Fisher pointed to his own chest and then indicated the gathered group of covert operators—"didn't have any say in that. As I recollect, *la jefa* herself insisted ya be brought in under pressure from your dear ol' daddy."

If indignation had a face, it would've been Eliza's. "Are you saying nepotism is the only reason I'm here? If you don't think I'm pulling my weight, Fish, I'd be happy to hear what you think I should be——"

"Now, hang on a minute." Fisher had the good sense to interrupt. Then he proved he didn't have any sense at all when he added, "Don't go gettin' your panties in a wad."

Eliza's top lip curled until her teeth showed. "I despise that phrase."

"Likely 'cause ya got a bit a class and talk of a person's britches goes *beyond the pale*." The last three words were said in a posh, East Coast accent that mimicked Eliza's. She opened her mouth to let him have it, but he rushed ahead. "My point wasn't that you're not good at your job. My point was that none of us had any say in the matter. That's all."

"Well, thank you *so* much for clearing that up." Her tone was the same one she'd have used had Fisher insulted all her ancestors.

Fisher Wakefield and Eliza Meadows were oil and water. Except, instead of not mixing, they mixed it up on the reg. The two of them couldn't be in the same room without bickering like siblings stuck in the backseat of the family Volkswagen on a long summer road trip.

Which, if Sam was being honest, was part of the charm of Black Knights Inc. The people who lived and worked there were more than coworkers or colleagues. They were family. The only family he'd ever known since he'd been the only son of a couple of South Side methheads and since his ex-wife had been little more than a stranger who'd accepted his ring and lived in his off-base condo for a short period of time.

His parents had spent his formative years cooking up the poor man's coke in the abandoned warehouse down the road from their shitty apartment. Which meant he'd been left to raise himself.

Feral. That was a good word to describe his pre-pubescent self. *Neglected* and *helpless* and *malnourished* all worked too. In fact, were it not for his high school baseball coach seeing something in him and giving him a purpose, he might've ended up another sad South Side statistic.

Lucky for him, instead of slinging dope he'd learned to sling curveballs. Not well enough to make it to the Majors, but well enough to get his team to the state playoffs two years running. Which is where he'd met a Marine Corps recruiter. Which is how he'd become a Raider. Which is the reason he'd popped up on Madam President's radar when she'd been looking to put together her very own fast-action response team.

And, yes, somewhere in the middle of that he'd popped the question, walked down the aisle—er, the steps at the courthouse—and *tried* as an adult to build what he'd never had as a kid. But that'd been little more than a blip on the radar of his life, over before it'd even begun. And his ex-wife *certainly* hadn't filled the hole left behind by his lackluster upbringing.

Which brings us full circle, all the way back to Black Knights Inc.

Sam celebrated the day two Secret Service agents knocked on the door of his quarters in Camp Lejeune and told him the leader of the free world was making him an offer he couldn't refuse. He celebrated because that offer hadn't just given him the opportunity to do the kind of work he'd always dreamed of doing—taking on the missions that were too hard, too hot, or too politically unwise for the armed forces or the alphabet soup of American agencies to handle—but it'd also made him part of a family.

A loud, sarcastic, often quarrelsome family. But a family all the same.

And sure, there were times he missed the routine and regimentation of the Marine Corp. Missed the structure and the stability that came from working under a strict chain of command. But he wouldn't trade the time he'd spent at BKI or the relationships he'd built there for anything.

The Marine Corp had given him people to fight beside. Black Knights Incorporated had given him people to fight *for*.

Turning his attention away from Fisher and Eliza, he avoided reaching for his phone by forcing himself to focus on his environment. On the *clink* of beer bottles and the smooth, driving beats of Chris Stapleton crooning from the jukebox. On the leather and denim covering the clientele packed into the place because it was 10PM on a Saturday night and everyone who was anyone in Chicago's biker scene considered Red Delilah's *the* place to be. On the aromas of hops and barley mixed with the saltier, earthier smell of the crushed peanut shells strewn across the floor.

Red Delilah's Biker Bar was a home away from home for the Black Knights. Owned by the wife of one of the original BKI operators, it was just about the only place where a group of big, bearded, leather-wearing men could gather without drawing attention to themselves. In fact, at Red Delilah's the Knights were just another band of tattooed, motorcycle-riding guys in a room full of tattooed, motorcycle-riding guys.

Okay, that's not exactly true.

It was *still* tough to blend in when every woman within thirty feet couldn't stop sneaking peeks their way. Blame it on Fisher, who looked like he should be on billboards hocking designer jockey shorts. Or Britt Rollins, who had the kind of boy-next-door face that made women want to ruffle his hair before taking him home to bounce up and down on his lap. Or Hewitt Burch, who'd been told he looked like Sam Heughan's beefier, handsomer brother. Or Graham Colburn, whose six-feet-five-inches of hardpacked muscle and dark, fulminating stares drew women in like moths to the flame. Or Hunter Jackson, who was…

Currently lip-locked with his fiancée.

Sam rolled his eyes at the couple snugged into the corner of the large booth the crew appropriated anytime they came to the bar. It afforded them unimpeded views of both the front *and* the back doors. Instinct, intuition, and too many missions to places where dangerous men toting deadly weapons might burst in meant the Knights couldn't turn off their training.

Even when they had a night off.

"You two remind me of teenagers in the back row of a dark movie theater," he told the canoodling pair, thinking it a wonder either of them had any skin left on their lips as often as they tried to eat each other's faces off.

Hunter came up for air, his hair mussed from Grace's busy fingers. "Jealous?" His grin was more than a little self-satisfied.

"If I'm being honest?" Sam nodded. "Yeah."

Ever since coming to live and work at the old factory building on Goose Island, he'd realized missions and mayhem, and the monotony of one-night stands, weren't enough to satisfy him.

He wanted more.

The kind of life he'd only ever seen on TV. The kind of life he hadn't thought he could have until he'd given up the career that had shaped him into the man he was—because if his ex-wife had taught him anything, it was that covert operations and matrimony didn't mix.

Then he'd seen Boss and Becky, Ozzie and Samantha, Christian and Emily, and all the rest of the OG Knights, and he'd come to realize that with the *right* woman, it *was* possible to make things work. And when Hunter—a man who epitomized the phrase *lone wolf*—told the group he was ready to settle down with Grace, that realization had been cemented.

Something Britt had recently said drifted through Sam's head. *"Whoever builds souls, built Hunter's and Grace's the same."*

Even though Sam wasn't much for religion—hell, he wasn't sure he even believed in the concept of a soul—he knew Britt was right. Hunter and Grace...*fit.*

And *that's* what he wanted.

To find the person who saw him for all he was, from his smallest weakness to his greatest strength. The person who would cry and laugh with him through all of life's sorrows and joys. The person who was as happy sitting beside him at a Sox game as she was sitting beside him on some romantic getaway.

The woman whose soul matched his own.

But where would I even begin?

The dating apps weren't helpful. A man in his line of work couldn't exactly be up-front in the whole *getting-to-know-you* game. And it wasn't as if he'd have any luck finding love at the office. The only women working at

Black Knights Inc. were either already married or…Eliza. And as beautiful and smart as Eliza Meadows was, he couldn't think of her as anything other than a sister from another mister and—

"Not to be cliché or anything." Grace dragged him from his thoughts. "But it'll happen for you when you least expect it." She squeezed his hand and he couldn't help but smirk at the proprietary spark that ignited in Hunter's eyes. "Take it from me," she continued. "One minute I was investigating the Michigan Militia. The next minute *this one*"—she jerked her chin toward Hunter—"moseyed into my life."

"I never mosey. And that's enough of that." Hunter snagged Grace's hand from Sam's and placed it inside his own.

Until Grace, Sam would've sworn Hunter didn't have a possessive bone in his body. Now? The former Green Beret seemed to be *made* of possessive bones. Or, at the very least, greedy ones.

Hunter was happiest having Grace all to himself.

"Grace is right," Eliza chimed in from beside Sam. "With those ocean eyes and that John Hamm jaw, the minute you're ready you'll have no trouble finding someone to fall into your lap."

Tell that to the woman who refuses to text me back, he thought grumpily.

Although, if there was anyone on the planet he would *never* consider for the role of Mrs. Harwood, it was Hannah Blue. Hannah, whom he'd watched trade in her undershirts for training bras. Hannah, whom he'd consoled when the "cool girls" in middle school mercilessly teased her about her new braces. Hannah, who'd been the closest thing he'd had to family before BKI had come into the picture.

That's it. One little peek.

Flipping over his phone, he checked to see if one of those wonderful red numbers had appeared beside his Messages app.

Nothing.

What the hell, Hannah?

"Good lord, brother," Fisher muttered. "Ya got it bad."

Grimacing, he slammed his phone facedown on the table. "I don't *have it bad*. *Having it bad* implies I have romantic feelings for Hannah. Which I *don't*. She's like a kid sister."

Visions of Hurricane Hannah flashed through his head. Big, dark eyes that took up too much of her face. Small, Cupid's bow of a mouth that covered a set of train-tracked teeth. SpongeBob SquarePants pajama bottoms that were frayed around the hems from her walking on them.

Except…

That wasn't Hannah anymore, was it? That was the girl from sixteen years ago.

The woman she'd grown into had amazing purple hair, an hourglass figure, and porcelain skin that looked too soft to touch. The woman she'd grown into had come back into his life like a breath of fresh air, reminding him that not *everything* from his past was dark and disturbing. Reminding him there *had* been parts of his formative years that were sweet and uncomplicated. And then she'd disappeared without a word, taking that breath of fresh air with her, and leaving him with—

"I call bullshit." Once again, it was Grace who dragged him from his thoughts. "No one obsesses over their kid sister not texting them back. Take it from me. I *have* a kid sister."

"I'm not *obsessing*." He realized his tone might invite a response of *me thinks he doth protest too much*. He tempered his next words. "I just owe her a steak dinner for helping us out two weeks ago, and I'm trying to nail her down on a time. We're flying outta here in three days, and I hate leaving loose ends behind."

Especially because, in their line of work, there was no telling if they'd make it back home in one piece. *Or if we'll make it back home at all.*

"Whatever ya need to tell yourself." Fisher smirked.

Sam was usually immune to the good-natured ribbing that came with being part of such a tight-knit crew. But something about *this* ribbing hit a nerve.

He told himself it was because what they were insinuating gave him the ick. To think he could view Hurricane Hannah as anything more than the funny, sarcastic younger sister of his high school girlfriend was…well…*gross*.

"You guys dunno shit." His South Side accent had grown right alongside his temper. "Not every relationship has to look like *that*." He gestured toward Grace, who'd leaned in to catch Hunter's earlobe between her teeth. "Now, what were we talking 'bout before this discussion got turned on me?"

The look on Fisher's face made Sam think he was in for more ridicule. He was relieved then when Fisher only shrugged. "We were talkin' about how Graham here has been campaignin' for an ass whoopin' for years now."

Fisher nudged Graham with a not inconsiderable amount of force. "And how he just won the election by honin' in on my newest conquest. I mean, I go to the bathroom for two minutes and come back to find he's seduced the woman I've been makin' eyes at all night."

Sam lifted an eyebrow at Graham, awaiting the big man's response. He should've known better than to think Graham might rise to Fisher's bait.

To say Graham Colburn was the strong, silent type was an understatement. Graham rarely spoke. And when he did, it was more of a low grumble that forced everyone to lean in to listen.

Ignoring Fisher completely, Graham hitched his chin toward a dark-haired woman in skintight jeans who sat with a group of ladies two tables over. Raising his deep voice above the din of the bar, he called out two words. Just two. "You ready?"

The woman's face lit up like a kid whose Christmas wishes were about to come true. And the way she launched herself from the table, it was a wonder she didn't knock over her chair.

Graham was a little slower to his feet. The big guy spent most of his life moving at a snail's pace. Which just made his occasional bursts of speed that much more astonishing.

Sam remembered the time he'd watched Graham run across the Saharan Desert like a freight train pegged to full-tilt. A truckload of armed enemy fighters had been trying their level best to gun him down. And even as Sam had been laying down cover fire, his jaw had slung open to witness that much bulk moving so quickly.

Graham towered over the petite brunette when she joined him beside the table, her eyes wide with excitement as she stared up at him.

"I'm musical." Fisher pulled the harmonica he always had on hand out of his pocket and wiggled it at the brunette. "Does that change your mind?" When the woman only blinked at him, he sighed. "I get it. It's cuffing season. And according to SZA, all the ladies are lookin' for a big boy."

The woman's friends clapped and cheered when Graham placed his big, meaty mitt on the small of her back to escort her from the bar. And Sam caught the eye of one of her friends.

The blonde had a mouth made for sin. And the smile that curved her lips when their eyes collided could only be described as an invitation.

"See?" Eliza said from beside him, having caught the exchange. "The ladies are waiting in the wings, eager for you to say the word that you're ready to take the leap."

He waited for that burst of adrenaline, that kick of hormones that usually went hand-in-hand with a beautiful woman's come-and-get-me-big-boy look. But...nada. All he felt was irritation that his phone was resoundingly silent.

After tipping his chin toward the blonde in a gesture that conveyed a polite thanks-but-no-thanks, he flipped over his cell.

Damnit! Why won't she respond?

Casting his memory back to the day she'd come to the BKI compound, he replayed their conversations in his head. Saw her smile in his mind's eye. Recalled how her mouth had puckered into a perfect moue as she'd concentrated on the computer screen while her sparkly blue fingernails had clacked on the keyboard.

Aside from their teeny, tiny squabble over her not flirting with him because, while it'd been endearing when she'd been thirteen and trying out her feminine wiles, at twenty-nine it'd just made things awkward between them, he couldn't think of a single exchange that should've had her ghosting him.

And she is *ghosting me, isn't she? Or maybe...*

His blood froze when an alarming thought occurred.

Had she been hit by a cab while crossing the street? Had she fallen through a missing manhole cover and been trapped in the god-awful labyrinth of Chicago's sewer system? Had she been swept into Lake Michigan by a rogue wave?

"For fuck's sake, Hannah," he grumbled while quickly typing yet *another* text. **If you don't text me back in 5 seconds, I'll assume you've been kidnapped & I'll send the CPD out looking for you.**

He counted the seconds in his head. *One. Two. Three. F*— When he saw those three gloriously scrolling dots appear on his screen, a breath of relief gusted from him.

Of course, the instant her response appeared he was back to scowling. **I'm fine. Just not feeling carnivorous. Thanks for checking in. Goodbye, Sam.**

Goodbye, Sam? *Goodbye, Sam?*

Why did that sound so final?

CHAPTER 1

728 West Addison Street, Apartment 2B
Six months later...

"**W**hy do you look like someone peed in your fajitas tonight?"

When Cesar frowned at Hannah's reflection in the vanity's mirror, she fluttered her lashes and blew him a kiss.

"It was carnitas, not fajitas," he corrected. There were lines of bronzer streaked down both sides of his nose and a thin line of highlighter swiped down the middle. When he made a face at her, the expression looked ridiculous.

Normally, she would've grinned and told him as much. But normally, when he was getting ready for a show at the Kit Kat Lounge, he was all sunny smiles, seated dance moves, and belting out whichever pop songs he planned to sing. Tonight, something was up with him. He was quiet. Contemplative. Almost...*subdued.*

Very un-Cesar-like.

She kept her teasing to herself and instead asked, "What's the difference again?" Then she waved a dismissive hand. "Never mind. That's not the point. Whatever it was you ate with the grilled chicken and the corn tortillas, the look on your face says someone peed in it. But since you made it yourself, micturition is out. Surely."

He rolled his eyes. "I rue the day I bought you that Word of the Day calendar."

"Come on." She pointed to his reflection. "Tell your best gal pal what's got your mind tied in a knot. Maybe I can help you untangle it."

As was her routine, she'd sprawled on her stomach across his bed to watch him transform himself from Cesar, a devastatingly handsome man, into Cesarine, the city's most beautiful woman. It was like witnessing a caterpillar become a butterfly or seeing Cinderella go from coal-covered kitchen scamp to ethereal princess with the wave of a wand.

Or, in Cesar's case, with the wave of a mascara spoolie, a generous swipe of concealer, and the deft application of a half-pound of dark, sparkly eyeshadow.

Still no less magical than a fairy godmother in Hannah's estimation. And bonus, it was the easiest way to learn the latest makeup techniques since Cesar watched all the newest TikToks and YouTube videos and she watched Cesar.

Using a makeup sponge, he blended the bronzer and highlighter into his nose, taking the feature from average to snatched in ten seconds flat. Next he applied glue to an amazingly fluttery set of false eyelashes. But as he waved the lashes to make the glue tacky, he remained frustratingly mute.

"Wow." She blinked. "It must be bad if even Roy Orbison isn't enough to lift your spirits."

The low, velvety voice of The Big O crooned from the speakers in the living room. Along with the old Hi-Fi system, Cesar had inherited a substantial record collection from his grandfather. He spun oldies-but-goodies pretty much nonstop.

"This morning"—his voice was low and pensive when he finally spoke—"Pete told me he loves me."

She waited for him to get to the bad part, the part that was making his painted lips purse into a sour-looking moue. But he stopped there. The only sound to fill the room besides the music was the *clackity-clackity-clack* of the nearby train.

They lived six blocks from a leg of Chicago's famous transit system, affectionately known as "The L." Instead of subways, the city's trains ran above street level on elevated tracks. The L? Short for The El because they were *elevated*? Get it?

When her silence stretched on for too long, Cesar caught her eye in the mirror. His expression clearly broadcast, *Well? What do you think of what I said?*

What she thought was Pete—or, as she liked to refer to Cesar's boyfriend, *The Golden God*—was the GOAT. She'd never met a man kinder, funnier or, most importantly, more enamored of all things Cesar than Peter Olsen. And she was beyond happy to hear Pete had finally said the words she was sure had been perched on the tip of his tongue since week two of his relationship with her roommate.

If I ever meet anyone who looks at me the way Pete looks at Cesar, I'm going down on one knee and proposing to him on the spot.

"And you're not happy about this *because?*" She rolled her hand.

"Because falling in love scares the crap out of me." He pulled a long, black wig off the Styrofoam head sitting at the corner of the vanity and ably fitted the Cher-worthy hair over his wig cap. "I don't like feeling out of control."

Ah, yes. Her best friend was nothing if not controlled. He always rinsed his dirty dishes before putting them in the dishwasher. His damp towel never fell off the hook in the bathroom. And he made his bed every day. Every *single* day. Even on the weekends.

Who does that?

She screwed up her mouth and tried to remember if she'd made *her* bed that day?

Dollars to donuts, the answer was *no.*

Cesar was the orderly yin to her disorderly yang. And yet, somehow, they'd managed to live together for seven years without visiting violence upon each other's person.

Unless, of course, one counted the popcorn food fights they'd gotten into over who was causing the conflict in season one of *Queer Eye*. She was a firm believer Karamo was the culprit and Cesar swore Antoni had to be the one making all the behind-the-scenes drama.

"What did you think it was going to feel like?" She cupped her cheek in her hand, absently kicking her bare feet behind her as she watched him slip out of his dressing gown and into the padded girdle that gave him an hourglass figure. "They wouldn't call it *falling* in love if it wasn't a wild, uncontrolled plummet," she added.

After doing up the girdle's eyehooks, he stepped into her favorite cocktail dress. The color brought out the gold in his skin tone. "Exactly. And what's to stop me from breaking into a million pieces once I hit the ground?"

"Who says you have to hit the ground?" she countered quickly.

He pinned her with a knowing look. "Experience gained by watching friends and family crash and burn."

"Love isn't always a pitfall into destruction." She shook her head. "Sometimes it gives people the softest place to land."

He crouched on the floor of his closet to sort through the rows of high-heeled shoes. Lifting a pair of red pumps, he glanced at her expectantly. When she shook her head, he offered up a pair of blue ones and she nodded.

"Paired with your sapphire costume jewelry," she told him.

"See? You *do* have taste." He stood to balance on one foot then the other as he slipped into the pumps. "Which makes me wonder why you insist on running around in graphic T-shirts, ragged jeans, and Vans that look like they should be tossed into the nearest dumpster."

"Because I *like* graphic T-shirts." She pointed to her current cropped T-shirt printed with a picture of a possum that read: Live fast, Eat trash… "Ragged jeans are comfortable. And you couldn't pay me enough to teeter around in *those* torture devices." She hitched her chin toward the shoes that added a good five inches to Cesar's height. "Also, stop trying to change the subject. Familiarity doesn't *always* breed contempt. Sometimes love lasts."

"You mean like your love for one Mr. Samuel Harwood?"

Her smile was thin and tight. No teeth.

"Sorry." He grimaced. "It fell out of my mouth before I could stop it."

"I'm not in love with Sam."

"No?" He cocked his head right along with his padded, sequined hip.

"I had a crush on him in middle school. That's all. I mean, what thirteen-year-old girl *wouldn't*? You've seen his yearbook pictures."

"Crushes don't usually last a decade and a half."

"Absence makes the heart grow fonder. Isn't that what they say? I spent sixteen years building him up in my head."

"I might buy this whole *the reality of him doesn't measure up to my fantasies of him* tact except you forget what you told me the day you saw him again." Cesar pointed a cherry-red press-on nail at her nose. "When I asked if he was as yummy as you remembered, you said, and I quote, 'He's yummier.'"

"Doesn't matter." She shook her head, wanting the floor to open and swallow her whole when she thought of that day and the things Sam had said to her after she'd pressed a quick kiss to his lips. She'd been rejected before. But never had it felt as awful as when he'd had to gently explain to her that he'd never see her as anything more than his high school girlfriend's kid sister. "I've put him out of my mind. He's a part of my past and will never occupy a place in my future." She clapped her hands together as if dusting them off. "From now on, I'm keeping it one-hundred-percent in the present."

Although, purposefully avoiding thinking of Sam during the day hadn't stopped her from dreaming of him every night. And with the dreams had come a sense of need or hunger or...*heck, maybe it's just horniness*, she thought.

It'd been over a year since she'd been naked with a man. And even longer since she'd been naked with a man who knew what he was doing.

But maybe if she allowed the door to the past to swing open inside her head without immediately shoving it shut, turning the lock, and tossing away the key, she could trick her *unconsciousness* into taking a page from her *consciousness* and just...*letting go*. Letting *Sam* go so she could finally, *finally* move on.

And there's no time like the present.

She allowed the memory of the first moment she set eyes on him to bloom to life inside her head.

He'd still been in his baseball uniform when Candy had brought him home to meet their parents. His hair had been dark and shaggy, curling over his ears. His shoulders had been broad and well-muscled thanks to all the time his coach had kept him in the weight room. And his face had been classically handsome. Like the heroes in the old black-and-white movies her mother always watched—Clark Gable or James Stewart transported sixty years into the future.

But what'd made Hannah's pubescent heart go pitter-pat had been his eyes. Crystal blue and startlingly clear. Like Lake Michigan reflecting a cloudless summer sky. And the *expression* in them, mischief mixed with intelligence woven together with the kind of wariness that had come from growing up in one of the roughest neighborhoods in the city, had made her aware of parts of her body she'd been completely oblivious to before he'd walked into her life.

Sam had been a heady mix of bad boy from the wrong side of the tracks and jock with the confident smile and cocky swagger. And from the first moment she'd experienced all six-plus feet of his sinewy brawn and burgeoning charisma, she'd known what it was to lust after a man.

*Er…*boy *rather.* He'd barely been eighteen at the time.

Eighteen then, thirty-four now and *all* grown up.

When she'd hopped out of the cab on Goose Island six months earlier to find him leaning nonchalantly against the big iron gates surrounding the grounds of the old menthol cigarette factory, and despite all the intervening years, she'd recognized him immediately.

Recognized him and nearly swallowed her own tongue.

He'd been handsome as a boy on the cusp of manhood. But as a full-fledged man?

Well, not to put it too bluntly, but we're talking straight fire. Hashtag smash. Bow-chicka-wow-wow. Wink, wink. Nudge, nudge.

His face had lost the fullness of youth, his bearded jaw having been whittled down to hard planes and sharp edges. His steady teenage diet of chicken wings and cheeseburgers meant teenage Sam had been a little on the beefier side. But present-day Sam? Oh, present-day Sam was lean and mean, with the kind of physique that said he moved his body all day, every day. He'd replaced his youthful sneakers with steel-toed biker boots. An intricate tattoo depicting an eagle feather had peeked beneath the sleeve of his T-shirt. And the puckered scar across his neck had broadcast to the world that he was the rarest of specimens: a modern-day warrior.

Yes, thirty-four-year-old Sam was the kind of guy to make women suck in their stomachs and stick out their chests. The kind to make the minds of hetero ladies shoot straight to hot nights and tangled sheets. The kind that'd instantly made her forget he hadn't spared her a single, solitary thought since he'd left their South Side neighborhood to join the Marines sixteen years earlier.

Although, if she was being fair, it wasn't like he *should* have spared her a thought. He hadn't been *her* boyfriend. She'd only gotten to know him—and lose her thirteen-year-old heart to him—because he'd been too nice to tell her to buzz off when she'd sidled up beside him on the front porch swing of her parents' house all the times he'd waited for her older sister to finish blow-drying her hair, or putting on mascara, or changing outfits for the eighty-fifth time.

And yet… Hannah had missed him every single day since the day he'd left. And she'd just about given up hope of ever seeing him again when, out of the blue, he'd called with a request for her help on a job.

To say she'd *jumped* at the chance was an understatement. On the entire fifteen-minute cab ride from her neighborhood to Goose Island, she'd thought, *Huzzah! Now's my chance! He'll look at me and see the woman I've become instead of the snot-nosed eighth grader with the knobby knees and training bra.*

Boy-oh-boy, she couldn't have been more wrong.

"I'm finally ready to let go of my girlish fantasies when it comes to Mr. Samuel Harwood." She shook away the memories of him and gently closed the door on them. "The past is a place to learn from, not to live in."

When Cesar opened his mouth, she expected him to naysay her. To tell her she was fooling herself if she thought that, after all these years, she could so easily let go of her hopes and dreams. She was relieved when he only dipped his chin. "Right. Which means you should change out of those ridiculous pajama bottoms and come to the club. You need to get out. You need to get *laid*."

"Wait. How did this get turned on me?" She sat up and frowned. "Weren't we talking about you and Pete? I mean, you *do* love him, don't you?"

Cesar waved a hand through air redolent with the smells of nail polish, perfume, and face powder. "Of course I do. The man is perfect." He screwed up his mouth in consideration. "Well, maybe not *perfect*. He wears cotton boxers with sports logos on them, which gives me total *suburban dad* vibes." He shuddered as if suburban dads were akin to flesh-eating bacteria. "But we can't have it all, can we? And Pete is more than I'd ever hoped for."

"So *tell* him. Take the risk. Take the plunge. And if there's heartbreak in your future, well…" She shrugged. "You know what they say. It's better to have loved and lost than never to have loved at all."

"You're full of overused adages tonight, aren't you?" His brows knit together. "And do you *really* believe that?"

She thought back on her decade-and-a-half of unrequited longing for

Sam. Sure, it hadn't been *love* love. It'd been *puppy* love. Even still, she could say without a doubt that she wouldn't trade the time she'd spent with Sam back in Englewood, or the years since which she'd spent missing him and fantasizing about him, for anything.

She was a better person for having known him. And she had a far clearer picture of the kind of man she wanted in her future for having spent so much time daydreaming about him.

"I *do* believe it." She nodded. "I think loving someone, even if that love doesn't end up lasting, is a miracle. One of the *only* miracles we get to experience in life."

Cesar continued to look skeptical. But instead of arguing, he said, "If I promise to don your rose-colored glasses and give love a chance, will you go put on your dancing shoes, remember you're young and fun and living in one of the most exciting cities in America, and come to the club where you might meet Prince Charming? And if you're really, *really* lucky, maybe he'll take you home and give you a couple of O's that'll turn that frown you've been wearing for the last few months upside down."

"This frown has nothing to do with lack of O's. For your information, I had an orgasm just last night."

His mouth flattened until all she could see was the outline of his lip liner. "Reading a chapter from your alien porno novel and going a round with your vibrator isn't the same as letting a man flick your bean until you scream."

"It's not a porno novel!" She crossed her arms in afront. "It's *erotica.* There is plot and characterization and snappy dialogue and…and…*plot.* Also, you realize the Kit Kat Lounge is the last place on Earth I'm likely to meet a man who has any interest in my bean, right? Drag shows are basically straight man repellent. They're like Deep Woods Off for cishet dudes."

"True." He tapped one fingernail against his cheek. "Too much latex, Lycra, and sequins for them."

"It's not that. There's plenty of latex, Lycra, and sequins in strip clubs, and heaven knows I've known plenty of guys to frequent *those.*"

"So is it that our latex, Lycra, and sequins stays *on*, do you suppose?" Cesar tilted his head.

"It probably has more to do with the fact that seeing men dressed as beautiful women makes your average, everyday straight dude question the intractability of his sexuality."

"Which would explain all the shootings and protests outside our clubs." Cesar shook his head sadly.

"Mmm." She agreed, but only partially. "I mean, I think the discomfort and anger has always been there for these Neanderthals. But their violence can be laid directly at the feet of the politicians who're vilifying the entire community. These assholes can't get elected based on their policies, so they have to get elected by giving people an out-group to hate on."

"The jokes on them, though." Cesar's smile was heartbreakingly sweet. "In the end, love always wins out over hate."

Hannah, who lived in terror that some crazy man with an AR-15 would burst into the Kit Kat Lounge and start spraying bullets, only sighed. "I love your eternal optimism, my friend. And I hope you're right. Because The Lounge"—that's how Cesar and his fellow performers referred to the club—"is the happiest place on Earth and I want it to stay that way."

He wrinkled his perfectly contoured nose. "Isn't the happiest place on Earth supposed to be Disneyland?"

"Nah. The Lounge has better costumes, better music, and unless it's Friday or Saturday night, far shorter lines to get in the door."

"True," he conceded with a chuckle. "It *is* a pretty magical place, even if I do say so myself. Which brings us full circle. Come with me tonight! We can go straight-guy hunting after my last set." His brow furrowed. "Where does one go to pick up a *bro*? A sports bar? A brewpub? God, please tell me we don't have to go to one of those clubs that smells like Red Bull, Axe body spray, and toxic masculinity."

She curled her lip. "I'm too old to be traipsing around town chasing dick until all hours of the morning."

"You're not even *thirty*."

"I will be in a month. Besides, I'm happy here. My erotica is better than any bro could hope to be. And my vibrator never finishes before I do." She frowned. "As long as I remember to charge it. Also, I don't want to go through that whole *getting to know you* phase. I swear on all that's holy, if I have to listen to another guy drone on about his ambition to conquer the world one Bitcoin at a time, or how rad his gaming buddies are, or how many flasks he has in his collection, I might—"

Boom!

It sounded like a hand grenade had gone off. The whole building shook. The ancient double-paned glass rattled in the sash. And a puff of foul-smelling smoke drifted in through the open bedroom door.

Hannah bolted off the bed at the same time Cesar leapt in her direction. They had their arms around each other, their hearts thundering in unison, when she whispered, "A gas line you think? Or maybe The L jumped its tracks?"

He didn't have time to answer before a trio of men in Kevlar vests emblazoned with the letters FBI burst into the room. It was then she realized the *boom* had been the explosives the agents had used to breach the front door.

"What the—" That's all she managed before she was staring down the deadly ends of three evil-looking handguns.

"On the ground!"

"Hands in the air!"

"Don't move!"

All the body-cam videos she'd seen of people being shot by authorities who couldn't coordinate their shit flashed through her head.

"Which is it?" She was careful to keep her tone modulated even though adrenaline-fueled blood singed her veins. "Do you want us not to move or to get on the ground or to put our hands in the air?"

"Hands in the air! Put your damned hands in the air!" The agent closest to them shouted.

She was many things. A fool wasn't one of them. She didn't hesitate to comply.

As soon as she raised her hands, however, she wished she'd donned a different outfit. Her cropped T-shirt barely covered the undersides of her boobs and her loose pajama bottoms slung low around her hips, leaving her entire midriff bare.

"Get on the floor! Face down!" the closest agent added as Roy skipped in the living room, repeating over and over again, "Pretty woman, walkin' down…Pretty woman, walkin' down…"

The girdle and tight cocktail dress made his motions stiff and awkward, but Cesar managed to join her in a prone position on the floor. His voice was hoarse when he whispered, "What's going on?"

"Maybe something to do with that job Sam called me in to help with?" She grimaced. The adrenaline had coated her tongue with its sour taste. "Which means this is all a big misunderstanding."

If she hadn't hacked into the emails of the director of the FBI, the authorities never would have found the government mole who'd recruited Americans to act as online trolls to spread Russian misinformation and propaganda.

With my help, hundreds of double-agents are either awaiting trial or have otherwise copped plea agreements and are doing time.

But perhaps these guys didn't realize her sneak-a-peek had been deemed a necessary evil. Maybe they'd stumbled upon her little cyberpunk stunt and didn't know she'd been cleared of any wrongdoing by none other than the director himself.

"Just do everything they say until I can get this straightened out," she whispered, pressing her cheek against the rug. "Don't give them any reason to shoot you."

"Wasn't planning on it." His face was turned toward hers and she tried to don an expression of calm confidence even though she was feeling the exact opposite.

"Hands behind your head!" the agent who took up a position above her commanded.

Once again, she was quick to comply. After she'd laced her fingers together over the back of her skull, she heard her best friend yell, "Ow! You fucker!"

One of the agents had planted a none-too-gentle knee into the middle of Cesar's back. The adrenaline in her blood turned to pure, fiery rage. "Hey!" she snarled even as hard plastic cinched around her wrists. "Get off him! He's complying! You don't have to—"

That's all she got out before the agent who'd cuffed her wrapped a hand around her ties and yanked her to her feet. The move was so sudden, she thought for sure she'd feel warm blood dripping down her arms from where the plastic ties had dug into her flesh.

"Easy!" She snarled. "There's no reason for—"

"Shut the fuck up!" The fed spun her around and shoved her backward until her back hit the wall where Cesar's framed and signed photo of Lady Gaga hung in a place of prominence. The breath whooshed from her lungs and the photograph jumped on its nail. *Thankfully*, it didn't come crashing down on top of her skull.

"There's been a m-mistake," she sputtered. "If you'll talk to Director Morgan, you'll see I helped you guys bag one of the biggest busts this country has—"

"Take the director's name out of your treasonous mouth." The agent pressed her bound wrists above her head with one hand while placing his opposite forearm across her throat. White stars populated her field of vision when her windpipe was crushed. "He wouldn't be caught dead in the same room with someone who conspired with Red Square to target Dominion Pipeline."

Perhaps it was the lack of oxygen getting to her brain but, try as she might, she couldn't make sense of his words. Red Square? The ransomware syndicate that sold their services to affiliate malware gangs on the dark web? And Dominion Pipeline? The largest fuel supplier to the Eastern Seaboard?

She'd never had occasion to deal with either entity in her work for Cyber Crimes.

"Do you deny it?" the agent demanded, his face barely an inch from hers. She could smell the stale coffee on his breath and feel the wet heat of his words fanning over her cheeks.

Yes, I deny it, you toad-eating cockwaffle! She wanted to scream. But the only thing she could manage was, "You're ch-choking m—"

"We're not here to hurt you, Miss Blue," said the agent who'd been abusing Cesar. She glanced past the beast holding her hostage to see her best friend was on his feet. His wig was askew, there was fear and confusion in his eyes, but otherwise, he seemed mostly unharmed.

"Tell th-that to your p-pal h-here," she wheezed and then cut her eyes to the fed in front of her. His dishwater-blond hair was trimmed military short. A muscle clenched in his jaw. And she would swear she saw cruelty and…*pleasure* in his beady brown eyes.

He gets a kick out of using his credentials and his authority to terrorize people.

Her hunch was confirmed when the other agent—she suspected the man holding Cesar was the *lead* agent—admitted, "Agent Waller gets overzealous sometimes. Especially when it comes to a government employee using her position and security clearance to line her pockets while putting this country at risk. But I'm sure Keith will be happy to release you if you'll agree to come peacefully and admit what you've done."

The stars in front of her eyes were going supernova. And the loud buzzing in her ears made the agent's words sound tinny and far away. Even still, her inner smart-ass jumped into the fray.

"I'm being m-manhandled by a guy named *Keith*? Just wh-when I thought my night couldn't get any w-worse."

The pressure on her throat increased and her oxygen-starved brain conjured up her sister's face. Candy's words drifted through her head. *Why do you always have to make things so much more difficult?*

It was a refrain she'd heard a lot growing up. What she'd always thought but had never said aloud was, *Not everyone is born with an angel's face and a runway model's body. Some people have to rely on brains, wit, and sarcasm to make it in this world.*

Despite her best efforts to log every move the agents made and remember every word they said—she planned to file a harshly worded complaint once this mess was straightened out—she couldn't stop her eyelids from fluttering. And just when her eyes started to roll back in her head, she heard Lead Guy say, "That's enough, Waller."

She expected the pressure on her throat to ease, but it didn't. And Roy's voice now sounded like it was drifting in from a hundred miles away. "Pretty woman, walkin' down... Pretty woman, walkin' down..."

It took the lead agent barking, "Keith, I said enough!" for the rabid government dog to take his arm off her throat.

The blood rushed to her head so quickly it made her dizzy. And the sound her windpipe made when she raked in a lungful of air was half gargle, half gasp.

"Let's get her loaded up," the lead agent added. "Maybe she'll be more cooperative back at headquarters."

"Wait!" Cesar yelled when she found herself being frog-marched across the room. "What about her Miranda rights?"

"They're the FBI," she said hoarsely as she was hustled by him. "They don't have to abide by the same legal requirements as local law enforcement."

"Do you know what they're talking about? Did you—"

"No." She shook her head even as Overzealous Johnny Lawman— Overzealous Keith Lawman just didn't have the same ring—shoved her toward the bedroom door. "But it sounds like I'm in trouble and I can think of only one person who can help me out of it."

Cesar gave her a subtle nod, indicating he'd received her message loud and clear. And that helped stave off the panic attack clawing at the back of her brain.

The private government defense firm Sam worked for was small enough to have to share space with a custom motorcycle shop, but the job she'd done with him had ended up with her on a phone call with the FBI director himself.

Like they say, she thought a little desperately, *when it comes to getting out of a jam, it's all about who you know.*

Samuel Harwood might not be willing to admit she was nearly thirty instead of thirteen. He might not have spent the last decade and a half fantasizing about her the way she'd been fantasizing about him. But one thing he *did* do was pay his debts.

He owed her. And she was calling in that IOU.

CHAPTER 2

Black Knights Inc., Goose Island

"**H**e nearly shot my dick off!"

"Well, if he'd managed to hit a target that small, I'd have called him up and recruited him to our side."

Sam stopped running the shammy over the chrome exhaust pipe of his pride and joy—his black-and-white Harley chopper named Pale Horse—to see Fisher grin at Eliza.

Instead of getting bent out of shape that BKI's secretary, den mother, and onsite chef extraordinaire had maligned his manhood, Fisher simply wiggled his eyebrows. "I like knowin' ya think about what I'm packin' in my pants, doll face."

"Oh…" Eliza batted her lashes. "I *do* think about you, Fish. In fact, you were the first thing I thought about when I woke up this morning."

"Yeah?" Fisher flashed a hundred-watt grin.

"Yeah." Eliza nodded. "I thought of you and I was reminded to take out the trash."

Sam chuckled and then laughed harder when Fisher shot him a quelling glance.

"Hey!" He lifted his hands. "Don't get mad at the audience for enjoying the show."

"Don't ya have anything better to do than encourage her to take chunks out of my ego?" Fisher gestured toward Eliza.

"As a matter of fact, I don't. 'Cause I had to fly back here with you instead of staying down south with the others. I coulda been on a beach in Aruba being served umbrella drinks by a dark-eyed beauty. But instead I'm here in the Great White North listening to you two fight like children."

"The next mission requires precision ballistics. Who better than you, our resident marksman, to help me finetune the logistics?" Fisher was quick to retort.

"I can almost smell the coconut oil and rum." Sam's tone was purposefully petulant. He made sure his expression said he was thinking of how the other three members of their team—only three because Hunter was on his honeymoon—were sunning themselves in the Caribbean instead of being back in Chicago freezing their dicks off.

"I can sing ya some Jimmy Buffett and pour some sand in your sheets if that'll make ya feel better," Fisher offered.

Sam flipped him the bird before pulling a watermelon-flavored Jolly Rancher from his pocket and popping it into his mouth. He'd been partial to the candy as a teenager. But he'd kind of forgotten his penchant for the sugary little snacks until six months earlier when Hannah had reminded him by secretly slipping one into his pocket—a trick she'd obviously learned from her older sister.

Hannah…

For sixteen years, he hadn't given her more than a passing thought. Then she'd popped back into his life and he'd thought of little else since.

He wanted to blame that on the surprising speed with which she'd then adiosed herself right back *out* of his life. But that was a lie. The dreams he'd been having *proved* that was a lie.

Dreams he made himself forget the moment he woke up.

"And speakin' of missions." Fisher swung back to Eliza and distracted Sam from his thoughts. "I got one for ya." He reached into his pocket and pulled out a folded sheet of paper, handing it over with a flourish.

After giving him a critical look, BKI's girl Friday unfolded the note. "This is a grocery list." Her tone was the same one she might've used had she said, *"I just stepped in dog shit."*

"You know I'm not allowed inside Costco. I'll come out with six new shirts, a television we don't need, and a rotisserie chicken you'll turn your nose up at and feed to the cat."

"Beer, alpha whiskey," Eliza read aloud from the list, not batting a lash at Fisher's use of military slang when referring to toilet paper. "Hot dogs, hot sauce, potato chips, Twinkies. More beer." She lifted an eyebrow.

Fisher made a face. "If it's nice, buy it twice."

"Except for the beer, you have the palate of a thirteen-year-old boy. You realize that, right?"

Fisher shrugged. "I don't know. I liked beer at thirteen too."

"That explains a lot. Specifically your chronic case of immaturity. Your developing brain was stunted by alcohol consumption, you poor thing."

"Why are ya always bustin' my balls?" Despite his words, Fisher's grin was good-natured.

"Uh, maybe because you whip them out so often? Correct me if I'm wrong, but I could've sworn I saw a redhead slinking through the front gates this morning. I thought we agreed it's too much of a security risk to bring our dates back here. Or, in your case, your latest one-night stand." Cocking her head, she eyed Fisher up and down. "Surely you can do your business elsewhere. I mean, a guy like you must have a standing reservation at some off-brand motel of the no tell ilk."

"First of all, what do ya mean *a guy like me*? What kind of guy do ya think I am?"

"The kind who probably has half a dozen sex trophies running around with his hazel eyes and Tom Hardy mouth."

"Please," Fisher scoffed. "Give me some credit. I know how to use a condom."

"Which are only ninety-eight percent effective at preventing pregnancy. At the rate you've gone, you're bound to have run up against the short side of that statistic a time or two."

"At the rate I've gone?" Fisher pretended offense. "Are ya callin' me a slut?"

She shrugged, her button-down shirt looking as freshly starched at the end of the day as it had at the beginning. That was one of the wonders of Eliza Meadows. She always looked the picture of perfection. Not a hair out of place. Not a wrinkle to be found. "If the shoe fits, wear it," she declared. "What's the second thing?"

"Huh?" Fisher scowled.

"You said *first of all* which leads me to believe there was a second of all coming."

"Oh. Right. Second of all, I didn't bring her *here*." Fisher waved a hand to indicate the three-story factory building housing the world-renowned custom motorcycle shop that provided the cover for the true work of Black Knights Inc. "I took her out to the cottage." He gestured toward the two giant garage doors that opened to the outside where a ten-foot-tall brick wall topped by razor wire enclosed a two-acre plot of land that included the old factory building, various outbuildings, and the little stone cottage that'd been home to the foreman's family back when the place had been making menthol cigarettes instead of badass bikes.

Eliza's lips twisted. "That's splitting hairs and you know it. Besides, I would've thought after the close call you just had you'd take at least *one* night off."

She was referring to their most recent mission to South America. They'd helped Colombian forces take out a cartel leader who'd been systematically maiming and killing the locals who'd refused to fall in line with his brutal authoritarian tactics.

Unfortunately, the intel the Knights had received about the job had been bad. Instead of the kingpin having fifteen guards roving his compound, he'd had nearly fifty.

The ensuing firefight had lasted half the night. And near the end of the siege, a bullet had grazed Fisher's hip, barely missing his favorite body part.

"It was *because* of that close call that I was so quick to hop back in the saddle." Fisher dipped his chin. "When you're two inches away from losin' your best feature, ya come to appreciate it that much more."

Eliza rolled her eyes. "If you have nothing else, Fish, at least I can always count on you to have the audacity."

"Thanks, doll face."

"I told you not to call me that." Sam watched Eliza's nostrils flare. A sure sign she was reaching her wit's end when it came to Fisher's relentless bullshit. "And it wasn't a compliment. I was alluding to your moral turpitude."

"You call it moral turpitude. I call it *livin'*. You should try it sometime."

"No thanks. I find one-night stands shallow and unfulfilling."

"Then ya aren't doin' them right. I'd be happy to show ya how profound and gratifyin' they can be. Just say the word."

Eliza's dark eyes flared with an unholy light and Sam knew Fisher was in for it.

"Fisher, what I'm about to tell you I say with my whole chest and every ounce of my conviction. I would rather sit naked on a hot grill and have dull shish kabob skewers shoved through my brain than ever have intercourse with you. I mean, as much as you spread yourself around, you've got to be a petri dish full of sexually transmitted infections."

Fisher's sense of self was made of Teflon. So Sam wasn't surprised when he only chuckled and admitted, "The only STI I've had was chlamydia. Caught it from a nice lady in Belize and cleared it up in two weeks with antibiotics."

Sam coughed into his fist to cover up his laugh at the look of revulsion that came over Eliza's face. She blinked twice before shaking her head and declaring, "You're hopeless, Fish. Absolutely *hopeless*."

The former Delta Force sergeant major grinned until all his teeth showed. Then he grew serious. "'Hope is the thing with feathers that perches in the soul.' Emily Dickenson. A woman who knew there's no such thing as hopelessness."

Eliza turned to Sam, her face the picture of incredulity. "One minute he's admitting to catching the clam and the next he's quoting poetry. Who does that?"

"Hey." Sam held up his hands. "This isn't one of those audience participation shows. Don't drag me into this. I—"

"Yo!" A call from above cut Sam off. Lifting his chin, he saw Ozzie leaning over the railing of the second-floor balcony.

Ethan "Ozzie" Sykes was a former Navy SEAL, a computer genius holdover from the original Black Knights, and an eighties hairband aficionado known for blasting Bon Jovi, Quiet Riot, and Def Leppard at insane levels until someone screamed at him to *shut that shit off!*

He was also usually gone by this time of night, home with his lovely wife, Samantha, who was five months pregnant with their first child.

"What are you still doing here?" Sam called up to him. "Figured you'd be long gone by now. Isn't this 'bout the time you should be making an ice cream run?"

According to Ozzie, it didn't matter if it was negative ten degrees outside with snow swirling in all directions. Samantha's pregnancy hormones had her craving cookies and cream and butter pecan double scoops on the daily.

"Samantha's editor has her working late on a story," Ozzie explained. Samantha Sykes was an investigative reporter for the *Chicago Tribune*. "Thought I'd stick around and finish up the CAD drawings for the new bike designs Becky came up with. But that's neither here nor there." He pointed to the small screen mounted to the wall between the two large garage doors. It showed camera footage of the front gate and the guardhouse manned by one of the four huge, redheaded Connelly brothers whom BKI paid to keep an eye on the perimeter. "Toran just called to say someone is here and asking to see you."

Sam shoved up from his squatted position and glanced at the screen in curiosity. He hadn't the first clue who would be looking for him at nine o'clock on a Friday night. His parents had died two years after he'd joined the Marines—their addictions having finally caught up with them in a terrible meth lab explosion. And it wasn't like any of his friends from the old neighborhood would be coming to visit since most of them were in jail.

Marching over to the mounted TV, he leaned toward the screen to get a closer look. The instant he saw the woman in the long fur coat and sparkly dress, he decided Ozzie had made a mistake.

"Hey Fish!" He gestured for his teammate to join him. "Pretty sure this one's for you."

"Oh, for the love of..." Eliza didn't bother finishing her sentence. Neither did she vamoose herself upstairs to her room. Curiosity had her trailing Fisher toward the TV screen as she added, "Another one?"

Sam watched Fisher's eyebrows draw together once he got a look at the black-haired beauty. Confusion had Sam asking, "Is she *not* one of yours?"

"Not that I recall," Fisher admitted.

Eliza rolled her eyes so hard Sam thought it a wonder she didn't give herself a headache.

"She's not here for Fish!" Ozzie called down to them. "She says she's here for you, Sam!"

"Me?" Sam's chin jerked back so hard he almost gave himself whiplash.

"Good for you, Sammy!" Fisher clapped a hand on his shoulder. "Ya been woefully short on female companionship lately. It's about time ya got back on that horse after it bucked ya off."

Sam ignored his teammate as he headed for the front door. His curiosity was piqued—who was the woman and what could she possibly want with him? Also, what the fuck was Fisher talking about? He hadn't been short of female companionship.

Had he?

He racked his brain, searching for a memory of the last time he'd gone home with someone, and realized with a shock it'd been almost seven months.

Holy fuckballs! How did that happen?

Grabbing his leather jacket off a hook on the wall and shoving a black stocking cap down over his ears, he gritted his teeth and wrenched open the front door. As expected, the icy breath of a Midwestern February blew across his face.

Sipping boat drinks, baking in coconut oil, and charming a pretty tourist who'd break my recent streak of abstinence. That's what I should be doing right now, he thought grumpily.

After zipping his jacket, he shoved his hands deep in his pockets and started making his way across the grounds toward the gates. There was no snow on the pavement, but the frosty blacktop still crunched under his boots. He craned his head over his shoulder when he heard footsteps pounding behind him.

Fisher was in the process of pulling on his own stocking cap. And Eliza was hot on Fisher's heels, hastily doing up the buttons on her camel-colored peacoat.

Sam stopped and waited for them. When they caught up, he gifted them with his best frown of disapproval.

"What?" Fisher blinked. "Ya didn't think we'd let ya meet a woman who looks like *that* all by yourself, did ya?"

"I'd hoped," Sam muttered. "'Cause in my experience, women who look like that can be trouble."

"Women who look like that are *always* trouble," Eliza corrected. "Which is why you need backup."

Sam shook his head. "Made Marine Raider quicker than any other recruit, did countless tours in countless war zones, and been running missions for Madam President for over three years now. But sure. I need help handling one high-heeled female."

"*Woman*, if you please," Eliza corrected as they resumed their journey toward the front of the property. "*Female* is derogatory. It reduces a woman to her sex instead of viewing her as a whole person. Do you ever refer to other men as *males*? No. You call them *men*. You respect their whole personhood."

Sam frowned as he considered her words and couldn't find fault in them. Still, he couldn't help pointing out, "You just said women who look like her are *always* trouble. Now you're defending her?"

"Sure." Eliza hitched a shoulder, her warm breath frosting the air. "One doesn't cancel out the other. I can agree she's trouble and also believe words and labels matter. Which is why it takes every ounce of self-control I possess not to rip off Fisher's arm and beat him with it every time he calls me doll face."

"I don't mean to give offense." Fisher's Louisiana drawl sounded particularly thick in the cold night air. "Ya *have* a doll face. All pale and big-eyed and—"

"Sam?" The mystery woman standing beyond the gate called and Sam was struck by the depth of her voice. Had he not been staring right at her, seeing the swell of her cleavage above the neckline of her dress, he would've sworn she was a dude.

"Huh." He heard Fisher whisper from beside him.

"Do I know you?" Sam didn't have to raise his voice. Like the Big Apple, there were parts of Chicago that didn't sleep, parts that partied all night, every night. But Goose Island wasn't one of them. The streets might as well have been rolled up after 8PM for all the use they got.

"No." The woman shook her head, causing her long, black hair to swish over her shoulders. "But you know my best friend. And she needs your help."

Apprehension lifted the hairs on the back of Sam's neck. When he picked up his pace, Fisher and Eliza matched his steps. "Who's your friend?"

"Hannah Blue," the exotic beauty said. "But I think you call her Hurricane Hannah."

Sam's boots glued themselves to the pavement at the same time his heart tried to exit his body through his throat. "Toran!" he called to the big, ruddy Chicagoan manning the guardhouse. "Open the gates!"

CHAPTER 3

Southpark Hotel, Austin, Texas

"She has been arrested."

Vincent Romano sat back in his chair and let loose with a small sigh of relief. "That's good. So the plan is still a go?"

The immediacy of the response that came through his cell phone's speaker comforted him further. "Yes. I am waiting for my contact to give me the go-ahead. But there appear to be no further impediments in our path."

"Right." Vinny nodded even though the man on the other end of the call couldn't see him.

What was Yang, exactly? His *handler*? That's what all the spy movies called guys in Yang's position.

Then again, all the spy movies Vinny had ever watched revolved around the CIA. And Yang? Well, he worked in some capacity for a *Chinese* intelligence agency. Although, Yang was coordinating with his counterpart in the U.S. government, which probably meant the term *handler* could still be applied to him.

Look at me, Vinny thought with no small amount of pride. *From a two-bit criminal hacker to a government asset in the span of a few months. Nanna will be so proud.*

He couldn't wait to tell her all about it. Just as soon as he finished with the job. Just as soon as he ditched the Lone Star State and returned to the mean streets of New York City.

Just as soon as I get paid...

"The evidence you planted on her work computer gave the feds all they needed to take her into custody. Nice job."

"You gave me the documentation. I just did the dirty work of inserting it into her system."

"Regardless, it was an unexpected bump in the road, and you helped us navigate it without blowing a tire."

Vinny bit the inside of his cheek. Yang's metaphors always sounded odd and slightly forced. Maybe it was his accent.

"Hey, is this Red Square deal legit?" he couldn't stop himself from asking. "Have they really seized the East Coast pipeline? Or is this more joint maneuvering to prove weaknesses in our infrastructure?"

Yang's response was clipped. "The less you know, the better, Vincent."

"Right."

"I will phone you with any updates."

Before Vinny could respond, the line went dead.

Just as well, he thought when the alarm on his phone chimed.

It was time for his nightly check-in with his grandmother. And if he was even a few minutes late, she'd worry.

CHAPTER 4

FBI Field Office, 2111 West Roosevelt Road

"We have you dead to rights, Miss Blue." The lead fed had turned out to be named *Agent Mulder*, of all things.

"But I didn't *do* this." Hannah pointed to the laptop screen that clearly showed she *had* done what they were accusing her of. According to their evidence, she'd given highly sensitive information to Red Square, which the group had then used to hack into the computer system controlling the Dominion Pipeline and the flow of refined oil to the East Coast.

Red Square was demanding a half billion dollars in ransom from Dominion or else they threatened to shut down the pipeline. Which wouldn't simply result in a gasoline shortage at the pumps. It would result in a scarcity of the oil many people were using to heat their homes during one of the coldest winters the eastern seaboard had ever seen.

"How much is your cut?" Mulder asked casually. "How much of that five hundred million is Red Square paying you?"

"Someone's throwing shade," she insisted, hoping the agent could read the truth in her eyes.

He frowned. "Is that some sort of hacker lingo?"

"It means I'm being set up. *Framed.* If you'll just let me…" When she reached for the laptop, Mulder snatched the machine toward his side of the table.

"Nice try." He slapped the lid shut before sitting back in his chair, crossing his arms over his chest. The move caused his black tie to bunch in a little arc. Black suit. Black tie. Black loafers. The guy was really leaning hard on the whole MIB vibe.

The only thing he's missing is a neutralizer, she thought a little hysterically because she was *this close* to losing her damn mind.

How? *How* was she sitting in FBI headquarters being accused of selling out her country?

It felt like a dream.

No. A nightmare.

Wake up, Hannah! Wake up!

She pinched herself and was sorry to say the pain didn't miraculously have her bolting upright in bed. Nope. She was still firmly seated inside the bleak interrogation room Agent Waller had frog-marched her to after frog-marching her out of the car, across the parking lot, and into the ten-story building.

Apparently, Agent Waller was a big fan of the frog-march.

"I'm not letting you anywhere near this evidence." Mulder tapped the closed laptop lid. "I've read your file. I know what you're capable of when you get a keyboard beneath your fingertips."

She was still barefoot and wearing the sleepwear she'd had on when the feds had burst into the apartment. Even so, when her teeth chattered, she wasn't sure if it was from her lack of appropriate attire or the trouble she was in.

Who's setting me up?

It was a question she couldn't answer unless she was given a chance to look at the evidence.

Which left the question of *why*? Why would someone want to frame her?

She'd helped bring down plenty of criminals in the two years she'd worked for the Department of Defense. Had one of them somehow traced their apprehension back to her? Were they now seeking revenge in the best way possible, by making her out to be the thing she hated most? A lowdown, dirty criminal?

Which, of course, brought her back around to her original question. The question of *who* would—

A sudden thought occurred and she nailed Mulder with a diamond-hard stare. "Who tipped you off to my *supposed*"—she flicked a finger toward the laptop—"involvement in this ransom scheme?"

Mulder's chin jerked back with incredulity. "Do I need to remind you *I* am the one asking the questions here, Miss Blue?"

"I just find it strange that this afternoon I found proof that a group of Chinese hackers have discovered a way to insert malware inside the computer system controlling Texas's power grid, and now here I am being accused of conspiring with the very people I'm paid to hunt down."

Ignoring her, Mulder said, "If you cooperate, if you help us take down Red Square before they can kill the pipeline, I'm sure we could work out a deal on your charges. Get them lessened." He sat back again and gave her a friendly smile that didn't reach his eyes. "I mean, it's possible we could even get them dropped. How does that sound?"

"I would *love* to help you take out Red Square. Problem is, I don't know who they are or how to find them. If I did, I wouldn't have conspired with them. I would've nailed the bastards to the wall."

For a long moment, the fed said nothing, simply regarded her through narrowed eyes.

She tried her best not to squirm. But it was damned difficult considering she was barely dressed. And considering if it was more than sixty degrees inside the room she'd eat her favorite WiFi Pineapple whole, including its five radio antennae.

"You're very convincing, Miss Blue," Mulder finally said. "But I've been doing this job long enough to know all the good criminals are. Tell me." He cocked his head. "Have you been playing the long game this entire time? Two years with the D.O.D. just to get to this point? Or were you a good little cog in the machine until you saw an opportunity to make a little extra scratch?"

This is going nowhere, she thought impatiently as another uncontrollable shiver made her teeth clack together.

Rubbing her hands over her exposed arms didn't do a thing to ease the goose bumps peppering her skin. And when she glanced around the room, looking for a vent in the hopes she could go stand under the heat, she realized there wasn't a duct to be found. Just four drab, gray walls. One cold tile floor. And the uncompromising metal table in the center of it all where she sat opposite a man who refused to believe a word out of her mouth.

"Can someone get me a coat or something?" She hated the pleading in her voice when what she really wanted was to fly across the table and choke Mulder with his own tie until he *listened* to what she was saying.

If this whole Red Square/Dominion setup *was* related to the intel she'd uncovered about the Chinese hackers, time was of the essence. According to the information she'd stumbled upon, the hackers planned to have their inside man attack Texas's grid in the next twenty-four to forty-eight hours.

"Agent Waller?" Agent Mulder turned to look at the two-way mirror that showed Hannah's pale and shivering reflection. "Bring Miss Blue a blanket, would you? She's not dressed for this weather."

Not dressed for this weather because you didn't let me change or grab shoes, you blackhearted bastard, she thought.

Aloud, she asked, "Can you at least tell me if the information regarding the Chinese hacker group made its way to my superiors?"

She'd sent her gathered intelligence through the coded channels she always used. But given her current predicament, it was possible she'd been followed out of the depths of the dark web and reverse-hacked, then framed so that doubt would be cast on her character.

If that was the case, she thought it highly likely her message for the big fish inside the D.O.D.—the nameless, faceless group that took her information and ran with it—had been intercepted and sent to that limitless, virtual garbage bin in cyberspace.

"I've played the shell game before, Miss Blue," Mulder tsked. "But I'm not going to let you distract me. No sleight of hand is going to turn me away from the issue of Red Square and your association with them."

She sighed. Or shuddered. A sigh mixed with another full-body shiver automatically became a shudder, right? Continuing to try to convince Mulder she was innocent was a waste of her time. He'd made up his mind about her.

Changing tactics, she curled her toes against the cold, tile floor and asked, "Is it possible for me to speak with Agent Floyd? He knows me from a job I assisted the FBI with a few months back."

After she'd played a key role in helping the Black Knights expose the Russian-backed troll farm, she and Agent Timothy Floyd had gone out to dinner. They'd soon learned their similarities stopped at their mutual love for Carpi Sun, however, and there hadn't been a second date.

Even still, he'd been on the call with her and the director. Surely he'd be willing to try to convince Agent Mulder to at least *consider* what she was saying and investigate whether or not her intelligence had been received by the higher ups in the Department of Defense.

"Agent Floyd transferred to the Cincinnati office three months ago," Mulder informed her with a self-satisfied shrug.

Yeah. She remembered Tim mentioning something about missing his family and being homesick for Ohio.

So much for that idea.

Changing tactics again, she asked, "I'm assuming you plan to book me tonight?"

"We have more than enough to hold you with or without your confession." Mulder's expression morphed from self-satisfied into what could only be described as smug.

"So I get a phone call, right? A chance to talk to my lawyer?"

As soon as she mentioned the L-word, irritation flamed in the agent's eyes. He knew as well as she did the instant a suspect demanded their counsel be present, the interview was over.

The gray metal door leading to the hallway opened and Agent Waller— *man, how I haven't missed him*—walked into the interview room. He had a ratty blue blanket that looked like it belonged on the bed of a Civil War prisoner.

She wondered if he'd found it in the dumpster outside.

"Not that you deserve it, *traitor*." He threw the blanket on the table in front of her before stomping out of the room.

She couldn't bring herself to care about his vitriol. Not when her freedom—maybe her very *life* and the lives of many others in Texas and across the country—could be at stake.

Unfolding the blanket, she quickly wrapped it around her shoulders. It wasn't long enough to tuck around her feet, so she pulled her legs up and sat crisscross-apple-sauce in the uncomfortable metal chair until she could snug the blanket beneath her frozen toes.

Better, she thought once the only part of her remaining visible was her head.

Although better was a far cry from good. She still couldn't keep her teeth from chattering or her limbs from shivering so hard she worried she might shake them loose from her body.

"You'll have to excuse Keith," Agent Mulder said. "His wife works for Apple. She had to deal with that ransomware attack by REvil back in—"

"2021," she cut in. "Yeah. I remember that hack job by the Kremlin. It resulted in unprecedented schematic leaks."

"Right." Mulder nodded. "Which means Keith's wife was working around the clock for months trying to clean things up. Not seeing each other took a toll on their marriage. They're still not fully recovered. You can understand how he'd hold a grudge against people like you."

"People like me?"

"People who think just because they don't run into the street with an automatic rifle and gun down innocents in a hailstorm of bullets that what they do doesn't hurt people. There are real world consequences to this kind of online warfare, Miss Blue."

"I did *not* scheme with Red Square to take down Dominion Pipeline!" It was the dozenth time she'd repeated the words. And it had the same impact on Mulder as it'd had the eleven times before. Sighing, she shook her head. "You don't take after your namesake, huh?"

His eyebrows pinched together.

"The truth is out there?" When he shook his head, she added the second most famous line from the series. "I want to believe?"

"Are you talking in some sort of code again, Miss Blue?"

"It's from *The X-Files.* You know, Agents Mulder and Scully out to explain the unexplainable? Surely I'm not the first person to point out that you share the name of the FBI agent from one of the longest running Sci-Fi series ever."

The line between Mulder's brows deepened and she sighed again.

Was it a requirement that newbie FBI agents hand over their senses of humor and their subscriptions to Netflix when they walked through the doors at Quantico, she wondered?

"I don't have much time for television, Miss Blue," Mulder said as if he deserved some sort of medal.

"Right." She rolled her eyes before adding, "Can I get my phone call now?"

"As you wish." He pushed up from the metal table and motioned for her to precede him toward the door.

She considered making a reference to *The Princess Bride*. But she'd learned her lesson about using pop culture references and didn't waste her breath.

She really *hated* the idea of uncurling from the infinitesimal amount of warmth she'd found snugged inside the blanket. *But needs must.* Physical discomfort was temporary. Being able to clear her name and possibly save the state of Texas—and the country at large—from a disaster of incalculable proportions would last a lifetime.

Sack up, Hannah, she coached herself as she gingerly placed her soles back on the floor. Her feet were no longer numb. But she wished they were because the tile might as well have been an iceberg. The cold was so intense it burned.

After wrapping the blanket as tightly around herself as she could, she limped after Agent Mulder as he led her from the room and down a narrow, featureless hallway. Keeping her chin down, playing the submissive suspect, she covertly checked out the security around her.

It wasn't much. There was only one camera mounted to the ceiling above a metal door that boasted a red and white "exit" sign.

Apparently, the FBI wasn't too concerned about their prisoners escaping.

Which was exactly what she planned to do if Sam couldn't call in a favor to get her released.

CHAPTER 5

Black Knights Inc.

S am watched, mesmerized, as Cesarine became Cesar.

Hannah's best friend and roommate pulled the black wig off his head, peeled a set of wispy lashes off his lids, and used a handful of tissues from his purse to wipe what looked like ten pounds of makeup off his face. But even without all the props and beauty aids, he was still dazzlingly beautiful when he smiled at Eliza while accepting the steaming mug of coffee she handed him.

Eliza shook her head and said in an awe-struck voice, "Even without the hair and makeup, you're still absolutely gorgeous."

"Thank you, darling." Cesar winked as he blew over the top of his coffee.

After taking a greedy sip, he sputtered and set the cup on the table a good foot in front of him. Then he eyed the beverage like he was afraid it might explode. Or grow legs, walk across the table, and forcefully pour itself down his throat.

"Yes, um, sorry." Eliza wrinkled her nose. "I should've warned you. The coffee around here is more like espresso on crack. It's tolerable if you mix it with creamer in a 50/50 ratio." She hitched her chin to the creamer sitting on the serving tray in the center of the table.

"High-octane liquid life." Fisher took a healthy gulp from his own mug of straight black java. "It'll put a pep in your step and grow hair on your ass."

"Just what I want." Eliza made a face. "A hairy ass." She cocked her head as she reconsidered her words. "Although, if it'll keep you from propositioning me, then maybe I *should* consider the merits."

"If ya think a little hair on a derriere would stop me from givin' a woman the love she's cravin', then ya don't know me at all."

"If *only* that were true. I would *love* not to know anything about you and your various exploits with—"

"Children, children." Ozzie patted the air. "We've lost the plot."

Sam hid a grin. Most of the OG Black Knights had seven to ten years on the new crew. But Ozzie was only thirty-four—the same age as Sam. Which meant it was highly hilarious when he tried to act like BKI 2.0's senior statesmen.

"The question remains"—Ozzie stared hard at Cesar—"what exactly is it you think we can do to help?"

Hannah's roommate had been quick to fill them in on the FBI raid. He'd been even quicker to assure them it had to have been a mistake.

"Hannah might not be the picture of a patriot that everyone expects," he'd said. *"She doesn't wear the flag on her chest and she's not a lifetime member of the NRA. But she* loves *this country. She believes* in it. *She'd never sell her soul for quick cash."*

Sam agreed. And he might've thought *the truth always prevails in the end,* thought *the FBI will figure out they're wrong about her,* if he hadn't spent the last decade and a half working for the government.

Like beauty, sometimes the truth was in the eye of the beholder. And when it came to games of international intrigue, national security, and espionage, the powers that be occasionally got it bass ackwards. When that happened, innocent people paid the price.

He was ready to move heaven and earth to make sure Hannah didn't pony up one single red cent.

"I don't know." Cesar shook his head. "Hannah just said she was in trouble and that *you*"—he pointed directly at Sam—"were the one person who might be able to help her out of it."

"It'd be easier if we could find out exactly what's going on," Ozzie said.

"Like, what proof does the FBI have that she's guilty of the thing they're accusing her of?"

"I bet Grace could help us find out," Fisher submitted.

"Grace is an FBI agent here in Chicago. She also happens to be the wife of one of the guys who works with us," Eliza explained for Cesar's benefit.

"Unfortunately, she left for her honeymoon yesterday," Ozzie was quick to add. As soon as Hunter, Fisher, and Sam had come back from Colombia, Hunter and Grace and packed their bags and headed for Greece for a long-overdue celebration of their nuptials. "And I don't know about the rest of you"—Ozzie looked around the table—"but I like my teeth the way they are and don't care for the idea of Hunter rearranging them. Which he'll do if we call and interrupt him now."

"Right," Sam agreed. "We need to find another way to figure out what the hell is going on and why the hell the FBI is so sure Hannah is involved in this plot."

"Hannah said you all have—" Cesar was cut off mid-sentence when Peanut, the alley-cat-turned-rotund-indoor-fluffball, landed on his lap. "Well, hello there," he cooed at the notch-eared devil.

Sam had to hide a grin when Peanut's yellow eyes slitted at the sound of Cesar's voice. Peanut loved women. Men he only tolerated. And it was clear the cat couldn't decide which he was dealing with when it came to Cesar.

The instant Cesar scratched Peanut's cheeks with his long, red fingernails, however, the cat leaned into the caress and started purring.

Since Peanut had a motor big enough to give Pale Horse's supped-up V-twin a run for the money, Cesar had to raise his voice to be heard over the racket. "Don't you guys have government contacts? I mean, from what little Hannah told me about the job she helped you with a few months back, I thought for sure you'd be able to make a call and get her out so we could see what's what."

If only it were that simple.

Since Madam President wanted to keep it on the DL that she employed a group of highly trained, highly skilled commandos to sometimes circumvent traditional military pursuits, it wasn't like the Knights had the freedom to drop the president's name and spring Hannah from FBI custody.

Quite the opposite, they did their best to *avoid* getting on anyone's radar. Especially the radars of people whose very job it was to investigate anyone or anything they found suspicious.

"Unfortunately, we don't have that kind of clout." Ozzie ran a hand through his unruly head of sandy-blond hair. He was wearing one of his countless *Star Trek* T-shirts. This one was printed with a picture of Spok's favorite hand gesture. Stamped beneath the picture were the words: Stay Weird.

Ozzie's words had Cesar visibly deflating. In his dejection, he absently stopped scratching Peanut. This gave the cat time to turn his head and get an eyeful of the long black wig piled atop the table.

Sam saw what would happen before Peanut even batted his crooked tail. But he wasn't fast enough to grab the cat before Peanut jumped on the wig with an ungodly *yowl*.

What followed would've garnered a million views on social media had anyone thought to whip out their camera and start recording.

Peanut attacked the hair by falling to his side and sinking his teeth into the strands, kicking his back legs along the long tresses as he continued to howl and hiss so loudly Sam's back teeth began to itch. It eventually became clear to the tom, however, that the hairy black mass wasn't a rival, that it wasn't even *alive*. At which point Peanut stopped his attack and glanced around at the shocked faces staring back at him with various expressions of humor and horror.

Looking embarrassed by his mistake, Peanut righted himself. Unfortunately, a hank of hair had gotten caught in the metal bell attached to his collar. When he took a step away from the wig, the wig went with him.

That's when all hell *really* broke loose.

With a hiss of terror, Peanut proceeded to dart around the conference table, knocking over coffee mugs and the bottle of creamer along the way and dragging the wig through the mess. Everyone hopped from their seats with yelps of surprise.

Cesar yelled, "Oh, my god! My favorite wig!" at the exact moment Sam caught Peanut by the scruff and stopped the carnage.

With a quick twist of his wrist, he pulled the wig free. But the damage had been done.

Holding out the tangled, coffee-and-creamer-drenched hair toward Cesar, he winced. "Can you, uh, shampoo it? Does it work that way?"

Cesar gingerly caught the wig between two fingers. His expression was a mixture of dismay and resignation. "It does. But it'll take me three hours to restyle it."

Sam winced again and then turned to scowl at Peanut. Instead of being grateful Sam had saved him from the wig, the bastard cat turned his head and sank his needle-like teeth directly in Sam's wrist.

"Ow!" Sam tore his arm free, dropping the tom onto the table with a *thud*. Peanut didn't hesitate to launch himself onto the floor, landing with enough force to rattle Sam's chair.

As Peanut scurried toward the stairs leading to the third floor, Sam understood how the phrase "more than one way to skin a cat" might have become part of the human lexicon. Because it took every ounce of self-control he possessed not to give chase.

Instead, he satisfied himself with shaking a fist at Peanut's wide, retreating backend. "Stupidity and bad tempers aren't crimes, you little shit! So I guess you're free to go!"

When he turned back to the table, rubbing his wrist—which sported four tiny holes beading with blood—he saw Ozzie trying his best to hide his grin. "Uh. You okay, bruh?"

"Sure." Sam walked over to the bank of computers that was the beating heart and firing brain of BKI's clandestine endeavors. He snagged a tissue from a metal holder atop the desk. "Just living the dream," he added sarcastically, followed by, "Someday I might have to kill that cat."

Ozzie grimaced. "Which would break Becky's heart. Which, in turn, would make Boss kill *you*."

Ozzie was right, of course.

Becky—the lead mechanic and wunderkind designer of the badass bikes that gave the civilian side of their operation legitimacy—*loved* Peanut. Her love was evidenced by the cat's size. Because even though she swore she fed Peanut vet-prescribed diet kitty chow, for the last three-plus years, Sam had witnessed her slipping the fat feline treats on the daily. And Boss? Well, Boss was the head of the original crew of operators. But, more importantly, he was Becky's husband.

The man became six-and-a-half feet of bulk, buzzcut, and bad temper when anything so much as made Becky's eyebrows knit together.

Dabbing at his puncture wounds, Sam said, "So maybe I won't kill Peanut. Maybe he'll simply jump the back wall and *accidently* drown in the Chicago R—"

The rest of his sentence was cut off by the sudden sound of Lady Gaga singing about lovers in the night.

When Cesar's eyes jumped to the side, Sam made his way back to the conference table. He was careful to avoid the spilled coffee dripping from the table onto the floor when he asked, "What is that?"

"My phone." Cesar's eyebrows—which weren't as thick and arching as they'd been when he'd been wearing the face of Cesarine—drew together over his nose. "But I don't know who'd be calling. My partner thinks I'm performing tonight. And it wouldn't be anyone from the club. When I called to tell them I wouldn't be coming in, I said it was because I had a family emergency." Cesar screwed up his lips. "Maybe it's a wrong number? Spam or something?"

"Answer it," Sam advised. When he realized he'd inadvertently used his military voice, he softened his tone. "It might be Hannah."

"My god," Cesar wheezed. "You think?"

Cesar didn't wait for Sam to answer before diving into the sparkly purse he'd slung over the back of the chair.

It seemed to take the man forever and a day to locate his phone. *And those two-inch fingernails aren't helping matters,* Sam thought impatiently. He was poised to step forward and take over the task when Cesar finally came up with his cell.

Pressing the device to his ear, he said, "Hello?" Followed immediately by, "Oh my god, what—"

That's all he managed before snapping his mouth shut and nodding his head at the group, letting everyone know Sam had been right. It *was* Hannah calling.

Sam wanted to yank the phone from Cesar's ear and press it to his own. He only managed to keep his hands to himself by shoving them deep into the front pockets of his jeans.

Hannah's voice was small and tinny-sounding through the phone's speaker. He couldn't make out her words, but the fear and desperation in her tone were as clear as bells.

"Yes." Cesar's eyes darted to Sam. "He's here with me. Or, I should say, I'm here with him."

Sam stepped forward to take the phone. But Cesar shook his head. "I don't think he can pull the strings you thought he could, Hannah. It doesn't sound like he'd able to just waltz in there and get you out without—" He stopped talking and listened.

A pit formed in Sam's stomach as he watched Cesar's eyes grow wide.

"No." The man shook his head. "No, Hannah. That's nuts! Don't you dare—" He blinked and briefly looked down at his glowing screen before returning the phone to his ear. "Hannah? Hannah? Damnit! She hung up on me!"

"What did she say?" Sam's military voice was back. He couldn't help it.

Cesar's Adam's apple bobbed in his throat. "She said there might be more at play here than just Red Square and Dominion Pipeline. She said since you can't get her out, she's making a break for it because the clock is ticking and people could die if she doesn't convince someone to listen to her."

The pit in Sam's stomach grew spikes and cut into his spleen. Surely, *surely* she wasn't thinking of attempting to escape from the Federal Bureau of Investigations?

Then again, he hadn't dubbed her Hurricane Hannah for nothing. Even at thirteen, she'd been a whirlwind. All feisty and rash and fiercely determined to do…well…whatever she had her mind set on at that moment.

Fuck!

"She said she needs you to be waiting for her at the back of the FBI field office in thirty minutes," Cesar added, looking directly at Sam.

"Holy shit!" Eliza's eyes were round. "She can't be serious."

"She's serious." Sam was already on the move, his boots thudding against the metal floor as he bolted for the stairs.

"Wait!" Fisher called. "What's the plan? Ya can't go off half-cocked!"

"Hannah didn't leave us much of a choice in that, did she?" Sam called over his shoulder as he took the stairs two at a time. "Ozzie?" he yelled above the thunder of his own footfalls. "Kill the CCTV cameras between here and the FBI field office if you can! If she somehow manages not to get herself shot making her escape, we don't want the feds tracking her back here! Cesar, go home! Hannah doesn't want you mixed up in what's gonna happen next!"

"I'm comin' with ya!" Fisher called, already following Sam down the stairs.

Sam stopped, his heart—usually metronome steady—was going wild inside the cage of his ribs. "No." When Fisher opened his mouth to argue, he shook his head hard. "I need you here helping Eliza and Ozzie think of all the things I don't have time to consider. Like what the hell we're gonna do to hide an FBI fugitive."

CHAPTER 6

Eliza had already begun her ritual pacing and rubbing of the locket she wore around her neck when Ozzie grabbed a seat at his bank of computers, his fingers flying over the closest keyboard.

The little heart-shaped locket held her mother's photo and brought her comfort anytime she was stressed. And hoofing it was how she did her best thinking. Something about moving her body in a repetitive path encouraged her brain to disconnect from the world so it could run through scenarios, weigh consequences, and mull over the infinitesimal details that could mean the difference between a successful mission and one where the men she'd grown to know and love came home in body bags.

She *had* grown to know and love each and every one of the Black Knights. Hunter for his ability to stay calm even when the entire world was turning upside down. Sam for treating her like a long-lost sister from the first moment he met her. Graham for understanding that silence was golden and *never* attempting to mansplain anything to her. Britt for his obsession with fun and adventure. Hewitt for his love of books and his comically pessimistic outlook on life. And Fisher for…well, that was a whole other story.

The Black Knights had given her a place to belong. They'd given her a purpose, a direction, a reason to get up in the morning with the goal of making the world a better, *safer* place for everyone. But most importantly, they'd given her people to care for. People to pamper and spoil. People who had favorite meals she could prepare. Who'd sit around the table playing cards after the holiday dishes were put away. Who lived with her day-in and day-out and thus knew all her frailties and foibles and adored her anyway.

Having grown up almost entirely in boarding schools, she'd longed for the stuff she'd seen depicted in those sweet, sappy movies that played on the Hallmark Channel, the things she'd heard other girls at school talking about but had never experienced herself.

To put it simply, BKI had given her a family. And she was bound and determined to make sure all *her guys*, as she liked to call them, made it out the other side of this particular career path with all their body parts still intact.

If the original Knights could do it, so could the new crew.

But to ensure that happened, she had to stay frosty. Vigilant. *Careful* when it came to helping plan missions and organize transportation and scour intel.

Her father had made it clear from the beginning he and Madam President expected BKI to operate as independently as possible. "

The president and I need plausible deniability should the truth of Black Knights Inc. ever reach the media," he'd said the day he'd told her about his desire to install her in a position within the company. *"I expect to be kept apprised of the details regarding the men and their missions, but that's where I'd like my involvement to end. Are we clear on that?"*

They'd been clear. Her job was to pass along the information about the Knights and their assignments, but if the BKI boys ever found themselves in a bind, the last place they should look for help was the Oval Office.

That fact had been hammered home recently down in Colombia. When her guys had found themselves fighting for their lives, it would've been the simplest thing for her father to call in an exfil from the U.S. naval base in Cartagena. But when she'd phoned him in desperation, asking him to do exactly that, he'd told her, *"This op is strictly off books. Local military doesn't even know it's going down. I'm sure your guys can handle themselves. Aren't you always bragging they're the best of the best?"*

It wasn't bragging. It was a statement of fact.

And yet, she'd been scared. Scared by how badly the Knights had been outnumbered. Scared of the local law enforcement who'd been helping them on the op because, like anywhere else, a man in a uniform couldn't always be trusted—a badge didn't make a man immune to corruption. Scared that her guys might've found themselves in a situation too hot and too heavy for even their mad skills to navigate.

She'd never been particularly close with her father. How could she have been when the only times she'd seen him during her growing up years were the Thanksgiving and Christmas holidays and the few weeks during the summers when she hadn't been shuffled between one camp or another? But even though they'd never been close, she'd always loved him, respected him, had wanted to do whatever it took to make him proud.

That night, on that call, things had changed. That night, on that call, she'd realized when push came to shove, her dear old dad really *was* just a political animal. More worried about his position within the government than he was the lives of six courageous men who never questioned or complained about the sometimes *insanely* dangerous jobs Madam President assigned them.

That night, on that call, Eliza had wanted to reach through the phone and throttle the man who'd given her life.

In the end, however, he'd been right. Her guys *had* managed to handle themselves. They'd put a period on the cartel leader's life and escaped without any of them sustaining serious injuries. But it'd been a close thing.

Too close.

She *still* couldn't understand how the intel they'd received from their source inside the CIA had been so wrong. If she were a conspiracy theorist, she'd swear they'd been set up. But she was pragmatic enough to know that even the Central Intelligence Agency, ostensibly the best information gathering group in the world, sometimes got shit wrong.

Speaking of getting shit wrong...

"Sam!" she yelled, dropping her locket as the roar of a V-twin engine filled the factory building. "Wait!" Flying down the metal stairs, she hissed, "Move!" as she shoved by Fisher who had taken up a position in the middle of the staircase. Against her will, his aftershave tunneled up her nose and made the hairs on her arms lift in awareness.

Why does he have to smell so good, all smokey and sweet like fine scotch?

Why can't he smell like the man-ho he is, like cheap cologne and 3-in-1 hair and body wash?

"Hey!" he called after her. "What's the rush?"

She ignored him as she raced across the shop floor toward the yawning black hole that led to the secret entrance—or in this case, *exit*—to the BKI compound. Sam had already nosed the front tire of his big, heavily chromed out bike over the lip of the tunnel. His back brake light sent a wash of red into the shop, making the large space with its rows of bike-lifts and horde of tools look eerie, like the set of a horror movie where a serial-killer mechanic tortured his victims.

"Sam!" she called again. "Wait a second!"

But Sam couldn't hear her over the motorcycle's massive engine. With a twist of his wrist, the bike lurched into the tunnel and was immediately swallowed up by the darkness.

She skidded to a halt at the entrance to the Bat Cave, as they lovingly called the channel dug beneath the Chicago River. It ended in a lightly used parking garage on the opposite bank. Like the back taillight, the sound of the motorcycle was quickly consumed by the steep curve of the tunnel. And within seconds, all she could hear was the steady *drip, drip, drip* of the moisture leaking off the thick walls and hitting the cement floor.

"Shit," she muttered as she took her cell phone from her pocket to shoot Sam a quick text. Not that she held out much hope he'd actually *look* at his phone before making the trek to FBI headquarters.

The expression he'd worn when Cesar explained Hannah's plan had said he was one-hundred-percent focused on getting to Miss Blue with all due haste. And when Sam focused, he *focused*. It was almost trance-like. His pupils pinpointed. His breathing grew slow and deep. And his movements, which were always athletic and coordinated, became swift and efficient—no wasted movement.

It was sort of like watching a jungle cat home in on its prey.

After she hit "send," she walked over to the wall where a large red button was concealed behind a rolling Craftsman toolbox. The air belching up from inside the tunnel wasn't nearly as frigid as the air outside, but neither was it warm. She was anxious to close up the wall.

Smashing the button with her palm, she stepped back and watched the pop-out section of the brick expanse slowly slide back into place until the gaping maw of the tunnel was concealed. When the bricks knitted themselves together with a solid-sounding *thunk*, the illusion was complete.

Nothing to see here, folks. No secret passageway. Just a solid wall.

If not for the lingering aroma of wet concrete mixed with a hint of fish, no one would ever know anything of interest lay behind the old factory building's east facade.

Except *Cesar* now knew.

"What in the world?" he breathed. He'd come to stand beside her, his dark eyes wide and unblinking.

She was a stickler when it came to civilians entering the shop. She couldn't do anything about the occasional reporter who wanted to interview Becky about building bikes or the various deep-pocketed, golden-spoon types who came in to actually *request* one of BKI's custom jobs. And, truly, both of those things were *boons* to the business. They upheld the illusion that Black Knights Inc. was exactly what it was purported to be, a badass chopper shop. But she tried her best to mitigate any other potential security breaches. Which was why she'd implemented her *No Dates Allowed* policy.

Well, that and because I hate it when one of Fisher's conquests struts into the kitchen the morning after and I have to make her coffee.

It wasn't that she thought Cesar would ever *intentionally* become a security breach. But sometimes people popped off at the mouth before they realized what they were saying. And anyone outside "the life" had no clue just how much trouble they could cause if one misplaced word landed in the wrong ear.

It was bad enough Cesar knew the truth about the Knights. Him knowing about the Bat Cave made all her internal alarms blare simultaneous warnings.

"I'm sure it goes without saying you aren't to share anything you've seen or heard here with anyone outside this building." She worked hard to keep her voice steady, but a hint of a threat still snuck into her tone.

Apprehension made Cesar's beautiful eyes widen further. "Who would I tell?"

"Don't know." She shook her head. "A friend. Someone in your family. Your partner, perhaps? But you have to understand that these men"—she waved a hand to indicate Fisher, who'd made his way to the bottom of the stairs, and Ozzie, who was upstairs rattling away on keyboard—"do the kind of work that makes them targets of some very nasty people. If you tell one person what you've seen here, and that person tells one person, and so forth and so on, there's no telling where that information ends up. Maybe in the ears of people looking to hunt these fine men down like dogs." Her gaze was unmistakably direct when she added, "These men who are, at the very least, risking their reputations by helping Hannah. And perhaps even risking their lives."

Cesar's voice was hoarse when he nodded. "I understand. I won't mention any of this"—he gestured toward the brick wall and then widened his hand to include the entirety of the old factory building—"to anyone."

When she narrowed her eyes, not sure she could believe him, he added, "I was seven years old the first time I realized I was gay. But I didn't come out to my staunchly Catholic parents until I was twenty-two. I know how to keep a secret."

"Good." She jerked her chin once, feeling somewhat relieved. "Now, Sam's right. Hannah wouldn't want you anywhere near here. Go home. Plausible deniability when the feds come knocking and all that."

"But…" He shook his head. "I'd like to stay. I'd like to make sure Hannah's okay and—"

"She'll be a whole hell of a lot better knowin' she hasn't dragged ya into somethin' ya might not be able to get out of." Fisher had made his way over to them. He clapped a hand on Cesar's shoulder. "She did right by tellin' ya to come to us. Now let us take it from here. I'll have Toran out at the gate call a cab for ya."

Cesar hesitated. But he must've seen that no amount of arguing was going to change their minds. "Will you call me once she's here? Let me know she made it?" he asked hopefully, twisting the damp wig he held in his hands.

"If she manages to escape, the first thing the feds will do is come to you," Eliza was quick to explain. "They'll assume she's headed back home. Or, at the very least, that she's telling her best friend and roommate where she *is* headed. So, we won't be able to call you. It's a sure bet one of the first things the FBI will do is requisition your phone logs."

When Cesar visibly deflated, Fisher added, "But ya should take silence as a sign. If ya don't hear from us, it'll mean she's here. It'll mean we got her and she's safe. And I promise ya, as soon as it's feasible for her to make contact, she will. In the meantime, when the feds come knockin', ya just play dumb. And if they get pushy, ask to have an attorney present. Ya got someone ya can call for legal representation?"

Cesar nodded. "I have a friend who's a criminal defense attorney when he's not doing a bang-up impersonation of Katy Perry."

"Perfect." Eliza smiled encouragingly.

Cesar's return smile was a little wobbly. Then it disappeared completely as a deep line appeared between his perfectly plucked eyebrows. "I worried when she took that job with the D.O.D. that she might get caught up in something dangerous. I just never imagined... *this.*"

"We all get to go about our ordinary, borin' days because folks like Hannah do the dirty work of crawlin' through the dark side of the internet catchin' the cyber criminals who'd like nothin' more than to make our lives a livin' hell. But that just means she's tough. And tough people don't go down without a fight." He took a deep breath and finished with, "Everyone here at BKI is a fighter too. If there's a way to get your girl out of this mess, we'll find it."

Fisher reveled in being a world-class ass. Which just made it that much more astonishing when he whipped out the exact right thing to say at the exact right moment.

It makes no sense, Eliza thought. *And yet, it makes all the sense in the world.*

It was cliché, but Fisher was an onion. He had layers. There was light and dark in him. Flattery and snark in him. He was irreverent to the point of insolence, but at his core lived a big, squishy heart that was absolutely *full-to-burstin',* as he would say, with compassion.

And *that* was her kryptonite. It's what had made her fall in love with him.

Yes, despite them fighting like cats and dogs, Eliza Meadows was ass over teakettle in L.O.V.E with Fisher Wakefield. Or maybe *because* she was so in love with him was *why* they fought like cats and dogs. Because she knew her love was hopeless.

Fisher wasn't the type to settle down with one woman. Why would he when he had dozens panting after him everywhere he went?

And she had too much pride and self-respect to allow herself to become just another notch on his bedpost. So she kept her feelings to herself, and every day she searched for ways to fall out of love with him.

After Fisher escorted Cesar to the front door, she trotted to the bottom of the stairs and yelled up at Ozzie, "What can I do to help?"

Whitesnake blared from the second floor, David Coverdale wailing, *"Here I go again on my own!"* Eighties hair bands worked on Ozzie the way pacing worked on her.

"Coffee!" he hollered above the music. "Lots of it!"

"Copy that!" When she turned, she saw Fisher bent over in the doorway.

A gust of frigid February air had blown a dead leaf into the shop. He picked it up to toss it outside and after closing the door, he caught her staring. Or...*ogling* was probably a more apt description.

"See something you like?" He grinned that Fisher grin that was all charm and male magnetism and so, so much sex appeal.

She *did* see something she liked. Very much.

He had one of those high, round asses that begged to be squeezed. And his jeans were tight enough that she'd seen the delineation of the muscles in the backs of his thighs when he'd been bent over.

Oh, how she wanted to straddle those thighs. How she wanted to grab that ass. How she wanted to drag him up to the third floor and take him up on all the pleasure he'd been promising her for years if she'd just agree to sleep with him.

He's a lady-killer, she staunchly reminded herself. *He'd bed you and leave you in the dust just like he does all the others.*

Considering she'd spent six years in therapy working through her abandonment issues—even though her father would never see shipping her off to school after her mother passed as abandonment—she knew being slammed-bammed-and-thank-you-ma'amed by the man she'd lost her heart to would crush her. Would make all that childhood trauma rear its ugly head and set her back to the beginning on her healing journey.

So she tamped down the lust that fired low in her belly, batted her lashes, and fell back on her only two weapons of defense against Fisher. Derision and sarcasm. "You know what they say about big egos, right, Fish?"

"No." He shook his head and sauntered toward her. Fisher sauntered *everywhere,* his natural gait all loose-limbed and confident. "But I'm sure you're goin' to tell me."

"It's said big egos are big shields for lots of empty space."

He stopped a foot in front of her. Far enough away not to invade her personal space. But close enough that she could feel the heat coming off his big body.

"Ya sayin' I got no substance?" His eyes bored into hers.

She hated when he did that. Really *looked* at her. She always feared he might *see*.

See the truth of her feelings for him. See that all her sarcasm and cynicism was just a smokescreen for what she really wanted to say, which was that she'd never met a man who'd made her *want* the way he did.

She avoided his question by brushing past him. "I need to make a fresh pot of coffee for Ozzie. You know he's at his best when he's hopped up on caffeine."

Escaping down the hall and into the kitchen, she tried to force her brain away from BKI's resident playboy and toward the task at hand. But focusing on the task at hand was impossible when he stopped in the doorway.

His black T-shirt—he was *always* in black—pulled tight across his shoulders and chest when he hung onto the top jamb so he could casually lean into the room.

The hem of his shirt lifted enough to reveal a couple of things. One was the glinting chrome top of the harmonica he carried with him in his front pocket. The other was the two inches of tanned flesh beneath his belly button. It sported a line of curly hair that was a good three or four shades darker than the wavy, light-brown mop crowning his head.

She had the nearly overwhelming urge to walk over there, kneel down, and follow that line of hair with her tongue.

Her nipples hardened without her permission. They were a mutinous pair, to be sure. So she turned toward the sink, glad for the excuse of needing to fill the coffeepot with water.

"Why are you following me around like a puppy dog?" she asked over her shoulder as the water flowed into the insulated carafe. She usually preferred to use a French press. It made the strong coffee taste richer, creamier, and less acidic. But it took time for the grounds to steep, and Ozzie needed liquid life *stat*. So the industrial-size Bunn coffee maker the Knights kept in the corner of the kitchen for caffeine emergencies it was.

"Just wonderin' when you're goin' to call your daddy and let him know the president's personal henchmen are about to run afoul of the Federal Bureau of Investigations."

"I hate it when you refer to the Knights that way." She frowned as she poured the water from the pot into the coffee maker. "You're not henchmen. You're…guardians of democracy, protectors of American interests, the president's first line of defense when it comes to the missions the military can't touch with a ten-foot pole."

"You say tomato; I say mercenaries."

She frowned harder. "The difference between mercenaries and soldiers comes down to who's cutting the checks. It's a small but important distinction. Also, when it comes to us running afoul of the feds…it won't be the first time. We've already done it once this year."

Fisher had been out on assignment when Hunter had brought Agent Grace Beacham back to BKI after she'd been accused of killing her partner. But he'd been home for the sit-rep after the fact. He knew Hunter and Sam had kept Grace safe not only from the FBI but also from the infamous Russian assassin who'd been hot on her trail.

And now look at us. About to house another *fugitive.*

Fisher arched an eyebrow. "I can't help noticin' ya didn't answer my question."

Damn him! He liked to pretend he was nothing but a big, dumb grunt. An army bullet-sponge good for nothing but taking orders and spraying lead. But there was a reason he could quote John Keats and Sylvia Plath. He had a mind as sharp as a sword. Nothing escaped him.

"What?" She planted a hand on her cocked hip. "You think I should wait to let Dad know what's going on until *after* we get Hannah here?"

"Hey. Don't ask for my advice. I've fucked up just about every decision I've ever made in life." He lifted both hands in a shrug before resuming his grip on the doorframe.

I will not look at his love trail. I will not look at his love trail. Shit! I looked at his love trail.

Her mouth was watering again. As for her nipples? Yep. They were doing their thing, broadcasting loud and clear that she wanted to make him her Superman-sized lollipop and lick him from head to toe…paying *particular* attention to what was halfway between.

When she ripped her eyes away from the lovely line of hair delineating his stomach, she saw a strange expression in his eyes. It was…sad, maybe? Or…regretful?

Very un-Fisher-like considering he was the King of Cool, always with that laid-back air of amused indifference.

"You want to expand on that?" she prompted.

"Not really." He hitched a shoulder and she did *not* notice that it caused his shirt to inch higher. No, she did *not*. "Just makin' the point that ya should never ask me what ya should or shouldn't do. Because if devils are made from bad decisions, bad deeds, then I am, unquestionably, the devil incarnate."

The lust she'd experienced moments before morphed into concern. "I feel like there's something you're trying to tell me, Fish." His gaze caught and held hers until she found herself taking a step toward him. She was careful to keep the stinging sarcasm she usually reserved for him out of her tone when she asked, "Am I right?"

A muscle twitched in his jaw. If she hadn't been watching closely, she would've missed the subtle dip of his chin.

"Okay then." She nodded. "I'm all ears."

His voice, usually so low and smooth, turned rough. "I did somethin' on our last mission I'm not particularly proud of. Somethin' that's been eatin' at me ever since. But if I tell ya, I'm afraid it'll go into the next report ya send your pops. And I'd just as soon keep this particular clusterfuck off my record."

"Your record is sealed. Not even the Joint Chiefs can access it," she assured him.

"Even so." He hitched his shoulder again and dropped his gaze to the tile floor in front of him.

She liked it better when they were bickering. *Then* she knew what to do. What to say.

"Does this…uh…thing you did have any bearing on the outcome of the mission?" she asked hesitantly.

He shook his head.

She let loose with a sigh of relief. "Then there's no reason I'd need to report it to my father."

When he glanced up, the look of sadness in his hazel eyes nearly had her falling to her knees. It made all her softer feelings rise to the surface. Made her want to walk over, wrap her arms around his trim waist, and hug him.

Of course, the instant she was that close to him she knew she'd be tempted to take things beyond a hug. She'd be tempted to go up on tiptoe and see if his lips tasted as delicious as they looked.

She'd never seen a more beautiful mouth on a man. His lips were plump and pink, with the top one sporting a perfect Cupid's bow and the bottom one looking like a little pillow meant for nibbling.

The better angels of her nature kept her rooted in place. And as she waited for him to elaborate, the silence grew in the large kitchen until it seemed to take on mass, to press in on her from all sides. It was only broken by the distant notes of music—Ozzie's playlist had moved on to Mötley Crüe's "Kickstart My Heart"—and the gentle hum of the coffee maker as the hot water filtered over the grounds and filled the carafe.

Her voice was purposefully soft when she finally ventured, "I don't have any accreditation or anything. But I had plenty of practice playing the part of amateur counselor in boarding school. I mean"—she grinned at him encouragingly—"you get that many teenage girls together in one place and inevitably you end up having a big group therapy session."

The muscle twitching in his jaw began working double-time. He'd dropped his hands from the doorframe to shove them deep inside the front pockets of his jeans.

"I let a man be killed in cold blood the night of the raid." This was said through gritted teeth.

A chill stole up her spine, but she made sure to keep her features schooled into impassivity. "You were down there on a mission sanctioned by Madam President herself. The man you took out had been leaving a path of death and destruction behind him for months. And the guards who worked for him? They were as crooked and culpable as he was. Hell, they were the ones who'd been helping him do all his dirty work."

"But I'm not talkin' about Miguel Blanco or his men. I'm talkin' about a local law enforcement officer. One of the policemen who went on the raid with us." The words poured out of his mouth like poison from a vial and burned when they hit her ears.

She nearly recoiled but stopped herself by biting the inside of her cheek. In all the time she'd worked with Fisher, she'd never known him to be anything less than honorable.

He's even up-front with the women he dates. He tells them point-blank he's not relationship material and is only in it for the fun.

Making sure to keep her expression open and encouraging, she walked over and gently placed a hand on his arm. His skin was warm. The muscles beneath were hard and flexed at her touch.

"It's okay, Fish. You can tell me what happened."

CHAPTER 7

What the fuck are ya doin', man?

It was a question Fisher had asked himself more than once since following Eliza into the kitchen. Now he finally knew the answer.

It was there in her soft, dark eyes. There in her beautiful, compassionate expression. There in the tenderness of her hand on his arm.

He wanted to unburden himself. To absolve himself. To be told the horror he'd allowed to happen down in Colombia was right and just and not simply his childhood trauma coming back to bite him in the ass.

"Ya know what a shitshow it was down there." His voice was harsh with emotion. "By the time we breached the compound, we were tired, low on ammo, and runnin' on steam."

"And you were shot." Her gaze tracked down to his hip. The path the bullet left behind still smarted like a sonofabitch if he moved the wrong way.

"I was *grazed*," he corrected. "But that's neither here nor there. The point is, I was angry and probably not thinkin' straight when we split up to search the grounds for stragglers. Because when I went to clear the kitchen and saw that Colombian bastard—" His voice hitched.

Her palm, so soft and warm, rubbed up and down his arm.

How many nights had he lain awake *fantasizing* about her touching him? How many times had he imagined all the different scenarios that ended with her running those long, lithe fingers over his arm not out of annoyance, like she did after he'd said something particularly obnoxious, but with affection and care?

Too many to count.

And here she was doing exactly that. And here he was about to ruin it all by confessing the truth of what'd happened on his last mission.

Even still…he couldn't stop himself.

He had to know if he'd become the monster he'd always feared. Or was it possible there *was* justice in the choice he'd made?

No matter how many times he'd turned it over in his mind, he'd been unable to sort through the static to see things clearly. He had too many emotional scars. Was incapable of separating the sins of his father from his own motivations.

He needed a second opinion. A second set of eyes to look at what he'd done and tell him the truth about himself.

He could've asked his teammates. They were all decent, noble men. But they were also soldiers, hardened by life and the atrocities they'd seen. They had little compassion left for anyone who stepped over the lines of decency and honor. And that Colombian police officer had certainly done that by a good country mile.

So that left…Eliza.

Eliza with her clear head and open heart. Eliza, who'd grown up gently and *genteelly* and therefore hadn't been callused by the world. Eliza, whom he could always count on to tell him exactly what she thought of him, no holds barred.

"When I walked into that cartel leader's kitchen, I saw one of the Colombian officers rapin' a girl," he admitted lowly, the words feeling like they came with poison tipped barbs that scoured his throat as he spoke them. "I think she was one of Blanco's cooks or housekeepers or somethin'. She couldn't have been more than sixteen or seventeen. Lord"—he ran a hand through his hair—"she looked like a baby."

Eliza's pretty face paled as she dropped her hand from his arm. The kitchen air felt cold against his skin compared to the warmth of her touch.

He wondered if that was the first and last time he'd ever feel her fingers on him and chastised himself for not hesitating a bit longer before starting his tale. For not allowing himself a few more seconds to revel in the softness of her skin and the comfort of her touch.

"That sonofabitch had the girl pinned down on the floor. She was strugglin' and screamin' like—" He stopped himself as the awful scene replayed in his mind's eye.

He saw the policeman's naked, hairy ass pumping away between the girl's skinny legs as her feet scrabbled uselessly against the tile. Saw the blood streaming from her nose and the bruises blooming to Technicolor life on her jaw because the brute had punched her to gain her submission. Saw the look of horror and humility and…*brokenness* that'd come into her eyes.

It was a look he'd recognized well. A look that'd haunted his dreams since he'd been fifteen. A look he'd seen in his mother's eyes right before—

"I grabbed a fryin' pan and whacked the bastard on the back of the head so hard it was a wonder I didn't send his brain shootin' out his nostrils. I knocked him clean off the girl," he gritted from a jaw that'd locked down tight at the memory.

Even now, days later, all the muscles in his body clenched in fury when he thought back on what that sadistic motherfucker had been doing.

"While he was howlin' like a coyote and holdin' onto his head," he continued, "I snatched his weapon from his holster, pulled the clip, and threw his sidearm out the window into the koi pond."

There was confusion in Eliza's eyes. The questions she wanted to ask were obvious. *Why unload the weapon? Why not point it at the policeman and hold him hostage until he could be handed over to his superiors and brought up on rape charges?* But instead of voicing those queries, she waited for him to finish.

He could still remember the smells in that kitchen, cooked beans mixed with hot spices. And underneath it all, the scent of fresh blood. When he'd reached a hand toward the girl, she'd flinched and scampered backward like a crab, stopping when there'd been nowhere left for her to go. The cabinets had cut off her escape.

Her expression as she'd stared wide-eyed at him had made it clear she'd expected him to take over where the other man had left off. And even now bile climbed into the back of his throat at the thought.

He'd known what he was going to do the moment he'd walked into that kitchen and seen the brokenness in that girl's eyes. Even still, it'd seemed like someone else's legs carrying him over to the opposite counter. It'd seemed like someone else's hand reaching for the blade.

"I yanked a butcher knife out of the block and tested it with my thumb." A hard knot formed in the center of his throat. His words rasped around it. "It was razor-sharp."

The coffee machine had done its job. Now the kitchen was quiet enough to hear Eliza's throat work over a hard swallow. "You…you *stabbed* him?"

"No." He shook his head. "I gave the knife to the girl. Then I walked away."

Eliza blinked. A little line appeared between her delicately arched eyebrows. "You didn't stick around to make sure the officer didn't go after her again?"

Fisher jerked his chin side to side. "Didn't need to. I knew she was takin' care of the problem. The sound a knife makes when it's tearin' through flesh is unmistakable. So were the policeman's screams when I closed the door behind me."

"Dear god." Her hand jumped to cover her mouth.

"I know." He hung his head. His gaze was glued to the steel toes of his biker boots, but he wasn't really seeing them. His mind was still back in that other kitchen. Still seeing the dawning realization on the girl's face when he handed her that blade. "I shouldn't have done that. I should've—"

"What happened to the girl?" Eliza interrupted.

His eyes jumped to her face. He expected to see revulsion there. Disgust. He was a little surprised when all he saw was concern. "What do ya mean?"

"I mean did the authorities catch her? Is she being held in some sleazy Colombian jail for killing her rapist?"

"No." He shook his head. "I don't know where she ran off to, but she was nowhere to be found by the time the local boys discovered that bastard's body. They assumed he'd been taken down by one of Blanco's guards."

"Good." She blew out a rough breath and fished her locket from inside her blouse so she could rub her thumb over the golden heart. She did that anytime her emotions ran high. "That's perfect," she added.

His chin jerked back. "I let that girl kill that policeman. Worse, I handed her the weapon to do the job. Which means I may as well have done it myself. I *should* have done the job myself. I wasn't thinkin' about the added trauma I caused her by—"

"No." She cut him off by slicing her hand through the air. "It's better it was her who did it."

He blinked so quickly her grim expression took on a strobe effect.

"Rape is an abuse of power. A *theft* of power." Her harsh tone matched her expression. "You gave that girl her power back. And better than that, you allowed her to violate that policeman the way he violated her. You let her *enter* him without his permission just like he'd entered her."

Fisher was taken aback by the vehemence, the *viciousness* of her reaction. "Most…uh…civilized societies don't punish rape with death."

Her upper lip curled. "Maybe they should. Maybe then women would feel safe jogging alone or wearing their favorite sundress on a hot summer day or leaving their drink on the bar when they go to the restroom."

"So… ya don't think what I did was…" He licked his lips and slipped his hand into his pocket, feeling the cool steel of his harmonica. The instrument always brought him a level of peace. She had her locket. He had his mouth harp. "Evil or…immoral or…" He searched for the right word and couldn't find it. He ended up shrugging.

"I'm sure there are people who would argue the morality of what you did. Or"—she frowned—"it's more like they'd have to argue the morality of what you allowed that girl to do. But I'm not one of them. And I doubt anyone who's been raped would pass any judgement on you."

He was tempted, just for a moment, to tell her about his mother. To admit he'd handed that girl that knife because he *hadn't* been able to do the same for his mom. To explain that even though it'd been a Colombian police officer committing that awful act, all he'd seen when he'd looked in that man's face was his father's sweaty, rage-filled visage.

But then she'd know me for what I truly am. She'd see all the muck and mud I come from.

Keeping his mouth shut, he let his eyes travel over her. Her face was heart-shaped and soft. The black hair, high cheekbones, and a pointed chin she'd inherited from her Greek mother gave her a slightly exotic look. And she enhanced the almond shape of her eyes with black eyeliner and played up the plumpness of her mouth with lipstick the color of a dusty rose.

She was tall for a woman. Five eight or five nine would be his guess.

And her figure was trim and efficient. Nothing extra, but nothing missing either.

Simply put, Eliza was one of the most beautiful women he'd ever seen. *Classically* beautiful. Like an old black-and-white photograph that'd been digitally enhanced and filled with color.

The fire in her eyes when he returned his gaze to her face was something he hadn't seen before, however. It begged the question, "Have ya..." He stopped and reworded. "Did someone hurt ya, Eliza?"

Her nostrils flared. When her chin trembled, he only stopped himself from pulling her into his arms because he wasn't sure she'd welcome his embrace.

"No." She swallowed loudly and the wave of relief that washed over him was shocking in its size. "But my best friend..."

She turned her face to the side and worried her locket between her fingers. When she blinked three times in rapid succession, he knew she was fighting back tears.

Again, the urge to pull her into a hug was so strong he had to shove his hands into his pockets to keep from reaching for her.

"Aveline and I were roommates the last four years of boarding school," she whispered. "Aveline was a runner. She had legs like a gazelle and could go for hours. And one morning..." She trailed off again. It was as if she couldn't speak the awful words aloud and had to skip forward in the story. "Anyway, when she dragged herself back to the dormitory, she was so bloody and bruised I thought she'd been hit by a car."

"Fuck," he cursed, feeling the muscle in his jaw start twitching again.

"I held her on the ride to the hospital," she admitted hoarsely. "I held her when she was forced to strip naked so a nurse could take pictures of her injuries. And I held her hand as they took the samples for the rape kit. She never cried. Not once."

She turned back to him then and her brown eyes were swimming with unshed tears. "But once we got back to the dormitory, she didn't *stop* crying for three days."

"I'm so sorry, Liza." It was the first time he'd used her nickname. But it sounded right in that moment. It *felt* right in his mouth. "Did they ever catch the guy?"

Her hands were shaky when she wiped away the tears that slipped over her lower lids. "Yes. But sometimes I wish they hadn't. Sometimes I think it would've been better for Aveline if he'd just remained some faceless, nameless stranger."

When Fisher frowned, she explained. "She had to go through the horror of a trial. She had to get on that witness stand while that bastard of a defense attorney painted her as the school slut because she'd had a boyfriend she'd been intimate with. That lawyer even had the audacity to mention how short her running shorts were that morning. And even though he didn't say the words, everyone in that courtroom could read between the lines. He implied she'd been *asking* for it."

"Jesus." Fisher's stomach churned with revulsion.

"And you know what's worse?" Color rode high in her cheeks. "That fat, old, misogynistic judge bought it. He bought the sob story the defense painted of a rich frat boy whose parents had spoiled and coddled him and who hadn't taught him the difference between right and wrong. That judge said Aveline's rapist *deserved a second chance to make something of himself.*" She made air quotes. "And so he gave the twenty-two-year-old *man* who beat and brutalized and raped my friend time-served, community service, and probation. *Probation* for dragging her into an alleyway, punching her in the head until she was nearly unconscious, and then shoving his cock inside her while she struggled and bled onto the dirty ground."

Tears streamed unchecked down her cheeks now. But they weren't tears of sorrow. They were tears of rage.

He understood them.

He'd cried plenty of tears just like them in the days and weeks following his mother's murder.

"If I'd had a knife the day of the sentencing, I would've used it to carve up that sonofabitch," she snarled. "And more than that, I would've *enjoyed* it. So no." She shook her head. "I don't think what you did down in Colombia was wrong. In fact, I'm not sure you could've done anything more right."

It was as if a weight was lifted from his shoulders. "Ya don't think it makes me a monster?"

She used the backs of her hands to wipe away more tears. "Fisher, I think you're a tomcat and a player and a terrible tea maker. But a monster you are *not.*"

He'd only made her tea once. The time she and Sam had come down with the stomach flu together.

"What's wrong with the way I make tea?" he demanded. She was attempting to lighten the mood and he happily followed her direction.

"You have to let the tea bag *steep* for three to five minutes. Otherwise you just get colored hot water."

"Oh..." He scratched the stubble on his cheek. "I thought you just bobbed the bag up and down a couple of times." He made a face. "It's the thought that counts though, right? I still get brownie points for tryin'?"

"Mmm." She shook her head and sniffled. But there was a small smile playing at the corner of her mouth. "I suppose."

He chuckled and then sobered when he realized it was the first time they'd had a conversation that hadn't ended with one of them insulting the other. "Look at us. Bein' all friendly." When a snippet of a poem blossomed in his head, he recited it aloud. "'Friends will think of ways to make you smile. So you can be happy for a while.'"

She cocked her head. "So we're friends now, are we?"

"Aren't we?" he countered.

"Hmm." She flattened her mouth. "I suppose so. Which just drives home that old saying, *with friends like these, who needs enemies?*"

He chuckled again. And before he could think better of it, threw an arm around her shoulders to steer her toward the coffee maker. "Oh, come on. I'm not *that* bad, am I?"

"No." She shook her head. "And that's the problem. You're not bad at all."

He stopped and glanced down into her upturned face. He expected to find the usual teasing light in her eyes. He was confused when instead she just looked...earnest.

"Why's that a problem?"

"Because I don't *want* to like you, Fish. It's better for me when you're actively giving me reasons to *dis*like you."

"I don't understand." He shook his head.

"Don't you?"

He frowned as confusion gave way to an impossible idea.

Did she...*like* him? Like, *like* him like him?

No way, he quickly squashed the thought. It was too absurd.

Eliza came from money. He'd been born as poor as a church mouse. Her family had been part of American politics for generations. His family name was considered a swear word by some in north Louisiana. She had three degrees. He'd graduated high school on a wing and a prayer.

But he'd swear the look on her face said—

"Eliza!" Ozzie's voice echoed from the second floor. "If I have any hope of taking down all these damned CCTV cameras, I need caffeine! Tout de suite!"

"Right!" she hollered in response. "On my way!"

Fisher felt oddly bereft when she slid out from under his arm to grab the coffee carafe. After snagging a mug big enough to second as a soup bowl, she jogged from the kitchen, leaving him to stare after her retreating form.

What the hell just happened?

He replayed the scene in his mind and came up with a big ol' handful of nada.

Shaking his head, he decided, *I'm tired. The groove in my hip is burnin' like hellfire. And I've just been put through the emotional ringer after tellin' my tale and listenin' to hers.*

Eliza Meadows didn't like him. Not like *that*. In fact, she'd made it crystal clear on many occasions that most days it took everything in her simply to *tolerate* him.

Slapping both cheeks, he muttered to himself, "Get it together, son. Stop buildin' castles in the sky."

CHAPTER 8

Chicago's FBI Field Office

When Hannah cracked open the door of the women's restroom to find Agent Mulder with his back to her and his cell phone pressed to his ear, she blinked, momentarily discombobulated.

She'd expected to find him standing guard. She'd expected to have to do a juke move to avoid his grasp. She'd expected for it to be a footrace to the exit door and then a chase down the stairwell to the bottom level where, *hopefully*, Sam would be waiting to whisk her away to safety.

But if she could *sneak* her way out? Just slip through the cracks of FBI custody without them being the wiser?

Oh, that would be so much better.

Especially because her idea of exercise was hot yoga on Tuesdays and Thursdays followed by smoothies at the corner juice bar. She hadn't sprinted since… Well, the last time she could remember sprinting was in the fifth grade when Tommy Fiorintino had chased her around the playground with the slimy corpse of a long-dead frog.

Glancing at the door with its tempting red and white exit sign, she wondered if she'd given Sam enough time to make the journey to the Near West Side neighborhood where the FBI's Chicago branch was located.

Dear god, I hope so.

There was no way to know for sure, however, because there was no way for her to accurately guess the time. She didn't wear a wristwatch and her cell phone was still charging on her nightstand.

But she'd spent what surely had to have been fifteen minutes in the little anteroom off what appeared to be another interrogation room pretending to talk to her "lawyer." Her phone call to Cesar had only lasted sixty seconds, although she'd figured a real call to her attorney would've lasted far longer than that. And so she'd stayed standing with the phone pressed to her ear while she'd counted the seconds and listened to the dial tone.

Afterward, she'd gone about implementing step two in her plan to stall her booking.

"I, uh, need to use the facilities," she'd told Mulder after exiting the privacy of the anteroom to find the fed waiting for her in the hallway. *"Now."* She'd made sure her expression screamed the situation was dire before adding, *"All this stress has loosened my b—"*

Mulder had raised a hand. *"Please spare me the details, Miss Blue."*

He'd shown her to the women's restroom and there she'd stayed for what she'd *hoped* was an additional fifteen minutes. Agent Mulder had checked on her once, pushing open the door and calling, *"Look, Miss Blue. Let's get this show on the road and—"*

That's all she'd allowed him to get out before she'd groaned from inside the stall like her bowels were being chewed on by a sewer rat while simultaneously dropping the wet wads of paper towels she'd taken from the hand dispenser near the sinks into toilet bowl so they made *sploosh, sploosh, sploosh* noises.

Mulder had quickly changed his tune *"Uh…take your time. I'll be waiting outside."*

She'd done exactly that. Taken her time. All the time she'd dared.

She hadn't really been surprised to discover Sam hadn't been able to pull strings to get her released. Given the mountain of evidence piled against her, even if he could've persuaded one of his government contacts to consider her case, one look at what she was accused of was all it would've taken for that contact to back away, shaking their head.

No one was stupid enough to put their reputation on the line to help an accused criminal conspirator. And self-serving political animals? They were the *least* likely group of folks to risk their necks.

Which left only Sam to aid in her escape.

Sam, whom she didn't doubt for a second was either already waiting for her outside or busting his ass trying to get to her. Sam, who would believe her when she said she hadn't done what they said she'd done. Sam, who would do everything in his power to help her clear her name.

He might not feel for her half of what she felt for him. But he was as steadfast and as loyal as they came. The kind of guy a gal could depend on no matter what. A real-life knight in shining…uh…biker boots.

She stared again at the exit sign. It beckoned like a beacon, and she tried to remember how many floors she'd have to race down before she reached the exit. Three? Four?

She couldn't recall what number Agent Waller had pushed on the keypad when they'd been inside the elevator on the way up to the interrogation room. She'd been too focused on the cruel hand he'd kept on her wrist, squeezing the joint until she'd thought for sure he was trying to break her bones.

Waller really was a bastard. And she hoped like hell she didn't run into him while making her escape. His hatred for her, and his confidence in her guilt, assured her he would be more than happy to shoot first and ask questions later.

The thought of just *how* dangerous her plan was had her hesitating in the bathroom's doorway a second longer.

Maybe this is a mistake. Maybe there's another way for me to…

She stopped the doubt in its tracks.

If she wanted to save Texas, figure out what the *hell* was going on with Red Square and Dominion Pipeline, and, you know, clear her name of treason, she needed *out*. Then she needed a laptop, a secure, untraceable internet connection, and about fifteen pots of regular coffee or one pot of the caffeinated swill they served at Black Knights Inc.

Girding her loins, she told herself, *This is the only way. And it's now or never.*

As she slipped soundlessly from the bathroom, stomach acid burned the back of her throat, leaving an acrid coating on her tongue. Her blood pounded in her ears, reminding her of the *whir* of an old solid-state hard drive. And fear had turned her legs into a couple of wet noodles.

How do spies and soldiers do this? How do they function when terror is a living thing with razor-sharp teeth gnawing on their amygdala?

Her initial shaky step backward had her watching Mulder with eagle-eyed focus. But he gave no indication he'd heard her silent footfalls. So she took another step. Then another.

The agent laughed and the sound cracked through the stillness of the hallway like thunder. It also afforded her enough acoustic cover to take three hasty steps closer to the stairwell door.

She would swear the hallway telescoped. No matter how much progress she made toward the exit, the door seemed to get farther and farther away. But just when she wanted to scream—the tension inside her pushing her to the breaking point—she found herself standing in front of her means of escape.

She should've been relieved.

She wasn't.

Now she had a *new* set of problems.

The exit was one of those fireproof doors with the horizontal bar across the center that acted as the locking mechanism. There was no way she'd be able to press that bar without it making at least a *little* noise. Also, it was very possible the stairwell doors came equipped with alarms.

Only one way to find out.

Grimacing, she gently pushed on the bar, and then blinked when the door cracked open without a sound.

Thank you, Lady Luck! she silently crowed as she slipped through the crack and quickly shut the door behind her.

The stairwell was indistinguishable from any other. Concrete steps. Metal railing Unflattering florescent lights. The stale air smelled faintly of cigarette smoke—someone snuck in on their break to indulge their nicotine habit.

Wrapping the blanket securely around her shoulders, she wasted no time beginning her descent. If she'd thought the tile in the hallways was cold, it was nothing compared to the painted concrete steps. Her bare feet stung as she raced down, down, down one floor. Then another.

Since she wasn't sharing a hallway with Agent Mulder, she didn't attempt to quiet her breathing. It sawed from her lungs, dry and raw-sounding. And every time she hit a landing, she expected to see agents waiting on the stairway below, weapons drawn. With every step closer to the exit, she expected to hear a door open above her and the sound of jackboots giving chase.

Not that FBI agents wear jackboots. More like oxfords or wingtips, but—

Her thoughts skidded to a halt at the same time her feet did.

She'd made it to the ground floor.

Holy flying shitstains!

She hadn't really expected to get that far.

The door to the outside was no different than the door to the stairwell. And when she pushed it open, the bitter winter air stole her breath. It was the kind of cold only people from the Midwest—*or maybe Siberia*—could appreciate.

She nearly slunk back inside the vestibule. Standing trial was surely less awful than stepping out into the frigid February night.

Then she saw the figure parked on the access road just beyond the fence. A darker shadow among the dark shadows of the trees lining the roadway.

She might've thought she was imagining things—thought her desperate mind was conjuring up a hallucination—except for a nearby streetlight glinted off the chrome of the motorcycle's exhaust pipe. And there was only one place in the whole country that built bikes like that.

Black Knights Inc.

Sam! Her heart screamed.

CHAPTER 9

Sam flipped up the visor on his helmet when one of the two rear exits on the FBI building opened.

He'd parked beneath the trees outside the fence, which meant he was a good sixty yards from the building itself. But floodlights glared from the rooftop, turning the empty, paved expanse between him and FBI headquarters as bright as day, and spotlighting the moment Hannah appeared on the threshold.

Despite the distance, there was no mistaking her pale, heart-shaped face. And she was the only person on the planet with hair that was every shade of purple under the sun.

Why is she wrapped in a blanket? he wondered. Before he could answer that question, an even more alarming one blasted through his head. *Holy fucknuts! Is she barefoot?*

Bastards! He railed against the agents who hadn't thought to let her put on shoes before whisking her away into the night.

Just as with any other body of law enforcement, the Federal Bureau of Investigations attracted results-oriented types. Meaning sometimes FBI agents were so eager to *get their man*, or in this case *their woman*, they overlooked compassion and basic human decency.

Bastards, he thought again.

Cesar hadn't mentioned anything about what she'd been wearing—or *not* wearing—when the FBI had taken her. If he had, Sam would've come prepared with…well, not with a car. No one at BKI drove four wheels except for Becky, and the only reason *she* did was because she needed room for two car seats. Everyone else was the proud owner of one of her fantastical creations.

Tooling around town on a quarter-ton of polished steel and sex appeal wasn't just fun as shit, it was also a way for them to be rolling advertisements for the business. And when the weather got inclement? They did as every other city dweller did and took the train, hailed a cab, or called an Uber.

Of course, a taxi or an Uber was out of the question when it came to a prison break. And the nearest train stop was six blocks away. Which meant Pale Horse had been his only option.

But if he'd known Hannah was so underdressed for the weather, he could have at least brought extra clothing. And *shoes.*

Waaahhh-woo-waaahhh!

His jaw clenched when loudspeakers mounted to the sides of the building let loose with a squall that turned the cold night air into a wall of sound.

The guardian angel who'd helped Hannah make it this far had just spread her wings and flown the coop. Or, as the guys in his old regiment used to say, *Looks like we got ourselves a bit of a snafu.*

As in…situation normal, all fucked up.

The feds knew their prisoner had escaped. And they were happy to let the whole world know too.

"Hannah!" He waved to catch her attention. But she was already heading in his direction. Her bare feet pounded across the pavement. Her brightly colored hair flew out behind her. And the ends of the blanket flapped like the wings of a drunken bird.

He was off the bike in a flash after toeing out the kickstand. And he'd made it to the fence when the first responding agent rounded the corner of the building, weapon up and at the ready.

"Halt!" the man yelled.

Or at least that's what Sam *thought* he heard over the cacophony of the wailing alarm.

He had unzipped his coat and placed a hand on the butt of his Glock

19 before he'd consciously made the decision to move. Muscle memory was a beautiful thing.

"Stop! Get on the ground!" Another agent called. This one appeared in the doorway she'd recently vacated.

Pulling his sidearm from his shoulder holster, Sam alternated his aim between the two agents all while keeping a close eye on Hannah's progress.

That's it! he silently encouraged her. *Keep those little legs moving!*

For such a short woman, she could *run*. Then again, terror had a way of lending the human body an unnatural amount of speed and strength. One need look no further than the stories of mothers lifting whole-ass cars off their trapped children to know that much was true.

"Halt or I'll shoot!" the first agent shouted and Sam refocused his aim as a ball of dread hardened in his stomach.

If the bastard pulled his trigger—forcing Sam to pull his—there was no telling if he could hit the weapon in the agent's hand. Because even though he was the best marksmen the Raiders had ever seen, the distance to the agent was substantial. And the difference between putting a bullet through the fed's service sidearm and sending a slug straight through the man's hand, probably ending his career, was a matter of inches.

"Don't do it," he grumbled under his breath. "Don't you fucking do it, you sonofa—"

He saw the muzzle flash before he heard the weapon's report. His response was immediate.

Again, muscle memory.

And years of putting a thousand pounds of lead downrange.

He'd taken his shot and was already returning his attention to Hannah when the fed yelped as his weapon caught Sam's round and flew from his fingers.

Hannah stumbled too, the blanket falling from her shoulders.

For a split second, Sam thought she'd been hit. And in that split second, a wrecking ball slammed into his chest. Then she righted herself, leaving the blanket on the pavement behind her, and continued her mad dash across the blacktop.

His desperate eyes roved over her hurtling form. But he could see no blooming red flower to indicate she'd taken a bullet. There was no hitch in her step. No cry of pain.

He nearly dropped to his knees in relief.

His respite was short-lived, however, because a stream of feds—he counted five in all—joined the remaining agent at the exit before bubbling out of the building like ants racing from an anthill.

"Faster, Hannah!" he bellowed, climbing onto the bottom rung of the fence. It was one of those fancy wrought-irons jobs, made up of straight posts held together by two horizontal bracing bars. Thankfully, it was only five-feet tall.

"Sam!" The sheer terror in her voice had him gritting his teeth.

"Keep coming, sweetheart!" He made a come-hitcher motion with one hand even as he kept his aim on the group of agents chasing her across the brightly lit expanse.

All of them had their weapons up and aimed. Six government-issued cannons of death bull's-eyed on her back.

Anyone who said spec-ops guys were fearless, hearts black as stone and nerves made of steel, were either completely full of shit or dumber than dirt. Because Sam had known fear plenty of times.

That time when his unit had been sent in to take out a local Islamic State leader only to get cut off from their designated extraction site and then chased by the entire IS army for two full days. That time he'd nearly lost his head—literally—when his instincts had failed him, and he'd let an enemy combatant with an eight-inch blade sneak up on his six. And most recently, down in Colombia, when he and the rest of the Knights had been outnumbered five-to-one in a firefight that'd been chaotic and seemingly endless.

Fear was something men in his profession lived with. Lived *on*. It was as familiar to them as the weapons they lovingly cleaned or the scars they carried on their bodies. But nothing, *nothing*, had prepared him for the sheer terror of watching Hurricane Hannah running her ass off through a frigid February night with six federal agents looking to light her up.

Boom!

The fed at the front of the pack opened fire and Sam didn't hesitate to do the same. His trigger was worn smooth by years of use. It reacted to even the slightest pressure from his gloved fingertip. And in three seconds he'd riddled the pavement in front of the agents with shots.

Two, three, four, five…

He kept count of each slug.

His magazine was a fifteen plus one. Meaning he only had sixteen shots before he'd have to reload. And in that split second between dropping the mag and slamming in a new one was when Charlie Foxtrot tended to make his appearance.

AKA, Mr. Cluster Fucked.

Six. Seven.

The group of agents scattered. Three ran for cover around the side of the building. One kissed the pavement like it was a long-lost lover. But two more simply swerved around his fire and continued their pursuit.

Drawing in a steady breath of frigid night air that was perfumed with the acrid aroma of burned nitroglycerin—modern "gunpowder" was basically sawdust soaked in nitro and coated with graphite; it was the nitro that burned hot and left a distinct smell—he sighted down his barrel and fired.

Bam!

The bark of his weapon echoed over the open expanse, a sound as familiar to him as the beat of his own heart.

Switching his aim, he went through the motions again. *Bam!*

His second shot wasn't as accurate as his first. He'd missed the ground in front of the second agent and nicked the fed's foot with his round.

Damnit.

But he satisfied himself that neither man was truly injured, and he'd managed to stop their forward momentum. Both of them lay on the ground, the uninjured one crawling toward the other who was grimacing in pain and gripping his bleeding toe.

"S-S-Sam!" Hannah cried once she'd closed the distance to him.

Shoving his sidearm into his waistband, he grabbed her under her arms. With a heave, he had her over the fence—she was just a little thing after all. Then his weapon was back in his hand as he gave her a nudge toward Pale Horse.

"Go!" he hissed.

She sprinted across the grassy expanse and hopped onto the back of the bike like a cowgirl showing off her trick riding skills.

One last look over his shoulder assured him the agents who'd ducked and covered were more interested in running to the aid of their colleagues than continuing to give chase. He re-holstered his weapon and three running steps brought him to Pale Horse and Hannah.

Her eyes were so wide they looked like they were about to swallow her face. Goose bumps peppered the exposed skin on her arms. And her poor bare feet were bright pink from the cold.

He wanted to strip off all his clothes and cover her in them. But there was no time. All he could do was throw a leg over the seat, use the heel of his biker boot to slam back the kickstand, and smash the ignition with his gloved thumb.

The instant Pale Horse roared to life, he laid on the throttle. The motorcycle's rear tire spun, sending up caustic-smelling smoke before it gained traction and shot them forward like an arrow fired from a bow.

Hannah squealed and nearly lost her grip on him. He kept her on the bike by snaking an arm back around her waist. Which meant he had to one-hand the handlebars and wrestle the motorcycle through a tight curve in the road.

Once he was assured she wasn't going to fall off, he let her go so he could concentrate on getting them the fuck out of Dodge. With a twist of his wrist that sent a surge of fuel to Pale Horse's hungry engine, the big bike proceeded to eat up the pavement.

The west side of town was nearly as deserted as Goose Island. He was glad for it. It meant he could plow through red lights and speed down side streets without worrying about cross traffic or wandering pedestrians.

Every fiber of his being that *wasn't* focused on the road and the patchy pavement that came part and parcel with living in the upper Midwest where the snowplows and salt trucks wreaked havoc on all things asphalt was centered on his passenger. On the feel of her thin arms locked tight around his waist. On the pressure of her lithe legs clamped like a vice around his hips. On the feel of her shaking so hard he worried she might shatter her own bones. And then...

She *wasn't* shaking. She was still.

And that was so, *so* much worse.

He needed to put more miles between them and the feds. He needed to duck down more side streets to convolute any trail he might be leaving behind. And he *definitely* needed to get her back to BKI where he could wrap her in a million blankets.

But the miles and the trail and the destination would have to wait. Because she couldn't wait any longer.

Hypothermia was no joke. Left unchecked, it could quickly lead to heart failure.

Cutting the engine so he wouldn't wake the people living in the buildings on either side of the alleyway he'd found—the *last* thing he wanted was the CPD shoving a nose up his ass because someone had called in a noise complaint—he coasted the bike past a dumpster, an empty paint bucket, and a stray pizza box. When he was assured they were out of sight of any passing cars, he squeezed the brakes and brought them to a gentle halt.

Out went the kickstand. Off came his helmet. And within two seconds, he'd shrugged out of his winter-weight coat to carefully drape it over Hannah's hunched shoulders.

Her skin was as pale as death. Her lips were so blue they were almost purple. And her eyes were glassy looking when she lifted her chin. "I didn't do it, Sam," she whispered hoarsely. "What they say I did, I didn't—"

"I know you didn't, sweetheart. I never believed it for a second." He threaded her stiff arms into the sleeves of his coat because she seemed incapable of doing the job herself.

And no wonder. She was a human Popsicle. One-hundred-twenty pounds of frozen flesh and icy blood.

After zipping the jacket to her chin, he turned his attention to his boots. She watched him numbly, seemingly unaware of what he was doing or *why* he was doing it when he unlaced the first one. But when he tackled the laces on his second, she blinked and shook her head. "No. You need your shoes to—"

"If we don't get something on your feet, you're gonna lose a fucking toe," he interrupted. "I'll be fine in my socks."

Not *fine*, fine. He was already feeling the effects of the icy air when he planted his soles against the frigid concrete. But his socks were wool. And they only had another fifteen minutes to ride before they'd be inside the heated halls of BKI. So he'd survive.

"Come on." He motioned for her to extend a leg. "I'll help you get 'em on."

He nearly cried out when he grabbed her foot and saw the condition it was in. Her toenails were painted with the same sparkly blue polish she wore on her fingernails. But that didn't hide the fact that the skin all around the nails was ashen.

He'd said that thing about her losing a toe so she'd shut up and let him do what needed to be done. Now he worried his words might turn out to be portentous.

With as much care as he could muster, he slipped her foot inside the dark mouth of his steel-toed biker boot. Her trim ankles required him to cinch the laces as tight as they would go. Even then he wasn't sure the boot wouldn't slip off.

Her opposite foot was in even worse shape. She'd cut the end of her pinky toe during her escape, and the entire sole of her foot was covered in frozen blood.

She didn't whimper when he shoved the boot over the mess. Which told him her feet had lost all feeling.

Not good, he thought in alarm. *Not good at all.*

At eighteen below zero, frostbite could set in in as little as fifteen minutes. It wasn't quite eighteen below. More like three. But close counted in hand grenades, horseshoes, and hypothermia.

"Last thing." He gently placed his helmet over her head and tightened the chin strap until the metal clasp couldn't cinch any more.

"Thank you, Sam." Her dark eyes were so full of gratitude, he almost wept.

"Anything for you, kiddo." He chucked her on the chin before flipping down the helmet's visor.

When he stepped back to view his work, he decided she looked like a little girl who'd played dress up in her daddy's closet. Everything was huge on her. But at least she was no longer completely exposed to the elements.

He wasn't calling it a win. They were far from finished playing the night's game of cat and mouse. But he was calling it a goal. Major points for getting her covered.

His nose and ears already stung from the cold when he straddle-walked the bike to the mouth of the alley. By the time he cranked the engine and gunned them back onto the street, it felt like someone was shoving needles into his exposed cheeks.

How Hannah had kept from crying out in pain during the first part of the ride, he'd never know.

Except…he *did* know.

She'd always been a tough cookie. And her stubborn streak had been a mile wide, even as a middle schooler.

Pale Horse chewed up the streets like the badass beast it was. Which allowed him to whittle down their journey from fifteen minutes to a little over ten. Even still, by the time they made it to the parking garage housing the secret entrance to BKI's backdoor, he was nearly frozen.

The tears that'd streamed from the corners of his eyes had iced in the hair at his temples. He couldn't feel his lips or the tips of his toes. And he could tell he'd lost at least two degrees of core temperature because he could. Not. Quit. Shivering.

By the time he rolled up to the hidden mouth of the Bat Cave, he could barely keep the handlebars straight.

Hannah tightened her grip around his waist when he tipped the motorcycle's front tire over the lip of the tunnel. And when they started going down, the wet cement walls encroaching in on them, Pale Horse's engine sounding viciously loud in the enclosed space, he thought he heard her whimper.

Who can blame her?

The Bat Cave was freaky as fuck. Not only was it dark and dank and smelling of fish, but it also had the feel of a tomb. That earthy, quiet, *underground* atmosphere that conjured up all sorts of flashbacks to horror films.

"A-almost th-there!" he chattered above the rumble of the motorcycle's engine when they hit the end of the tunnel and what appeared to be a solid brick wall.

Except it wasn't solid. High up on the left side was an inconspicuous red button. He smashed it with his gloved palm and the bricks popped forward to slide back like the plastic on the TV dinners he'd lived on as a kid when his folks had had enough functioning brain cells to stock the freezer.

A rush of warm air and the smell of grease guns hit him in the face when the interior of the shop came into view. The lights blazing overhead were overwhelming after the darkness of the tunnel. And the expressions on the faces of the people lined up and waiting for him reflected varying degrees of the urgency he felt.

With one last twist of the throttle, Pale Horse crawled out of the tunnel and onto the cement floor of BKI's headquarters. He maneuvered the bike into its spot alongside the other fantastical motorcycles and nudged out the kickstand with a foot that felt like a block of ice.

The moment he cut the engine, Eliza peppered him with questions.

"Did you run into any trouble? Do the feds know she's escaped? Ozzie was able to hack into the city's camera system, but he's still working to get into the FBI's security feed, so do you think their cameras were able to catch your license plate? I texted you to take it off, but I wasn't sure you'd get it."

Eliza Meadows wasn't simply the daughter of the current chief of staff and therefore an integral part of their team because of her familial ties. She was an integral part of their team because she had a mind like a steel trap. She was always thinking. One step ahead.

At the moment, he hated her for that.

The cold had turned his brain to icy slush. All he could think was how badly he hurt.

It felt like someone was shoving red-hot needles into the places where his skin had been exposed to the elements. And his teeth chattered so hard he wouldn't be surprised if he'd cracked a filling.

The last thing he wanted was to grind the frozen gears of his brain into answering questions. But he managed, "G-got your text," as he attempted to dismount. *Attempted* because it took him two tries to swing his leg over the bike. His muscles were in lockdown and not listening to what his gray matter was telling them. "Left my plates in th-the garage. S-someone sh-should go get 'em. B-b-but right now, w-we n-need to g-get warm."

Eliza blinked as if she'd just realized he was shoeless and coatless and Hannah was still sitting on the back of the bike, hunched into a tiny ball with her arms wrapped protectively around herself.

"Oh, my god!" She nodded rapidly. "Of course. I'm so sorry. What should we—"

"T-tub," he cut her off, shivering so hard he thought for sure his organs were getting pureed inside his body. "H-hot water."

"Right." She didn't waste time turning to race for the stairs.

He shuffled over to Hannah on feet that ached so badly he thought maybe they were busted. Could the cold do that? Could it break bones?

"C-can y-you dismount?" he asked.

She hadn't removed his helmet. And the visor was still down, so he couldn't see her face. But he caught her subtle nod.

Of course, the instant she stepped off the bike, her muscles failed her. She fell into his arms, and because his muscles were in the same shape as hers, he fumbled to catch her. In fact, he only managed to keep her from slipping through his grip and onto the floor by going down on one knee and folding her close against his quivering chest.

"Here." Fisher laid a hand on his shoulder. "Let me, brother."

Before Sam could object, Fisher lifted Hannah into his arms and turned for the stairs. Hannah's feet, made cumbersome by Sam's big boots, bobbed with each of Fisher's steps. And her helmeted head fell onto Fisher's shoulder as if the effort to hold it up was too much.

Sam blamed the pain shooting through his socked feet as he followed in Fisher's footsteps for the growl that built in the back of his throat. But somewhere in the furthest reaches of his frozen brain, a little voice whispered, *That's not really what's bothering you, is it? You don't like seeing Hannah in Fisher's arms.*

Okay, fine. But it wasn't because he was *jealous*. It was because Fisher was a charming sonofabitch who seduced every woman he met.

Sam didn't want the handsome bastard to get any ideas regarding *Hannah*. Because Hannah deserved more than a quick roll in the hay. Hannah deserved...

Everything.

CHAPTER 10

Hannah was only distantly aware of her surroundings as she was carried to the third floor of the old menthol cigarette factory.

But it wasn't because she was distracted by how nice the stranger who carried her smelled or by the certainty she'd become a bona fide damsel in distress—*barf*. It was because her brain had morphed into cold molasses.

No matter how hard she tried to move her consciousness forward, her thoughts stayed stuck in place. And she was nearly overcome by the urge to sleep.

Truly, she couldn't remember a time she'd been so exhausted. She wasn't sure if it was the letdown of adrenaline or if the cold was about to send her comatose. But it took everything she had just to keep her eyes cracked open.

She sort of, kind of, *maybe* registered a large television room at the top of the second set of stairs. And she thought for sure she saw a long hallway interrupted by more than a handful of doors. But she *definitely* couldn't have said which door the man who carried her entered.

In fact, she might've fallen asleep at the entrance to the hall, only coming awake when the stranger stepped inside what turned out to be a bedroom. She blinked blearily through the helmet's visor and saw a picture hanging above a bed. But, again, she couldn't say what it was of. And the bedspread could've been red, green, or tangerine for all she knew.

"I'm goin' to set ya on your feet now, little one," the man said after he'd ducked into an adjoining bathroom.

Any other day, his Southern drawl would have delighted her. As it was, she only noted his accent as an aside.

When her borrowed boots hit the floor, pain shot up from the soles of her frozen feet. It was enough to have her crying out in shock.

"Easy there." The man helped her to the toilet and caught her by the elbows so she could slowly sit atop the closed lid instead of crashing down when her knees buckled.

"I'm goin' to take this off, okay?" He knelt in front of her and pointed to the helmet. It took all her strength to simply lift her chin so he could unhook the clasp.

Once the headwear was gone, she blinked into the man's sympathetic face.

Wow.

To call him handsome was an understatement. His chiseled jaw, pouty mouth, and hazel eyes belonged on the silver screen.

She might've felt a flicker of interest were she not a human ice cube. As it was, he could've been Quasimodo and she would've had the same reaction to him unzipping her borrowed coat and carefully pulling it off her.

"Blocks of ice," he muttered when he caught her hands between both of his and softly chafed the frozen skin.

"Poor thing."

Hannah glanced over to find the dark-haired woman from downstairs perched on the edge of the tub. She was filling it with hot water so that moist, comforting steam rose into the air.

Hannah remembered the sloe-eyed beauty from the last time she'd been at BKI. But her sluggish brain couldn't conjure up a name.

"But you'll be okay." Currently-Nameless smiled encouragingly. "Just as soon as we get you warmed up, you'll be right as rain."

Hannah nodded numbly and then hissed when the handsome man pulled the boot off her left foot.

"Sorry." He winced, turning her foot over in his large hands. "You've got a nasty cut here."

"H-Hannah." Sam appeared in the doorway looking ghostly pale and shaking so hard she could hear his teeth chattering.

"*Sam!*" she cried out, and then shocked herself by immediately bursting into tears.

"Whoa," the handsome man kneeling in front of her drawled. "The dam's sprung a leak."

"I'll t-take it from h-here." Sam nudged the man aside so he could squat at her feet.

"I'll go down and get some hot chocolate going," the pretty black-haired woman said as she rose from the tub and headed for the door. Before she stepped into the bedroom, she turned and lifted an eyebrow at Mr. Tall, Tan, and Handsome. "You coming?"

"Be right there." Mr. Movie Star now stood beside Hannah and used his thumb to wipe a tear from her cheek. "You're a brave little thing, aren't ya?"

Brave? She blinked up at him in confusion. No. She'd been the opposite of brave. She'd been absolutely terrified.

Opening her mouth, she was poised to admit as much. But Sam cut her off by emphasizing, "I *g-got* it, Fish."

"Alright. Alright. Message receive." The man lifted his wide hands in a gesture of surrender as he headed for the door.

After he—had Sam called him *Fish*?—and the woman disappeared into the adjoining bedroom, Sam turned back to tackle the laces of the boot on her right foot.

She didn't have the strength—or the will—to lift her hands to brush her tears away. Which meant they ran down her face, dripped off her chin, and plopped onto her shirt.

"I'm s-so sorry," Sam said as he gingerly removed the last boot from the five-toed iceberg that was her foot. His hands were shaking so hard he dropped the boot the instant it came free. And she wondered why *she* wasn't shivering. She was absolutely frozen. Shouldn't she be quaking like him? "I kn-know you're hurting, 'cause I feel like s-someone's shoving f-frozen pokers into me, and you were more exposed than I was. B-but hang on a little bit l-longer, okay?"

"That's not why I'm crying," she whispered.

"No?" He cocked his head.

"I'm just…" She sniffed. "Thank you, Sam." She hiccupped as a new sob shook her entire body. "You saved me."

"You mostly s-saved yourself. I just d-did the d-driving."

"No." She shook her head, wanting to tell him how much she appreciated the risk he'd taken in coming for her. Wanting to explain how much it meant to her. But no matter how hard she tried, the words wouldn't form. What came out of her mouth was, "I feel like I only have two brain cells functioning, and they seem to be fighting each other for third place."

One corner of his mouth twitched. "There sh-she is, the funny, flippant H-Hurricane Hannah I know and l-love."

The instant the word *love* left his lips, fresh tears welled. She'd waited her whole life to hear him say that. And now he had.

But he hadn't meant it.

Not the way she wanted him to.

"C-come here." He gathered her close and she thought he was going to hug her. She was more than a little disappointed when instead he scooped her into his arms so he could quickly transfer her into the tub, T-shirt, pajama bottoms, and all.

"No!" she yelped. Her brain went from slow and sluggish to blaring *danger, Will Robinson! Danger!* The water was burning tongues of fire licking over her skin. "It's too hot!"

He kept her in the tub with a firm hand on her shoulder. "It only f-feels that way 'cause your sk-skin is f-frozen."

Every instinct told her to jump from the lava bath lest her flesh melt right off her bones. But she trusted him. Gritting her teeth, she stayed put. And then watched, dumbfounded, as he peeled his White Sox sweatshirt over his head before tackling the zipper on his jeans.

Once he was down to black, thermal long johns that hugged his muscular body like a second skin, he stepped into the tub.

"S-scoot forward," he instructed.

When he lowered himself into the tub behind her, his big body made the water rise. Every new inch of skin it touched burned like blue flames. She only managed to keep from hissing her pain by biting the inside of her cheek.

"Now l-lean b-back." He patted the place over his heart and she gingerly reclined until her back was pressed against his chest.

His long legs bracketed hers. His bare feet looked huge beside her much smaller ones. And his arms came around her—which was when she could truly appreciate how hard his muscles spasmed in an effort to warm his body.

"T-try to r-relax and let the w-water work," he told her, but she thought maybe he was really coaching himself.

Any other time, she would've been delighted to be in a tub with Sam. But the hot water no longer burned. Now it felt like every inch of her skin was being stabbed by hypodermic needles.

She whimpered.

"It's okay," he soothed. "Th-that's just your body heating b-back up. D-don't fight it. L-let it happen."

The running faucet continued to fill the tub higher and higher until she was submerged up to her chin. Some distant part of her brain noticed the ends of her hair floated around them like purple ribbons. And when the water slipped over her chin and licked at her lower lip, Sam used his bare toes to turn the knob and stop the flow.

For long minutes, they sat there. Her, feeling like a pincushion belonging to some sadistic seamstress. Him, shaking so hard little streams of water sloshed over the side of the tub to splash onto the tile floor.

If she concentrated on the misery of her body, she was afraid she might go insane. So instead she concentrated on the fresh scent of his fabric softener as it wafted up from his wet long johns. It mixed with the smell of his cologne—some wonderful infusion of salted caramel and blackberry musk—to create a bouquet of aromas that might have lulled her to sleep if her body hadn't decided at that moment to turn into a human cocktail shaker.

Her eyes became pinballs. Her teeth sounded like an entire brick of Black Cat Fireworks going off. And her body quaked so hard she worried she might be having a seizure.

"Thatta girl," he murmured, rubbing his hands up and down her arms. "This is good."

How can this possibly be good? she wanted to demand. But there was no way to form words with her teeth making all that racket.

She had no idea how long she quivered and quaked. It felt like an eternity. But eventually the tremors eased, leaving her feeling as wrung out as an old dishrag.

"Almost there," Sam said. "We just need to get some more hot water in this tub."

She barely registered when he used his big toe to flip the little handle that opened the drain. Her eyelids were weighed down with anchors. Her limbs, which moments earlier had been jerking around like they'd been attached to marionette strings, were dead weights hanging from their sockets. Her reheated blood rushed through her veins and pulsed rhythmically, *soothingly* in her ears.

Warm, dark oblivion beckoned.

She thought maybe she dozed off because the next thing she knew Sam was reclosing the drain and half the water was gone from the tub. Again he used his foot on the knob until hot water surged from the faucet and sent fresh steam billowing into the air.

She felt drugged. Like the time she'd gone in to have her wisdom teeth removed and the oral surgeon had added the anesthesia to the IV in her arm. A warm rush of contentment turned all her muscles to pudding. And somewhere in the distance came the soft, melancholy sound of...*Is that a harmonica playing "Heart of Gold"?*

Cesar sometimes spun Neil Young on the turntable, and she was of the opinion that vinyl was really the only way to appreciate The Godfather of Grunge.

"Cesar!" She bolted upright. The water fell off her shoulders in sheets. "What happened to him? Where is he?"

"Shh." Sam pulled her back against him. "He's fine. I sent him home. Figured you didn't want him any more mixed up in this than he already is."

"But the feds will go looking for me back at the apartment and—"

"I'm sure the others"—he made a vague gesture toward the open door—"gave him strict instructions to have an attorney present before answering any questions."

The sudden tension that'd gripped her body released. "He'll call Marco. And Marco is as good at twisting officials into knots as he is at impersonating Katy Perry."

Sam's soft laugh was comforting. "You live an interesting life, Hannah Blue. Has anyone ever told you that?"

"Mmm," she hummed noncommittally and let her head fall back against his shoulder. Thoughts drifted in and out of her mind like cirrus clouds through a summer sky, wispy and ephemeral.

Then he started to hum. Lowly. Softly. Not much more than a rumble of sound that originated in his big chest and echoed up through his tanned throat.

She'd always loved his voice. So deep and sonorous. If he hadn't gone into the Marines, he could've made a living in radio. Or as a book narrator.

Oh! How she would love to hear him read aloud from one of her alien romance novels.

Especially the spicy parts, she thought drowsily.

With her body no longer wracked by spasms, her skin no longer besieged by invisible needles, and her teeth no longer trying to pound themselves to dust, she could concentrate on the heavenly embrace of the water. On the soothing wetness of the steam. On…Sam.

Sam who was so broad and hard behind her. Sam whose callused palms felt wonderfully delicious on her skin as he chafed her arms. Sam who hummed a tune that drowned out the distant notes of the harmonica.

"And I would've stayed up with you all night," she sang along softly.

She'd been in love with The Fray the entirety of her eighth-grade year. "How to Save a Life" had been her theme song.

"You remembered," she murmured sleepily.

"How could I forget? You played that song for me…what? A hundred times? Two hundred?"

The raspy feel of his beard atop her head was soothing. And the *safety* of being in his arms had her giving in to the oblivion that'd been whispering her name all along.

She was asleep before she could answer.

CHAPTER 11

The first indication Sam had that Hannah had drifted off was the subtle lolling of her head to one side. The second was the way her hands floated up to the surface of the water. But the true-blue clincher was her snoring.

Hannah snores.

It wasn't obnoxious or grating. It was soft and low, reminding him of the sound a contented cat made.

He snuggled her tighter, noting how small she felt in his arms. And yet, despite her smallness, she was solid. Not delicate and frail, but sturdy and compact.

When Shakespeare coined the phrase, "though she but little, she is fierce!" he was talking about a woman like Hannah.

Hannah who'd had enough courage to bust out of FBI custody. Hannah who hadn't uttered a word of complaint even though he knew how badly she'd been hurting. Hannah who's first thought after she'd beaten back the cold wasn't herself but her best friend.

Before he could stop himself, he dropped a kiss on top of her head, breathing in that unique scent that would always remind him of her. It was citrusy and sweet, like orange blossoms mixed with warm vanilla.

When she'd been a girl, that smell had been overpowered by the scents of drugstore lip gloss and Noxzema cleansing cream. As a woman, it took center stage.

Using his foot beneath her heel, he carefully raised her injured toe out of the water and eyed the cut along the top of the tiny digit. Warm droplets ran from the wound, tinged faintly pink by her blood. But he was reassured the gash wasn't deep enough to require stitches.

Settling against the slanted back of the tub once again, he let his head rest on the tile wall. Reality would force them to deal with the mess that was their current situation soon enough. For the moment, he was content to hold her while she slept.

Her short shirt had worked its way up her body, exposing her entire midriff. And he noticed two things. One, her belly button was a perfect oval. And two, tendrils of a tattoo snuck around her flanks.

What sort of ink did Hannah choose? he wondered.

She was girlie enough for flowers but countercultured enough for skulls and crossbones.

When she stirred, he thought she was waking up. But instead, she simply turned onto her side, her little hand coming up to pillow her cheek against his chest, her left leg settling over his right thigh.

He curved his hand around her hip to keep her from sliding down in the water. Since her wet pajama bottoms rode low on her frame, his thumb rested against the flesh of her side.

Before he knew it, he was rubbing his thumb in a circular motion, reveling in the velvety softness of her skin.

The water made it difficult to see, but when he tilted his head to the side, he could just make out the design of her tattoo. It was a garden scene, filled with colorful flowers, flitting butterflies, and the occasional honeybee.

It wasn't made up of soft, fluffy blooms like roses or carnations, however. It was a garden of harsh, spiky flowers, like thistle and delphinium. The butterflies weren't delicate and fluttery. They were highly stylized, partially mechanical, and totally badass.

It suited her, he decided. Captured her femininity as well as her rebellious side. And the flowing lines followed the contours of her body, emphasizing the dip of her waist and the flare of her hips.

She stirred again. This time snaking an arm around his neck and turning until they were breast to chest. When she tucked her face into the crook of his neck, her breath was warm and wet against his skin.

Unlike the last time she adjusted herself, this time he didn't snuggle her close. Because unlike last time, this time he couldn't deny the girl in his arms wasn't a girl at all, but a full-grown woman with curves in all the right places.

His body responded by kicking up his heart rate and filling his cock with blood.

No. He closed his eyes and tried to forget what she looked like now. Picturing, instead, what she'd looked like at thirteen.

But *that* was a mistake. He *could not* think of a pubescent girl while sporting a hard-on.

She went and made everything worse—or *better?*—by snuggling closer and whispering his name in her sleep. "Sam."

Against his will, his mind dredged up scenes from the dreams he'd been having. Dreams that saw her stretched out on a bed, beckoning him closer with the crook of a finger, or kneeling between his legs and staring up at him with a seductive expression hooding her big, dark eyes.

He always shook himself awake before the dreams could go further. Because how could he lust after the girl who'd scrunched up her nose while telling him boys were covered in cooties? The girl who'd come home from school after getting her first period to regale him with stories of the diaper-sized pads the school nurse kept on hand? The girl who was the baby sister of the woman who'd claimed his virginity?

Except…

That was just it, wasn't it?

Hannah *wasn't* that girl. Not anymore.

"Sam," she murmured again, her leg crooking higher so that her thigh rested precariously close to his throbbing cock.

He knew the kind of sleep she'd fallen into because he'd experienced it plenty of times himself. The body and brain had a way of shutting off after a harrowing experience.

If adrenaline was a stimulant, then the let-down that followed could only be described as the mother of all depressants.

He'd fallen asleep in huge transport planes that roared like freight trains and tumbled him around so much he may as well have been flying inside a clothes dryer. He'd gone full-on comatose in the bed of a pickup truck while it'd bumped eighty miles per hour down a dirt road in Egypt. And he'd once conked out in the middle of a sit-rep with his superiors. Just... head down on the conference table and lights out.

He *knew* this sleep was her body's way of coping with the trauma and rebooting itself. And yet he couldn't take having her sprawled atop him a second longer. He didn't trust himself not to...

He stopped his thoughts in their tracks.

"Hannah." Rubbing a hand over the small of her back, he did his level best not to notice the slight curvature that led to her plump ass.

Fuck! Why do I know her ass is plump?

Oh, right. Because when she'd been at BKI six months earlier, she'd been wearing a figure-hugging pair of jeans and he'd looked.

He hadn't wanted to. He hadn't even been aware he'd been doing it. But he'd looked.

And what he'd found was a plump, perfect, peach-shaped—

Double fuck!

"Hannah." This time when he said her name he squeezed her hip.

"Mmm." She grumped, turning her face more fully into his neck.

Her mouth was pressed against the skin over his pulse point. Her little tongue flicked out to lick her lips except the gesture caught him instead.

His dick flexed so hard he was amazed it didn't lift her right out of the water.

"Hannah!" This time he slapped her ass.

"Wh-what happened?" She bolted upright to blink at him blearily as water sheeted off her shoulders and arms.

"You zonked."

A line formed between her dark eyebrows. "I did?"

"Mmm." He nodded. "And I'd love to let you sleep. But I'm turning into a prune." He lifted his hand with his wrinkled fingertips as proof. "Plus, we gotta figure out what the hell is going on with you and the feds and this Red Square business."

"Right." She shook her head as if trying to jostle the cobwebs from her mind. Then she scrunched up her nose. "Holy fart-catching ass-monkeys, I've never had to pee so bad in my life."

If he hadn't been concentrating so hard on trying to tame his erection, he might've laughed. She'd always had a rare talent for coming up with colorful curses.

"That's part of it," he assured her.

"Part of what?"

"Nearly dying of hypothermia." When she frowned her confusion, he explained. "When you get cold, the thermoreceptors in your skin tell your hypothalamus, which acts like the body's thermostat, to get to work. One of the first things it does is tighten the blood vessels in your extremities. The basic tenet being a decrease in blood flow to your arms and legs means a decrease in systemic heat loss *from* those areas."

She slow blinked twice. "What does that have to do with me needing to pee like a Russian racehorse?"

"Because of all that vasoconstriction, fluid gathers at your core. That causes your brain to go, 'Hey, how's about you get rid of some of that fluid by peeing?'"

"Fascinating. Why do you know so much about hypothermia?"

"Part of Raider training was cold-weather drills in Alaska in January. The Marine Corps prefers their jarheads to be jacks-of-all-trades and masters of none."

"I'd love to delve more into that if I wasn't about to turn this bathwater into lemonade."

"Hop out." He gestured to the towels Eliza had piled next to the tub. BKI's Girl Friday thought of everything. "I'll give you some privacy so you can turn the toilet water into lemonade instead of the bathwater. How's that sound?"

He had to keep his eyes down when she splashed out of the tub. Her T-shirt had gone see through, and even though he'd done his level best to keep his eyes on her face when he'd been explaining about the hypothermia, his peripheral vision had clocked the points of her nipples and the way her dark areolas pressed against the wet cotton.

Plus, you know, her soggy pajama bottoms were hugging her butt as she bent to grab a towel and the *last* thing he needed was to get an eyeful of *that*.

While she was distracted wrapping the towel around herself, he pushed up from the tub and quickly grabbed a towel of his own. Holding it in front of his hard-on—the damn thing refused to go down—he stepped out of the water.

"Just throw your wet things over the shower rod," he said as he headed for his bedroom, leaving large puddles on the tile. "I'll see what I can find in the way of dry clothes for you," he added before gently shutting the door behind him.

Then he was standing in front of his bed, dripping water onto his rug, and trying *not* to imagine her peeling herself out of her wet clothes.

"For fuck's sake," he muttered. "Get your head outta the gutter and remember she's like a kid sister to you."

After shedding his soaking long johns, he used the towel to vigorously scour the water from his skin. His hard-on thanked him for the attention by bobbing happily. Then he walked over to the armchair he'd pushed into the corner of the room, spread the towel across the seat, and arranged his long johns so they'd dry.

When he heard the toilet flush, he didn't think much of it. But then the bathroom door opened, and he swung around to find Hannah standing in the threshold.

She'd ditched her wet clothes and wrapped a bath sheet under her arms, doing that quintessential *woman* thing of tucking the ends between her breasts. Her damp hair was tousled. Her cheeks were pink from the steam. And the most devilish grin split her face when he yelped and grabbed his dick and balls with both hands.

Because of his hard-on, it was difficult to get everything covered. But he managed to position his arms in such a way that the head of his eager cock was hidden behind his forearm.

"Don't worry," she teased. "You don't have anything I haven't seen before. Although, dat ass?" She winked. "Top ten, for sure. Probably top five."

He made a face. "I don't wanna think of you seeing other men in the raw. You're too young. You should be playing D and D and eating cheese puffs by the fistful."

She threw back her head and laughed.

He didn't notice how it made her pale neck look totally lickable. No he did not.

When she lowered her chin, she was still grinning. "Oh, I still play D and D and eat cheese puffs. But I also like to—"

"Lah, lah, lah!" he sang over her, wishing he could plug his ears. But that would require letting go of his junk and *that* was a terrible, horrible, no good, very bad idea.

She shook her head. "I swear, Sam, I'll be sixty and you'll still look at me and see an eighth grader."

He could've countered with *you have no idea how wrong you are.* But he didn't want to encourage further conversation considering…you know… he was standing there in his birthday suit.

"I…uh…I can bring you those dry clothes if you'll give me a minute." He hitched his chin toward the bathroom door, indicating she should slide back inside and close it behind her.

"I came out to ask about Band-Aids." She gestured toward her injured toe.

"There's a first aid kit under the sink."

"Great. Thanks." She nodded and turned away.

His covert sigh of relief was cut short when she swung back.

Biting the inside of her cheek, she gestured up and down his length. "It's not just the ass that's top five. The whole kit and kaboodle is pretty damn good. Maybe good enough to rate top two."

Two? That meant there was some sonofabitch out there whom she thought was better looking than—

No. He shook his head. He wasn't going to think about that.

And he *definitely* wasn't going to address the little spurt of jealousy he felt. No, he was not.

"I think you're enjoying having me at a disadvantage just a little too much," he grumbled.

"Nonsense." She shook her head. "When it comes to enjoyment, there's no such thing as too much." Then, with a flirty wink, she disappeared inside the bathroom.

As soon as the door snapped shut, he let loose with a breathy sigh. "You"—he stared down at his happily hard cock—"are *not* helping matters."

But his dick was immune to recriminations. Which meant all he could do was shove it inside a pair of boxer briefs which he then stuffed inside a pair of jeans.

By the time he'd donned fresh wool socks and a clean hoodie, he *mostly* had his thoughts under control. Which allowed him to focus on rooting around in his drawers and closet for something that might work for Hannah.

The top was easy enough. One of his hoodies would swallow her, but at least it'd keep her warm. The bottoms were another matter. There was no way a pair of his jeans would fit.

"Something with a drawstring," he decided and pulled a pair of gray joggers from a drawer.

He was all out of panties and bras, so she'd have to go commando.

Before he could stop it, his brain conjured up images of her nipples rubbing against the inside of his hoodie and her sweet, soft p—

"Stop it!" he hissed, clenching his fists in an effort to wrangle his unruly libido.

"Did you say something?" her voice called through the closed bathroom door.

"Just trying to find you some clothes!" he was quick to come back, pulling a pair of socks from a separate drawer and adding them to the pile in his hand.

Fisher's right. I need to get laid.

Maybe if he hadn't been on an inadvertent sexual hiatus, his gray matter wouldn't be jumping at any excuse to go all Pornhub on him now.

That's it, he decided with a determined jerk of his chin. *I'm sexually frustrated. That's all. And it wouldn't matter who was in that bathroom. As long as they were sporting double-X chromosomes, my body would be reacting this way.*

Feeling decidedly better about himself and the whole situation, he knocked on the bathroom door. "Hannah?"

"Come in," she said and he opened the door to find her on her knees beneath his sink.

He almost pulled back and marched directly downstairs. Just raised the white flag and surrendered.

"Why anyone needs this many rolls of toilet paper is beyond me," she muttered. "And who keeps three extra deodorants, five extra tubes of toothpaste, a two-pound bag of Jolly Ranchers, and four extra bottles of shaving cream on hand? Are you a Costco nut or something?"

"Eliza does most of the shopping," he admitted, looking everywhere but at the curve of her butt because he thought he could see the *faintest* line of her ass crack through the terry cloth.

This is hell, he decided, stepping fully into the still-steamy bathroom. *I'm in hell.*

"I can't find it." She backed out from under the vanity and adjusted the towel more securely beneath her arms as she stood.

"I'll take a look." He shoved the clothes toward her. "None of this'll fit. But it's the best I got to offer."

"Thank you." She held the folded garments to her chest.

Thank keerist she'd covered her cleavage. He'd been having a helluva time not staring.

Turning toward the vanity to go in search of the recalcitrant first aid kit, he was thwarted from dropping to his knees when she placed a hand on his wrist. The bath had warmed her palm but the tips of her fingers still held on to a bit of the night's cold.

He had a brief flash of those cool fingertips trailing up his naked chest before he forcefully slammed the door shut on *that* imagery.

"No. I mean it," she insisted. "*Thank you.* And not just for the clothes. I know the danger you put yourself in tonight. I know the danger you're *still* in."

"I owed you," he told her simply. "But even if I hadn't, I'd still have come. The ties that bind can be stretched and frayed, but they never break. You and me?" He booped her button nose like he'd done when she was a kid. "We got history. And that means no matter how much time passes, if you call, I'll come."

Something softened in her eyes. When she tried for a cheeky grin, it came out a little wobbly. "So what you're saying is we're even?"

"What I'm saying is, between you and me, there's no reason to keep score."

Her eyes suddenly looked overly bright. "I've missed you, Sam."

"And who's fault is that?" He pasted on a stern expression. "I don't recall sending *you* a goodbye text six months ago."

"No." She shook her head and her damp hair brushed across her milky-white shoulders. "I don't just mean recently. I mean all along. Ever since you left Englewood. I've *missed* you."

He wanted to pull her into a hug. But given she wasn't wearing any clothes, and given the eagerness of his Johnson, he thought it better just to keep his grubby hands to himself.

"I've missed you too, kiddo. You're the only one who gets my movie references. Apparently, the Coen brothers aren't as universally beloved as we always thought."

"No accounting for taste, I guess." She shook her head sorrowfully and then quoted from *O Brother, Where Art Thou*. "It's a fool who looks for logic in the chambers of the human heart."

He chuckled. "Ulysses Everett McGill. One of the greatest characters every written."

"The paterfamilias."

"Long may he live in cinematic infamy."

There they stood in the still steamy bathroom, grinning at each other like a couple of dopes, lost in their own little world. The world they'd created sixteen years earlier when they'd been young and naive and green to all the happiness and heartbreak life had to offer.

She was the one to drag them back to the present. "First aid kit?"

"Shit." He ran a hand through his hair. "Right away."

He fished around under his sink through the supplies Eliza kept stocked until he located the square, plastic container. It'd been in the back corner, hidden under a pack of Charmin.

After gesturing for her to take a seat on the toilet lid, he knelt in front of her and opened the case. "Lemme see it." He patted his leg and tried not to notice how the towel climbed above her knees when she placed her foot on his thigh.

He wasn't a foot person. But he could appreciate how pretty Hannah's were. Thin and white, with delicate arches and the sparkly blue nail polish that caught the overhead light and glinted.

With as much care as possible, he applied ointment to the wound on her toe and then closed it with two butterfly bandages. He topped the butterfly bandages with a Band-Aid to cushion the cut and provide an extra layer of protection.

Even still, he warned her, "Shoes are probably gonna be a problem for a while."

"Good thing I don't have any with me." She made a face.

"Those goddamn feds. What were they thinking dragging you out barefoot in this weather?"

"I think they were thinking they'd bagged themselves a bona fide traitor."

"Which brings us full circle." He stood, realized he could see down the top of her towel, and hastily averted his eyes. "Get dressed and come down to the second floor. Everyone's eager to hear just how much trouble you're in, and how much trouble *we're* in by association."

"It's not good," she warned. "And I'm sorry I dragged you all into this. But I didn't know where else to—"

"Don't apologize. I've been in the middle of messes a whole helluva lot bigger than whatever this is."

"Maybe." A dark cloud moved over her face. "But you only know the half of it."

"Ain't that usually the way?" He gave a resigned shake of his head. "When the shit hits the fan, it tends to come from left, right, and center."

She swallowed noisily while nodding her agreement.

Deciding that was his cue, he escaped the bathroom and his bedroom, but ran into Fisher in the hallway. The man had two steaming mugs of hot chocolate in hand.

"Eliza sent me up with these," he said.

"We're headed down for a sit-rep." Sam took both mugs and indicated with a hitch of his chin that Fisher should proceed him back downstairs.

"*We?*" Fisher looked past Sam's shoulder. "All I see is you."

"Don't sound so disappointed. She's putting on dry clothes."

"Pity." Fisher shook his head. "I liked her in that little crop top." The grin he threw Sam over his shoulder as he turned and headed down the hall was absolutely devilish. "*Live fast, Eat trash,*" he quoted the slogan from Hannah's T-shirt. "Your girl is funny. And cute. You failed to mention how cute she is."

"First of all, she's not my girl." Why did a knot form in Sam's stomach when he said that? "And second of all, I get that most women look at your red flags and think it's a carnival, but Hannah isn't most women."

"I think I'm offended." Fisher pressed a hand to his chest as they passed the TV room. "I think you're sayin' I'm not good enough for your girl."

"She's *not* my girl. And don't forget I've known you long enough to recognize when you're cooking up some ill-conceived, half-formed plan to seduce a woman."

Fisher slid him a considering look. "My plans of seduction are *never* ill-conceived or half-formed. But I don't reckon that matters in this case. Because somethin' tells me Miss Hannah Blue is immune to any of my tricks."

If only that were true, Sam thought grouchily, remembering the reverence in her face as she'd stared up at the sergeant major when he'd called her brave.

"Please," Sam scoffed. "You're like catnip to women. None of them are immune. So hear me when I say *stay away from Hannah.* She's not for you."

"Gotcha." Fisher nodded. "Consider your territory pissed on."

"That's not what I'm saying."

"No?" Fisher cocked his head. "You're *not* claimin' her for yourself? Then I don't see the problem in my givin' it a go."

"The *problem* is that if you try, I'm gonna have to cut off your balls and feed them to you."

"Oohh." Fisher chuckled. "You've gone and whipped out your big, bad Marine Raider voice. I'm shakin' in my boots."

Sam was done with the conversation. "Do me a favor, Fish, and go play with your dick."

"Temptin'." Fish rubbed a hand over his stubbled jaw. "But see? It's so much more fun when someone else does it."

Sam considered dumping both mugs of hot chocolate over Fisher's head, and only managed *not* to by gripping the handles hard enough to have his knuckles turning white.

After he'd followed Fisher to the second floor, Fisher turned and said, "So is it just me in particular? Or are ya sayin' ya want men in general to stay away from Hannah? Because if it's the latter, I should warn ya, that's a losin' battle. She's fine as frog's hair. Ain't no way you're goin' to hold off the whole of the male population. Even you aren't that good of a marksman."

"I don't have to hold 'em all back." Sam took a seat at the conference table. "Just the one's like you who have dishonorable intentions."

Fisher grabbed his heart. "Ya wound me. Why would ya think my aim toward Miss Blue would be anything but honorable?"

"History." Eliza answered before Sam could. She stood at the top of the stairs with a tray full of snacks. "And the long line of broken hearts strung out behind you."

"Horseshit," Fisher scoffed. "I haven't even *scratched* a heart, much less left one broken."

"Only 'cause you've never been with any one woman long enough for her to fall in love with you," Sam insisted.

Fisher lifted a hand like he was a Roman orator addressing the senate. "Romantic relationships are like avocados. They're perfect for about twenty-four hours. After that, they start to spoil."

Eliza opened her mouth, no doubt to tell Fisher off, but Ozzie interrupted from his seat in front of the bank of computers. "It's official, folks. The FBI has a picture of Sam and Hannah leaving on Pale Horse." He hit a key and a grainy photo appeared on one of the monitors. The angle showed it'd been taken from a security camera on the roof of the FBI building.

"If that's the best image they have, we're home free." Eliza dropped the tray into the center of the table.

"I was able to hack their system and erase their security footage for the ten minutes surrounding Hannah's escape. But apparently they have a couple old analog cameras that record straight to tape. That's how they got this photo." Ozzie tapped the monitor's screen.

"No real identifying factors then," Eliza insisted. "I mean, it's obvious whoever raced to Hannah's rescue drove a souped-up motorcycle. But it's impossible to discern any details from the image. There's no way the feds will be able to trace the bike back here."

Ozzie looked skeptical. "They could use old city CCTV footage of motorcycles that've been caught on traffic cams to contrast and compare. I bet they'll come knocking on our door sooner or later to see if the motorcycle they caught on camera matches one of ours." He flung his arm in the general direction of the lower floor. "We should park Pale Horse in the Bat Cave."

"Agreed." Sam nodded, staring hard at the photo on the monitor. He could make out Hannah's form huddled against his back and shuddered at the memory of just how bitterly cold it had been and how *little* protection she'd had against that cold.

"I've also been monitoring the online chatter surrounding the escape," Ozzie added. "Seems the feds consider Miss Blue public enemy numero uno. They've just looped in local law enforcement and put out an APB."

"It's no wonder," Hannah said from the bottom of the stairs. "Red Square is demanding half a billion dollars from Dominion or they're threatening to shut down the pipeline. The FBI is convinced I can help them get to Red Square before that happens."

Sam hadn't realized the sweatshirt he'd taken from his closet was the one he'd gotten in 2014 when his favorite first basemen, Paul Konerko, had retired from baseball.

Or maybe he *had* realized it, subconsciously. Maybe somewhere in the far reaches of his mind he'd *chosen* his most cherished hoodie for her because he felt like wrapping her in something that *meant* something to him.

Regardless, he'd never be able to wear the hoodie again without thinking of her and the way she looked right then with the sleeves pushed up her forearms and the hem hanging nearly to her knees.

What *was* it about a woman wearing a man's shirt that made that man's inner caveman roar to life?

Was it just that it was a stark reminder that the fairer sex tended to be physically smaller? Was it somehow tied to growing up in a patriarchal society and therefore it made a man feel proprietary? Like, *she's wearing my shirt, and that's a signal to all you bastards she's mine.* Or was it something as simple as knowing that something that had touched his skin was now touching hers?

Whatever the reason, he decided he'd never seen Hannah looking more beautiful.

"Hannah." He was quick to escort her over to where Ozzie reigned supreme. "Let me introduce you to Ozzie. You two have a lot in common. He's a white hat hacker too."

Ozzie grimaced as he pushed up from his rolling chair to shake her hand. "I mean, I'm not sure my enemies would label me such. To them I'm definitely a threat actor."

"And I'm Fisher, by the way," Fisher called from his seat at the conference table. "We met unofficially earlier, but I reckon we can make it official now. Good to see ya with some color in your cheeks." He stood and pulled out the chair next to him, indicating with a flourish that Hannah should sit there.

If it were possible to kill a man with a look, Sam would've put Fisher six feet under.

"Thanks for the ride earlier," Hannah told Fisher as Sam steered her unerringly toward the chair next to *his* spot at the conference table.

"Happy to oblige." Fisher inclined his head toward Hannah. Then he shot Sam a knowing grin before adding, "If you're ever up for another... *ride*, just say the word."

Hannah blinked, startled by Fisher's blatant flirting.

When Sam spoke, it was more of a snarl. "For fuck's sake, Fish. I'm starting to wish that Colombian had had a better aim."

"What Colombian?" Hannah glanced back and forth between them.

"The one who tried to shoot Fish's dick off," Sam clarified.

When her eyes automatically pinged down to Fisher's fly, Sam instantly regretted his words.

But Fisher? The bastard's grin only widened.

"Not sure how the man managed to miss such a large target," Fisher drawled. "But I thank my lucky stars he did."

"You'll have to excuse Fisher," Eliza said from her seat at the head of the table. "He's great for reconnaissance. Which is why we keep him around. But his mental maturity was stunted. And now he's basically a thirteen-year-old boy stuck in thirty-four-year-old's body."

"Got to take the good with the bad," Fisher submitted, completely unphased by Eliza's recrimination.

Sam pulled out Hannah's chair and waited for her to sink into it before taking his own seat. When he shoved the mug of hot chocolate in front of her, he hoped to distract her from the flirty smile Fisher sent her way.

"Get a couple sips of that in you," he instructed, "and then fill us in on what's going on. Upstairs you said I only know half the story."

She nodded before tipping the mug to her lips. Her tentative sip turned into a gulp.

"Holy shit," she gasped. "That's the best hot chocolate I've ever tasted."

"Thank you." Eliza beamed. "The trick is to use a mixture of cocoa powder and chocolate chips."

"Mmm." Hannah took another healthy slug and then grunted when Peanut jumped into her lap.

"Oh, hello." She smiled at the cat, who immediately butted his head under her chin. "I remember you. Still as sweet and adorable as ever, I see."

Fisher snorted. "I doubt your friend Cesar would agree with that."

"Why?" Hannah looked sharply around the conference table. "Did something happen?"

"Let's just say there was an incident with a wig," Sam admitted with a grimace.

"Oh, no." She winced. "Not the Cher hair. That's his favorite."

"He assured us it could be salvaged. Now, tell us what sort of trouble you're in so we can figure out how to get you out of it."

She kissed Peanut before beginning her tale. And Sam did *not* relive the moment when her mouth was pressed against the side of his neck.

No he did not.

CHAPTER 12

Southpark Hotel, Austin, Texas

"The D.O.D woman has escaped."

Vinny's fingers hovered over his keyboard as he glanced at his lit phone screen, unsure if he'd heard his contact correctly. Yang had a thick Chinese accent, after all, making his consonants sharp and his vowels staccato.

"She escaped from the *FBI?*" If his tone sounded incredulous, it was because he was fucking-A *incredulous*.

The answer that came through his phone's speaker was a clipped and succinct, "Yes."

Astonished, he leaned back in the rolling chair. "You're telling me a cyber rat like myself somehow slipped the noose of the Federal Bureau of Investigations?"

Again, the answer was one word. "Yes." And then Yang added, "She is gone. No longer in custody."

Vinny stared out the window at the cars rushing past on the freeway outside. So many people going about their daily routine, oblivious to the dark dealings and dangers all around them.

"How does a desk jockey pull one over on the feds?" he said to himself.

Even still, Yang answered, "You Americans give too much credit to your police forces. Your movies have made them into heroes when the truth is, they underperform more often than not. And when they *do* solve a big case, it is usually through luck or confession. I am told the woman simply walked out the back door."

Walked out the back door, Vinny thought with a shake of his head. *Just that easy.*

Vincent Romano had been fourteen years old when he'd dipped his toes into a life of crime. It'd been a simple scam, an SIRF—stolen identity refund fraud. He'd filched the identities of his friends' parents by snatching their business mail straight out of their mailboxes. Then he'd filed tax returns using their pilfered information and pocketed the refunds the IRS mailed to them.

Four grand. That's what he made that year. And even though his nanna, who'd raised him after his parents died, would never condone such behavior, he'd been hooked on easy money ever since.

After that first SIRF scheme, he'd set about teaching himself to code and hack. Sitting at a desk to do his deeds was far more pleasant than getting his hands dirty in the trades, like so many of the boys from his neighborhood were forced to do. Plus, unlike his first victims, his online prey were always strangers. Faceless, sometimes nameless entities that didn't seem all that real. Only a list of digits or a few lines of code.

With a fundamental grasp of the finer points of cybercrime, he'd embarked on a career of credit card fraud, online wire transfer fraud, and banking fraud. He'd even spent a year in his early twenties as a "romance scammer," creating fake dating profiles and establishing online relationships with women where, after a little wooing, he'd coerced his targets into sending him money or reloading his digital wallet.

But he'd soured on that avenue of income pretty quickly. For one, the ROI was shit. He'd had to invest a ridiculous amount of time on each target for a payout that sometimes only netted him a few hundred dollars. Plus, it'd felt *wrong* to take the money of desperate women. Especially after he'd spent weeks getting to know them.

So he'd gone back to concentrating on his other endeavors. Purposefully keeping himself humble, keeping his jobs small to avoid the laser-focused eyes of the feds.

Or so I assumed *their eyes were laser-focused.*

Given how they'd just let the D.O.D. woman slip through their fingers, maybe he'd been playing it too safe, worrying too much about their cunning and reach.

Of course, his current plot was *far* from small. In fact, if everything went according to plan, two million smackaroonies were headed his way. Two million bones to help pay off the mortgage on his nanna's third-floor walkup in Queens and buy him that suit he'd been eyeing at Brooklyn Tailors.

He cast his mind back to where it'd all started, in his favorite deli two blocks down from his nanna's place. He'd been enjoying pastrami on rye with mustard and a sour pickle when a little man with a soft smile but hard eyes slid into the seat across from him.

New Yorkers were notorious for invading the space of others. That's what happened when you packed eight million people onto a thirty square mile plot of land. But even New Yorkers didn't share tables without asking.

Vinny had opened his mouth to say something quintessentially New York, like, *"Yo. What the fuck, bruh?"* But the little man with the hard eyes had beat him to the punch.

"Hello Vincent. Or would you rather I call you Vinny?"

The man's thick accent was one Vinny had recognized from his trips to Chinatown for dim sum.

"Who the fuck are you?" he'd demanded, looking around the deli to see if the little man had friends.

He hadn't.

At least none that Vinny had seen.

"My name is not important. But my offer is."

The sandwich Vinny had been mowing down turned to a stone at the bottom of his stomach.

"I know this is New York," he'd said with what he'd hoped looked like casual boredom. *"And I know I'm Italian. But this ain't* The Godfather. *No man can make me an offer I can't refuse."*

A confident, knowing expression had spread across Yang's face—although it wasn't until later that Vinny had learned the little man was called Yang—as he sat back in the chair and cocked his head. *"You can refuse it. But I do not think you will want to."*

"Oh, yeah? Why's that?"

"Because my offer comes with a two-million-dollar paycheck."

Even though Vinny had worked hard to keep his expression blank, he hadn't been able to stop his right eye from twitching with sudden interest. *"What's the catch?"*

When it came to two rocks, there was *always* a catch.

"You must move to Texas, get a job at a power plant outside of Austin, and when the time is right, plant some malware." The little man had patted his breast pocket and Vinny's eyes had recognized the outline of a thumb drive.

"Right." He'd nodded. *"Except I don't want to move to Texas. I have a grandmother who depends on me to do her shopping. Plus, guys down there fuck their cows and their sisters."*

"It will not be for long. Three months, maybe. Four maximum. And you can use an app to have your grandmother's food delivered."

Vinny's heart had started pounding at the thought of making two million simoleons for three, maybe four months of work.

"Okay. But then there's the problem of me not having any experience working in a power plant. I'm no electrical engineer or—"

"We have fabricated all the experience and credentials you will need for the job," Yang had interrupted.

Glancing around the deli again, Vinny had noted the couple seated at a table by the front window—tourists by the looks of their sneakers. They'd been more interested in making googly eyes at each other than watching the uncomfortable exchange between the two men sitting in the back.

Returning his attention to the stranger sitting across from him, he'd asked the one, all-important question that'd been burning in his brain since the offer had been made. *"Why me?"*

Again that soft smile. It had been incongruous when paired with Yang's flinty, soulless eyes. *"Because you are the right color. You are the right sex. And you have the skills we will need to make this endeavor successful."*

Vinny had opened his mouth to ask another question, but Yang had added, *"Plus, we have been watching you for a while now. You are smart and careful. You lay low and do not draw attention to yourself."*

"I obviously drew your attention," Vinny had countered.

"Yes. But that is only because we have eyes everywhere."

That pronouncement had made Vinny's stomach sour. *"Who are you? Who do you work for?"*

"All in good time," Yang had promised. *"For now. Think about my offer."*

He'd slid the thumb drive across the table and Vinny had instinctively curled it into his hand. *"I will contact you again in three days."*

Before Vinny could object, Yang had pushed up from the table and exited the deli.

Turned out the little man with the soft smile and hard eyes worked for some shadowy Chinese intelligence group. And they, along with their partner high up inside the U.S. government, a man who went by the code name Bishop, were planning an attack on Texas's power grid.

Not to engage in espionage, as it'd been explained to Vinny in the information on the thumb drive. The scheme was government sanctioned, a partnership between the U.S. and China to convince Texas's electric reliability council there was a weakness in their system.

We're talking real inside spycraft shit, Vinny thought now, pride filling his chest.

He still found it hard to believe the powers that be had tapped him to participate in the intrigue. After all, wasn't this a job for the CIA? Or the NSA?

Then again, when the federal government was looking to pull one over on a state government, maybe it *was* smart to co-opt a civilian. Less red tape. More plausible deniability.

That was the thing, though, wasn't it? Vinny wasn't just any civilian.

When he'd asked Yang three days later, *"Your U.S. source knows what I do for a living, right?"* Yang had only shrugged.

"They understand that sometimes it takes a criminal to stop criminals. This is your chance to do something sanctioned. Your chance to answer the call of your country. Are you in?"

Vinny had been in. *More* than in, he'd been freakin' *pumped* at the chance to do some real-deal undercover work backed by Uncle Sam himself. A *legitimate* paycheck.

Nanna will be so proud.

He'd packed his bags and flown to Austin the next day. And he'd been living in a hotel by the airport and working at the power plant ever since.

His job left much to be desired. Being part of the janitorial team wasn't exactly glamorous. But the government-approved espionage made up for the drudgery of mopping floors and replacing the urinal cakes in the men's bathrooms.

He'd learned the layout of the plant and the schedules of the various workers. He knew exactly how he was going to get the malware uploaded when the engineers changed shifts. All he'd been waiting on was Yang to tell him it was go-time.

Then that D.O.D. chick had stumbled upon their plan.

Vinny wasn't real clear on how all that had come about. Something involving her finding the encrypted communications between Yang and Bishop. But it'd culminated in them deciding the best way to clear her piece off the board and ensure she kept her mouth shut was to frame her for some shady shit guaranteed to have the feds locking her away.

It'd been easy enough to create a dark web trail from the D.O.D chick's work computer to the contact person Yang's handler had given to Vinny, ostensibly someone associated with Red Square. And it'd been even easier to fabricate communications between the two that had made it appear as if the D.O.D woman was passing along highly classified Dominion Pipeline information. Then, it'd just been a matter of Yang planting a bug in the FBI's ear via an anonymous tip. And voila! The frameup was complete.

Except, the woman had thrown a potential wrench in the works by escaping.

"What does this mean for us?" he asked Yang now. "Does it change anything?"

"Bishop asks you to be prepared to move on the target at a moment's notice."

"I'm ready now."

"Good." Yang sounded pleased and Vinny felt another punch of pride. "Stay by your phone. I will contact you when it is time."

After the call clicked off, Vinny sat back and grinned, excited his job in Texas was almost finished.

Wide-open spaces, ten-gallon hats, and everyone smiling at him all the time had lost their charm. He missed dirty sidewalks and good bagels and cabbies who yelled out the window that he was a motherfucker when he crossed the street in front of them.

No one's called me a motherfucker in three months, he thought grumpily.

It was starting to affect his mental health.

CHAPTER 13

Black Knights Inc.

"You think the Chinese plot to knock out the Texas power grid is somehow linked to Red Square taking the Dominion Pipeline hostage?" Ozzie asked as he pecked away at the keyboard on the laptop he'd brought with him to the conference table.

Hannah wasn't offended by his split-attention. As a cyberpunk herself, she knew it was possible to surf the web, code, or do a little light hacking while also attending a conversation.

Most hackers had the ability to multitask. Oftentimes, in the land of spyware, spear phishing, and trojan horses, there were multiple data streams to contend with and one *had* to be good at keeping more than one ball in the air.

Of course, anytime she explained as much to Cesar, he always nodded and said, *"Sure. It's that or all you computer geeks have ADHD. You get jittery when you're not focusing on twenty things at once."*

"You say poe-tay-toe, I say poe-tah-toe," was her standard comeback.

"I mean"—she shrugged now and scratched the base of Peanut's tail while he made biscuits on her thighs—"I can't know anything for sure until I get in there and start pulling strings to see how things unravel." She hooked a thumb over her shoulder to indicate the bank of computers behind her before continuing. "But imagine the devastation should both things happen at once? The entire eastern seaboard loses access to fuel at the same time Texas goes dark? Either incident would be crippling to our country. Put them together?" She mimed her head exploding.

Annoyed she'd stopped scratching, Peanut meowed his discontent.

"Sorry," she told him before obediently resuming her duty, which activated his purr mechanism. He rumbled so loudly she had to concentrate to hear Eliza's question.

"I get how the pipeline going down could be catastrophic, but isn't our national power grid set up to withstand outages? I thought that was the whole point. That if a plant goes down in one area, a plant from another area can ramp up production and cover the loss of electricity. Assuming there's no equipment failure at the substations or on the power lines, of course."

"The national grid *is* set up that way," Hannah was quick to agree. "But Texas is on its own grid. It's called the Texas Interconnection and it's managed by ERCOT, the Electric Reliability Council of Texas."

"Right." Eliza tapped her chin with a red-tipped finger, her mouth screwed up in consideration. "Now that you mention it, I remember the headlines about ERCOT price gouging its customers when that big ice storm hit. When was that? 2020?"

"2021," Hannah corrected.

"Right," Eliza said again. "The property damage alone was in the billions. But wasn't that damage mostly due to the freezing temps and the ice and not so much the power outages?"

"It was both. But I'm not talking about one-third of the people being without power for a day or two," Hannah explained. "I'm talking about a statewide blackout that could last for weeks. Think of all the patients in hospitals hooked up to machines that will die as soon as the generators run out of fuel—fuel that might already be scarce if Dominion is shut down. Think of injured or ill people unable to get the life-saving surgeries they need because surgeons can't operate in the dark."

Peanut had doubled his biscuit-making efforts and she winced when a claw found its way through her borrowed joggers.

After carefully adjusting the cat into a more comfortable—and less dangerous—position she continued. "Then there are the longer-term effects. The elderly or infirmed living in the high-rise apartments in Dallas or Houston who'll be unable to walk down the dozens of flights of stairs to get food. The pumps that just about everyone relies on to send water to their homes will shut down, leaving people to seek out unsanitary options like rivers and streams. Dysentery, Giardia, and E. Coli will begin to run rampant within a handful of days. And the diarrhea, vomiting, and dehydration that accompanies these diseases will be enough to make some people seriously ill while actually *killing* the very young, very old, or those already living with compromised immune systems."

Saying the words aloud made them real and had the hot chocolate in her stomach threatening to curdle. Glancing around at the faces staring back at her, she made sure her expression as much as her words drove home just how dire the situation could be. "The 2021 winter storm in Texas had 290 confirmed deaths, with unconfirmed deaths reaching as high as 1000. This outage will affect far more people for a far longer period of time. We're looking at a potentially devastating loss of life."

"Good god." Eliza pressed her hand to her chest as if to keep her heart inside her body.

"It's happened before too." Ozzie ran a hand through hair that looked like it hadn't seen a good brushing in well over a week. "In 2019, Venezuela experienced a nation-wide blackout for five days. Just *five days*. And thousands of people died as a result."

"That's just the humanitarian crisis," Sam added grimly. "We haven't even *touched* on the financial repercussions."

His wide-palmed hands were wrapped around a coffee mug emblazoned with the White Sox team logo. Despite her best efforts, Hannah's center melted at the memory of those same hands rubbing up and down her arms.

Now that she wasn't nearly comatose from hypothermia, she could appreciate just how intimate they'd been upstairs. His big arms had been so strong and warm as he'd held her tight. His breath had felt so hot and comforting against her scalp when he'd pressed his mouth to the crown of her head. With him surrounding her on all sides, she'd felt safe and...most importantly...*cared* for in a way she never had before.

It was strange. Though she'd had sex with men, there'd never been one who'd made her feel as cherished as Sam had in that bathtub.

Although maybe that wasn't so strange. Because that was the true definition of intimacy, wasn't it? Not the insertion of one person's body parts into another person's body parts. But someone making another person feel protected and treasured and secure?

Taking a fully-clothed bath with Sam was better than the best sex I've had, she decided.

Of course the thought of fully-clothed Sam immediately brought to mind fully *un*clothed Sam.

When she'd walked out of his bathroom, she'd been momentarily stunned to be getting an eyeful of the lovely expanse of his naked back.

He had the prettiest skin, olive-toned and freckle-free. His broad shoulders tapered to his waist to create that quintessential male V-shape. And his ass was high and tight. One of those gym-bro butts that graced the glossy covers of fitness mags—although she would bet her left tit any iron Sam pumped was so he'd be strong and fast for the job and not because he was trying to get swole. Then there were his legs. Long and heavily muscled and sprinkled with crinkly black man-hair.

When he'd turned, her momentary astonishment had exploded into shock. She'd thought she'd gotten a glimpse of his penis before he'd hastily covered himself. But she didn't trust her eyes. Because it'd looked like… Well, it'd looked like he'd been hard.

Long and thick and *hard*.

But that couldn't be right. He wouldn't have been hard after her harrowing rescue. After nearly freezing to death. After having her fall asleep in his arms like a little kid conking out on her daddy.

She snored.

She knew she snored.

Cesar derived an annoying amount of pleasure in reminding her of that very thing on an unnecessarily frequent basis.

So no. He hadn't been hard. It'd just been her mind—and all her fantasies for the last sixteen years—playing tricks on her.

Of course, if she'd thought his backside was epic, then there wasn't a word in the English language to describe his frontside.

Pecs for days. Those delicious square-shaped numbers topped by flat brown nipples and peppered with more of that crinkly, black man-hair. A flat stomach rippling with muscles. And his Adonis lines?

The stuff dreams are made of.

Wet *dreams.*

Yet, despite the visual smorgasbord, the things that'd *really* grabbed her attention were the bruises mottling his skin. Their green and yellow hues told her he'd recently been put through the wringer. And then there were his scars. A jagged line here. A puckered circle there. Some looked fairly new, still raised and red. Others were obviously old, having faded to white.

She knew his work was dangerous. But the evidence left behind on his body told her just *how* dangerous.

He called himself a private defense contractor. But that was just a prettied-up name for what he really was.

A warrior.

A man who put his body in the path of peril as a matter of course.

And the most startling proof of this was the puckered, angry-looking scar on his neck. A scar that said, at least once, he'd come close to losing his life.

She tried to imagine a world without Sam in it. But the idea was so horrific she shoved it aside and returned her attention to the conversation.

"The thing is, we're not just talking about the financial repercussions for Texas." She dutifully rubbed her chin against Peanut's head when the cat butted her for attention. "A calamitous failure of the state's infrastructure would send shockwaves throughout the entire country. They have the second largest GDP in the U.S., after all."

"So why frame you for Red Square and Dominion when what you were focused on was the threat to Texas?" A line appeared between Eliza's dark, arching eyebrows. "I mean, why not make it look like you were in cahoots with the Chinese in the plot to take down the Lone Star State's electrical grid?"

Hannah frowned. "I've been thinking about that. The only thing I can figure is that, unless I'm wrong about all this and my report to my superiors regarding Texas actually made it up the D.O.D food chain, then no one but me...and now *you* guys...knows about the danger to the Lone Star State. Trying to make it look like I was helping the Chinese would draw attention to the scheme. But Red Square? They've already implemented a zero-day attack on Dominion. The feds know about it. I'm sure the president and her joint chiefs know about it. Heck, it'll probably be in the papers tomorrow morning. So why not link me to *that*, right?"

She punctuated her thinking by lifting a finger. "If I'm in FBI custody for helping Red Square take down Dominion, I'm not going to be out here raising a ruckus and checking to make sure Texas takes their vulnerable power plant offline before it can be hit by the malware."

"Two questions." Fisher raised a hand, his heavily lashed eyes bright with intelligence.

"Shoot," she told him, scratching beneath Peanut's chin, causing the cat's eyes to roll back in his head.

"What's a zero-day attack?"

She opened her mouth, but it was Ozzie who answered. "It's a cyber-attack that exploits a previously unknown vulnerability in a computer application."

"Ah." Fisher nodded and pinned his gaze on Hannah. "Okay, so ya said it's one power plant that's vulnerable. How does one vulnerable power plant take down the state's entire grid?"

She was struck once again by just how pretty the man's mouth was. And not only his mouth. The whole of him was almost too beautiful to look at, like Jude Law and Alex Pettyfer got put in a blender and swirled together.

Serious eye candy.

Too bad she was still smitten with Sam and therefore had no real interest in Mr. Tall, Tan, and Tasty.

There was no use continuing to deny it as she'd done with Cesar earlier. Sam was sitting a foot away from her, but every single one of her cells leaned toward him like he was a magnet and she was metal.

Of course, her preference for Samuel Harwood over Fisher could be blamed in no small part on her preference for scruffy types. Give her a full beard and hair that could use a cut any day over a clean shave and a face that was so glorious it was like staring into the sun.

Which was why even though Sam had made it clear he'd never like her *like that*, she was still drawn to *him* and not Fisher. Fisher, who was making it just as clear that even though he wasn't Mr. Right, he'd be more than happy to play the part of Mr. Right Now.

"Hannah?" Mr. Right Now pulled her from her thoughts.

"Huh?" She blinked at him.

When he grinned, she noticed he had the faintest hint of a dimple in his left cheek.

Okay, sometimes it's nice to stare into the sun, she decided.

She must've made a sound or a face of awe or something because Sam slammed his mug down on the table with enough force to make Peanut hiss unhappily and jump from her lap. Startled, she blinked over at him and found venom in his expression.

"What?" She barely refrained from shrinking in her chair. "What's that look for?"

"He's a walking, talking red flag." He hitched his bearded chin toward Fisher.

"Hey!" Fisher protested.

If it were anyone other than Sam she'd suspect jealousy. But it *was* Sam. Which meant he was going all big brother on her and warning her away from a guy she'd already pegged as a heartbreaker.

Which, yeah, pissed her off. Mostly because big brother was the last role she wanted him to play. But also because she *hated* someone thinking they could tell her what to do.

Or who *to do.*

"How do you think I made it to the ripe old age of thirty without recognizing a red flag when I see one?" was her counteroffer.

"Hey!" Fisher tried again.

Sam shook his head. "You're not thirty."

"Might as well be. My birthday's just around the corner. Speaking of, I think everyone can agree a thirty-year-old woman qualifies as fully grown and fully capable of deciding if she wants to wave around a red flag for a little while."

"Now we're talkin'." Fisher crossed his arms, grinning broadly. "I do enjoy a good…*wavin'.*"

"Breaking news just in, Fish." Eliza's expression broadcast her disgust. "There's promiscuity and then there's flat-out depravity. Since you can't seem to keep from seducing every woman you meet between the ages of eighteen and eighty, I'm thinking you fall into the second category."

"Aw, don't be jealous, doll face." Fisher chucked her on the chin. "There's enough of me to go around and always enough left over for you."

"What? And risk catching the clam?"

"I told ya antibiotics cleared that up."

Hannah ignored the bickering pair and instead asked Sam, "Why do you care anyway?"

"Don't wanna see you waking up in the morning with regrets is all." His words were smashed together in that classic *Sam* way.

"If it'll set your mind at ease, I'm more concerned with clearing my name and stopping a catastrophic power failure in Texas than I am with taking Pretty Boy"—she flung a hand in Fisher's direction—"up on his not-so-subtle offer of a good time."

"Boo. Hiss. Spoilsport," Fisher teased. "Also, why is everyone convinced all I'm ever after is a fling?"

"Once again," Eliza chimed in, "the answer is *history*."

"I don't get no respect." Fisher feigned a pout.

"Okay, Rodney Dangerfield, that's enough out of you." Ozzie pointed a finger at Fisher then used it to draw an invisible circle in the air. "Let's get back on track."

"Right." Fisher winked flirtatiously at Hannah before frowning at Ozzie. "Wait. Who's Rodney Dangerfield?"

"Who's Rodney Danger—?" Ozzie looked positively apoplectic. "New York comedian big in the 80s? His catchphrase was *I don't get no respect*? Played in *Caddyshack*?" When Fisher only blinked, he added, "*Easy Money? Back to School?*"

Fisher shrugged and Ozzie's jaw slung open. "Did you live under a rock in Louisiana? Those films are cult classics."

Sam disregarded the tangent by keeping his eyes on Hannah's face. She felt his gaze like a physical touch, but determinedly avoided the sensation so she could shake her head at him.

"No matter how hard this is for you to believe." She kept her voice low so the conversation stayed between them. "I'm not a little girl anymore. I can take care of myself."

His voice matched her own when he informed her, "Despite his allusion to the contrary, Fish doesn't play for keeps."

"Who says I'm looking for keeps?"

The look of astonishment that came over Sam's face was almost laughable. Then, he changed tactics. "He's too old for you."

She glanced briefly at Fisher, still deep in Rodney Dangerfield conversation with Ozzie. "How old is he?"

"Thirty-four."

"Your age. Which is only four years older than me."

"Almost five," he corrected.

"Okay. Almost five. Would it shock you to learn Candy married a man nearly eight years her senior? Are you ready to turn my brother-in-law in to the authorities for *corrupting a minor?*"

"That's different."

"How so?"

"Your sister wasn't a minor when she met her husband."

"And I'm not a minor now. Neither is Fisher. So explain to me again what the problem is?"

She'd just beat him at his own game. The expression on his face said as much.

"Look, Sam." She sighed. "I get you're having a hard time admitting I've grown up. But I spent six years in college getting two degrees. I have a career and an apartment and a 401K. I've had boyfriends and lovers and friends with benefits. So how about you drop the big brother act. Because I am not, and never have been, your little sister."

The way he blinked reminded her of the YouTube videos she'd seen of old Commodore 64 computers trying to crunch data. Slow and cumbersome.

Grunting her annoyance, she returned her attention to the group. Ozzie had moved on to the subject of *Saturday Night Live*. He was telling Fisher the best cast were the 70's members, including Chevy Chase, Gilda Radner, and Dan Akroyd.

"No, no, no." Fisher shook his head. "The absolute *best* SNL cast was the one with Maya Rudolph, Amy Poehler, Will Forte and—"

"To answer your question, Fisher"—she jumped in because she thought she might have to wait all night if she didn't—"that one vulnerable power plant is connected to all the others through a system of proprietary software. If the Chinese upload the malware to the vulnerable plant, it opens the doors to all the others. Then we're talking a catastrophic cascade of failures until eventually…" She snapped her fingers. "Lights out, Texas."

"Hell." Eliza's eyes were large and unblinking. She pulled a locket from inside the collar of her blouse and rubbed it between two fingers.

"It *will* be hell." Hannah nodded. "And nobody should be surprised. For years China has been working on ways to shut down the U.S. power grid. I think this is an experiment. It'll act as a test for what will happen nationally should the Chinese decide to make a broader incursion."

"Attacking a nation's power grid is considered an open act of war." Sam's dark eyebrows pulled into a V.

Ozzie wore a matching expression. "Which will result in a kinetic response."

Hannah had been so preoccupied with the consequences for Texas, she hadn't considered the international repercussions. She wouldn't have thought it possible after the freezing cold of the motorcycle ride but sweat popped out on the back of her neck. "Wait. Are you saying what I think you're saying?"

It was Eliza who answered. "The U.S. position is that digital attacks will be met with physical attacks."

"Meaning war?" Hannah's words were hoarse.

"Meaning war." Sam jerked his chin down once. "With China, which has the largest standing military on the planet."

Her stomach didn't just drop then. It hit the frickin' floor with so much force she wouldn't have been surprised to hear a *splat*. "Holy knuckle-dragging shit-gibbons," she breathed as the hair all over her body lifted as if in warning of a lightning strike.

"Right." Ozzie pushed back from the table. "So first things first. We make sure your superiors got the intel regarding Texas. If they have and are taking measures to prevent the attack, then we can turn our attention to figuring out who fingered you for working with Red Square."

As much as she didn't like the idea of being labeled a criminal conspirator for one minute longer than was absolutely necessary, Ozzie was right. They had to ensure Texas was safe—*and apparently head off World War III*—before they could turn their attention toward clearing her name.

"You okay if I use your equipment?" She jerked her chin toward the bank of computers.

"Be my guest." Ozzie threw an arm wide in welcome. "But stay away from the second machine from the left. That's my newest baby. I'm just now breaking her in."

"Noted." She pushed up from the conference table, eager to get started.

Before she could take a step, however, Sam stopped her with a hand on her wrist. She tried not to notice how warm and rough his palm was. How easily his fingers encircled her joint. "What can I do to help?"

"I second that question." Fisher pushed to a stand as well.

"Me three." This from Eliza.

"I'd love to grab one of those Capri Suns," Hannah told Eliza, gesturing toward the tray in the center of the table that held snacks. "I could use the extra kick of sugar."

"Be my guest." Eliza smiled. "I added those to the pile because I remembered you liked them. You and Agent..." She screwed up her face. "What was his name?"

"Timothy," Hannah automatically supplied. "Timothy Floyd."

One of Eliza's eyebrows arched and she touched the side of her nose. "I thought maybe I smelled some chemistry between you two when you were both here."

Sam grunted—or maybe *growled?*—beside Hannah.

The devil in her wanted to exaggerate her connection with Agent Floyd. But lying was anathema to her nature. Instead, she shrugged. "We had one date. It was uninspiring. And now, apparently, he's moved back to Ohio."

"Too bad." Eliza shook her head. "He was cute."

"Hey!" Fisher snapped his fingers. "Enough girl-talk about handsome FBI agents. We've got work to do. What do ya need me to do, Hannah?"

"Stay far, far away," she told him with a grin. "You're a terrible distraction."

He winked, that faint dimple shadowing his cheek. "Flattery will get ya nowhere, darlin'."

"Really?" She cocked her head and grinned. It was impossible not to grin back at Fisher when he was grinning at her. The man *oozed* charm.

"Well..." He relented with a shrug. "It'll get ya *somewhere*. Where were ya thinkin' you'd like to go?"

It was a blatant proposition and she felt Sam's hand tighten around her wrist.

"How 'bout you go grab my plates outta the parking garage, huh?" he growled at Fisher—really, that was the only way to describe the rumbly timbre of his voice. "And park Pale Horse in the Bat Cave while you're at it. That'll keep you outta everyone's hair."

"Copy that." Fisher gave him a sarcastic, limp-wristed salute. Then he returned his attention to Hannah. "I'm not as bad as they're makin' me out to be. Just so ya know."

"Except you *are*," Eliza interjected.

Fisher turned to BKI's... *What is Eliza's role here? Office manager? House mom? Social secretary?* It was all rather vague. "You are *determined* to rip me a new asshole tonight, aren't ya?"

Eliza rolled her eyes so hard Hannah was surprised they didn't pop out of her head and go tumbling across the floor. "Don't act like everything I say doesn't bounce off you like a rubber ball off blacktop," she countered.

"Not true." Fisher donned sad, puppy-dog eyes. "I'm as thin-skinned as they come. One big ball of sensitivity and insecurity."

"Pfft. Right. Thing is, Fish, after checking my receipts, turns out I never bought any of your bullshit."

Fisher threw back his head and laughed. "I love it when that porcelain veneer of yours cracks and we all get to see a little of the *real* Eliza beneath." When Eliza opened her mouth, Fisher jumped ahead. "Ah, ah, ah. Don't go gettin' your knickers in a knot. That was a compliment."

He tossed an arm around Eliza's shoulders and herded her toward the stairs. Hannah thought for sure she saw something flicker in Eliza's eyes. But before she could study it, Sam distracted her with, "Really. What can I do to help?"

See me! she wanted to scream. *See me as I am now, you big, hairy, frustrating idiot!*

Some of what she was feeling must've come through in her expression, because he tilted his head. "Come on. Out with it. I can see you've got something on your mind."

Deciding there was something to be said for that old phrase, *If you can't beat them, join them,* she fluttered her lashes and told him, "I was taught to respect my elders, so I'll refrain from saying what I was thinking."

He chuckled. The sound was low and throaty and made butterflies take flight in her stomach. "I'm pretty sure I can read your mind. And I'm pretty sure you're dragging my name through the mud."

"In that case, I'm sorry you heard that."

He chuckled again. "I'll make you a deal. I'll stop hovering over you like an over-protective big brother if you promise not to fall victim to Fisher's charms. I'm serious. That man is trouble."

"But see?" She lifted an eyebrow. "I *like* trouble."

All the teasing fled from Sam's eyes as a muscle went to work in his jaw.

Figuring it was best to quit while she was ahead, she turned for the bank of computers and left him staring after her.

CHAPTER 14

There was little point in replying to Hannah's last declaration, so Sam was left to watch her pad over to Ozzie's computer station in her socked feet.

As she took a seat in one of the rolling chairs, scooting herself close to a keyboard, her words drifted through his head. *"I am not, and never have been, your little sister."*

Good thing, too, he thought uncomfortably. *Considering the dreams I've been having.*

He realized Ozzie had come to stand next to him when he felt a hand clap on his shoulder.

Ozzie kept his voice low enough not to reach Hannah's ears, but it resonated in Sam's like a knell of truth. "Speaking of red flags, you telling Fisher to steer clear of Hannah is like waving one in front of a bull's face. You get that, right?"

"Yeah." Sam ran a hand through his hair in frustration, hearing Pale Horse rumble to life below. The big motorcycle's engine filled the cavernous space so he didn't have to worry about the volume of his voice when he added, "But what should I have done? You know Fish. He's the MVP of the Players Club."

The thought of Hannah with Fisher didn't just turn Sam's stomach. It twisted it into knots.

Ozzie cocked his head. "Why does the thought of her with Fish bother you so much?" When Sam opened his mouth, Ozzie pressed ahead. "And don't give me any of that *she's like a kid sister to me and I'm trying to keep her from getting hurt* bullshit. You know Fish. He wouldn't harm a fly. If he and Hannah started something, he'd make sure she knew where it'd end. Also, just so you're aware, *no* big brother looks at his little sister the way you look at Hannah. At least none that don't require an emergency intervention followed by a boatload of therapy."

Horror at his own transparency rose to the surface. "Jesus," he rasped, rubbing a hand over his beard.

Ozzie was quick to reassure him. "Don't beat yourself up. You'd have to be blind not to notice she's a purple-headed smokeshow. And she *isn't* your kid sister."

Sam frowned as the sound of his motorcycle grew quieter, the Bat Cave eating up the noise of the engine the same way it devoured light. He found his thoughts pulled in two different directions.

On the one hand, Ozzie was right. He *had* noticed how beautifully womanhood had settled on Hannah's shoulders, curves in all the right places with that little edge of counter-culture rebel shining through. On the other hand, so what? So she was no longer a metal-mouthed teen? So she'd grown into a fiery, fascinating woman full of sarcasm and sex appeal?

It wasn't like that *changed* anything.

I still dated her sister. Slept *with her sister. I still knew her when she was just a kid. Which means nothing can ever happen between us because—*

He wasn't aware he wanted to ask the question that popped out of his mouth until it was hanging in the air between them. "What are the rules for dating sisters, do you think? I mean, is it ever permissible?"

Holy fucknuts? Do I want Hannah?

It was too outrageous to fathom.

Except, he *was* fathoming it. *Had* fathomed it, even if he'd refused to admit it to himself.

Ozzie frowned, giving the topic the consideration it was due. Eventually, he shrugged. "I think the rules are probably different depending on the situation and the sisters in question. How would your old girlfriend feel about you getting it on with her baby sis? And how would *you* feel knowing you'd…uh…really gotten to *know* both of them?"

"Dunno." Sam answered honestly, running a hand over his beard again. "I mean, what happened with Candy was teen stuff, right? It was a million years ago, and we're both different people now."

He was no longer the high school jock with too much swagger and too little sense, and Candy was no longer the reigning prom queen champing at the bit to find a way out of the old neighborhood.

"Guess the thing to do then would be to ask Hannah how *she* feels, huh? You might be tying yourself into knots for nothing."

Before Sam could respond, the sound of the front door springing open distracted him with its familiar security *beep* followed by a slight *hiss* and a *pop*. The door was made of reinforced steel and pressure-sealed itself when it closed.

The Black Knights cut no corners when it came to security.

Following Ozzie over to the railing, he looked down to see Samantha, Ozzie's wife, walking across the cement floor with two large pizza boxes and two gallons of ice cream balanced atop her ever-expanding belly.

"If there's anything sexier than a woman bearing my child," Ozzie said as an aside to Sam, "it's a woman bearing my child who's also bearing ice cream and pizza."

Samantha, looking as cute as a hobbit with her head full of mink-brown ringlets, grinned up at her husband. "Your text said it might be a long night. Figured you could use the fuel!" she called.

"Woman, I love you more today than I did yesterday! And I'll undoubtedly love you even more tomorrow!"

Samantha blew him a kiss and he pretended to catch it and eat it. Then he nudged Sam. "Go help her. She shouldn't be carrying things in her condition."

"What's wrong with your arms?" Sam demanded.

"I need to go help your woman." Ozzie hooked a thumb over his shoulder toward the computer station. "So it stands to reason, you should go help mine."

"She's *not* my woman," Sam insisted through a clenched jaw. "I don't know why everyone keeps saying that."

Ozzie's words were, "It's a mystery." But the look on his face said it was anything but.

Feeling decidedly out of sorts, Sam stomped toward the stairs. He was down the steps before Samantha had climbed the first tread.

One look at his face had her chin jerking back. "Whoa. Why are you wearing a face like a smacked ass?"

"Because all the self-satisfied know-it-alls around here keep sticking their noses into my business."

"I smell a story." She tapped the side of her nose after she'd handed him the pizza boxes.

When he tried to fry off her eyebrows with his molten stare, grumbling, "Not you, too," she rolled her eyes.

"Fine. I promise not to pry if you promise not to tell Ozzie I already downed a pint of Rocky Road on the ride here. He's worried I'm getting too much sugar in my diet."

"Your secret is safe with me," he assured her, happy to know at least *one* person at BKI would refrain from getting all up in his shit.

The pizza boxes were warm, and the smell of pepperoni had his mouth watering. A frozen rescue mission followed by a bath that highlighted his unmitigated horniness had combined with his perturbation at his teammates to leave him famished.

It's been a helluva night. And something told him it was just getting started.

Before he could lug the pizza and ice cream upstairs, Samantha stopped him with a hand on his forearm. "There it is again." Her eyes were huge with wonder.

"There *what is* again?" Apprehension made his tone harsh.

"The baby. She's moving."

Just a week before, Ozzie and Samantha had announced Samantha's most recent sonogram revealed she was having a girl. The celebration at BKI that night had included pink cupcakes, strawberry cookies, and Hawaiian Punch—spiked with Ozzie's favorite flavored rum, naturally.

"Here." Samantha pulled on Sam's arm and he was forced to one-hand the pizza boxes and ice cream so he could cup his palm around the little mound of her belly.

The awkwardness of touching another man's wife was quickly replaced by awe when he felt a tiny ripple of movement against the tips of his fingers.

New life. Created by two people who think the other hung the damn moon.

It was so beautiful a lump formed in his throat.

But he was a big, macho man. He'd run through a field while mortars *whumped* at launch and hit the ground around him. He could use an Israeli bandage to stop critical battlefield blood loss. And he could clean and load both his primary and secondary weapons with his eyes closed.

He was *not* supposed to get choked up by a pregnant woman's belly.

Clearing his throat, he donned what he hoped passed as a smirk. "You sure that's not gas?"

She swiped at his arm. "That's what I get for sharing the wonder of burgeoning life with a Carl Everett fan."

Samantha Sykes was a born and raised Southsider like Sam. Which meant she was a tried-and-true Chicago White Sox fan. But they'd parted ways over Carl Everett, a homerun hitter who, despite being a key to the White Sox World Series victory in 2005, was more known for his whackadoodle ways on and off the field.

"I never said I was a *fan*," he corrected. "I just said we wouldn't have gone all the way without him."

"The man denied the existence of dinosaurs. He called the Apollo moon landing a hoax."

"He also hit twenty-three homers and drove in eighty-seven runs that year."

She rolled her eyes. "Anything for a win, right?"

"Not *anything*. But, babes, it was the freakin' World Series!"

"I heard that!" Ozzie hollered from the second floor. "No one calls my woman pet names but me!"

Sam rolled his eyes and motioned for Samantha to proceed him up the stairs. When she alighted on the step next to him, he whispered conspiratorially, "He's a little proprietary, doncha think?"

She made a face. "And it's only gotten worse with little Hazel on the way." She placed a protective hand on her belly the way pregnant women had been doing since the beginning of time.

"I vetoed Hazel last night, remember?" Ozzie yelled. "It sounds like that old aunt who comes to Thanksgiving toting fruitcake and smelling like mothballs!"

"You can't veto *every* name I choose!" Samantha hollered back, stomping up the steps.

Sam watched her go with a half grin on his face and a mile-wide ache in his heart.

There'd been a time at the beginning of his marriage when he'd wanted nothing more than to start a family of his own. To fill his life with all the laughter and love he'd missed out on as a kid. But his ex had insisted, *"I won't bring a child into this world knowing they might have to grow up without a father. The day you quit the Marines is the day I get my IUD removed."*

As it'd turned out, it hadn't only been his job that'd kept her from wanting to bear his children. It'd been the next-door neighbor who'd warmed her bed every time he'd been deployed.

He'd forgotten that sense of longing in the years since his divorce, that desire to hold a child of his own in his arms. But feeling the baby move inside Samantha's belly brought it all screaming back.

There was something missing in the center of him. A great, gaping hole he'd been desperate to fill his entire life. And no matter how far he sank into his job or his hobbies, or how much time and effort he gave to his friends and teammates, nothing filled the void because it was a space reserved specifically for the woman he'd love with this whole heart and the children he hoped they'd make together.

Will I ever find the one whose soul matches my own? he wondered.

When the memory of Hannah standing in the doorway to the bathroom with her purple hair all around her shoulders bloomed to life inside his brain, he quickly shoved it aside.

Even if somehow she *could* get past her older sister having been the one to take his virginity, even if *he* could get past the fact that, for many years, he truly *had* thought of her as a kid sister, he couldn't start something with her because what if it didn't work out?

What if, despite his best efforts, their romance crashed and burned?

He hated the thought of losing her as a friend. Hated thinking about how the sweet memories he had of her as a girl might be tainted if they were to start something that ended badly. Hated the idea of hurting her when all he'd ever wanted was to see her happy and whole and thriving.

The only way to make sure that happens is to never begin in the first place, he thought with a decisive nod as he made his way up to the second floor. *The best thing I can do for Hannah is keep my hands and my heart to myself.*

The instant he stepped onto the landing, however, he saw Samantha bending over Ozzie's shoulder so she could plant a kiss on his mouth and doubt crept into Sam's brain…

But what if?

What if he tried with Hannah and things worked out? What if she *was* the missing puzzle piece that could make the picture complete?

Is the reward worth the risk? Is it really better to have loved and lost than never to have loved at all?

"I love you, too, you furry little rascal." Samantha's words dragged him from his thoughts, and he looked down to see Peanut winding himself in a figure eight around Samantha's legs.

The silly cat loved women, but pregnant women? Peanut couldn't get enough of them.

As if on cue, after Samantha grabbed a seat at the conference table, propping her feet on the chair next to her, Peanut hopped into her lap.

The cat made gentle biscuits on her belly while Sam hooked a left to take the ice cream to the mini fridge they kept in an office-turned-breakroom. While he was there, he grabbed a sleeve of paper plates. By the time he returned to the conference table, Fisher was back from his errands and Eliza had arrived with a giant thermos of hot chocolate and enough mugs to go around.

"Look at them go." Eliza gestured with her chin toward Ozzie and Hannah.

The two computer geniuses sat at their machines, leaning forward to get their faces closer to their monitors and rattling their keyboards as their fingers flew through the motions.

"It's like seein' master artists paint. Or watchin' a prima ballerina dance," Fisher observed.

"You see beauty and poetry in everything, don't you, Fish?" Samantha said.

"Were all the stars to disappear or die, I should learn to look at an empty sky and feel its total darkness sublime, though this might take a little time," Fisher quoted. "W.H. Auden. Who had a far better way of sayin' that, for a guy like me, finding beauty and poetry in all things comes with the territory."

"And what territory is that?" Eliza asked.

"When ya grow up hard and in a place where most things are out to bite ya or sting ya, you learn to look for rhyme and grace in the world."

"There you go again." Eliza shook her head. "Making it impossible for me not to like you."

"Still not clear on why you're so set on tryin'." Fisher frowned, but Sam stopped listening and instead pulled a couple slices off the pie closest to him.

After sliding them onto a paper plate, he walked to where Hannah sat typing away. Not wanting to distract her, he was quiet as a church mouse while placing the pizza beside her elbow.

All the same, before he could return to the conference table, she glanced up and caught his wrist in her hand. Her fingers were soft and cool as she gave his joint a squeeze. "Thanks."

The loveliness of her heart-shaped face, that delicate prettiness that was so different from her sister's striking beauty—and yet no less enchanting—struck him mute.

All he could do was nod before making his way back to the others, rubbing the spot on his wrist where her fingers had been as if to hold on to the memory of her touch.

Yes. I want her.

The certainty of it hit him in the solar plexus like a frag grenade.

He *wanted* Hannah Blue not because he was suffering a dry spell. But because she was *her*. A smart, sassy, sexy as hell woman whom he'd liked and appreciated when she'd been a tender-aged thirteen. And whom, at the decidedly *grown-up* age of nearly thirty, he admired, respected, and absolutely *lusted* after.

All he could think was…*Fuck.*

CHAPTER 15

Distracted with patting grease off the top of her pizza slice with a paper towel, Eliza was unprepared for the feel of Fisher's leg brushing against her own.

Lightning.

That's what struck her anytime they touched.

Not little sparks of electricity. Not a zap to the system that made her sit up straight. But a full-on firebolt that fried her brain and turned her insides to molten lava.

A gasp shot out of her before she could stop it. Embarrassed by her involuntary outburst, her eyes jumped up to find him staring at her.

"What's wrong?" A deep line appeared between his eyebrows. "Is something the matter with your leg? I barely touched ya."

Her pulse beat in her neck like a butterfly's wings. With him laser-focused on her, she worried he'd notice.

Although, he probably won't, she thought.

Just because *she* registered every minor detail about *him*, the tiniest change in his expression or the slightest quickening of his breath, that didn't mean he did the same with her. A person only laser-focused on the object of their obsession, right?

Rubbing a hand over her throat, she cleared her voice. "No. I was in my own world and you startled me. That's all."

"Are ya jumpier than usual tonight, or is it just me?"

It's because you keep touching me! she could've wailed.

Why he'd suddenly taken to throwing an arm around her shoulders whenever he pleased she'd never know.

Or, rather, she *did* know.

Their little heart-to-heart in the kitchen had apparently made him think they'd become bosom buddies.

And yet…

He's as much of a scoundrel as ever, she reminded herself. *He can be amazingly empathetic and kind-hearted. But in the same breath, if it weren't for Sam throwing up roadblocks, he'd probably have Hannah upstairs and undressed.*

She'd watched him eye-bone dozens of women over the years. Had listened to him flirt and tease. Had stood by while he worked his magic and ended the night with another woman on his arm. And yes, she always felt a little frisson of jealousy. How could she not?

His blatant attempts to seduce Hannah, however, had turned that frisson of jealousy into a green-eyed monster the size of Godzilla.

Maybe because, for the first time, he was attempting to woo someone on her home turf. Maybe because, after their conversation in the kitchen, she felt closer to him than ever before. Or maybe because it was becoming increasingly impossible to distance herself from the power of her feelings for him.

"Eliza?" He dragged her from her disquieting thoughts.

"Hmm?" She blinked, wondering if he'd ever use her nickname again.

She'd always been indifferent to being called *Liza* until she'd heard the two syllables rolling around in his mouth. Now, that's all she wanted him to call her.

"What's got ya so wound up tonight?"

"Yeah. What the hell is going on around here?" Samantha asked, slipping a pepperoni to Peanut. The cat gulped it down like he hadn't eaten for days. "My beloved husband's text didn't get into specifics."

Eliza was glad for the conversational detour. It meant she didn't have to answer Fisher's question.

After she'd given Samantha the Cliffs Notes version of Hannah's predicament, Samantha raised an eyebrow and fed Peanut another slice of pepperoni. "I can see why you're jumpy. This *is* a fine mess."

"When that cat has explosive diarrhea, I'm telling Becky she has you to thank," Sam warned.

"Be my guest." Samantha shrugged. "She doesn't frighten me like she does all of you."

"*She's* not the one we're afraid of," Sam insisted with a grimace. "It's the man she's married to."

"Boss?" Samantha rolled her eyes. "Please. He's the biggest teddy bear there is."

"Right." Fisher shook his head. "A big ol' teddy bear with a buzz cut and a bad attitude."

"He doesn't have a bad attitude," Samantha argued. "He just has a low tolerance for bullshit."

Plus, he has a habit of spinning his KA-BAR on his desk. And it makes everyone with a working brain cell decidedly uncomfortable, Eliza thought.

It was no secret Frank "Boss" Knight could hit a target twenty yards away with little more than a flick of his wrist. Add that to his old-school military man gruffness and the combination was...intimidating. To say the least.

"Do you see—"

"Yeah. Just let me—"

Ozzie's and Hannah's shorthand distracted the group from their conversation and all heads turned toward the pair at the computer station. It was obvious by the change in Ozzie's posture and the way Hannah scooted closer to her keyboard they'd found something in that dark and mysterious dimension known as the World Wide Web.

"There!" Ozzie crowed, pushing away from the desk and pointing at his screen. "You were right. Your report was caught and flushed before it ever made it over the first firewall."

"Can you tell *who* intercepted it?" Hannah was still rattling away at her station. "Because I can't—"

She stopped and stared hard at her monitor. Eliza waited with the others, breath bated, to see how the drama would play out.

"The trail goes cold." Hannah's tone dripped disappointment. "Whoever back-hacked me and hijacked my report was using TAILs."

"What's TAILs?" Fisher asked around a mouthful of pizza.

"It's a Linux operating system that fits on a USB flash drive," Hannah explained. "A person can plug it into any computer anywhere, and because they're using an operating system on a flash drive, none of their programs or internet history will show up." She pointed to her screen. "Ozzie and I can see *what* was done. But there's no way to know who did it. Although, that's really neither here nor there. Because now we know my intel never made it to my superiors. Which means the Texas plot still needs to be foiled."

"Can you resend your report?" Eliza did her best to ignore the way Fisher licked grease from his fingertips. The move should've been gross. But it was Fisher, so it was sexy.

"Unfortunately, no." Hannah shook her head. "All my evidence was in that report and the report is gone. Whoever back-hacked me wiped my work hard drive, and because of the sensitive nature of the evidence I collect, it's not like I can ever store anything in the Cloud. And if I try to contact my superiors now without the evidence I gathered, and given my FBI's Most Wanted status, would they even believe me? Or would they turn me over to the feds quicker than any of us could spit?"

Eliza frowned. "Which means we need to prove the interception of your report was somehow tied to you being accused of helping Red Square. Prove the evidence against you was planted."

"Exactly." When Hannah nodded, it made her amazing purple hair dance across her shoulders. Eliza *wished* she could pull off something like that. But she couldn't shake the feeling that colored hair or cool tattoos or badass piercings would make her look like she was *trying* to be edgy as opposed to actually *being* edgy. "Let's hope proving the evidence was planted will be as easy as figuring out my report got yeeted."

Hannah swung around to her keyboard. Before she could delve back into the online world, however, the real world interrupted by way of a loud buzz that echoed around the lofty space.

"That would be Rafe calling," Ozzie pressed a few keys until Rafer Connelly's freckled face showed on his monitor.

"I thought Toran was working tonight," Sam wondered aloud to no one in particular.

"His wife came down with the flu and needed him home to look after the kids," Fisher explained. "Rafer came in to relieve him an hour ago."

Eliza loved the Connelly brothers. The four big, burly native Chicagoans never forgot to send her flowers on her birthday. And they devoured the sweets she baked as if she'd conjured up mana from heaven.

"What's up, Rafe?" Ozzie asked the guard.

Rafer's Windy City accent was thick, his words gruff and no-nonsense. "Feds are here."

"Fuck," Ozzie cursed. "That was quicker than I'd hoped."

"You've got to clean up your mouth before the baby arrives or else some of Annabelle's first words will be curses," Samantha scolded.

"Says the woman who knows fifty different ways to call a man an asshole." Ozzie chuckled. "And I told you Annabelle sounds like she should be milking cows and wearing gingham. No. Just no."

"I refuse to name this child Nyota!" Samantha shot back.

"Why not? Nyota Uhura was a trailblazing character! Our daughter would be lucky to share her name."

"I let you keep that *Star Trek* poster in the living room. But I put my foot down at naming our firstborn after anyone on that stupid TV show."

Ozzie grabbed his heart as if to keep it from falling out of his chest. "Take it back. Take it back right now." When Samantha only shook her head and blew him a kiss, he reluctantly pretended to catch it and eat it. Then, he fell serious and turned back to the monitor. "Stall as long as you can, Rafe. Then send them on up."

When he switched off his computer screen, Hannah was fast to follow suit.

"Quick," Eliza motioned for Hannah to stand. "You need to hide in the Bat Cave."

"By myself?" Hannah's face paled.

Eliza couldn't blame her. The tunnel dug under the Chicago River was seriously creepy. She'd only been inside a couple times herself, and she could honestly admit that was two times too many.

"I'll go with you." Sam was already up and reaching a hand toward Hannah.

"What did you do with your clothes?" Eliza's mind had leapt ahead to the possibility the feds might have arrived with a warrant.

"Hung them over the shower rod upstairs," Hannah answered.

"Right." Eliza was already headed for the stairs. "Hannah and Sam, hide. Fisher, go meet the feds. Ozzie and Samantha, act like we're just enjoying some late-night pizza. I'll go hide Hannah's clothes."

She didn't wait around to see if everyone followed her instructions. She knew they would.

Halfway up the stairs, however, she heard Fisher say as an aside to someone, "She's hot when she's bossy, isn't she?"

"Spare us the details of your kinks, Fish." There was laughter in Samantha's voice.

Any other woman would've been charmed by Fisher's compliment. But Eliza knew he tossed honeyed words out like float riders tossed beads in a Mardi Gras parade. So all she felt was tired.

And hollow.

I thought love was supposed to fill a person up, she thought dejectedly as she jogged up the stairs to the third floor. *Turns out loving someone who'll never love you back does the opposite. It carves out your insides until you're left with nothing but a shell.*

CHAPTER 16

Fisher donned his biggest, brightest, down-home, aw-shucks grin when he opened the door to the three federal agents.

Even without Rafer's warning, he'd have pegged them for G-Men based on their loafers alone. And why couldn't they spice things up with a colorful tie or a swaggy pocket square? Why did they always look like pallbearers at a funeral?

And yes, as a man whose closet was full of black clothes, he appreciated the irony of his own thoughts. But the difference between him and the feds was that he dressed in black as a reminder he'd once been a coward and now he'd spend the rest of his life in mourning. *They* dressed in black because they were trying to…what? Imitate Tommy Lee Jones?

Someone should tell them no one pulls off a black suit like Agent K.

The icy breath of February whispered in through the open door, and he was struck by the utter silence that cloaked the night outside.

In Louisiana, even in the dead of winter there was still life. Birds chirped. Gators growled. The sound of the mighty Mississippi rumbled.

Not so in the upper Midwest where winter wasn't simply a reprieve from the heat of summer but was instead a frigid fucking *force* to be reckoned with. Anything with blood and breath had long since found a burrow to hide in. The Chicago River, running along the back of the property, had been frozen over for weeks. And it'd been *months* since he'd seen anything moving around outside what wasn't a random brown leaf or a piece of refuse pushed by the relentless winds that swooped down from Canada.

At times like this, he missed home. Missed the sway of Spanish moss in the moonlight. Missed the soft sounds of the people when they spoke. Missed the taste of sweet tea and the smell of Cajun cooking.

But only at times like this.

Because, for the most part, home had only brought him heartache.

Heartache and horror and death.

"Come in." He ushered the agents inside. "It's too cold to be standing out there."

"Thank you," the tall, dark-haired fed said, flashing his badge while Fisher firmly shut the door. "I'm Agent Mulder with the Federal Bureau of Investigations."

"Mulder, huh?" Fisher turned to the blond man standing next to Mulder. "Please tell me that makes you Agent Scully."

Either the agents had heard the joke one-too-many times, or they'd left their senses of humor back at FBI headquarters. The second agent, whose high-and-tight haircut made Fisher wonder if he and Boss patronized the same barber, didn't so much as blink.

"I'm Agent Waller." Blondie flashed his own credentials.

"And this is Agent Moretti." Mulder indicated the last man, a short, dark-eyed gentleman who seemed to shrink into the background compared to the other two.

"Pleased to make your acquaintances." Fisher bobbed his chin. "You boys are out kind of late, ain't ya? What brings ya to our neck of the woods?"

Playing the part of the affable Southern gentleman came as easily to him as falling into bed at the end of a long, hard day. Which was a boon when he wanted to trick uptight Midwestern types into assuming that he had a slow way of talking that translated into a slow way of thinking.

"Justice never sleeps." Waller's tone was arrogant. Something about the pinched look in the dude's eyes told Fisher the man could probably benefit from having the stick removed from his ass.

"I reckon that's true." He shoved his hands in the front pockets of his jeans, unconsciously curling his fingers around his harmonica. "So what can we do ya for, gentlemen?"

"We're looking for this motorcycle." Mulder pulled a glossy 8X10 from inside his long, wool coat.

Fisher leaned forward to study the photo like it was the first time he'd seen the image, even though he'd gotten a good gander at it when Ozzie had blown it up on his computer screen.

"Mmm." He frowned at the blurry image. "Could be one of ours. It's definitely a Harley with some custom modifications. May I?" He gestured toward the photo, and when Mulder nodded, he took the image and squinted down at it. "No way y'all could clear it up?"

"It's too grainy." Mulder took the picture back. "The pixels are too big and too few. When we sent it through our software, it just got more distorted."

"Welp." Fisher grimaced. "I'm sure sorry to say it, but unless ya have a clearer image, there's no way I can tell for sure if it's one of ours."

"When we compared it to traffic cam footage, we thought it looked very similar to this bike that was caught on camera last fall." Mulder removed another 8x10 from his coat and handed it to Fisher.

The new image showed Sam sitting at a red light, leather jacket looking slick and shiny, black helmet obscuring his face from the camera's all-seeing eye. Pale Horse's gas tank gleamed like a giant pearl beneath him.

"The license plate on this machine," Mulder tapped the picture in Fisher's hand, "shows it's registered to Black Knights Inc. LLC. That's you guys, right?"

"Sure is." Fisher nodded convivially. "And that's one of our mechanics sitting on the back of it. But see here." Fisher pointed to the handlebars in the photo. "This bike has low drags. That first picture ya showed me has keystone-style handlebars."

He was glad Sam had recently switched out the handlebars on his ride, having decided the keystone style was too cumbersome.

"And see that." He pointed again at the photo in his hand. "This bike has a two-in-one exhaust, and that other image looked like it was a true dual exhaust. Although"—he shrugged—"it's too blurry for me to know for sure."

"So where is *that* motorcycle?" Waller hitched his chin toward the image Fisher held before turning to catalog the badass bikes lined up on the shop floor like good little soldiers.

Fisher had been careful to move his motorcycle, which usually sat at the end of the row of bikes, into the space reserved for Pale Horse. Nothing more suspicious than an obvious hole in the ranks.

"Your guess is as good as mine, my man." He redonned his down-home, aw-shucks grin. "We build and sell a lot of motorcycles here. Chances are good this one"—he shook the photo for emphasis—"went out the door months ago."

Mulder's eyes alighted on something over Fisher's shoulder when he asked, "And who here could tell us who bought this particular bike?"

Fisher turned to see Eliza, looking as fresh and fine as a daisy, gliding down the stairs. Her black slacks and button-down shirt made it seem as if she should be running a corporate office downtown, not whiling away the hours with a bunch of gun-toting grease monkeys on Goose Island.

"That would be Becky," she said to Mulder as she made her way to Fisher's side. "Our lead designer. She's the one who keeps the records of who orders what and who buys what."

"Is she here?" Waller sounded impatient and Fisher decided his initial instinct about the guy was right. Waller was a dick.

"Long gone, I'm afraid." Eliza laced her fingers together in front of her. Her placid expression managed to look both wide open and completely closed off which, for some reason, reminded Fisher of British royalty. He reckoned, being the chief of staff's daughter, she was as close to *American* royalty as it came. "She's usually out the door at five sharp," she added. "She's got two small children, you see."

When Waller and Mulder exchanged frustrated glances, she quickly added, "But she'll be in bright and early tomorrow morning. You gentlemen are welcome to come back then and talk to her. I'm sure she'd be a lot more help than we are. Fisher here"—she tucked an arm through Fisher's, and he was ridiculously aware of his elbow touching her side-boob—"is good with a wrench, but he doesn't touch the sales side of things. And I run the offices, but I'm hands-off when it comes to customers."

"How about those two?" Waller hitched his chin toward the second floor, where Samantha and Ozzie casually munched on pizza and watched the exchange below.

"That's Ozzie and Samantha Sykes," Eliza explained. "Ozzie's a designer as well. His wife isn't employed here, however. She's an investigative reporter for the *Chicago Tribune.*"

Raising her voice, Samantha called down, "Anything you'd like to put on the record, agents? I could have a story running in tomorrow's online edition if you have something juicy for me!"

Mulder blanched and Fisher only refrained from smiling by biting the inside of his cheek.

"No, thank you!" Mulder called up. "This visit is strictly off the record!"

Samantha only shrugged, not agreeing or disagreeing. Fisher could see how much that irritated Mulder. A muscle twitched in the man's right cheek.

"You guys sure have a lot of security and computing power for a simple motorcycle-building outfit." The agent tried to make the statement sound offhand, but there was no missing the hard speculation in his eyes.

"I can assure you, Agent Mulder, there is nothing *simple* about this operation. We have millions of dollars in equipment and bikes on site." Eliza's chin-lift could only be described as *haughty*. "Becky's production bikes sell for anywhere from fifty to ninety grand. But her custom jobs? Motorcycles like you see here?" She swung her arm to encompass the line of choppers whose sparkling chrome and fantastical paint jobs gleamed in the florescent lighting. "If you want one of these, it'll set you back a cool quarter mil."

"The hell you say." Waller's eyes flew wide with disbelief.

"It's true." Eliza nodded. "And Becky and Ozzie use some pretty high-powered software and high-tech equipment to design these rolling works of art. Hence the need for the guardhouse, the gate, and the razor-wire. Now…" Her smile was saccharin, but it didn't reach her eyes. "Is there anything more we can do for you tonight gentlemen? It's getting late."

It was the nicest way Fisher had ever heard someone say, *Get the fuck out*. Again, he had to bite the inside of his cheek to keep from grinning.

"One last thing." Mulder turned his attention on Fisher. "We pulled all your employment records before arriving. It's odd that almost everyone working here has a military background, don't you think?"

"Not really." Fisher shrugged. "The guy who owns the place makes it a point to employ former fightin' men."

"Why's that?" Mulder cocked his head.

"I reckon it's because he was a Navy SEAL for over a decade. So he knows guys who've seen the darker side of life sometimes have a tough time reintegratin' into society. He knows life doesn't give many people second chances, but that, with a little help, it can give some folks a chance at a new start.”

"So he's cultivated a home for wayward soldiers here?"

"And wayward airmen and seamen and jarheads. Basically any fool who had the bad sense to sign up to serve Uncle is welcomed with open arms."

"Why *are* you looking for the motorcycle in that picture?" Eliza asked. "Has something happened? Something to do with a former military man or—"

"Somebody with a shit-ton of training made those shots. And it wasn't the tranny or his uptight lawyer," Waller muttered and then had the grace to tuck his chin when Mulder shot him a scathing glance.

So, the feds have already been to see Cesar, eh? And found the man lawyered up? How wonderful. Fisher hid another a secret smile. *I knew I liked Cesar.*

"What shots?" Eliza blinked at the agents.

"Yes!" Samantha called from the second story. "What shots?"

"Never mind," Mulder grumbled, taking the photo from Fisher and tucking it back into his coat. "We'll be back to talk to this Becky person in the morning."

"I'll let her know to expect you." Eliza slid her arm from Fisher's so she could open the front door. The instant they were no longer touching, he missed the feel of her softness next to him. "In the meantime, I hope you gentlemen find what you're looking for," she added with a cool smile.

The feds muttered their thanks, even Agent Moretti, whom Fisher had begun to suspect might be mute. Wrapping an arm around Eliza's shoulders when she shivered in the cold air, he watched with her until the agents were halfway across the lot. Then he closed the door and listened to it seal tight.

"Your questions had them itchin' to get out of here," he told her proudly. "Excellent work."

"Really? Was it my questions or was it the presence of an investigative reporter?" She hooked a thumb over her shoulder toward the second-floor landing.

"Never seen anyone as smart or as capable as you, and never seen anyone as *in*capable of takin' a compliment." He shook his head. "I swear, woman, it's like tryin' to kick water uphill."

"Maybe I only have trouble taking compliments from *you* because you toss them out like confetti."

"Do I?" He was taken aback.

Her lovely mouth flattened. "You praise and flatter every woman you meet."

"And that bothers ya?" he asked cautiously. "Ya always act like ya don't care."

"It's not an act," she said with a sniff. "I *don't* care. But I also don't take your compliments to heart because I know you don't really mean them. It's just one of the many tools you use to charm women out of their pants."

He reckoned she didn't realize how hard her words hit him, and he wanted to keep it that way. Swallowing down the hurt, he pasted on his most rakish grin. "And here ya stand with pants that are uncharmable." He tossed an arm around her shoulders to lead her toward the shop area. "I'm trying to decide if I like that."

"You are the most annoying man I've ever met. I definitely don't like *that*," she countered.

"Aw, come on." He gave her a friendly squeeze, breathing deeply of her crisp, fresh-smelling perfume that always reminded him of spring rain on a bergamia tree. "Ya love me. Admit it."

"Pfft." Even though he wasn't looking at her, he knew she was rolling her eyes. "I'm a good cook. But I refuse to feed your ego."

He chuckled at her wit and felt a little flurry of movement in the center of his chest. Too bad he'd learned from his past that his feelings in the shiny, sparkly women department had to be handcuffed and hogtied.

"Where are you taking me?" she demanded.

"Over to the Bat Cave. Sam and Hannah got to be itchin' to get out of there."

She stopped dead in her tracks, forcing his boots to take root on the cement floor next to her. When his arm fell away from her shoulders, he searched for a reason to grab her hand but couldn't find one.

He'd spent three years *not* touching her. Her cool, haughty demeanor didn't exactly scream *come 'ere and gimme a bear hug, big boy*. But now that he'd started touching her, he didn't want to stop.

"Let's give them a bit more time." She glanced toward the inconspicuous expanse of the brick wall.

"Why?" His brow furrowed. "No one wants to spend any more time in that dark, dank place than they have to."

"They need to work some things out between them. A few moments alone are just the ticket."

"And what things are those?"

"The way they feel about each other for starters."

"Sam says she's like a kid sister."

Her frown was severe. "I know you'd probably like to believe him because you have designs on her. But surely your own aims haven't blinded you to the way he looks at her."

No. He wasn't blind. In fact, he'd seen the truth of things months ago when he'd come home to hear the tale of how one pipsqueak of a D.O.D hacker had helped Sam and Hunter clear Grace's name. The way Sam's eyes had lit up any time he'd mentioned Hannah had told Fisher all he'd needed to know.

"And what if I told ya my *designs* on Hannah are just for show?" He crossed his arms and regarded her through narrowed eyes.

She looked taken aback. "Are they?"

"Ya think you're the only one who sees how much Sam needs a shove to get over himself?"

For a while after that, she was silent. Then she tsked. "Have you ever heard that old saying that whoever is stirring the shit should have to lick the spoon?"

He laughed. "I like to think of it less as stirrin' the shit and more as givin' everyone involved a little nudge in the right direction."

"Well, you sure had me fooled."

"Only 'cause you're lookin' for reasons to think poorly of me."

She'd been smoothing an invisible wrinkle out of her slacks, but that made her glance up.

"What?" He lifted a curious eyebrow. "Am I wrong?"

Her mouth twisted. "You have to admit, you aren't exactly doing your damnedest to be named Saint of the Year."

"Saints are borin'. Not to mention pompous and pious and judgmental. Sinners take ya as ya are and allow ya room to mess up and grow. Give me the sinners any day."

"Is that what you're doing when you take home a different woman every night? Growing?"

"First of all, ya give me too much credit. It's not *every* night. I don't have it in me to do that much wooin'. Second of all, it's not *me* who limits things to one night. It's *them*."

When she made a face, he lifted a finger. "And don't ya go gettin' it in your head that I don't know what I'm doin' so they don't come back for seconds." Her smirk told him he'd read her mind. "It's just that they see me for what I am."

"And what's that?"

"Fun for now but not forever," he said simply.

"And yet, upstairs you claimed you want *more* than that."

"Wantin' it and findin' someone who's willin' to give it to me are too different things."

Women were smart. Once they heard about his background, they usually ran screaming for the hills.

"Maybe you're just looking in the wrong places. Ever think of that? Maybe skip the bars and the clubs and Tinder and try…" She shrugged. "Oh, I don't know. The library or something. You like poetry. Hang out in the poetry section. Maybe you'll find Miss Right."

He laughed. "Ya missed your callin', Eliza. You should be writin' romance novels. It's only in those books that folks meet like that."

"Not true." She shook her head. "I have a date next Saturday with a man I met while on a walk through Lincoln Park. We bumped into each other on the bridge over the duck pond. I spilled my coffee on my coat. He whisked out his pocket square to help me clean up. It was a *very* Hallmark moment."

He ignored the little stab of jealousy that sliced into him. Or at least he *tried* to.

In the three years she'd worked at BKI, he'd only known her to go on a handful of dates. And he'd *never* seen her looking so…wistful.

"Who is this lucky devil?" His tone came out more demanding than he'd intended. "Have you run a background check on him?"

"Don't need to." She shook her head. "He's Senator McClean's son. He's been vetted up one side and down the other."

"A politician's kid." He suddenly felt altogether unsettled. "So y'all got a lot in common."

"That's what the date is for. To see if we do. But that's my point." She lifted a hand and let it fall. "You should try the poetry section at the library. You might just have your own meet-cute."

"Meet what?" He frowned, trying desperately to remember if he'd ever seen photos of Senator McClean or his son.

"Meet-cute," she explained. "It's that moment in the books where the two lovers meet and sparks fly."

So sparks flew with McClean Junior, eh?

A muscle twitched under his right eye and his fingers automatically sought the cool comfort of his harmonica.

When it was clear he had nothing savvy or sarcastic to say about meet-cutes, she turned toward the rolling Craftsman toolbox concealing the button to the Bat Cave. "You think that's enough time alone for them?"

"Depends." He shrugged. "Is our aim to give them enough time to admit they're hot for each other? Or is our aim to give them enough time to *act* on things?"

"I think they're more than hot for each other." Her expression turned contemplative. "I think they might actually be in love."

"Heaven help them then. Every love story becomes a tragedy if ya wait long enough."

"God, that's a depressing thought."

"Oh, I don't know. There's some comfort in it too, I reckon."

"How do you figure that?"

"If ya go into love knowin' that, in the end, there's bound to be heartbreak, ya appreciate all the good times. Ya learn to revel in the happiness."

"Yeah. But then those good times and that happiness are tainted by the certainty of future pain, aren't they?"

"I don't think so. Ya know ya got an expiration date, right? We all do. Does that taint the life you're livin' now? Or does it make ya want to wring every last bit of joy out of every day?"

She frowned as she considered his point. "Actually, I think most people just stumble along without giving it much thought."

"And that's a cryin' shame. I'd rather look my inevitable end square in the eye and acknowledge its presence so I can truly enjoy the journey to get there."

She was quiet for a while after that. Eventually she shook her head. "I like you better when you're slinging bullshit and man-whoring your way through a quarter of the population of Chicago."

"Just a quarter?" He chuckled. "Reckon I better up my game." When she rolled her eyes, he hitched his chin toward the rolling toolbox. "Go let our wayward compatriots out of the hole. I need to head upstairs to check on something."

"Check on what?" she called to his back because he'd already turned toward the stairs.

"None of your business, nosy," he admonished, flashing a grin over his shoulder.

The instant he turned back, however, his smile faded.

He needed to google Senator McClean.

Or rather, Senator McClean's son.

CHAPTER 17

Hannah's stomach was a mass of cramps. And it was only partly due to the federal agents who'd come knocking at BKI's door.

She vaguely remembered the ride through the underground tunnel that was some sort of secret entrance to the old factory building on Goose Island. And why a private defense firm would *need* such a clandestine escape route was a question for another time. Because at the moment, her mind was fully occupied with beating back the urge to scream bloody murder.

The tunnel had been dark and spooky before. But at least it'd been alive with the glow of the headlight from Sam's motorcycle and filled with the rumbling sound of the big engine. Now the darkness was complete. Profound. It pressed in on her from all sides. And to add to the eeriness of it all, she could hear the distant, echoing sound of water slowly sliding off the concrete walls and falling to the floor.

Drip. Drip. Drip.

It was the musical score of every horror film she'd ever seen, the soundtrack to all her nightmares. And when mixed with the fishy, wet scent of the tunnel—a smell so fecund and ripe she could taste it in the back of her throat—it took every ounce of her self-possession not to scrabble around in the dark in search of the button that would re-open the wall.

And to hell with the federal agents waiting on the other side who'll haul me back into custody!

"Breathe." Sam's deep voice reached out to her in the blackness. "They can't hear us in here. You don't need to hold your breath."

Am I holding my breath?

She hadn't realized.

A wheezy exhale escaped her. And with her lungs empty, she could feel how painfully her heart beat against her ribs.

"Ever notice how terror tastes like gunmetal?" she whispered, hunching her shoulders up around her ears when her voice echoed downward and then was swallowed up by the curve in the tunnel as if there was something down there in the black depths that ate sound.

Her inhale was as shaky and wheezy as her exhale had been, forced as it was past the lump in her throat.

A light suddenly blazed to life, shining brightly in her face. Instinct had her blinking and lifting a hand to shade her eyes against the obnoxious glare. Which is when she realized Sam had turned on his phone's flashlight feature.

"I'm fine," she assured him. "I'm just scared. And cold. And—" The lump in her throat blocked the last of her words, leaving her to shake her head ineffectually.

Shoving the device into the front pocket of his jeans, he left the top peeking out from the denim so the little light could continue to cut a small circle through the stygian blackness around them.

She almost preferred the dark. She couldn't see the green and gray shadows dancing along the concrete walls then. Shadows that seemed to come from nowhere and take on a life of their own.

She shivered. Whether from the damp chill in the tunnel or the terror that clawed at the back of her neck with icy nails she couldn't say.

"Come 'ere." He grabbed her wrist and gave her a tug.

She fell willingly against his chest and buried her nose in the hollow at the base of his throat. Wanting to crawl inside his skin. Wanting to hide away from the trouble that stalked her and the nameless, faceless horror that seemed to inhabit the very air of the tunnel like a sentient miasma.

"You're shaking like a leaf." He ran his wide palms up and down her back and tucked his chin until his words were breathed into the crown of her head.

"It's been a long day." Her voice was muffled by the fabric of his shirt. She happily took in the smell of him, dryer sheets and aftershave and… *man*.

She prided herself on being tough. On being resilient and tenacious and independent. But in that moment, she couldn't deny she…*needed* him. Needed his warmth. Needed his strength. Needed his dogged determination to see this nightmare through until the end because she was starting to feel overwhelmed and a little hopeless about the sheer scope of shit raining down on her head.

It would have been so easy to go up on tiptoe and distract herself from her predicament by pressing her mouth to the scar that marred the perfection of his neck. She wanted to touch her lips to that wounded skin and whisper away the hurt.

Then he *would be the one slamming a hand on that button, to hell with the feds,* she thought dejectedly. *Either that, or he'd run screaming to the other end of the tunnel.*

"Why do you know what gunmetal tastes like, Hannah?" His words were low, barely reaching her ears. Even still, there was no mistaking the concern in them.

She instantly knew her mistake.

"Not for the reason you're thinking," she was quick to reassure him. "Cesar owns a pistol. Given the current political environment and the witch hunts that've been launched against drag queens, he'd be a fool not to. He's diligent about keeping his gun in top-notch condition. Anytime he cleans it, the smell lingers in the apartment and coats my tongue."

"Ah." That one word held a wealth of relief.

Tilting her head back, she looked into his shadowed face. His eyes, always so bright and piercing, were hooded by eyelashes so thick and inky her sister had spoken of them enviously and lamented how they were wasted on a man.

Hannah disagreed.

Nothing was wasted on Sam. From his thick head of mink-dark hair to his olive skin to his leanly muscled physique, he epitomized everything a man should be.

Not perfect. The scars on his body and the bump in the middle of his nose from the time he took a fastball to the face in game three of the state playoffs kept him from being perfect. But his imperfections made him even *more* attractive.

"Any good therapist would probably tell you that, like everyone, I have a host of issues I need to work through." She hoped he could see her teasing smile in the half-light. "But I can assure you, that's not one of them. I like my life too much to want to see it end. Plus, I have to stick around long enough to watch Candy fight the battle with aging. If I know my sister, she's going to go to war with it armed with the same determination she takes to the end-of-season sales at Saks."

He chuckled. "I think she's already been involved in a skirmish or two. I noticed her forehead didn't move when I ran into her in that steakhouse a few months ago."

Hannah widened her eyes. "Good god, no. Her forehead hasn't moved since she married Jared and could afford Botox."

He rubbed a thumb over the little lines on *her* forehead that'd formed after years of frowning at a computer screen. "That's too bad. Expressions give a person their character."

"I agree." She traced the laugh lines that crinkled the corners of his impossibly blue eyes. "But also, I think it's easier to age gracefully when you were never perfect to begin with."

His eyebrows pinched. "Who told you you're not perfect?"

"Please." She rolled her eyes. "I grew up with Candice Blue as a sister."

"Candy has always been…beautiful," he admitted slowly and she hated the little jab of jealousy that poked at her heart. "But her beauty is spotless and—" He winced. "I hate to say it, *boring*. You stop seeing it after a while. But you?" He cocked his head and let his gaze roam over her features. "You have a face that—"

"Has eyes that are too big and a mouth that is too small and a forehead that is too wide," she finished for him. Being the younger—and *lesser*—Blue sister meant she'd gotten really good at reciting her flaws.

"No." He shook his head, causing a dark lock to curl over his forehead, Super Man-style. "I was gonna say you have the kind of face a person could look at every day and every day still find something new to admire. Yours is the kind of beauty that'll change with time but will never fade. And I'm happy to hear you like your life," he finished with a soft smile that showed the barest hint of his straight, white teeth. "The world is a better place with you in it."

His words warmed her as much as his big body. But since she was terrible at receiving compliments—Cesar accused her of being allergic to them—she fell back on sarcasm.

"Are you feeling okay?" She hoped he couldn't hear how husky her voice was as she pressed the back of her hand to his forehead—and sneakily transferred the Jolly Rancher she'd taken from the bag under his vanity into the front pocket of his jeans. She felt just as thrilled and giddy as she'd been when she'd done the same thing at thirteen. "You're being *nice* to me."

He frowned. "I'm *always* nice to you."

"Admit it. When you're around me, you scowl. And growl."

"I do not."

When his frown deepened and his words came out all growly, she bit the inside of her cheek.

"Fine." He tossed one hand in the air. "Maybe I do, but it's only 'cause you seem hell bent on finding trouble. And I can't help feeling it's my duty to at least *try* to steer you clear of it."

"Are we back to talking about Fisher?" She grimaced.

"If that bastard breaks your heart, I promise I'll fucking nail gun his. Which is going to make working together afterward real awkward."

"Good thing I have zero interest in him then."

The line between his eyebrows deepened. "But you said—"

"I *know* what I said," she cut him off and shoved out of his arms. "But that was just to piss you off."

He stood to his full height, his eyes cutting through the low light like two blue lasers. "Why would you wanna go and piss me off? I *saved* your ass tonight and nearly got frostbite for the effort."

All the pique drained out of her, making her shoulders droop. The thought of having dragged him and his coworkers into her mess, the thought of having dragged *Cesar* into it as well, had the lump solidifying in her throat once again.

"You're right. I shouldn't be antagonizing you. But sometimes you make me want to throttle you."

His chin jerked back. "I've done nothing—"

"And that's the problem." She pointed at his nose. "You've done nothing to change the way you see me. You've done nothing to change the way you treat me. I'm a perpetual thirteen-year-old girl to you, and it drives me insane because…" She swallowed and shook her head, unable to go on.

When he crossed his arms, his biceps bulged against the fabric of his sleeves. "Because what? You may as well finish your thought."

There was something in his voice. Something that made her stomach flip. Glancing at him sharply, she was frustrated when his expression remained unreadable.

"Because I want you to see me as I am *now*," she admitted sullenly.

"Why?"

Screw it, she decided. *He must suspect how I feel about him, how I've always felt about him. It won't change anything if I come right out and say it.*

"Because I *want* you, Sam," she blurted. And then for good measure, and so there was no way he could misconstrue her words, she added, "And not in the puppy love way I wanted you when I was in middle school. I want you the way a woman wants a man. With all the accompanying nakedness and sweat and the exchanging of fluids."

Even in the low light, there was no mistaking the path his Adam's apple took up the length of his throat.

"I lost my virginity to your sister." The words were rough, like they'd been dragged over sandpaper on the way out of his mouth.

She waved a dismissive hand. "So what?"

"So doesn't that mean I'm off-limits?"

She blinked. And then remembered what he'd said months ago. That because he'd dated Candy back in high school, it meant he was more or less her brother-in-law.

She'd scoffed at the notion then. She wasted no time telling him what she thought of it now.

"I mean, if you'd actually *married* her and become my brother-in-law, then yeah. Or if *Candy* would have a problem with it, then sure. But a high school fling that began and ended a million years ago? And a sister who doesn't care about much besides the good standing of her membership at The Metropolitan Club? Pretty sure that means you're fair game."

"Candy might not care," he insisted. "But don't *you?*"

"Why would I?" She canted her head. "I spent my entire life being given

Candy's castoffs. All her old clothes. All her old makeup. Heck, I even got her old Honda Civic when she married Jared and he bought her a new Mercedes. I kind of feel like it's only fitting that I should lust after her old boyfriend."

Her words elicited the response she was after. One corner of his mouth quirked. "Why do I feel like you just called me Sloppy Seconds?"

"Are you sloppy?" she teased. "I'd just assumed you'd learned a thing or two since the days when you groped my sister on the park bench at Jackson Park."

His jaw slung open. "She *told* you 'bout that?"

"Not at the time," she assured him, deciding she was going straight to hell for having such fun at his expense. "I was too young. But once we were both adults? Over bottomless mimosas? Sure. I heard the stories."

"For fuck's sake." He ran a hand through his hair and then paced about ten yards down the tunnel to where Fisher had parked the motorcycle. The light from his cell phone haloed him in a circle of white. "And *this* is why a man should never date sisters," he muttered. "They compare notes."

"I hate to break it to you, but it isn't just sisters. All women share their experiences. It's one of the ways we protect ourselves since we're forced to date our only natural predators."

That stopped his pacing. "Your only natural predators?"

"Think about it. When you hear about a woman being assaulted or killed, is your first thought that the perpetrator was a mountain lion or a man?"

"Jesus." He shook his head. "When you put it that way, it's amazing any of you step foot outside your front doors."

"The urge to mate is strong." She sighed breathily. "Unfortunately."

He really played up the whole Super Man theme by shoving his fists onto his hips and taking up a wide-legged stance. "Is *that* the reason you want me? Because I've been vetted and deemed safe?"

"Oh, for—" She threw her hands in the air. "Are you serious?" When he refused to answer, simply stood there glowering, she was forced to go on. "I want you because you're smart and sexy. Because you like the Coen brothers and because your sense of humor matches mine. I want you because of *you*, you big, dumb…dummy."

She shook her head when her insult made that one corner of his mouth twitch again. For good measure, she added, "As for being safe? You're probably the most dangerous man I've ever met."

The part she kept to herself was, *And not because you can shoot a rifle or jump out of an airplane. But because you could break my heart without lifting a finger.*

Like it or not—and she was pretty sure she did *not*—there was no more denying exactly what she felt for him. It wasn't simply lust mixed with admiration swirled together with unrequited longing.

It was love.

She was in love with Samuel Harwood.

She'd *been* in love with him since the eighth grade. And neither time nor distance had done anything to squelch that love. On the contrary, it had only grown.

"Hannah." He shook his head, his expression pained.

"It's okay." She ignored the agony that sliced through her heart. "I get it. You've never felt about me the way I felt about you. I'm a big girl. I can take rejection. Just…lay off the big brother schtick, okay? It makes me feel small and ineffectual. You might look at me and see a thirteen-year-old girl. But that's not how I want the rest of the world to see me."

"That's the problem, though," he muttered so lowly that were it not for the oppressive quiet in the tunnel, she might not have heard him at all.

She frowned. "It's a problem that I don't want the rest of the world to—"

"No." He sliced a hand through the air with enough vehemence to have her blinking. "The problem is I *don't* see a thirteen-year-old girl when I look at you. I've *tried*. I've told myself that's how I *should* see you."

She was too scared to hope, so she simply looked at him expectantly, waiting for him to elaborate. To her complete frustration, he remained mute. Just stood there glowering at her like she should be able to read his mind.

Shaking her head, she muttered, "I swear on all that's holy, trying to figure you out is a million times harder than untangling code and unmasking cyber villains. You are a mystery wrapped in an enigma covered in facial hair."

"Well, let me clear things up." He stomped toward her, his biker boots *thumping* against the concrete floor with enough force to make each step rumble down into the tunnel like thunder.

"What…?" Instinct had her stumbling back until her spine hit the brick wall and there was nowhere left to run. He looked like he wanted to bend her over his knee and spank her ass. Either that or—

Her thoughts came to a halt at the same time he did. The tips of his biker boots touched her sock-covered toes. He pressed his palms flat against the wall on either side of her head.

"Sam?" she squeaked when he brought his face level with hers. "I didn't mean to upset you or—"

"You're playing with fire here, Hannah." His words were low. A warning. But what was he warning her of?

And then, she knew.

Or, at least, she *thought* she did.

Was he…?

Did he…?

When his steely gaze tracked down to her mouth, she had her answer.

Holy shit! He's going to kiss me!

He'd always had the ability to hyper-focus. It's what made him such a great pitcher in high school. He could drown out the sound of the heckling crowd, ignore the merciless heat of the high-summer sun on his shoulders, and concentrate on one single, solitary action. She assumed it was that same ability that'd turned him into a decorated marksman after he joined the Marines.

Never had *she* been the center of all that eagle-eyed focus, however. Now that she was, she could say with one-hundred-percent certainty, it was intoxicating.

"Fire doesn't scare me, Sam." Her voice was a bare whisper. "Fire can be fun."

"It also burns, Hannah." His words were gruff.

For the first time ever, when the urge struck she didn't stop herself from reaching for him. She framed his jaw, felt the deceptive softness of his beard against her palms, and listened to the shaky breath that leaked out of him at her touch.

He *wanted* her.

She barely dared to believe it. But there was no denying the hungry look in his eyes. The way his pulse hammered in his throat. How his gaze stayed glued to her mouth when she spoke.

"True." She felt breathless and over-oxygenated all at the same time. "But what's life without a little risk, right?"

He sounded like a bear then. A big, growly grizzly. And all her fantasies didn't hold a candle to the reality of his kiss.

When he took her mouth, it wasn't tentative or gentle. It wasn't reluctant or tame.

Hell, no. It was possessive. Deep and wild and toe-curlingly *thorough*.

He was right. Fire burned.

She was absolutely *branded* by the warmth of the hands he'd brought up to frame her face. Seared by the heat of his big body pressed so dominatingly against her own. Scorched by the flick of his hot tongue as he greedily set about mapping her mouth.

CHAPTER 18

What the fuck are you doing?

The question screamed through Sam's brain even as he pressed his body tight against Hannah's.

He reveled in the way she went up on tiptoe to meet him lick for lick, suck for suck. The way her fingers dug into his hair, her nails pricking deliciously against his scalp. The way she arched against him as if the minuscule amount of space left between their bodies was too much and she wanted more, more, *more*.

More of his passion. More of his lust. More of *him*.

All of him.

This is Hurricane Hannah! he tried to remind himself. *What the fuck are you doing?*

Hurricane Hannah. The nickname held a whole new meaning.

She wasn't some pillow princess happy to sit back and be ravaged. She was a hot-blooded storm of a woman who gave pleasure with as much fervor as she received it.

He was swept up. Blown away. His senses so consumed by her that even though he knew there was a reason he shouldn't be doing what he was doing, for the life of him, he couldn't remember what it was.

When her tongue dipped into his mouth, he caught it and sucked it greedily. Showing her exactly what he planned to do with other parts of her body. With her fingers. With her nipples. With that sweet, hidden bundle of nerves at the top of her sex.

Ripping her mouth free, she rasped his name. And what she did next shocked the ever-lovin' shit out of him.

She pressed her warm, damp lips to the scar on his neck. Then she flicked out her little tongue to trace the length of his puckered flesh.

His heart flipped. His stomach cramped. His knees nearly buckled.

"Hannah." Her name was dragged from the back of his throat.

"Just let me…" She didn't finish, simply pulled him harder against her and continued to map his scar with her greedy little mouth.

"Fuck," he groaned, having to curl his hands into fists to keep from pulling down her borrowed joggers, opening up his fly, and taking her right there against the dirty brick wall inside the dank, dingy tunnel.

"I've wanted to do this since I saw you leaning against the gates outside," she whispered against his throat, still following the line of his scar with her hot, talented tongue. "How'd you get it?"

"I can use my mouth in one of two ways." He tucked a tendril of purple hair behind the little shell of her ear, lingering briefly with her earlobe caught between his thumb and forefinger. *Soft.* Like the rest of her. "To answer your question or to leave a string of kisses from your lips down to your throat and then…lower." He palmed the sides of her face so his next words were breathed against her lips. "You decide."

"The latter."

The immediacy of her answer made him chuckle. "I hoped you'd say that," he rasped before reclaiming her mouth.

The way she moaned when he dipped his tongue into the honeyed interior, once, twice, three times?

Fuck me, it's the song of a siren.

Nothing could have stopped him from doing his damnedest to consume her then. Starting with the sweet pillow of her earlobe, moving to the soft skin below her ear, and ending with the delicate flesh that fluttered over her pulse point.

The taste of her tingled on his tongue. And the feel of her body moving against him in that sinuous, sinful motion that was as old as time had every rational thought falling out of his head.

He was acting on instinct when he yanked his phone from his hip pocket and dropped it to the cement floor. It shined up and spotlighted the two of them as he hooked his hands behind her knees. It was animal impulse that had him wrapping her legs around his waist and pressing her back against the brick wall. And it was the most feral form of lust he'd ever known that made him grind his turgid cock into the soft fabric that covered her warm, waiting folds.

The heat of her, the wonderful, humid *heat* of her seeped through the joggers and the denim of his jeans to tease his dick with hints of what was to come. Hints of soft, hot, slippery flesh that would bathe him in her deliciously sweet juices.

He wouldn't have thought it possible, but he grew harder. So hard he considered it a wonder he didn't split his own skin. And then, to his surprise, she softened. Just went languid and loose in his arms.

A surrender, he realized.

Made more powerful because for a woman like Hannah—the ball-busting, taking-no-prisoners type—letting go was the ultimate form of submission. An unequivocal show of her trust and faith in him to give her what she wanted.

What she needed.

"Touch me, Sam." She pleaded into his hungry mouth. "Please. I need to feel your hands on me."

She didn't need to ask him twice. Keeping her pinned to the wall with his hips, he found the hem of her sweatshirt and slipped his hand inside.

Her skin was warm and silky smooth. The muscles in her belly quivered when he skated his rough palm up her midriff, over her delicate ribs, until the tips of his fingers brushed the underside of her breast.

She gasped at the first hint of such an intimate touch. And when he gently cupped her, weighing her tender flesh, he swallowed her shuddering sigh.

She was a small woman, yet her breasts were large enough to fill his hands. He rubbed the edge of his thumb over her nipple, groaning when it hardened into a pebbled peak that begged to be sucked.

"Sam." Her nails cut into his scalp as she undulated her hips against him, seeking friction. Seeking pleasure. Seeking release.

"You're so damned sexy." The words came out more of a guttural growl than actual speech. The smell of ripe, ready woman tunneled up his nose and made him want to beat his chest, drag her off into his lair, and *ravage* her until he'd imprinted himself upon her. Until every inch of her body bore the scent of his skin, the mark of his teeth, the lingering shadow of his touch. "I want to tear off your clothes and sink into you over and over again until you melt around me."

"Yes." There was desperation in her voice. *Pleading.* "Please, Sam."

If he'd been able to think, he would've realized the Bat Cave was no place to make love to a woman. He would've stopped what they were doing so he could lay her down in a soft, warm bed where he could take his time and learn every fascinating inch of her decadent body.

But he couldn't think. And so it was pure impulse that had him lowering her left leg to the ground.

"Hook your heel into the back of my knee and open up to me, Hannah," he instructed between the string of kisses he left along the side of her warm neck.

Her breath shuddered out of her, but she didn't hesitate to obey. Her heel found purchase behind his knee and the sole of her foot molded itself to the back of his calf. Then she let her thigh fall wide.

"That's it," he praised, nipping lightly at the curve of her jaw. "Now, relax and lemme make you feel good."

He reveled in her little whimper of acquiescence when he reclaimed her hot, wanton mouth. Then he slowly pulled on the string at the waistband of the joggers.

It was ripping the ribbons off a Christmas present. It was unboxing a long-awaited Amazon delivery. It was pulling the paper down on the world's most delicious cupcake. Only better. Because the thing that waited for him beneath the layers was Hannah.

Sweet, warm, *willing* Hannah.

Slipping his hand inside the joggers, he once again marveled at the softness of her skin. How the lower curve of her belly had been made to fit his palm. How the muscles there quivered and spasmed under the gentle pressure of his touch.

The instant his fingers brushed the small triangle of hair at the top of her sex, she cried out.

He nearly cried out too. Cried out at having to be patient when what he really wanted was to pillage and plunder. Cried out at having to be gentle when what he needed was to rut and ravage.

"You're so soft," he whispered into her mouth as he slipped one finger, then two, between her slick, feverish folds. "So wet and sweet."

And then, he lost the ability to speak because he was totally focused on her.

On the slightest catch in her breath. The subtlest jerk of her hips. The tiniest change in the pulse that beat like a butterfly's wings in her throat.

Locating Hannah's clit was easy enough. The little nub was turgid and ripe. When he circled it gently, she hummed her pleasure. But when he softly pressed it up and down, she tossed back her head and gasped.

"Good girl," he encouraged, fitting his mouth over her pulse-point. Wanting to feel how her heart raced. Wanting to know if he did something to make it skip a beat.

For long moments, he simply studied and learned, holding back his own desires, ignoring how his dick flexed and begged. And only when he felt her getting close to the edge, only when her pulse hammered hard against his tongue and her hips flexed mindlessly, did he slip a finger into her heated, grasping interior.

"Sam!" She fisted his hair in her hands.

Before she could catch her breath, he pressed a second finger inside.

She was hot and welcoming, just as he'd known she would be. She was also snug. Her sheath a tight fit that let him know when it was time for him to truly make love to her, he'd need to take it slow. He'd need to sink into her gradually, inch by inch, allowing her body time to adjust to his intrusion.

Time to melt and make room for him.

For now, he simply used his thumb to work her clit the way he'd learned she liked while simultaneously pumping his fingers inside her. Changing his angle, changing his pressure, until he found the perfect combination that had her hips working counter to his ministrations and her breaths coming hard and fast.

"That's it, Hannah," he encouraged. "Just like that, sweetheart. Cum for me. I want to feel it. I want to hear it. Give me all you got."

Delving his free hand under her shirt, he found her nipple pebble-hard and waiting. When he pinched it gently, she flung herself into the breach.

Her release wasn't soft or rolling. It wasn't the surf washing onto the

168   JULIE ANN WALKER

beach. *Oh, no.* It was an explosion. A .50 caliber fired from a Browning machine gun. *Boom!*

Her back arched, her thighs clamped tight around his marauding hand, and she screamed his name so loudly he worried—despite the soundproofing— the people on the other side of the brick wall might have heard.

Seeing her unravel, *feeling* the way her sheath clenched and sucked his fingers had him longing for the moment when he could be inside her. When he could experience the exquisiteness of her completion with the part of himself that most longed for her.

She would send him over the edge, he knew. Her orgasm would trigger his own explosive release.

He was careful to match the motion of his hand to her body's subsiding convulsions. Slowing the pump of his fingers. Gentling the press of his thumb. Softly releasing her nipple and cupping her breast as the final ripples shuddered through her. And then, with one last shiver of delight, her foot fell to the ground and she lifted her head.

In the spotlight of his cell phone's flashlight, her eyes were half-lidded and glazed. Her mouth was swollen and shiny from his kisses. And her chest rose and fell in rapid succession.

He didn't want to lose the sensation of her soft flesh holding his fingers, but her body needed a break. And so, as gently as he could—and having to bite his tongue to keep from crying out his disappointment—he slowly slid his hand from inside her joggers.

The urge to lick her essence from his fingertips was intense. But the first time he tasted her, he wanted his head between her thighs. So he planted both hands flat against the wall on either side of her head.

In typical Hannah fashion, she whispered, "Shit on a monkey-buttered biscuit, Sam."

He wouldn't have thought it possible, but he found himself laughing. Thirty seconds earlier he'd been enmeshed in an experience that was mind-bendingly erotic. And now he was laughing.

Leave it to Hannah, he thought and then winced before adjusting himself into a more comfortable position. It was either that or risk permanent harm because he was diamond hard and aching so much he'd lost the ability to decipher pleasure from pain.

Her eyes brightened as she followed the movement of his hand. And when she glanced back up, she wore an expression that had all the air wheezing from his lungs.

"Turn about is fair play." She reached for the waistband of his jeans and snapped her fingers so that the top button on his fly slipped open.

"Good god, Hannah," he rasped. "Where the hell did you learn to do that?" She arched a seductive eyebrow, but he lifted a hand. "Never mind. I don't wanna know."

"Jealous?" One corner of her kiss-swollen lips quirked. When she gave his fly a gentle yank, the remaining three buttons popped free and the entire length of his dick, covered only by the fabric of his boxer briefs, sprung into the breach.

"Fuck yeah, I'm jealous," he gasped when she turned her hand upside down to gently cup him. "I don't wanna think of you with other guys when you're with me."

"Would it help to know that lots of times when I was with those other guys *you* were the one I was thinking about?"

He groaned when she gave him a squeeze. "Is that true?"

She leaned forward to capture the skin of his neck between her teeth. "I've fantasized about you a million times." Her tongue darted out to soothe the nip of her teeth. "Dreamed of all the things you'd do to me. All the things I'd do to *you*."

While she'd been distracting him with her words, she'd pulled out the waistband of his boxer briefs. Now, she thrust her hand inside and wrapped her fingers around his erection.

"Show me how you like to be touched," she whispered, her mouth close to his ear. "I want to make you feel good, Sam." When her tongue swirled inside the hollow of his ear, his eyes rolled back in his head.

Curling his hand around hers, he taught her how to fist him. Then he pumped his hips until she stroked his cock just how he liked. With that perfect pressure. With that perfect rhythm.

The skin of her hand was softer than his, making the experience so much more enjoyable. And when she thumbed the tender, round tip of his penis, spreading the silky drop of wetness she found there around his head and down his shaft, he whimpered.

"You're so hard and hot," she breathed. "I want to feel you filling up my mouth. I want to taste you on my tongue."

Letting go of her fingers, he flattened his palms against the brick wall again. She didn't need his help anymore. She was a quick study. And the thought of her going down on her knees to suck him into the warm, hot haven of her mouth had his *own* knees threatening to buckle. He needed the support to remain upright.

"I want to pull you deep into my mouth." She continued to torture him with her hand, with her words. "I want to feel you bump against the back of my throat. I want to rub my tongue along the base of your cock and then lick up your entire length."

"Jesus," he wheezed.

With her free hand, she reached down into his boxer briefs to cup his balls. Then, with another little nip at the skin over his pulse-point, she used her nails to softly scrape along his scrotum.

He nearly lost it.

His hands were back inside the waistband of her borrowed joggers, ready to shove them down her legs and take her, fuck her, make her *his* when the sound of the wall rumbling on its tracks stopped him cold.

"Cockwaffle," she rasped. "Talk about bad timing."

He whimpered when she removed her hands from his underwear. And it took him a full five seconds to gather enough of his wits to tuck the tip of his dick back into his boxer briefs and do up his fly.

The light of the cell phone showed the knowing smile on her face. "Don't worry. We'll pick up right where we left off." And then she punctuated her promise with a saucy wink.

When the wall completed its journey and the shop came into view, he still wasn't in complete control of himself. He used the excuse of bending to retrieve his cell phone to give himself a couple more seconds before facing his coworkers.

Er…rather, *one* coworker.

Only Eliza stood on the other side of the opening.

BKI's Girl Friday took one look at him then blinked over at Hannah. "Should I…" She cleared her throat. "Should I reclose the wall and let you guys finish?"

Yes! he wanted to thunder. Unfortunately, there were more important matters to deal with than easing the ache in his balls.

"What did the feds—" *Whoa.* Was that his voice? It sounded like he'd been eating gravel. He tried again. "What did the feds hafta say?"

Better. Still rough and ragged. But better.

Eliza gave them a rundown of the conversation she and Fisher had had with the FBI agents as she reclosed the entrance to the Bat Cave and motioned for them to follow her upstairs. By the time he retook his seat at the conference table, he thought he had himself in hand.

Then Hannah reached over from the chair beside him, placing her hand high on his thigh so high that her pinky finger brushed the base of his dick, and he had to bite his tongue to keep from whimpering again.

When it came to Hannah Blue, the more he tried to hide his lust, the louder it roared inside him.

CHAPTER 19

*S*am just made me cum. Sam just made me cum. Sam just made me cum.
No matter how she emphasized the thought, Hannah couldn't make it sound like reality.

But it'd happened. *Oh man* had it.

And it was so much better than her fantasies.

Turned out her imagination—though exceptional—had failed to match the reality of Samuel Harwood. The hungriness of his kisses. The sexiness of his whispered instructions. The absolute *expertise* of his hands.

The man had *skillz*. Mad ones.

She was so lost in her memories, she didn't realize she'd skated her hand up until she was cupping his length beneath the table. She was only pulled back to reality when he threaded his fingers through hers to place her hand back on his thigh.

Glancing at his face, she was gratified to find his nostrils flared with desire and a deep flush staining his cheeks.

Sam wants me. ME! Hannah Blue!

She was tempted to hop on the table and do a victory dance that started with The Carlton and ended with some Nae Nae. She might've thrown caution—and any sense of decorum—to the wind and done exactly that if he hadn't flicked her a quick look, his ocean-blue eyes telling her two things. One, you're driving me crazy. And two, pay attention.

Right.

She dragged in a covert breath and forced her focus back to Eliza, who'd grabbed a seat at the head of the table. Ozzie and Samantha sat on the opposite side from Hannah. As for Fisher? He was nowhere in sight.

"…mentioned Cesar had his attorney present when they stopped by your apartment."

"That's good." She nodded, and then made a face of anguish. "I wish I could call and tell him I'm okay. I hate the thought of worrying him."

"He knows you're with us." Sam squeezed her hand beneath the table. "And he's got his lawyer and his partner to keep him company."

The thought of Pete and Marco being there to see Cesar through things brought comfort. She returned Sam's gesture, squeezing his fingers in silent thanks.

"Okay, first things first." Ozzie absently massaged his wife's shoulders with one hand even as he used the other to peck at his laptop's keyboard. "Since the D.O.D. never received Hannah's intel, that means the fate of Texas rests with us. How are we planning to save the Lone Star State from a devastating blackout?"

Hannah sat up straighter. "In the exchanges I intercepted between the Chinese and their mysterious contact here in the U.S., they spoke of where the breach in the system was located and how a skilled hacker could exploit it. If I could somehow gain access to the plant's control center, I could pinpoint the problem and code in a firewall to patch up the weakness. And just to make things *extra* secure, I could plant a Trojan Horse that'll fry the system of anyone trying to circumvent the firewall. It'll take me…" She screwed up her face as she thought. "Thirty minutes, maybe? Forty-five tops?"

She slumped back in her chair when she realized the logistics of her plan were a nightmare. "Except it's not like I can hop on a plane. I'd never make it through security at the airport. I'm sure my name is on every watch list there is. And even *if* somehow I was able to make it to Texas, how would I gain access to the power plant?"

"Pretty easily, actually," Sam said and she blinked at him in surprise. He shrugged. "We know a couple of guys with private planes who'll fly us south, no questions asked."

"As long as one of them is available." Eliza pulled her cell phone from the pocket of her crisp slacks. After a quick scroll through her contacts, she lifted the device to her ear. Two seconds later, she said, "Ricky? This is Eliza with Black Knights Inc. We need transport for…" She held the phone to her chest and looked directly at Ozzie. "I'm assuming you'll be staying here to man the shop?"

"No out-of-town missions for me until this one"—he placed his hand on Samantha's belly—"makes her appearance."

"Right." Eliza nodded and raised the phone back to her ear. "That'd be transport for four to Texas tonight."

Hannah heard the man on the other end say something and Eliza's gaze landed on her. "Where in Texas would we be headed?"

"Austin," Hannah supplied, blinking myopically at how quickly things were moving. "The plant in question is right outside the city limits."

Eliza relayed the information and then grew quiet as she listened to the mysterious Ricky's reply. Her eyes darted back and forth as if she were cataloging the details of his response. Eventually, she nodded. "Perfect. That'll work. Standard rate?" She paused as Ricky answered, then flattened her mouth. "Don't pull any of that after-hours bullshit on me. Remember who you're talking to."

Whatever Ricky's response was it made Eliza laugh. After she sobered, she shook her head. "And that's why I love you, Ricky. You're nothing if not consistent. As for the return trip, let's play it by ear."

After thumbing off the phone, she explained, "Ricky can be fueled and ready to go wheels up at oh-three-hundred." She glanced at her phone's glowing screen. "Which means we have two hours to get everyone ready to roll with all the appropriate gear."

Hannah opened her mouth to ask *what gear* followed by *but how will we gain access to the power plant* but Fisher beat her to the punch. He'd suddenly appeared at the bottom of the staircase leading to the third floor. "Sounds like I missed somethin' important. What's happenin'?"

"We're gonna get Hannah into the vulnerable power plant so she can perform her hacker magic and put a Band-Aid and a booby trap on the spot where their system is vulnerable," Sam explained.

"Roger that." Fisher nodded. "When do we leave and what should I wear?"

"Leave here at oh-two-hundred. Wheels up at oh-three-hundred," Eliza told him. "And you should wear your best suit. You're going to be a fed."

"Oooh." Fisher rubbed his hands together. "I do like role playin'."

"What about her?" Sam gestured toward Hannah, who finally understood how laypeople felt when they were stuck in a group of hackers talking shop. Those around her may as well have been speaking a foreign language for all she could comprehend of their plan of action.

"She's going to be with ERCOT, I think." Eliza's eyes narrowed in contemplation. "If we try to say she's an agent like the rest of us, whoever's working security at the plant might get suspicious." Eliza winced and turned to Hannah. "It's the purple hair. Self-expression isn't generally encouraged in FBI agents. But, for the record, I think your hair is beautiful. Please don't be offended—"

Hannah raised a hand. "No offense taken." She started to ask…well, one of the hundred questions swirling through her head, but Sam interrupted her before she could snag one and get it out of her mouth.

"What's our cover story?" His crystalline gaze was pinned on Eliza.

Yes, Hannah thought. *What is our cover story? How the hell are we going to get inside the plant?*

"Not sure yet." A wrinkle formed between Eliza's eyebrows. "I have a vague idea, but I'll flesh it out on the flight down."

"Great." Sam clapped his hands together. "So everyone needs to shower, shave, and change."

"Wait." Hannah lifted a finger, her head absolutely spinning. "I don't have any clothes here."

"Mmmm." Eliza tapped her bottom lip. "Nothing I have will fit you. But you're about Becky's height. What are you? A size four?"

Hannah blew Eliza a raspberry. "I love you for that. But these babies"—she patted her hips—"squeeze into a size six, if I'm lucky."

"I think Becky should have something."

"Like what?" Fisher blinked. "I've never seen the woman out of coveralls and Chuck Taylors."

"I'm sure she has a dress or two that'll work." Eliza winced. "But that means someone has to call and wake her up." She, Sam, and Fisher touched their noses and burst out simultaneously with, "Not it!"

"Oh, for Pete's sake." Samantha dug into her purse. Then she dug some more. When she couldn't find what she was looking for, she dumped the entire contents onto the table. Loose change, a random M&M, and two mismatched buttons scattered, along with a tube of Chapstick, a wallet, a sunglasses case, various pens and pencils, and a couple colorful notepads. And, of course, a cell phone which she snagged with an, "Aha! There you are! Why are you always hiding from me?"

Waving a hand at the gathered group, she instructed, "You four go get cleaned up. And you?" She turned to her husband. "You get their IDs and badges made."

"Already on it." Ozzie nodded. "Just remotely switched on the 3D printer."

"Wait." Hannah lifted her hands, palm out, when everyone pushed up from the table. "What about Red Square and the pipeline? I still need to clear my name and—"

"I'll work on that while you're in Texas," Ozzie interrupted. He wasn't looking at her; he was focused hard on his screen. "Just leave your login information, passwords, security questions, etc."

Samantha picked a notepad out of the pile on the table and slid it, along with a pen, toward Hannah.

Tearing out a page, Hannah clicked the pen and began writing the required information. She desperately wanted to insist they slow down and fill her in on *exactly* what they had in mind. But since she was the one imposing on their time and resources, she was in no position to make demands.

It went against everything she'd been taught, all the NDAs she'd signed, and her pledge to never misuse her security status, but she folded the piece of paper and slid it across the table toward Ozzie.

He didn't even glance up from his laptop while slipping the note into the pocket of his jeans.

"Do me a favor and burn that after you're finished with it," she told him warily.

When he glanced up from his laptop and saw her troubled expression, his eyes softened. "You can trust me, Hannah. I'm good at what I do. I'll figure this out for you. In the meantime, you go take care of Texas."

She shook her head and laughed, but there was no real humor in it. "*Go take care of Texas.* Just that easy, huh? Son of a cockwaffling shitburger." She dropped her head into her hands. "How did I end up here?"

Sam wrapped his hand around the back of her neck and donned an accent. "It's a mess, ain't it, Hannah?"

Where had she heard that before?

Oh, right. *No Country for Old Men,* one of her top three favorite Coen brothers' movies.

She came back with the following quote, "If it ain't, it'll do till the mess gets here."

His smile was soft and warm. The same smile he'd always given her when they'd bantered back and forth with movie quotes. But there was something more there now.

A heat. A *hunger.*

They had two hours to prepare themselves for…well, whatever the Black Knights had in mind. But she could tell Sam didn't believe it'd take him two hours to get ready. Which left them time to finish what they'd started down in that dark, dank tunnel.

"Whoa." Fisher had moved to stand behind Eliza's chair, but his eyes pinged from Sam to Hannah. "I guess this means ya won't be wavin' this here red flag"—he hooked a thumb toward his chest—"around for a few hours?"

"Oh, for the love of lemons." Eliza rolled her eyes. "Read the room, Fish!"

"I was!" he exclaimed. "Which is how I found out I officially lost my chance with the lovely lady hacker." He wiggled his eyebrows at Hannah. "Although if this one"—he pointed to Sam—"fails to satisfy, ya know where to find me."

"Fish, the next time you're down in Louisiana, do me a favor and make sure you get a kiss on the neck from an alligator," Sam snarled.

"What?" Fisher blinked innocently. "I thought I was doin' everyone a favor by offerin' up my services to—"

"Close your mouth, Fish," Eliza cut in, "before I give in to my baser impulses and hit you over the head with a phonebook."

Fisher blinked. "Do they even make those anymore?"

"I'm resourceful. I'll find one."

Fisher came back with some sort of smart-ass response, but Hannah had stopped listening because Sam cupped his hand under her chin and turned her face toward his.

"Wanna come upstairs with me now?" he asked quietly.

Her throat dried up like she'd eaten one of the desiccant bags that came inside the packaging of new electronics. She wasn't sure she could form words, so all she did was nod her head.

"Good." His white teeth blazed bright against the darkness of his beard. "Let's go."

Life was strange. For months her days had looked the same. A routine of work, hanging out with Cesar, and getting her jollies by reading alien romance series.

Now look at her. In the space of a few hours, she'd been framed for selling secrets to a mysterious group of black hat hackers, arrested by and escaped from the FBI, and now was on her way to pull off some truly heroic shit. But before that, she was going to get naked and sweaty with the one man on the planet she'd never dared to dream she'd ever be able to get naked and sweaty with.

What is it they say? What a difference a day makes?

Unaware of her swirling thoughts, Sam pulled her from her chair. His hand was so warm and wide inside hers. When she remembered exactly what he'd done with those fingers, her knees nearly buckled. But she somehow managed to follow him to the staircase.

Holy cannoli! I'm going upstairs to make love to Sam!

They were halfway up the treads when a thought occurred. *Will he consider it making love? Or will this simply be sex to him?*

And hot on the heels of that worry came another. *What does he think this is?*

She'd assumed when he'd busted down the walls he'd built up against the idea of her having grown *all the way up* that their natural affection for one another combined with their newfound physical connection would mean things would inevitably lead to that little town she liked to call Relationshipville. And then maybe, after the appropriate amount of time, they'd try their luck in Marriagetown. Which, of course, would be followed up with them establishing a permanent residence in Happily-Ever-After.

But there's that old saw about assuming things, she reminded herself.

What if Sam thought they were simply scratching an itch? What if he thought that after they'd saved Texas and cleared her of any association in Red Square's plot against Dominion they'd go back to the way things were before? What if all he wanted from her was a one-night stand?

Her steps faltered, causing him to turn back to her when they topped the landing. "Hannah?" His expression held concern. "Do you not wanna do this?"

God, he had a wonderful face.

If this was a one-night stand, if he didn't want anything *beyond* this one night, she might never be able to see his face again. Because she knew herself. Knew it'd be too hard to be around him and not touch him, not *be* with him after she'd known what it was to do both.

Now was her chance to call it off. To stop things before they went too far. To go back to being his friend and his occasional emergency hacker contact.

But if she did that, she'd miss out on the opportunity to know what it was to fully give herself to the man who'd held her heart in his hands since before she'd even grown boobs. She'd give up her chance to know what it was to share her body with the one person on the planet whom she loved more than life.

What had she said to Cesar? It's better to have loved and lost than to never have loved at all?

"Don't be silly." She went up on tiptoe, framed his face with her hands, and pressed a soft, lingering kiss to his warm mouth. "Of course I want to do this. I've been fantasizing about doing this since I was old enough to understand what *this* is."

"Good." He slid his palms down to her butt, pulling her against him so she could feel his hardness pressing into the curve of her lower belly. "Because I don't think there's a shower cold enough to take care of this thing."

"Well then." She arched a provocative eyebrow. "How about we see what *I* can do to help?"

CHAPTER 20

Sam would've preferred to have the entire night to taste and touch and explore Hannah's body. Learn all the things that made her pant and purr. Catalog all her different flavors and textures. But they only had an hour before they needed to start getting ready to leave for Texas.

Sixty glorious minutes to put out the fire they'd started down in the cold darkness of the Bat Cave.

Or maybe, this is the kind of blaze that never burns out. A chemical flame with an endless supply that just rages and rages.

As soon as the thought ran through his head, he paused because…

What is this exactly? Where is it headed? And where can it possibly end?

Probably things he should've worked out *before* he tossed aside all his long-held misgivings and kissed her. But he was too far gone to back down now. His need for her was too strong, his passion for her too hot.

The only thing that would stop him from stripping her naked and plunging into her tight, warm body was if she herself hit the brakes.

Thankfully—for him—she wasn't a *brakes* kinda gal. She was more of the *pedal to the metal* type. She proved it by pulling him through the open door of his bedroom with a breathy laugh and a coquettish smile.

Like all things in life, he decided he'd deal with the consequences of his actions once those consequences arrived. For now, he kicked his bedroom door shut and tugged her hand so she turned to him. Another tug was her invitation to fall into his arms.

But she didn't fall; she leapt. Hitting him with all her momentum and wrapping her arms around his shoulders and her legs around his waist.

He let out a little *oof* while stumbling back, stabilizing himself with a hand on the doorknob.

"The last thing a woman wants to hear when she throws herself at a man is *oof*," she scolded.

He let go of the doorknob so he could use both hands to cup her wonderfully curvy hips. He loved the way his fingertips sank into her firm flesh when he gave her a squeeze.

"What I meant was…*oofucking* hell. You're the sexiest thing I've ever seen."

One corner of her decadent mouth hitched. "Nice save."

"Nice ass," he countered. "And nice tits. And nice mouth. And nice… *everything*."

"I inherited at least *some* of the same genetics as my sister," she teased. "So don't sound so surprised."

"Nothing about you surprises me." His words were grated between his teeth because she flexed her hips, rubbing their sexes together and creating an eye-crossing friction even through the fabric that separated them. "But everything about you delights me," he added, giving her hips another squeeze.

"Another good answer." Her grin was teasing. "You're really on a roll."

"And I'm just getting started." He punctuated his point by claiming her lips.

As he marched them toward his bed, her mouth was hungry against his own. Her hands got busy tunneling into his hair. And she continued to rub her body against him, teasing him with the promise of the pleasure to come.

When his shins bumped the side of the bed, he gave her one last, lingering kiss before tossing her onto the mattress.

She squealed in surprise, bounced once, and then laughed as she pushed her hair out of her face. She opened her mouth to scold him or tease him or say something outlandishly on-brand and Hannah, but he stopped her by launching himself on top of her.

"Sam!" She squealed.

"Sorry." He told her, glorying in the way she caught him in the cradle of her hips. "But this is whatcha do to me. You rip away all the charm and charisma I've cultivated over the years and make me revert back to my former Southside self. All grit and no glamour."

She twined her hands behind his neck. "Good. I like gritty, glamourless Southside Sam. He was my very first crush, you know?"

"And now?" He arced a teasing eyebrow.

"Now I'm *still* crushing on him. But I wish he'd shut up and get this show on the road. We have to be on a plane in—"

He silenced her with his mouth, reclaiming and remapping all the terrain he'd so recently explored.

Proving she was just as greedy, just as *needy* as he was, she pulled his sweatshirt over his head and tossed it to the floor beside the bed. The cool air of the bedroom felt nice against his heated skin. But not as nice as her hands when she ran them over his chest, using the edge of her thumbnails to flick at his nipples until they hardened.

"Take off your clothes, Sam." Passion turned her voice husky. "I need to feel all of you against all of me."

The image of his large, scarred body pressing tight against her small, perfect frame bloomed to life inside his head and tempted him to do as she asked. But when he remembered her whispered words about sucking his dick into the back of her throat, he thought it wise to keep his pants on.

Hannah was Hannah. She gave as good as she got.

If he got naked, her focus would turn to the part of him that needed her the most. The part of him that was so hard and hot and hungry that, were she to do even half of the things she'd described, he feared he'd go off like a fucking bottle rocket. *Zip. BOOM!*

"We have time," he promised, kissing his way to her ear. "There's no need to rush."

When she opened her mouth to protest, he silenced her by slipping a hand under her shirt and plumping her bare breast high. He'd known he'd find her nipple stiffened into a delicious point, but it was still gratifying to feel the flesh pebbled between his thumb and forefinger.

"You have sensitive nipples, don't you?" He rolled to her side and leaned up on one elbow so he could watch her face as he continued to play with her breast until he'd rubbed a moan out of her.

"Yes." Her eyes closed in ecstasy.

"Do you want me to suck them?"

Even riding the sharp edge of passion, she was still as clever as ever. "To ask the question is to answer it."

He chuckled. "Never let it be said I kept a lady waiting."

"Who are you calling a lady?" she demanded, but the last word ended on a hiss when he pulled up the sweatshirt, exposing one pretty breast, and immediately bent to suck her coral-colored nipple into his mouth.

Her hands were in his hair again, her nails biting into his scalp as he tongued and sucked and made love to the sweet point until she writhed and mewled and pumped her hips in a helpless entreaty.

He loved the way her soft flesh pillowed his cheeks. Loved more how her nipple grew longer when he tongued it to the roof of his mouth.

His cock throbbed at the sound it made when he pulled back and it popped free of his lips. And the sight of that sweet peak, all damp and achy from the attention of his teeth and tongue, was so incredibly erotic.

He could've sat back and stared at it all night. Memorized the exact shape of her breast, fixed in his mind the exact color of her nipple, counted every tiny variation in her ruched areola until, no matter how much time passed, he would always be able to recall everything about her in perfect detail. But the clock was ticking. He had to move things along or they'd never finish before they needed to leave.

Pulling his favorite sweatshirt over her head, he watched, mesmerized, as her purple hair spilled down like colorful confectioner's candy to fan out against his pillow. Her big, dark eyes were glazed with passion. And a beautiful blush stained her decolletage and the inner slopes of her pretty breasts.

Cradling her face between his hands, he thumbed her plump bottom lip. "You're beautiful, Hannah."

Something flickered in her eyes. He remembered what she'd said about being compared to her sister and falling short.

Where Candy was long and lithe, Hannah was compact and curvy. Where Candy's skin was honeyed and golden, Hannah's was pale and perfect.

She wasn't a rail-thin runway model. But she absolutely, positively *was* the womanliest woman he'd ever seen.

And all her delicate femininity called to every single atom of his masculinity.

He'd never wanted anyone more than he wanted her.

Words would be lost on her, though. Any compliments he might offer would be fanned away as flattery. And so he did the one thing that would make her a believer. The one thing beyond her dispute.

Crawling back on top of her, he found his place between her thighs. Thrusting his hips, he showed her just how hard she'd made him. How swollen and thick and *achy* he was.

"Feel what you do to me?" He watched the blush on her chest travel up her throat to stain her cheeks. "I'm so hard I hurt. Because of you, Hannah. Because you have the sweetest, prettiest, fuckin'-A *sexiest* little body I've ever seen."

To further prove his point, he rolled back to his side, hooked a hand into the waistband of the joggers, and pulled them free from her legs in one fell swoop. The wool socks he'd lent her bunched at her ankles but stayed on. And for some reason, he found that unreasonably adorable.

Of course, his thoughts turned a whole lot more carnal when his eager eyes traveled up her pretty legs to her soft thighs and the little piece of paradise that lay between them.

Her pubic hair was dark. Trimmed neatly into a triangle that arrowed down to her plump lips. Evidence of her passion glistened on the insides of her thighs.

"Jesus, Hannah," he breathed reverently. "I've never seen anyone who looks better in the raw."

He could've phrased his words better, he knew. Could've waxed poetic about how sexy it was that he could see tendrils of her tattoo snaking around the sides of her narrow rib cage. Or he could've gushed on about how the curve of her waist was something artists had been attempting—and failing—to accurately capture for centuries. But he was glad he'd lost the ability to harness his more bombastic side when she chuckled happily and reached for him.

He gloried in the eager press of her tongue between his lips, gloried more in the feel of her nude body skating beneath his palm as he learned the terrain of her soft hills and gentle valleys.

She murmured her disappointment when he eventually pulled his lips free. But that turned into a hum of pleasure as he began leaving a string of kisses down her neck, across her collarbone, only stopping once he reached her breasts. There, he feasted. Thoroughly suckling and licking her nipples until he could feel the throb of her heart in each tender peak.

When she pushed at his shoulders, her body twisting mindlessly, seeking ever more pleasure, he obligingly resumed his journey south. Mapping her ribs with his lips. Swirling his tongue into the delicate oval of her belly button. Catching the edge of her hip bone with his teeth and leaving behind a gentle love bite.

By the time he settled his shoulders between her legs, she was a live wire. Crying out unintelligibly. Absolutely vibrating with need.

The smell of her, the warm scent of ripe, ready woman filled his nose and nearly had his eyes rolling back in his head. And the taste of her when he closed his lips over the swollen button at the top of her sex? That salty, zesty *zing* of hungry, healthy woman? There was nothing like it.

"Sam!" she groaned his name at the first pass of his tongue. "God, yes! That feels so good!"

Having gotten the all-clear, he settled in and gorged himself.

She was so delicious, so slick and hot, that he wanted to tease and torture her all night. But after only a handful of minutes, he glanced up and saw she was already close to the edge. It was there in the way she grabbed her breasts and pinched her nipples. In the way her hips pumped mindlessly against the glide of his tongue.

And then her orgasm hit like the shockwave from a nuclear blast.

Her thighs clamped tight around his ears. His name was a keening cry that echoed around the room.

Tasting her release on his tongue was ecstasy. It was also agony. And had him grinding his dick into the mattress, seeking what small amount of relief that offered.

CHAPTER 21

Hannah was having an out of body experience.

Er... that wasn't right. Because her entire *existence* was her body. The pleasure pummeling it. The sensations shaking it. The sheer delight that detonated through her again and again.

It was so intense she lost track of time. Of where she was. Of *who* she was.

There was only physical bliss. And then...ever-so-slowly, synapse by synapse, her mind returned.

She was in Sam's room at Black Knights Inc. It was past midnight, although she didn't have the first clue how *far* past. And her name was Hannah Blue.

Hannah, the girl from Englewood. Hannah, Candy's little sister. Hannah...Samuel Harwood's lover.

Even with the tail end of her orgasm shimmering through her, it was still hard to believe. Even with him between her legs leaving gentle, open-mouthed kisses against her swollen, achy sex, she still had trouble wrapping her mind around it.

"That was..." She had to stop and swallow. "Pretty good."

He crawled up beside her. There was satisfaction and desire in his eyes. But also humor. "Just pretty good?"

"Well…" She panted, her breath still struggling to return. "I'm trying not to overinflate your ego."

"Well…" He parroted her inflection. "Guess I'll have to settle for pretty good then."

She hummed a small laugh and thought how lovely it was that, even though they were naked and doing terribly naughty things to each other— well, Sam was only half-naked; *boo*—they were still *them*. Still talking and teasing. Still…*friends*.

"But see?" She reached for the top button on his jeans. "The thing about pretty good is that it leaves room for improvement. I suggest we practice." *Pop.* The first button came loose. "*A lot*," she emphasized. *Pop, pop, pop!* Before she reached into his open fly, she quirked an eyebrow. "What do you think?"

She was playing. But she couldn't deny the hint of desperation as she waited for his answer. Waited to see if he agreed they would be doing what they were doing now for many nights—months? *Years?*—to come.

Which meant she was disappointed when all he said was, "I think you should pull off the socks and get comfy. Because I'm gonna fuck you better than you've ever been fucked before."

Coming from any other man, it would've sounded like bravado. Coming from Sam, it sounded like a promise.

Her sex, so recently sated, throbbed with renewed need. And she didn't waste time complying with his command.

When she turned back from pulling off her socks, it was to find he'd taken down his jeans and boxer briefs, kicking them over the side of the bed. But she barely registered the action because her gaze was riveted to his cock.

So large and swollen. So long and thick. So veiny and dark.

Her mouth watered as the urge to taste him, just as she'd promised down in the tunnel, returned with a vengeance.

When she pushed him onto his back, he stopped her from bending to take him into her mouth with a hand around her arm.

"No." He shook his head. "I want you too much. I don't think I can—"

"Hush," she told him. "Just a little taste. Turnabout is fair play, right?"

His Adam's apple bobbed in his throat. She could tell by the way his jaw tightened that he wanted to argue. But in typical Sam fashion, he acquiesced to *her* wants with a sharp, downward jerk of his chin.

Finding a place between his legs, she marveled at his big body stretched out before her like a smorgasbord of tan skin, hard muscles, and delicious man-hair. His dick was so engorged it arced off his body, holding itself aloft. And her fingers strained to circle his base when she took him in hand.

She could feel the heavy beat of his pulse in the large, ropey veins that throbbed against her fingertips. And she watched, mesmerized, as a drop of silky precum oozed from the slit at his tip.

All she could think as she angled him toward her mouth was...*man*. Big, beautiful man who made the woman in her melt.

Literally. A new rush of warmth bathed her sex.

He'd propped pillows behind his head so he could watch her. So, with a seductive smile, she held his gaze and slowly flicked out her tongue to taste him.

His hips flexed. A harsh hiss seeped from between his clamped jaw. And his eyes were superglued to her mouth. "Fuck me, Hannah."

"Soon," she promised. Then she swallowed his swollen head.

He was salty and sweet. And she quickly learned his contours with her tongue. Followed his straining veins as she sucked him deeper, deeper, deeper still.

By the time his plump crown bumped against the back of her throat, she was wet and ready and *eager* to get him inside her. To feel all that hard, hot flesh filling her up, stretching her out, *completing* her.

"Holy fuck, Hannah." His eyes were half-lidded as he watched. "I don't think I can stand much more."

"Mmm," she hummed and his eyes crossed. Literally *crossed*.

She might've smiled her victory, but her mouth was stretched too far around him. All she could do was reverse her caress, taking care to massage every inch of him before finally allowing his fat head to pull free of her suckling lips.

"Condom?" she asked breathlessly.

He broke the land speed record for fishing a condom from his nightstand. A split second later, he ripped open the foil package and rolled on the latex, grunting when the rubber ring squeezed tight around his base.

She might've taken her time kissing her way up his body, tonguing his navel and sucking the flat, brown discs of his nipples, but he hooked his hands under her arms and yanked her up beside him.

So eager, she thought, secretly delighted.

When he would've climbed on top of her, trepidation had her pressing a palm to his chest. "Can I be on top? You're rather…um…girthy. I'd like to be able to control the—"

Again, his Adam's apple bobbed. But he quickly nodded and rolled onto his back.

"Can't promise how long I'll last if I'm not in control," he whispered honestly. "I'm so hot for you, Hannah."

"Doesn't matter," she assured him, straddling his hips and spreading her thighs wide. "I've already had two. I think it's time you had one."

Grabbing his thick base, she angled him toward her entrance. His dick pulsed and strained against her hand, and she could tell by the way his long fingers fisted into the coverlet that it was taking everything he had not to thrust. Not to bury himself deep.

She took pity on him and didn't torment or tease. Instead, she immediately adjusted herself so she was directly over him. And then she lowered herself slightly so she could drag his plum-shaped head through her juices.

They hissed in unison at that first intimate contact. And then they moaned when she positioned his crown at her opening and sank onto him that first fraction of an inch.

"Slow, sweetheart." His hands gripped her hips. She could feel the indents of all ten of his fingertips pressing into her flesh. "Go slow." When she sank down another half inch, then another, he grunted. "Thatta girl. Just like that."

She had a praise kink. Or maybe she just had a *Sam* kink. Because hearing him say *thatta girl* was nearly enough to have her teetering on the edge. *Again*.

A hot flush stained his cheeks. A muscle worked in his jaw and made his beard twitch. And a glistening bead of sweat formed at his temple to trickle down and dampen his dark hair as she took him deeper. Deeper. Deeper still.

A flash of fear arced through her when she thought she wouldn't be able to take all of him. When she thought there was too much and she was too shallow. But the curves of her butt hit the top of his thighs at the same time his swollen head bumped into her cervix.

They moaned. Him with pleasure. Her with relief.

But she was too full. Too stretched. Too…preoccupied with how close the pleasure was to pain.

Either her face gave her away or he was so attuned to her that he knew. Because he grabbed her hips to lock himself tight inside her body.

"Just give it a second," he rasped. "You'll adjust."

"Sam, I—"

"Shh." He cupped her face with one hand. "Kiss me, Hannah. Just kiss me."

Like always, she obeyed.

The feel of his chest hair abrading her straining nipples was deliciously erotic. And the skill of his lips and tongue had her forgetting her discomfort and focusing on the joy of his mouth.

By the time he put his hands back on her hips and flexed into her slightly, she realized he'd been right. She *had* adjusted. Grown wetter, softer. Her body accommodating his in a way that was as surprising as it was natural.

Pressing up with one hand on his chest and the other braced on the headboard, she began to move. Slowly at first. Tentatively.

She didn't want that unpleasant feeling returning.

But after a few seconds, when all she felt was that wonderful slick slide of hardness inside welcoming softness, she quickened her pace. Lengthened her strokes. Strengthened the friction.

"Good," he praised, his hands helping her hips swing back and forth. "That's it, Hannah. Ride me."

If she hadn't already cum twice, she would've already careened over the edge. But her body was worn out from pleasure. Worn out and yet somehow still needing more.

Wanting more.

Craving more.

Greedy. That's what she was. Absolutely insatiable for the man who allowed her to use his body for her own pleasure.

She was full of him, every single nerve ending touched by him. Her downstroke had him bumping into the end of her channel. Her upstroke had her clit grinding against his pubic bone.

It was heaven. It was hell because she just…couldn't…quite…get—

"Sam!" she cried his name. "Help me, I—"

She needn't say more. He knew what to do.

Pulling her down to his chest, he claimed her mouth at the same time he locked his hands hard into the creases where her thighs met her hips. He worked their bodies in opposite directions until the friction was brain-melting. Until the pressure of him inside her was toe-curling. Until she felt the telltale ache of her release coiling ever tighter.

"Look at me," he demanded against her lips. "Open your eyes and look at me."

She reluctantly pulled her mouth from his until they were nose-to-nose and she could see the lust that rode him as hard as she did.

He was close too. Her body giving him so much pleasure the skin over his cheeks had tightened. And it was clear by the muscle twitching under his left eye and the way his jaw had clamped down tight that the only thing he was waiting on was her.

Knowing that was all it took for the first wave of orgasm to roll through her.

"Fuck yes, Hannah!" he howled when he felt her walls close tight around him. Then he followed it up with a string of deliciously filthy words that succeeded in having another wave of pleasure crashing over her. Rolling under her. Catching her up in its ecstasy.

Once again, she *was* her body. An instrument of elation. A thing of rapture.

And just when she thought she'd reached the peak and would begin sliding down the other side, she felt him explode inside her. Truly, he swelled to an impossible size and then bucked and pulsed as long, hot jets of ejaculate filled the condom.

His pleasure triggered more of her own. And for long moments they simply clung to one another as her orgasm milked him and his orgasm throbbed inside her.

It was the most sensual, most intimate thing she'd ever experienced. And then finally, with them both spent, she collapsed on top of him.

She wasn't sure how long they stayed that way, joined and slowly coming down from the throws of passion. But eventually, she registered the gentle glide of his fingertips along the groove of her spine. The steady beat of his heart against her chest. The way his breaths had gone from fast and gasping to slow and easy.

Her mouth automatically sought the warmth of his neck. And the instant her lips brushed the puckered skin of his scar, instinct had her pressing a gentle kiss there.

"How *did* you get it?" Her voice husky from passion.

He gave her ass a teasing spank. It was enough to make her sheath clench, and since he was still buried inside her, he felt it and groaned softly. "Really? We just had simultaneous orgasms and the thing you wanna talk about is my scar?"

"If you'll recall, I asked you about it earlier, but you refused to answer."

"I didn't refuse. I just gave you the choice between me using my mouth to form words or using my mouth to do other, far more pleasurable things."

She pushed up so he could see the teasing twist of her lips. "Are you being purposefully evasive? Is the subject of your scar a national security secret?"

"Just not something I'm very proud of." When she lifted an eyebrow, he sighed. "I was on the rooftop of a building in…" He frowned and she realized, despite her security clearance, there were details of his life he'd probably never be able to share with her. "A war zone," he finished, "waiting for a target to enter my crosshairs."

He reached up and scratched his beard. She smiled at the lovely *scritching* sound it made. Then he grimaced. "I was so focused on the view through my scope, I wasn't paying attention to my six. An enemy combatant snuck up behind me and had his blade to my throat before I even knew anyone was there. If not for one of my teammates arriving on the scene and shooting the fucker in the back, I probably woulda lost my whole head."

Her stomach turned at the thought.

The work she did was dangerous because there were nefarious creatures crawling through the dark web. But what *Sam* did for a living? That was peril set to overdrive and then raised to the power of ten.

Unaware of her thoughts, he continued, "It was still a close thing. The bastard managed to nick my jugular and I nearly bled out before I made it back to the evac site."

"Good god, Sam."

"Yeah." His lips twisted. "The good news is, I got to go back to the States for six weeks of medical leave. The bad news is, it really drove home just how dangerous it was to be a Marine Raider. My ex-wife took one look at me and put the kibosh on trying to get pregnant then and there. She was terrified of the thought of raising kids on her own."

Hannah blinked in confusion. Before she could form a question, however, he went on. "But all's well that ends well. Turns out having a coupla rugrats with her would've been a huge mistake. I'd have had to get a paternity test to prove they were actually mine."

Her confusion had climbed the ladder to pure bewilderment. He must've read it in her face because he explained, "She was sleeping with our next-door neighbor."

Ignoring how the idea of him having children with someone made her want to chew nails, she asked the question burning in her brain. "Was I supposed to know you've been married?"

"Didn't you?" He looked genuinely perplexed.

"No." She shook her head.

"Huh." He blinked. "Yeah. I kinda forget we didn't know each other for sixteen years. A lotta living gets done in that amount of time, I guess."

"Stay on topic." She poked his shoulder. "I need more details."

"Not much to tell." He shrugged and then tapped her ass. "Scooch off me, sweetheart. I'm afraid the condom might leak."

They both moaned when she lifted herself away from him and he slid from the warm, soft comfort of her body. Turning onto her side, she watched as he sat on the edge of the bed and pulled off the latex. When he walked into the bathroom to dispose of it, she appreciated the view of his high, tight glutes and his broad, tanned back.

Re-emerging, her eyes snagged on the towel he rubbed across his private parts. He had a second towel in hand, and she reached for it when he knelt on the mattress.

"No." He shook his head. "Let me."

Tossing his own towel aside, he gently used the spare towel to dry the evidence of her desire from the inside of her thighs and outside of her labia. She groaned when the terry cloth ran over a tender spot and his eyes shot to her face. "Sore?"

"A little." She nodded.

"You'd tell me if it was more than a little, wouldn't you?" The concern on his face, the way he wasn't skipping the aftercare, had a lump forming in her throat.

I love him so freakin' much!

She loved him until she thought her heart might burst with it. Loved him until all her bones ached with it. Loved him until she wanted to declare it right then and there.

Instead, she bit her tongue and went willingly into his arms once he lay down on his back and patted the space over his heart. With her cheek pillowed on his chest and her thigh thrown over his, she noted once again how lovely his body hair felt against her skin and how safe and comfortable she felt when his arm came around her waist.

This is intimacy, she thought. *Even more than the sex.*

"How'd you and your ex meet?" she asked quietly, still reeling at the thought of him having been married.

And yes, maybe a little jealous too. Who *was* this woman who'd won his heart enough to have him walking down the aisle?

"Met her at a bar six weeks before I finished Raider training." He absently twirled the ends of her hair between his fingers. "A month later, we were married."

She pushed up on her elbow and cupped her cheek in her hand. "That was quick." The green-eyed monster that'd hopped atop her shoulder gained ten pounds and grew fangs. "Must've been love at first sight."

He shook his head. "More like *lust* at first sight. And I was still so green I didn't know the difference. Plus, I had this crazy idea I was gonna make myself the perfect family. You know, the wife, the two-point-five kids, and the house in the suburbs. But I caught Chloe riding her Jody—" He stopped and explained. "Chloe is my ex. And a Jody is what us military types call the guy back home who's fucking your woman. Anyway, the neighbor's *real* name was Steve, and I caught her screwing him eighteen months after we said our I do's. We were divorced a day shy of our second wedding anniversary. As they say, easy come, easy go."

"Do you miss her?" She held her breath as she awaited his answer.

"Hell no." The harshness of his words convinced her even more than the look of disgust that came over his face. "The only thing I miss is the fantasy I had of living that Meredith and McDreamy life, you know?"

Her eyes rounded. "You did not just reference *Grey's Anatomy*."

His grin was a little self-conscious. "Look, being a Raider meant there were moments of balls-to-the-wall action. But most of the time, it was a game of hurry up and wait. I had to fill my hours with something. One of my bunkmates had the first ten seasons downloaded onto his laptop."

She blinked. "Only the first ten? Did you ever pick up after that?"

"No." He shook his head. "Why?"

She grimaced. "I'm not one for spoilers."

"*Why*, Hannah?" He poked her shoulder. "What happened?"

"You sure you want to know?" She turned to give him the side-eye. "I don't want to ruin the—"

"Oh, my god! Just tell me!"

"Derek dies in season eleven."

His face paled. "No."

"Afraid so." She winced.

"But why are there so many seasons after that? I mean, Derek and Meredith's relationship is the lynchpin of the whole show."

She shrugged. "It sort of focused more on other characters after that."

While he digested her bombshell, she was quiet. Then, tentatively, she ventured, "Do you still want that? The wife and the kids and the house in the 'burbs?"

He hitched a shoulder. "Someday maybe. But hopefully I'll be smarter the second time around. Choose with my heart and my head instead of trying to force a childhood dream into reality with the first woman willing to wear my ring."

She wasn't sure where the idea came from, but suddenly she couldn't think of anything else. "Do you have a picture? Of Chloe, I mean?"

He frowned. "Why?"

She shrugged. "Just curious about the woman you chose to mother your children, I guess."

"Women." He shook his head. "You guys are an endless mystery to me. I'm lying here with you naked and the absolute *last* thing I wanna look at is photos of your exes."

Normally, she wouldn't care about his exes either. Normally, she was a firm believer in *the past is in the past and there is no use rehashing it*. But there was something she needed to know.

When he realized she was serious, he slapped her ass. "Okay. Fine. Get up and lemme grab my phone. I think our wedding photos are still stored on the Cloud somewhere."

She rolled off him so he could snatch his jeans from the floor and fish his phone from the pocket. He sat on the edge of the bed as he located the pictures. When he finally stretched out next to her and handed her his phone, she took it with shaky fingers.

"We were married by a justice of the peace." He sounded disinterested. "So you won't see any fancy tux or five-layer cake if that's what you're thinking. Just me in my best suit and Chloe with a cheap grocery-store bouquet."

"Just let me…" She drifted off as she thumbed the screen so the phone would wake up. The second she saw the first picture, her stomach sank.

There was Sam, looking young and handsome and so much like the boy she'd known when she was thirteen that she couldn't help suffering a pang of nostalgia. And there was his wife, tall and tan and blond.

The woman actually looked enough like Candy that Hannah nearly did a double take.

"You have a type." Her voice was raspy thanks to the constriction in her throat. But that was nothing compared to the vice around her heart. "Tell me your ex-wife isn't the spitting image of my big sister."

He studied the screen. "Holy shit. You're right. Never noticed that before."

"Are *all* your exes blondes?"

He screwed up his mouth as he considered her question, then… "Come to think of it, a good portion of them are."

Whatever she'd been about to say was cut off by a knock at the door. "Sorry to interrupt." It was Eliza. "But I have clothes and shoes for Hannah out here. I'll leave them hanging over the knob."

"Thanks, Eliza!" Sam called. Then he smacked a quick kiss on Hannah's mouth and vaulted out of the bed. "Come on. Let's get ready. Fake identities and weaseling our way into state-run power plants requires attention to detail." He rubbed his beard and winced. "I think I probably gotta get rid of this to really pull off the look."

When he bent to grab his jeans, the Jolly Rancher she'd shoved in his pocket fell to the floor. After picking it up, he quirked an eyebrow.

"I take it Candy shared more than just my inexperienced park bench groping. You know, I'd done a bang-up job of getting rid of the sugar in my diet until *you* came back into the picture six months ago and reminded me of my addiction." His expression was teasing and more than a little accusing. "Now I keep a bag of these under my vanity like the dirty secret it is. I'm assuming that's where this came from?" He held the candy between his thumb and forefinger.

She couldn't tease back. "You really thought it was Candy slipping the Jolly Ranchers into your pocket back then?"

His eyebrows formed a V. "Wasn't it?"

She shook her head and thought, *"Men. They can't help but think the best of beautiful women."*

Aloud she said, "Since when did you *ever* know my big sis to do something for someone just because she knew it'd make them smile? I mean, she's a little less self-serving now. But back then? The world revolved around her and her alone."

"It was you?" Wonder and incredulity fought for supremacy in his expression. When all she did was nod, he ran a hand through his hair. "Well what d'you know." And then he turned and disappeared through the bathroom door.

She was left to stare at the empty space he'd left behind as all her hopes and dreams yeeted themselves right out the window.

Sure, he'd slept with her. What single, horny guy wouldn't when she'd made it clear she'd been panting after him for most of her life? But sleeping with her and wanting a relationship were worlds apart. And sleeping with her and falling in *love* with her? Well, those two things were *galaxies* apart.

Sam dreamed of the wife and the kids and the picket fence. But it was clear the picture in his head didn't include a purple-haired pipsqueak of a woman who ran around with drag queens and preferred ridiculous T-shirts and ratty Vans to sweetheart sundresses and self-tanner.

You knew the risks, a little voice whispered. *Better to have loved and lost than never to have loved at all, right?*

Wrong. And holy cheeseballs what an idiot she'd been.

Instead of listening to that tired old cliché, she should've taken to heart the one that went something like…*what a person doesn't know can't hurt them.*

Because now she knew. Knew what it was to give her body and soul to the man who'd long ago stolen her heart. Knew what it was to realize he'd *never* feel for her half of what she felt for him. Knew what it was to be forced to finally, *finally* let go of her silly, childish dreams.

CHAPTER 22

After dropping Becky's borrowed dress and shoes outside Sam's door, Eliza turned toward her bedroom. She'd made it to her own door when her cell phone blared to life.

Glancing at the screen, she grimaced. Considered not answering. And then remembered when the chief of staff called, not answering wasn't an option.

"Hey, Dad," she said without preamble, her hand automatically seeking the comfort of her locket. "It's late. Is everything okay?"

"You tell me." He sounded impatient.

What's new? He always sounds impatient.

Taking a deep breath, she reminded herself he had a very important job. And chances were good he was calling in the capacity of that job and not in the capacity of his role as her father.

"What do you mean?" She frowned unseeingly at her door, trepidation making her heart kick up a notch.

"A report just came across my desk. Apparently, that D.O.D. computer hacker— What was her name?" Over the airwaves, Eliza could hear papers shuffling. "Oh, yes. Here it is. Hannah Blue. Anyway, I just received a report she was caught leaking sensitive information to a rogue group of online vigilantes who are holding a major U.S. pipeline hostage. The FBI apprehended her there in Chicago earlier this evening, but she managed to escape custody and rode away on the back of a souped-up motorcycle after an all-out Wild West shootout."

Her heart went from a fast trot to a full gallop. With their plan hinging on them getting to the Lone Star State incognito, and then pulling off the mother of all cons by posing as feds, she *couldn't* bring her father into the know now.

He was the president's right-hand man, after all. He took the job of protecting Madam President *very* seriously. And the very *last* thing the president would want was her personal fast-action response team getting embroiled in a situation involving a suspected criminal conspirator.

With that certainty burning in her brain, she went against her honest nature and chose willful ambiguity. "Was anyone hurt?"

"One of the agents took a round to the foot. But it was only a graze. He'll be fine," her father reported. And then, in typical Leonard Meadows fashion, pressed forward before she could form a response. "Isn't Hannah Blue the same woman the Knights brought in to help bring down that Russian misinformation ring last year? Wasn't she the one on the phone that night when you called and begged me to set up a sit-down with the head of the FBI?"

"She was."

"So am I to assume it was Black Knights Inc. who helped her flee from the authorities tonight?"

"You know assuming things rarely works out well for anyone, Dad," she said evasively.

A deep, resounding quiet echoed from the other end of the call. It highlighted how loudly her blood pounded between her ears.

Her father was a wily sonofagun. One didn't make it as far as he had in political life without being whip-smart, uncannily shrewd, and in possession of the rare ability to sniff out a lie.

She nearly jumped out of her skin when he finally spoke. "Are you saying it *wasn't* BKI who absconded with Miss Blue?"

Instead of answering the question, she posed one of her own. "If we had an FBI fugitive in our midst, don't you think I'd have called you to report on the situation?"

"I would *hope* so, young lady." His voice boomed through the phone.

The little girl in her, the one who'd always been a little afraid of him, wanted to curl into a ball on the floor. "But I didn't get the details on Agent Grace Beacham's situation until you all had secreted her away somewhere safe."

"I called you as soon as we got a handle on things," she insisted and wanted to add *which is the same thing I'm doing now*. Instead, she slyly changed the subject. "And it's Agent Jackson now. Remember? I told you she and Major Jackson got married."

Once again, silence reigned from the other side of the call. And once again, she was left to listen to the rhythmic *woosh-woosh-woosh* of her own blood rushing through her veins.

She was about to lose her mind *and* her bravado, just blurt out the truth and ease her guilty conscience, when her father finally spoke up. "So I'm supposed to believe it's coincidence this Blue woman made her escape on the back of a motorcycle and all the men working at BKI *ride* motorcycles?"

"How about this, Dad. I'll have Ozzie look into these charges you've leveled against her. He might be able to find something the feds overlooked. If he does, you'll be the first person I call."

She was a master of conversational roundabouts. She'd learned from the best.

"Don't bother." The two words were staccato. "Let the FBI do their jobs. I don't want the Knights sticking their noses into this and bringing attention to themselves if there's no need for it."

"Okay." She waited a tick before asking, "Is there anything else?"

When he paused again, she worried he'd continue to poke and prod. But all he said was, "That's it for now. Get some sleep, Eliza. You sound tired."

Before she could sign off, the line went dead.

"Love you too, Dad," she whispered despite the disconnected call. "Hope you're doing well. Good night."

Sighing heavily, she told herself it was past time she let go of her girlhood fantasy that someday, in some way, she and her father could have a *real* relationship. You know, instead of the pseudo-business association they shared now.

It's a pipedream, Eliza. For a man like him, everyone is just a chess piece to be moved around the board. Including *his own daughter.*

She went to push open her door just as Fisher poked his head from the next room.

His hair was damp and adorably wavy. The five-o'clock shadow that usually darkened his square jaw had been shaved off. And his cheeks were rosy from the heat of his recent shower.

Yes, she shared a wall with Fisher. Yes, she could sometimes hear him playing his harmonica in his room or singing in his bathroom. And yes, she'd spent more nights than she cared to count imagining him sleeping not two feet from her.

That is when he isn't sleeping somewhere else. With someone *else.*

"Couldn't help but overhear." He cocked his head and eyed her closely. "Why didn't ya tell him we have her?"

"Because he would've done what he always does. Protect his own ass. Or, more accurately, the *president's* ass. He'd insist we stop what we're doing and hand her over to the FBI. And since I know there's no way Sam would agree to that, I thought it better all around if Dad stays in the dark until we have it handled. *Then* I'll tell him the truth."

"And *then* he'll know ya lied. What's that goin' to do to your relationship goin' forward?"

She snorted. "What relationship? I'm a cog in his machine, same as all of you."

When he searched her eyes, she tried to make sure her expression didn't reveal how much that knowledge hurt.

She must've failed because he grabbed her hand and tugged her toward him. "Come here."

"Fish, I—"

"Shut up." He stepped from his room and she realized he was naked from the waist up. He had on a pair of black suit pants, but that was all. His feet were as bare as his chest. "I know when someone needs a hug."

Oh, my god.

Before she could protest, her cheek was pressed against his naked chest and his muscled arms had folded her close. His skin was hot and smelled of fresh soap. His breath was warm as he dropped a kiss to the crown of her head. And his words were tender when he said, "I know this probably isn't any consolation, Liza, but he's the one who's missin' out."

There was that nickname again.

Why does it sound so good when he says it?

"You're so much more than a cog in a machine," he added. "If he can't see that, he's a fool."

Don't cry. Don't cry. Don't you dare *cry.*

Maybe it was the adrenaline that'd been burning through her veins all evening. Maybe it was the stress of lying to her father. But whatever the reason, she was incapable of stopping the tears that burned her throat and spilled hotly over her bottom eyelids.

One must've dropped onto Fisher's chest, because suddenly her face was framed in his big hands, and he forced her to look up at him.

At 5'8", she wasn't necessarily *tall* for a woman. But neither was she short. Even still, Fisher seemed to tower above her. Making her feel delicate and dainty in a way that had her questioning her membership in the I Am Woman, Hear Me Roar club.

"Oh, doll face." There was such sympathy in his hazel eyes. "I can't stand the sight of a woman's tears. And a woman I happen to admire?" He shook his head. "It's like a knife to the heart."

"Sorry." She sniffled, feeling foolish and soggy and...*foolish.* She was supposed to be BKI's pillar of poise and professionalism. "I don't know what's wrong with me."

"Ya got a hard and ruthless man for a father." His tone was compassionate. "Makes things difficult, because no matter how old we get, and no matter how much we accomplish, there's still the little kid who lives inside us who just wants the approval of our daddies."

She'd seen Fisher's file. The parts that hadn't been redacted, anyway.

She knew he'd lost both parents as a teen and had been bounced around from family member to family member until he'd graduated high school and joined the Army. But the *details* of what happened were a mystery. One she'd been curious about since the day she joined the Knights.

She searched his eyes but found no answers there. Then, of its own volition, her gaze traveled south, landing on his mouth. On his lips. Those full, firm, *beautifully* shaped lips.

The urge to kiss him was intense. So she did the only thing she could.

She pushed out of his arms and carefully tucked a stray strand of hair behind her ear. "You sound like you're speaking from experience. Was your father hard and ruthless too?"

His expression, usually so open and affable, grew hard and cruel. "The hardest, most ruthless man you could ever meet." There was something in his voice. A sharp edge she'd never heard before. "Thankfully, you'll never have to since he's doin' life without parole down in Pollock Penitentiary."

She blinked, dumbfounded. "He's still alive? I thought he died. Thought *both* your parents were dead."

"Mom's gone." A muscle worked in his newly shaved jaw. "But dear ol' Dad is still kickin'. Leastways he was the last time I checked. Which, to be honest, was probably about ten years ago now."

She desperately wanted to ask what his father was in prison for. But something told her he wouldn't be open to questions on the subject.

"If you're trying to make me see things could be far worse between me and my dad, point proved." She attempted a smile, but it fell flat.

Thankfully, he took pity on her and her pathetic attempt to lighten the mood by giving her a wink. "Nah. Your dad is a dick, if ya don't mind me sayin'. And I can't imagine what it was like growin' up with him."

"I didn't." She shook her head. "After Mom died, he shipped me off to boarding school."

"Like I was sayin', it's his loss if he doesn't want to be part of your life. You're amazin'."

As wonderful as it was to hear him say that, she was careful to temper her joy. "You think *all* women are amazing, Fish."

"True." He shrugged. "I mean, have ya seen y'all? All soft and curvy. But you're the cream of the crop. The cherry on top."

"Well, thank you." She slanted him a look. "But don't think all this kumbaya you and I have been sharing tonight means I'm going to stop calling you on your bullshit or letting you off easy when you're being a lecherous cad."

He chuckled and used a knuckle to tap her chin. The skin tingled at his touch. "Wouldn't have it any other way. Don't know what I'd do if I had to go a whole day without ya takin' a strip out of my hide. Now." He placed his hand on his bedroom door. "I need to finish gettin' ready. Meet ya downstairs in half an hour?"

She nodded, her heart so full of love for him it was a wonder the stupid organ didn't explode out of her chest. "Half an hour." When he went to push the door open, she stopped him with, "Hey Fish? Thank you."

His smile was so genuine, so sweet and warm, she wanted to die. "That's what friends are for, Liza. They got your back when ya feel like things are goin' pear-shaped."

His casual mention of their friendship had her gritting her teeth to keep from breaking down crying again.

As much as she liked the change in their relationship, she couldn't deny it made things more difficult for her. Now she couldn't hide her feelings behind derision and disgust. Now the only thing she had to hide them behind was a mask of practiced nonchalance.

Problem is, I've never had a poker face.

CHAPTER 23

Southpark Hotel, Austin, Texas

Vinny was one of those rare animals who didn't need much sleep. Three, four hours a night was about all he required. Which meant, when his phone rang at 5am, he'd already been awake for over an hour and was on his second cup of the dirty swill the hotel called *coffee*.

He could not *wait* to get back to NYC for a cup of java from his favorite roaster. There was a little café right off Queens Boulevard that brewed beans fresh out of Columbia.

He could almost taste that rich, nutty flavor on his tongue.

"Yo. Tell me it's go-time," he said into the phone in lieu of *hello*.

"You will plant the malware on your next shift," came Yang's immediate reply.

A surge of adrenaline fired through Vinny's blood, joining the caffeine already circulating there.

"Great." He nodded even though Yang couldn't see him. "And then what? What're the next steps?"

"For you? Go to the airport and fly home." A note of impatience had crept into Yang's voice. "Once we have proven to ERCOT there is a weakness in their system, your work in Texas is done."

"Right." Vinny nodded again. "But I mean, what about the money? How am I getting paid?"

He realized he probably should've asked that question a long time ago. But, honestly, he'd just assumed Uncle Sam would cut him a check.

"Once you are back home, you will open an account in the Cayman Islands. I will contact you for the account number. Bishop will deposit the money that is owed to you there."

Sitting back in the desk chair, Vinny's eyes tracked to the window and the intermittent headlights whizzing past on the highway outside. Traffic was light that early in the morning. Yet another reminder why he was itching to get back home.

For a guy who rarely slept, The City That Never Sleeps was perfect. Texas on the other hand? Felt like sleeping was all people did. They talked slow and walked slow and sometimes seemed to *think* slow.

I'll be back by tonight, he told himself. *Back in the land of yellow cabs, the Statue of Liberty, and drunken 4am stops at the kabob shop.*

He was nearly giddy with excitement at the thought of it. And at the thought of the look on his nanna's face when he told her he'd paid off her mortgage.

And yes. He wasn't an idiot. It was weird Yang was talking about him opening an offshore account.

If what he was doing was federally mandated, why wasn't he simply going to be paid the regular way? With a check after all the appropriate taxes had been taken out?

I mean, it's the government. *They always want their pound of flesh.*

Then again, maybe this was how it worked when it came to wearing the cloak of International Men of Mystery. Maybe that's why, when the IRS audited the Pentagon, they couldn't account for 220 billion dollars. Maybe that was because the spooks used that money to clandestinely pay off their assets.

"Okay." He pushed up from the desk so he could pace. He needed an outlet for the adrenaline/caffeine high. "I'll sneak into the control room during the shift change. The engineers always gather around the coffee station to gossip and fill each other in on the plant's status. I'll pretend to go around emptying trash cans and mopping the aisles and use their distraction to plant the malware."

"Very good." For the first time ever, Vinny thought he heard a note of excitement in Yang's voice. "Thank you, Vinny. We could not have done this without you."

Stopping his pacing, Vinny frowned at the phone lying face-up on the desk.

Why did that sound like a goodbye?

"Aw, don't act like we won't talk again. You still need to call for that account number, right?"

His momentary paranoia disappeared when Yang's answer was prompt. "Of course. Good luck this morning."

"No luck needed, baby," he boasted, once more imagining how his life would change in the weeks and months to come. "It's all skill."

Yang made a noncommittal sound and then the line went dead, leaving him to fish his suitcase out from beneath the bed.

There was a skip in his step as he packed his clothes. Just as soon as he uploaded that malware, he planned to bid an immediate and not-so-fond farewell to Texas.

New York City, here I come!

CHAPTER 24

Somewhere over Missouri, 40,000 feet up

Flying on private jets came with a few perks.

One, no security lines or need to check luggage through metal detectors. Two, a more direct route to their destination because they didn't have to follow the flight paths dictated to the commercial boys. Three—and probably the most underrated of all the benefits—private aircraft flew higher than their public counterparts, which allowed their occupants the rare wonder of enjoying clear, cloudless, awe-inspiring skies.

Truly, Sam had seen some beautiful shit in his life. He'd watched the sun rise over the "Rainbow Mountains" in China. The flowing red, yellow, and blue stripes of the craggy crests were the result of sedimentary materials laying down over time. But the effect didn't look scientific. It looked magical. And when those peaks were hit by the first rays of light? The colors were so bright they were almost blinding.

He'd hiked the ten miles to Havasu Falls near Grand Canyon National Park so he could swim in the beautiful blue waters that spewed from the orange rocks. And as he'd floated on his back in the pool at the bottom of the falls, he'd watched the moon slide over the sun. A total solar eclipse that'd turned the sandstone to blood-orange and the waters cerulean.

In the Land of the Midnight Sun, deep inside the Abisko National Park, he'd lain on his back in his sleeping bag while reindeer foraged around him and the swirling green, purples, and pinks of the northern lights danced and undulated above.

But this night sky out the windows of the tiny jet? So moonless and black and glittering with the diamond brightness of thousands of distant stars? Well, it ranked high on his list of natural wonders.

He amended his thoughts when his eyes drifted over to his seatmate.

But not as high as Hannah.

Becky had lent her a plain black dress, which Hannah had belted at her waist. It allowed the skirt to hang loose and flutter prettily around her calves. The shoes she'd borrowed had low heels and straps across the top of her feet that accentuated the delicate turn of her ankles. And she'd twisted her purple hair into a messy bun, eschewing her usual heavy-handed cat-eye makeup and ruby-red lip for a swipe of Eliza's mascara and a dollop of lip gloss.

She looked very put-together and professional. But if he was being honest, he preferred her hipster/punk rock style to this pretty, toned-down version. The tattered jeans and ratty Vans suited her. And he couldn't wait to put all this behind them so he could take her home and watch her transform herself back into the Hannah he'd been dreaming of for the past six months.

Speaking of my dreams...

They hadn't done the reality of the woman justice. She was far sexier, far *lustier* than even his wildest fantasies. And as she slept with her head rested against the side of the fuselage, he drank in her pretty profile.

High cheekbones, long lashes, and the most piquant little chin. So ethereal and elf-like. A otherworldly creature sprung to life and snoring softly.

The urge to pull her into his arms was strong. But he didn't dare wake her. She'd been put through the damn wringer and there was more fuckery to deal with yet.

He blamed the weight of her situation and their mad dash to Texas on the distance he'd sensed in her after they'd had sex. It hadn't been overt. She hadn't told him, *"Thanks for the O's, now fuck on off."* But when he'd asked to join her in the shower, instead of answering with an enthusiastic *yes*, she'd slanted him a side-eye and said, *"You know if we shower together, we're going to end up having more sex and be late for our flight."* And when he'd wrapped his arms around her waist as she'd stood at his bathroom vanity twisting her hair atop her head, instead of smiling at his reflection, she'd swatted at his arm and scolded him for being a *big, bearded distraction.*

Give the woman a break, he told himself now. *She's not used to life on the edge. She needs space. Room to breathe and process everything that's happening to her.*

Instead of leaning over and pressing a kiss to her pulse-point as every cell in his body urged him to do, or rubbing a thumb over her tender bottom lip to see if it was really as soft as he remembered, or bringing her fingers to his mouth so he could drop a kiss onto the tip of each one, he satisfied himself with simply watching her.

Watching as her chest rose and fell. As her mouth opened slightly on a particularly noising inhale. As her thick lashes fluttered before her eyes tracked back and forth behind her delicately veined eyelids.

His heart swelled at the thought of her lost in a soft, sensuous dream, an escape from her reality. It swelled further when she shifted and her hand landed on his thigh, palm up.

Careful not to wake her, he threaded his fingers through hers. Reveling in the contrast of their skin tones—his so sun kissed and golden, hers so pale and perfect. And he was delighted by the difference in their sizes. Her hand looked tiny inside his own.

But Hannah was no girl. As much he'd tried to convince himself she was so he wouldn't act on the lust that'd been riding him hard since the moment she walked back into his life, there was no denying Hannah Blue was *all* woman. All sweet curves and deliciously hot passion, with a mouth that was mind-bendingly talented and absolutely *made* for sin.

He replayed the moment she'd sucked his heated, straining head between her lips and felt himself grow instantly hard. Since the last thing he wanted was to spend the rest of the flight with a pup tent in his pants, he shook away the erotic imagery and went back to cataloging her features.

The little mole next to her collarbone. The way her eyebrows winged up at the ends. How small and delicate her ears were.

I'm happy, he thought. Not content. Not comfortable. But *happy.*

It was a novel sensation. And considering the trouble she was still in, considering how many unknowns still lay ahead of them, the emotion felt misplaced. Or, at the very least, mistimed.

Then, something Boss had once said came screaming back to him. *"If you're with the right person, even the bad times feel good."*

The look of love on Boss's face as he'd stared at his wife had been so poignant and intense, Sam had been nearly staggered by a thunderbolt of envy.

Envy and the undeniable truth of why his own marriage had failed.

He'd *never* looked at Chloe the way Boss looked at Becky. And he'd *never* felt like Chloe made the bad times good.

But Hannah did.

She always had.

Even back when she'd been a metal-mouthed twerp and he'd been dating her sister, anytime he'd found himself around her, he'd been smiling.

He should've guessed about the Jolly Ranchers. He should've *known* it was her and not Candy who'd sneakily slipped his favorite treat into his pocket, because Hannah was the thoughtful one. The kind one. The generous and impish and sassy and *wonderful* one.

The *most* wonderful woman he'd ever known, in fact, and—

Holy shit! Am I in love with Hannah?

He tried to dismiss the idea.

Sure, he liked her. Sure, he was absolutely *panting* with lust for her. Sure, she challenged him and made him laugh and *got* him in a way no one else did, but that wasn't love, was it? It was friendship and affection and—

Fuck. I'm in love with Hannah.

He suddenly knew it as surely as he knew the shape and feel of his trusty Glock. As surely as he knew the White Sox were in desperate need of a good DH if they had any hope of making it to the playoffs. As surely as he knew that even though the night sky was as dark as pitch, the sun in all its golden glory *was* going to rise in the east in less than an hour.

"Mmm." Hannah turned toward him in her sleep. Her head finding its way to his shoulder. Her hand falling over his chest. Over the heart that now beat solely for her.

He loved smelling his shampoo in her hair. Loved the little purring snore that sounded over the steady *hum* of the plane's engines. Loved *her*.

Was completely, totally, *madly* in love with her. Little Hurricane Hannah. His fellow Coen brothers fan. His sidekick. The bohemian yin to his more conventional yang.

"Mmm," she hummed again and then abruptly sat up, blinking blearily.

Her fingers slipped from his so she could push a recalcitrant strand of hair from her face. He was shocked by how bereft he felt without her touch.

"I fell asleep." It was a statement. But the little upward lilt at the end made it sound like a question.

"You did." He grabbed the travel mug of coffee he'd tucked into the pocket on the back of the seat in front of him and took a drink he didn't really want. He needed the distraction, a moment to look anywhere but into her dark eyes because he was scared his recent revelation would show all over his face.

"Did I snore?" She wrinkled her nose and glanced toward the other side of the plane where Fisher and Eliza sat dozing.

"It was more of a low rumble," he assured her. "Like a kitten getting its belly rubbed."

The look she sent him shouted her skepticism. "Cesar says I sound like I'm choking on a fish bone."

He grinned. "What are best friends for if not to exaggerate our flaws?"

"True," she conceded and then lifted her arms over her head in a long stretch.

He used the opportunity to employ a little tactical breathing. He *had* to get his heart rate under control or he was afraid the silly organ was going to beat right out of his chest. And then she'd be all, *"What's your heart doing sitting on the armrest, Sam?"* And he'd have to admit, *"The damn thing just wants to be close to you, Hannah."*

"How close are we?" She glanced out the window at the moonless night.

"'Bout halfway would be my guess." Could she hear the heavy thud of his heart? The huskiness in his voice?

"Only halfway?" She shuddered and scooted down in her seat so she could lean her temple against his shoulder again. "I'm going back to sleep then. When I'm sleeping I don't have to think about being a fugitive."

"It's gonna be okay." He bit the inside of his cheek to keep from blurting,

I'm gonna move heaven and earth to make sure *it's okay because I'm head over heels in love with you, you adorable, wonderful, crazy-making woman.*

"I hope you're right." Her uneasiness made her voice thready. "I just want this to be over. To go back to my quiet life."

"Quiet life? You work for the D.O.D. You live with a drag queen. I don't think anyone would look at your life and call it *quiet.*"

She pushed up from his shoulder and the low sound she made in the back of her throat was one of despair. "I was *shot* at tonight, Sam." Her jaw worked like she was trying to break the words instead of say them. "I'm about to go sneak into a state-run power plant, which I'm pretty sure is a felony. And I've dragged you and your friends"—she hitched her chin toward Fisher and Eliza—"into this mess with me."

"Don't worry 'bout us, sweetheart." He brushed back the strand of hair that kept falling from her bun. "We do this sorta thing all the time. Just another day at the office for us."

She shuddered. "I don't know how you do it. I'm a damned wreck."

"You get used to it. And it's not like this all day, every day. It's mostly boring, boring, boring interrupted by brief stints of balls to the wall."

"No, thank you." She shook her head before tucking it back onto his shoulder. And then her next words cut into him like tiny blades. "You can keep that life to yourself. I want no part of it."

His heart had been floating like a damn helium balloon since he realized he was in love with her. Now it sank like a lead anchor.

It took a special kind of woman to love a fighting man. He'd assumed Hannah was that kind of woman.

Was I wrong?

Something Chloe had said when they'd been sitting across from each other at the divorce proceedings echoed in his head.

"What did you expect, Sam? That I was just supposed to be fine on my own while you were out doing god knows what? That I was just supposed to keep a stiff upper lip even though I was scared to death that any day I was going to wake up to a knock on my door? That I wasn't supposed to have a shoulder to cry on?"

If he loved Hannah—and he knew he did just like he knew his name was Samuel James Harwood—then the last thing he wanted was to subject her to the kind of life that would make her miserable. To be the reason she cried into her pillow at night instead of waking up smiling every morning. To expect her to be fine with the danger and riskiness and uncertainty that went hand-in-hand with the life path he'd chosen for himself.

For a moment there, his future had bloomed before him like a flower, unfurling with possibilities. Now it was curled into a tight bud, bound by the contract he'd signed and the duty he owed Madam President.

He took another sip of coffee, but it didn't wash away the bitterness in his throat. Or the pain in his heart.

CHAPTER 25

Thousand Air Private Airport, Austin, Texas

As the little jet taxied off the runway toward the chain-link fence surrounding the small, private airport, Fisher slowly came awake and blinked blearily at the world outside his window.

The sun was beginning to show its face, the first golden rays peeking over the horizon and highlighting the Texas terrain. A stand of Mesquite trees was visible to the west. To the east he could see the Austin city skyline. And for some reason, that old James Taylor song, "Sweet Baby James," came to mind.

His fingers drifted to the harmonica in his pocket. He could imagine how he'd fold his hands to get the right notes, how he'd position his mouth to play the tune.

He might've given in to the urge, but he heard Hannah moan and come awake across the aisle. Behind him, Eliza did the same.

The private jet was equipped to transport six passengers. It had two sets of side-by-side seats on the left side of the aircraft and two single seats on the right.

Sam and Hannah had chosen the side-by-side option. But upon boarding, Eliza had been quick to snag a single seat and he'd been left to either grab the only other single seat in front of her or plant his sorry ass in one of the two seats situated behind Sam and Hannah.

Since there'd have been no way to ignore the canoodling pair had he chosen option B, he'd gone with option A. But that meant, from the corner of his eye, he could still see the moment Sam brushed a strand of hair behind Hannah's ear.

Sliding the couple a quick glance, he wasn't surprised to find Sam's eyes glued to Hannah's face.

Despite Sam's assertations to the contrary, it'd been obvious ever since Hannah had come back into his life, that Sam was smitten with her. Now, Fisher figured that infatuation had morphed into something more. Something bigger. Deeper. *Finer.*

Something that looked a lot like love.

Reckon we'll be havin' another weddin' soon, he thought, noting only the slightest pinprick of jealousy.

He was glad for his friend. Truly he was. Samuel Harwood was as solid and true as an old oak tree. No matter how hard you leaned on him, he stayed firm and straight. And absolutely *no* one deserved happiness more.

And yet…Fisher couldn't help wondering when it would be *his* turn.

"Mac and Delilah are already here." Eliza's voice pulled him from his dark thoughts and he tilted his head so he could get a better look out the window.

Sure enough. There was Bryan "Mac" McMillan, the former FBI investigative specialist turned original Black Knight turned Texas cattleman. And there was his wife, the infamous Delilah, owner of the Knights' favorite watering hole.

The pair split their time between their ranch there in the Lone Star State and Delilah's biker bar back in Chi-Town. And it was lucky they'd been in Texas when Fisher had called asking if they could help secure transportation from the airport to the power plant.

The happy couple stood side by side beyond the chain link fence. Delilah looking as lovely as an old Hollywood starlet with her waves of shiny, auburn hair and her dramatic hourglass figure. And Mac was looking like the Marlboro Man in his cowboy hat and Carhartt coat.

Fisher quietly sang a few bars of "Sweet Baby James"—*"There is a young cowboy who lives on the range"*—as he watched Mac's eyes, shadowed by the brim of his hat, track their progress while their pilot parked the plane.

He must've made a sound or something, because Eliza poked her head around his seat. "Hey? You okay?"

"Mmm." He nodded, pointing through the window. "Just thinkin' how good those two look."

"How good those *two* look or how good *Delilah* looks?"

"I mean…" He let his sentence dangle and shrugged innocently. That's what Eliza expected of him, after all.

And right on cue…

"You're such a cad." She rolled her eyes and unclasped her seat belt when the high-pitched *ding-dong* of the PA system told her it was safe to do so.

"Ya left out the *lecherous* part," he told her as he unhooked his own seat belt and stood to stretch his legs.

Flying in a private plane was a sight more comfy than flying coach on a commercial airline. But at nearly six and a half feet, there wasn't an airplane built to *truly* accommodate him.

Except for maybe the back of a C-5.

"The lecherous part is understood," she sniffed, pulling the strap of her oversized purse across her chest.

Dudded up in their black suits and with a pair of freshly shaved faces, both Fisher and Sam looked nothing like their usual selves. But Eliza? She was the same as always.

Her pantsuit was tailored to a T. Her button-up shirt was crisp and wrinkle-free. And her dark hair was pulled back into a sleek, professional-looking ponytail.

She always seemed so cool and untouchable. Which was why he battled the constant urge to touch her. To muss her. To see exactly what lay beneath her polished façade.

"I'm fine with assumin' the lecherous part is understood if we can also assume the charmin' part is understood," he told her. When she frowned her confusion, he explained. "*Charmin'* lecherous cad." He pointed to himself.

Her lips twisted. Then she shrugged. "I think that's fair."

He widened his eyes. "Was that a compliment?"

"Don't get used to it." Her lips flattened into a straight line. "I've no doubt you'll make sure any opportunities I have to compliment you are few and far between."

He bit the inside of his cheek to keep from grinning. "Ya have the most amazin' ability to make an insult sound nice."

"And you have the most amazing ability to annoy the hell out of me." She opened her mouth to add something more. Before she could utter a syllable, however, the door to the cockpit opened.

Their pilot, a former Air Force guy who'd decided he'd make a lot more money as a private air jockey, announced, "Ladies and gentlemen. We have successfully reached our destination. Thank you for flying Ricky's friendly skies. I'll leave the meter running until your return."

He tipped an imaginary hat as he opened the door to the fuselage and watched the steps unfurl. The cool morning air mixed with the scent of jet fuel as it wafted into the plane.

"Ladies first." Fisher waved for Eliza to proceed him up the aisle.

She cocked an eyebrow as she passed him. "What a gentleman."

His nostrils flared as he got a whiff of her fresh, crisp perfume. "Nah. Just want to watch your ass as we disembark. It's lookin' mighty fine in those slacks."

She turned and pointed a stern finger at his nose. "And there it was. The last comment you're allowed to make until we get to the power plant."

He mimed zipping his lips and nodded obediently. Then watched the haughty twitch of her hips as she moved toward the exit.

He *liked* the added level of flirtation and friendliness their relationship had taken on ever since his confession in the kitchen. And if the slight smile she wore as she stepped out of the plane was anything to go by, she was enjoying it too.

Will wonders never cease.

CHAPTER 26

Bleeker Creek Power Station

The sky was bluebird blue. Not a cloud in sight. And the gentle breeze blowing the branches of the trees wasn't bitter like it was in Chicago. It was warm and moist and filled with the promise of spring.

Hannah had been given a black, wool coat to wear over her borrowed dress, but even this early in the morning, she didn't need it.

Maybe I should get the hell out of Chi-Town, she thought as Fisher turned into the short drive leading to the plant's gated entrance. *I could get used to sixty degrees in February.*

Of course, as soon as she considered the idea, she discarded it. She couldn't leave her parents. It was bad enough Candy made little effort to see them with any sort of regularity. If Hannah took off and couldn't make their weekly Sunday dinners? They'd be devastated.

Plus, there was Cesar.

She didn't know how much longer they were going to be roommates. If things kept progressing with Pete, she had no doubt her best friend would be walking down the aisle within the year. But even if the two of them weren't living together, the idea of being a thousand miles away from him nearly made her green with homesickness.

She couldn't imagine watching *Queer Eye* with anyone else. And not meeting up for a gossip-fest on Taco Tuesdays or a weekly life check-in on Flirtini Fridays?

Can't do it. I'm a Windy Citizen 'til the day I die.

Which wasn't a bad thing, really. She adored Chicago.

Loved the hardworking, blue-collar gruffness of the citizens. The seemingly limitless expanse of Lake Michigan, especially in the summertime when the water matched the sky. The classic notes of blues and jazz that echoed out of the bars. And the sound of the crowds at Cominsky Park when summer ball was in full swing—the ballpark's name had been changed to Guaranteed Rate Field years earlier, but no Southsider worth their salt would ever call it that.

In fact, the only drawback to the City of Big Shoulders—besides the awful, endless winters—was that it was also home to one Mr. Samuel Harwood.

It was going to be absolute *hell* knowing he was a cab ride away but also knowing he'd never be hers. The photos of his wedding proved it. When he pictured his future, it wasn't with someone like her.

She wanted to crawl into bed and pull the covers over her head for a week. A *year*. But she couldn't give in to the bout of ice-cream binging, no-showering depression she deserved. Not when she had an electrical grid to save and her good name to clear.

Fisher brought the car they'd been furnished courtesy of the couple who'd met them at the airport to a stop.

Hannah had been surprised to learn Sam and his teammates weren't the first people to work as private defense contractors out of the old menthol cigarette factory. Apparently, before Sam's crew took over, there'd been another squad of guys who'd called Goose Island home.

Included in that original group was one Bryan "Mac" McMillan who'd married Delilah Fairchild, the owner of Chicago's most famous biker bar. And the love in the couple's eyes as they'd stared adoringly at each other had been so sweet and hot she'd had to look away. It'd just driven home the fact that no one had ever looked at *her* that way. And now, it was crystal clear the one man she'd always dreamed might do exactly that, never would.

"Howdy." Fisher rolled down his window, pulling her from her depressing thoughts. He flashed his fake credentials at the guard. "I'm Agent Mulder. These are Agents Waller and Moretti." He hooked a thumb at Sam who sat in the back with Hannah and then jerked his chin over to Eliza, who rode in the passenger seat.

He and Ozzie had thought it the height of wit to take the names of the agents who'd apprehended Hannah and use those names as their fake identities. She didn't really get the joke. But maybe that was because she was in no mood for levity.

"We're here on urgent business with Miss Violet"—again, a play on Hannah's *real* last name of Blue that she didn't find all that funny—"who works for ERCOT."

The security guard grabbed Fisher's badge, studying it carefully. "FBI?" Disbelief colored his voice.

Hannah held her breath, wondering if the fakes Ozzie had 3D printed looked real or sus.

I mean, they seem identical to the ones the feds flashed in my face last night. But it wasn't like I took time to study them.

Holy hell, had that just been last night? Her flight from custody felt like ten years ago. So much had happened since.

A little sigh of relief hissed out of her when the guard handed back the badge and, instead of reaching for the gun he kept in the holster slung low around his waist, he simply said, "What's this about, Agent Mulder?"

He had a thick, Texas twang that made *about* sound like it had three syllables instead of two.

"That's classified." Hannah wouldn't have thought Fisher capable of sounding so authoritative. But he was doing a bang-up job of channeling the *real* Agent Mulder. "It's a matter of national security," he added. "We need to speak with whoever is in charge here."

"That'd be Teddy Gonzales." The guard waved over his shoulder in the general direction of the plant. "He's the lead engineer for third shift."

"Get him on the horn, then." Fisher made a hurry-up-time's-a-wastin' motion with his hand. "Tell him we need to speak with him ASAP."

The guard hesitated, his eyes traveling over the plain black sedan Mac and Delilah had given them, coming to a stop on the license plate bolted to the front bumper.

It was a government plate. Hannah had noted that when Mac had handed Fisher the keys. And she was more than a little curious how the Black Knights had gotten their hands on a government car.

Or maybe it *wasn't* a government car? Maybe it was a regular car with government plates?

Either way, all she could say was that Sam and his coworkers had an amazing ability to conjure out of thin air whatever they needed. Convincing-looking laminated ERCOT badge with her smiling face on it? No problem. A last-minute private flight from Chicago to Texas? Easy breezy lemon squeezy. A shiny black sedan with government plates? Ain't no thing but a chicken wing.

As the security guy made his way to the guardhouse, a thought occurred and her blood ran cold. "What if he calls the local FBI office to verify your identity?" she whispered because Fisher still had his window rolled down.

Eliza answered quietly. "Ozzie's monitoring all calls in and out of the facility. If someone here tries to check our credentials, he'll be the one to answer and confirm."

"Oh." Hannah shook her head. "Wow. You guys think of everything."

"Not our first rodeo." Sam's grin was cool and confident.

"Right." She tried to channel some of his mojo by slowing the racing of her heart. It didn't work. Her adrenaline was too high. "And I repeat, I don't know how you guys do this day in and day out. I'm about to jump out of my skin."

Something flickered across Sam's face. Before she could study it, the guard returned. "Teddy's on his way." His drawl drew out the sentence. "Be here in a jiff."

"Appreciate it." Fisher gave a curt nod and then rolled up the window.

After the security guard returned to the guardhouse, Hannah sat back and closed her eyes, trying to center herself. To imagine what would happen next. *To get a damn grip.*

But with her eyes closed, her other senses heightened. She could smell the sweet, earthy scent of Sam's aftershave. Hear when he adjusted his shoulder holster. Feel when he shifted slightly in his seat.

It'd been like that from the beginning. Her...*awareness* of him. But after making love with him, it was ten times worse and—

"Showtime, folks." Fisher's voice cut off her musings.

She opened her eyes to see a white utility truck parked on the opposite side of the gate. A man in jeans, cowboy boots, and a blue polo shirt with the words Bleeker Creek Power stitched over his left breast hopped out.

He was dark-haired and dark-eyed. She would clock him in at around fifty. But it was hard to tell for sure since he had that sunbaked look of a guy who spent a lot of time outside.

The guard opened the gate wide enough to let the lead engineer through. And she wouldn't have thought her heart could pound any faster. But watching the man in the polo get closer proved her wrong.

"Everyone ready?" Fisher asked when the engineer stopped a foot from the front bumper.

She wanted to scream *no!* Cesar was the performer, not her. She had no clue how to be anyone but herself. She had no clue how to fake—

The question had been rhetorical. The Knights opened their doors and exited the sedan. And she was left with no recourse but to follow suit.

Because her blood was running high, the cool air felt like heaven against her exposed cheeks. If she'd had her way, she would've taken a moment to breathe deeply and compose herself, but Fisher was already making introductions.

She gingerly made her way around to the front of the car when he mentioned her name. *Er...*her *fake* name. Automatically, she reached to shake the engineer's hand.

It was only after Gonzales gripped her fingers she worried she'd made a mistake. Could he feel how badly she trembled?

Get your shit together, Hannah! she berated herself. *Don't ruin this! Too much is on the line!*

"What's this about?" The curiosity on Gonzales's face included an undercurrent of alarm.

"Mr. Gonzales, we have reason to believe ya have an employee workin' here who's been tasked by the Chinese government with gainin' access to your system. Their plan is to insert malware that will cause a deregulation of the flow of electricity." Fisher still employed his stern, authoritative tone.

Gonzales blinked. "No." He shook his head and the morning sun glinted off his dark hair. "I know this system inside and out. If anyone tries to insert malicious code, it automatically shuts the whole plant down."

"That's the way it's *supposed* to work," Hannah piped up because it was her cue. "But this plant is using an outdated operating system. It has a weakness that *can* be exploited, and the Chinese have found it."

"How?" Gonzales's eyes were keen with intelligence.

"There's been a recent uptick in cyberspace of surrogate criminal actors who work on behalf of nation-states. They're essentially cyber hit men for hire and they've been hacking into various infrastructures within our country, looking for weaknesses and ways to cripple us. They found one of those weaknesses here at Bleeker Creek."

A muscle ticked in his jaw. "I mean, how is the malware supposed to work?"

"It's a two-fold approach. First, it'll attack your generator by connecting it to the grid out of phase. Which, as you're aware, will lead to extreme torque and cause the machine to break down. Secondly, and this is the most insidious part, once it's in your system, it'll use the backdoor codes your plant uses to communicate with the other plants hooked up to the grid to gain access to *their* operating systems—a sort of Trojan Horse attack—which will start a chain reaction of cascading failures."

Gonzales sputtered. "Y-you're talking about a statewide blackout."

"Yes, Mr. Gonzales." She was glad he understood the severity of the situation. "That's exactly what I'm talking about."

"But who?" He looked over his shoulder as if the traitor might be listening in. "Who's working for the Chinese?"

"That's the thing." She shook her head. "We don't know. Could be a recent hire. Could be someone who's been here for years. The only thing we know for sure is that the malware is supposed to be implanted soon. Like, within the next twelve to twenty-four hours."

"Jesus," Gonzales wheezed. Then he crossed himself and apologized for the blasphemy. "How do we stop it?" He glanced from Hannah to the others. "Take the plant offline?"

"I know where the weakness is. If you'll allow me access to your system, I can program a patch that'll stop the malware in its tracks. It shouldn't take more than half an hour. You won't even have to slow down production."

Gonzales's eyes pinged down to the ERCOT badge clipped to the collar of her borrowed dress. For a second, she thought she saw hesitation in his eyes. Then he glanced over his shoulder. "Evan, open the gate. Let these good folks through."

"Right away, Mr. Gonzales." The security guard hit a button and the gate rattled on its track.

"If you'll follow me." Gonzales gestured for them to get back in their car. "I'll show you the way."

Fisher bobbed his head in thanks and then made a circular motion with his finger, telling the group to load up.

Hannah had barely slipped into her seat and secured her belt when Fisher laid on the gas. And, just like that, they were in.

Holy toad-eating fucknuts, she thought. *I can't believe it was that easy.*

Either she snorted her disbelief or Sam was reading her mind again. He reached over to pat her leg. "Most people believe whatever they're seeing with their own two eyes and hearing with their own two ears."

She lifted her hand to show how much it trembled. "I thought for sure I'd ruined things when I shook his hand. He had to have felt me shaking."

"You did great," Eliza assured her. "Hopefully convincing him to let us in was the hard part and fixing the flaw in their system will be a cakewalk by comparison."

Hannah took in the different parts of the combined-cycle natural gas power plant as they drove down the length of the sprawling complex. The first thing she saw was the gas turbine. It was 300 tons of compressors and diffusers and combustion systems. Next came the generator, where the magic of converting mechanical energy to electrical energy happened. Then, there was the bus duct, which took the electricity from the generator to a transformer that was hooked up to the grid. And finally, the control room.

The latter didn't look like much. Just a large metal building with parking out front and a single door in the center of its south face. Looking at its unassuming exterior, one would never know it housed all the high-tech equipment used to monitor and control every aspect of the power plant's operation.

When she exited the car, she half expected to smell the rotten egg aroma associated with natural gas. But the only scents to tickle her nose were the slightly chemical smells of industrial lubricant and the burned-metal aroma of mechanical processes.

It was the gas companies supplying gas to residential homes and businesses who added a chemical called mercaptan to their product to ensure their customers could always tell if they had a gas leak. Natural gas in its true state, like what was used at the plant, was completely odorless.

"You got this," Sam said when she swallowed audibly.

"Right." She screwed up all her courage and pushed forward toward Gonzales, who stood by the door. She hoped her straight back and high head looked like confidence instead of an overcompensation for a rabbiting heart.

When she stepped inside the control room, she found it was just as she'd imagined. Filled with screens scrolling through various data sets, workstations with assorted control panels, and the unflattering florescent overhead lights that seemed standard to all industrial and institutional buildings.

There were three plant employees at various stations in the room. They didn't attempt to hide their curiosity as their gazes traveled over the group of new arrivals. But Gonzales waved them away with a grim sounding, "I'll fill y'all in later. Right now just watch your stations. Make sure we're not seeing any anomalies."

Turning to Hannah, he gestured wide with his arm. "If you'll follow me, Ms. Violet. I'll show you where you can access the system."

Her borrowed shoes were a size too big and rubbed painfully on her injured pinky toe as she tailed the engineer to a workstation in the corner. He pulled out a rolling chair with worn upholstery and a squeaky wheel. Then indicated she should sit.

"Thank you." She gratefully sank into the chair, taking the weight off her problematic foot. "Like I said outside, this shouldn't take long."

"Sure thing." He bobbed his chin as she flexed her fingers and began the task of…saving Texas.

Within seconds, she was in the virtual world of algorithms, arrays, and functions, and the real world around her faded. She didn't smell the coffee Gonzales poured into paper cups for Sam and the others. She didn't hear the whispered words he spoke to his team as he went around explaining what was happening. And she didn't see the way every head in the room kept turning her way, checking her progress.

Her entire focus was consumed by the characters on her screen. As her fingers flew across the keyboard, her breathing grew slow and steady. No more nerves. No more shaking hands. No more fluttering heart.

"There you are," she muttered when she found the problem in the program and started patching it up with coded firewalls. Character by character, line by line she shored up the weakness until she'd assured herself there was nothing more she could do.

By the time she finished and pushed back from the keyboard, she wasn't sure if five minutes or five hours had passed. But when she blinked and looked around, she saw Sam had made his way to her side.

He lifted an eyebrow, asking a question without uttering a word.

"It's done." She nodded. "The plant is safe."

"Never doubted you for a minute." He winked and offered a hand to help her rise.

She wondered if he caught her hesitation. Touching him *hurt*. Because there was no ignoring the fact that very soon now she'd probably be touching him for the last time. But eventually she muscled up her moxie and settled her fingers inside his.

"What now?" Gonzales asked once she was on her feet. She curled her fingers into a fist to hold onto the lingering sensation of Sam's touch.

"Our work here is done," Sam said simply. "So we'll leave you to *your* work."

"But what about the traitor? The person working for the Chinese?"

Hannah froze. Right. Because if they really *had* been FBI, surely they'd have been eager to get their hands on the culprit.

Sam was better at subterfuge than she was—*thank goodness*. His answer was immediate. "We'll send in a second team who'll want to go through recent security footage and start interviewing the employees here. Our job today was simply to foil the plan to sabotage the grid."

"Right." Gonzales nodded. Then he made a face. "Would y'all mind sticking around for another couple minutes?"

Good god, no! Hannah wanted to scream. Now that the deed was done, all she could think about was getting the hell out of Dodge.

Texas might be safe, but *she* wasn't. The FBI still considered her persona non grata. And even though she knew Ozzie was looking for proof that someone had planted the evidence against her on her work computer, she'd still feel a million times better if she could *assist* him in that process.

If you want something done right, do it yourself. Right?

That was *especially* true for her when it came to all things techy and hacky.

"The thing is," Gonzales continued, "my shift replacement is due to arrive any minute and she'll need to know what's happened. I figure y'all can explain it better than I can."

"Of course," Sam nodded. "We'd be happy to hang out until she gets here."

Speak for yourself, Hannah thought as she begrudgingly allowed him to escort her toward the others.

Fisher and Eliza were posted up by the coffee station. They casually sipped bitter-smelling java like they had every right to be there and weren't trespassing on government property while impersonating federal agents.

Hannah shook her head when Gonzales offered her a cup. She was jittery enough. The last thing she needed was a belly full of caffeine.

"Probably should cut back myself," he said with a wry smile as he poured himself a full cup. "Doc says it's bad for my blood pressure. But it's one of the few joys in life, you know?"

She smiled because that's what was expected of her. But it felt brittle and thin.

Then her expression turned genuine when the door opened behind her and she thought they were one step closer to heading back to the Windy City.

Except, it wasn't Gonzales's counterpart who walked into the control room. It was a brown-haired man in blue coveralls. He pushed a mop and bucket in front of him.

"Hey Vick," Gonzales said and the custodian stopped to blink in bewilderment at the gathered group.

"It's okay," Gonzales reassured the man. "The FBI is here with this lovely young woman from ERCOT to help us fix a problem in our operating system."

The custodian blinked again.

Something was…*off* about the man. Hannah couldn't put her finger on it. But she sensed it all the same. Like a glitch in the Matrix.

"But I thought…" He started and then changed tactics. "I mean I haven't…" He abruptly stopped himself and shook his head. "Sorry. I'll come back later to mop and empty the trash cans."

Even though he'd only spoken a few sentences, there was no mistaking his thick New York accent. She would guess Long Island? Maybe the Bronx?

What was a guy from New York City doing way down in Texas? And, more importantly, what did he stop himself from saying?

Sam must've picked up on whatever had wiggled her antennae, because before the man could open the door and escape from the control room, he said, "Wait a minute there, Vick. What do you mean you haven't? Haven't *what?*"

"Nothing." Vick swallowed audibly and shook his head. "I mean…I don't know. I was just confused to walk in and see you guys here. I'll get out of your way."

"Hold up." Sam lifted a hand. "I have a coupla questions I'd like—"

That's all he got out before Vick shoved his mop bucket and bolted for the door.

The bucket was heavy and cumbersome. One of those industrial-sized jobs. It hit Sam in the shins, making him lose his balance and go stumbling back into Eliza. Who stumbled into Fisher. Who stumbled into the coffee station, knocking the carafe out of the coffee maker.

It shattered when it hit the concrete floor, sending molten hot java and sharp glass in all directions.

Maybe it was because she was the closest to the custodian. Maybe it was because she was the only one not going down in the long line of human dominoes. Or, more likely, it was because she was sick of feeling like a pawn in the game.

Whatever the reason, Hannah took off after Vick before she could think what a colossally *bad* idea it was.

Bursting through the door, she saw the man darting between parked cars. Her kitten heels clattered against the pavement, but she didn't hear them. Her injured pinky toe cried out in agony, but she didn't feel it. Every ounce of her focus was on the custodian in the coveralls who turned and looked momentarily flabbergasted that it was *her* dogging his heels and not one of the others.

If she was being honest, she too was a little astonished.

It was like a part of her was looking down at herself running like a harridan across the parking lot after a mysterious man and asking, *What in the world do you think you're doing, Hannah? What's your plan once you catch him?*

But she was like a dog chasing after a car. She wasn't thinking about the actual *capture*. She was one-hundred-percent focused on the pursuit. On gaining ground.

"Hannah!" she heard Sam call from behind her.

If she'd been thinking, she would've slowed her roll and let him take over the footrace. He was faster. Stronger. He was freakin' *armed*. But she *wasn't* thinking.

She was acting on instinct. On the need to gain some goddamned control of her life.

Had there been an NFL scout around, she might've been drafted. The way she launched herself through the air, tackling Vick to the ground, was a thing of beauty.

Air rushed out of the man's lungs with a loud *oomph* when she landed on top of him. Her chin bounced off his shoulder—good thing or else it probably would've bounced off the pavement. And her knee hit the ground hard enough to have her wincing in agony.

Maybe it was the pain that brought her to her senses. Or maybe it was simply having caught her quarry that had her snapping back to reality. Either way, she did her best impression of a wrestler, clinging to Vick with all four limbs, when he tried to shake her off him.

"Get off me, you crazy bitch!" he bellowed, somehow managing to twist around in her grip until they were face-to-face.

His dark eyes were bloodshot. His breath was foul with the sour stench of fear. And there was no mistaking the hard tip of the knife that suddenly poked into her side.

Cold dread washed over her, reminding her of the time Candy had pushed her into Lake Michigan in late March.

She leapt up to avoid the blade, but he matched her movement so they gained their footing at the same time. As she faced the custodian, chest heaving from the effort of her mad dash across the parking lot, she noted how the morning light glinted malevolently on the blade clutched tight in his hand.

She went to step back, but his eyes tracked over her shoulder and spied something that caused his nostrils to flare. The next thing she knew, he grabbed her wrist in a cruel grip.

Before she could react, he spun her around, snaked one arm around her waist and used the other to press the tip of his knife into the space between her ribs.

"Hands in the air!" Sam bellowed. He'd skidded to a stop not six feet from them and had assumed a shooter's stance. "Let the woman go and put your hands in the air!"

With his beard gone, she could see the hard muscle ticking in his jaw. His breaths were deep and rapid. And there was no mistaking the fiercely determined gleam in his eye.

Movie-quoting Sam was gone. Love-making Sam was gone. Hell, even baseball-watching Sam was gone.

All that was left was the soldier. The fighter. Sergeant Samuel James Harwood, Marine Raider and marksman extraordinaire.

"Throw down your weapon or the woman gets it!" Vick screamed, his shrill voice making her eardrum rattle.

The blade dug deeper into her side, making her cry out as hot blood seeped from her flank to dampen the fabric of her borrowed dress.

She was going to owe Becky a replacement.

Of course, buying one meant she had to get out of this situation alive. And at the moment, that outcome seemed iffy. The way the custodian was careful to keep her in front of him, he'd left Sam with little to aim at.

Up to that point, Sam hadn't spared her a glance. He'd been zeroed in on the man behind her. Now his gaze shot to her face, and the confusion she read there told her he couldn't see what Vick had in his hand.

"He's got a knife," she whispered and watched the blood drain from his cheeks just as Fisher and Eliza skidded to a stop next to him. Their weapons were up and at the ready.

"I'm on your side!" Vick yelled. "I haven't done anything wrong!"

"If that's true," Sam was quick to counter, "there's no reason not to cooperate. Just step out from behind the woman, drop the blade to the ground, and put your hands in the air."

"No way!" She could feel Vick shaking his head. "The minute I let go of her, you'll shoot me! All you pigs are trigger-happy fucks!"

"Don't know if anyone's ever told you this or not, Vick," Fisher drawled, looking almost bored, "but when ya bring a knife to a gunfight, the odds aren't on your side."

Hannah's heart scrambled around in the cage of her ribs like a wild animal. Her breaths were rapid and shallow, but even still, she didn't seem to be getting enough oxygen.

Why had she run after Vick? Why hadn't she waited on Sam and Fisher to right themselves and give chase? They were trained to deal with bad guys with weapons. She was *not*.

"I'm sorry," she whispered, her eyes begging Sam to forgive her for screwing things up.

"Not your fault, sweetheart." He gave her a wink. No sooner had he finished the gesture than the world exploded.

Or, at least, she *thought* it did.

A loud *boom* cleaved the quiet morning in two. Vick screamed like he'd been shot. And when he stumbled backward, he dragged her with him.

They hit the ground together, the custodian landing on his back, her landing on top of him.

She expected to feel the blade sink into her side. Feel the *pop* of her lung. So she was a little surprised when the next thing she knew Sam was yanking her to her feet.

"Wha—?" was all she managed before he holstered his weapon and ran his hands over her face, down her sides, grimacing when he found the blood soaking through the fabric over her flank.

"How bad is it?" His baby blues were fixed on her face. His voice was so filled with violence, instinct almost had her stumbling back.

"Nothing fatal. Maybe some stitches—" was all she managed before Fisher yelled, "Shit!" He followed that up immediately with, "Fuck, Sam! Ya must've nicked something vital. He's bleedin' like a stuck pig!"

She blinked down to find Fisher straddling Vick's waist, his hands applying pressure to a wound high up on the custodian's chest near his shoulder.

It was then she realized Vick had screamed like he'd been shot because Sam had *shot* him. Sent a slug straight through the shoulder of the arm that'd been holding the knife to her side. Now, the blade lay on the pavement five feet away.

"Should I call 9-1-1?" Gonzales stood in the center of the parking lot, his hand lifted to shade his eyes against the ever-strengthening sun.

His coworkers filled the control room's door behind him, their eyes wide, their expressions ranging from horror to fascination.

"No!" Sam barked. "We'll take him in ourselves and hopefully get some answers outta him along the way. Where's the closest trauma center?"

CHAPTER 27

I-35 South, Fifteen Minutes from Dell Seton Hospital

"**H**ow's he doing?" Eliza yelled from the driver's seat as she sped down the highway at breakneck speeds, honking at cars that didn't get out of the passing lane quickly enough.

Hannah was in the passenger seat. And Sam and Fisher were both crammed into the back with Vick.

"It's slowed!" Sam told Eliza, continuing to apply pressure to the custodian's wound. No. Vick wasn't a custodian. He was a conspirator. A *traitor*. "But he's not outta the woods just yet. Don't let off the gas!" he added.

"Wasn't planning on it!"

Sam felt the car lurch as Eliza put the pedal to the metal.

Vick's cheeks were no longer pink with pain and exertion. They'd taken on a grayish cast. And his lips were so pale they would've blended into the skin of his face were it not for their cracked texture.

"Don't let me die," the man pleaded, fisting the lapel of Sam's suit jacket in his bloody hand.

"You're not gonna die," Sam assured him. "If you'll just keep still and keep that wound from opening up."

Silently, Sam cursed himself for his shitty aim.

He'd been six measly feet from the man, for fuck's sake. His bullet should've gone through meat and gristle and missed anything major.

But his fear for Hannah had made his hands shake. *Him*, Sam Harwood, the man known for his eagle-eyed focus and nerves of steel. He'd been trembling like a newborn colt all because the woman he loved more than life had winced in pain when the knife nicked her side.

I shoulda waited, he silently berated himself. *I shoulda centered my breaths, calmed my heart, and taken my shot when I could guarantee my aim.*

But the instant the custodian had given him an opening, when he'd thought Sam was preoccupied with winking at Hannah, Sam had taken his shot.

Look what that got me! The fucker might die before he gives us the intel we're after!

Sam had known the custodian had answers the minute he walked into the control room. A decade and a half of running spec ops had imbued him with the ability to spot when someone had mischief and mayhem in mind.

And Vick?

Vick had had both.

Lifting his hands away from Vick's chest, he noted the bleeding had almost stopped. *Thank fuck.* Although, he wasn't sure if it was due to Fisher's tourniquet or due to Vick running low on fuel.

Glancing over, he saw Fisher still had his phone out and recording.

Fisher might come off as a fool, what with all his clowning and craziness, but the man had a mind like a steel trap. They could be in the middle of a warzone and he had the amazing ability to keep his wits about him.

This mission was unsanctioned. Which meant they were going to need *proof* for Eliza's father and for Madam President that they'd had cause to come to Texas, impersonate federal agents, and...you know...shoot a man.

Vick and his wackadoo story about the Chinese partnering with the U.S. was that proof.

"Let me see if I have this straight," Sam said. "You were hired by a man named Yang who claimed to work for the Chinese government. And this Yang dude told you he was working jointly with his counterpart here in the U.S. to plant malware inside the Texas power grid. But the aim wasn't to take down the grid. The aim was simply to prove to ERCOT they had a weakness in their system."

"Yes." That one syllable was windy sounding and Vick's subtle nod was more of a twitch.

"And why would they do that? Why not just have the feds go to the powers that be in Texas and say, 'Hey guys, you got yourselves a problem and here's how you fix it'?"

"Yang said the current p-political..." Vick trailed off, wincing with pain. When he reopened them, his pupils nearly eclipsed his irises. A sure sign he was getting close to going lights-out.

Urgency had Sam gritting his next words through his clenched teeth. "Come on, man. Finish what you were saying."

Vick coughed and cried out. "I thought I was on the right side for once!" Hot tears leaked from the corners of his eyes. "I thought I was *helping*."

"You were duped." Sam tried to keep the growing impatience from his tone, but he wasn't sure he was totally successful. "China and the U.S. *do not* engage in joint ventures. And they certainly don't engage in joint ventures on U.S. soil against a U.S. state. But keep going. What were you saying about the political environment?"

"Yang said the current political environment is too fucked. That the Texas government didn't trust the federal government. That Texas would require *proof*."

"And you were supposed to provide that proof. Upload the malware. Expose the weakness. Bada bing, bada boom."

"Yes." Vick nodded...er...*twitched* again.

"So why choose *you*?" Fisher piped up, his eyes on the screen of his phone as he continued to record.

"I know how to c-code." More tears leaked from Vick's eyes. A snot bubble formed in his right nostril and Sam experienced a stab of pity for the poor gullible fuck. "And I'm the right gender and the right color is what Yang said," he finished on a hard sob that popped the snot bubble.

Vick's blood was beginning to dry on Sam's hands, making the skin beneath feel tight and uncomfortable. He ignored it. "What were you offered in return, Vick? What did Yang promise you? I mean, you weren't doing this outta the goodness of your heart."

"T-two million," Vick breathed.

Fisher snorted and Sam let loose with a humorless laugh.

"That shoulda been your *first* clue." He shook his head and noted Eliza had started slowing down to take an exit ramp. "Uncle Sam is a stingy bastard." Then, because Vick's eyes were beginning to roll, he added, "And what about Hannah? How does she fit in to all this?"

"Who?" Vick blink blearily. He wasn't even gray anymore; he was chalk white and panting shallowly. "Who's Hannah?"

Sam gestured over his shoulder. Hannah had turned in her seat so she could watch the goings-on in the back. Her expression was one he recognized, shock mixed with emotional exhaustion mixed with hours-old adrenaline.

He wished he could reassure her they were near the end, that this whole horrible ordeal was just about over. But he didn't have the time.

"The D.O.D cybercrimes specialist who got wind of your little scheme and who was framed for handing over classified information to a ransomware syndicate," he clarified for Vick.

The man lifted his chin, spied Hannah, and blinked in astonishment. "You're...her?"

Hannah made a face. "In the flesh."

The wounded *flesh*, Sam thought, fighting back the urge to peel off her dress and check her knife wound. But she said she was fine. And he had to take her word for it since they currently had bigger fish to fry.

"But...but," Vick sputtered, "Yang said you *escaped* the FBI. Why are you here working with them to..." Vick's eyes grew round as he glanced back at Sam and then over at Fisher. "You're not feds, are you? Who are you? Where are you taking me?"

When he started to struggle, Sam pressed a hand in the center of his chest. "Don't move, man. You'll open that wound again, and this time you'll probably bleed out."

"Where are you taking me?" Vick repeated. If his voice had been windy sounding before, now it was absolutely *wheezy*.

"We're taking you to the hospital," Sam assured him. "I promise. Now... back to Hannah."

Vick shook his head. "She wasn't *supposed* to be part of this at all. Yang told me she stumbled across some exchanges between him and his U.S. contact. So Yang had me back hack her computer, destroy the report she sent to her superiors, and plant evidence against her. But just to shut her up and keep her quiet until we could finish."

"And how do ya reckon Yang knew about Red Square and their plot to hijack the Dominion Pipeline?" Fisher asked. "It never occurred to ya that Yang might be part of *that* scheme as well? That he might be trying to disrupt our country's infrastructure on multiple fronts?"

Vick's eyes tracked back and forth as he considered things. Eventually, he screwed tight his lids and pressed his fingers to his eyes. "Yang was so convincing. He said Bishop was—"

"Wait," Sam interrupted, the hairs on the back of his neck lifting. "Did you say *Bishop?*"

But Vick chose that moment to pass the fuck out. His arm fell to the seat. His head lolled to the side. And his mouth fell open.

At least Sam *hoped* the bastard was only unconscious. He pressed two fingers to Vick's carotid and heaved a sigh of relief when he felt an answering *thud.*

"Did he say *Bishop?*" Hannah's eyes seemed to take up her whole face. Disbelief colored her voice. "As in...*the* Bishop? The former secretary to the director of the FBI? The guy we took down months ago?"

Sam was a little disbelieving himself. "No way that was coincidence, right?"

"We're going to have to talk about that later," Eliza jumped in. "We're sixty seconds out from the hospital and I need to know what the plan is."

"Plan?" Hannah frowned.

"If we go into a hospital with an unconscious man sporting a bullet wound, the feds will be called. The *real* feds. They're going to want to know who we are," Eliza explained.

"So we drop him off outside the emergency room and haul ass to the airport," Fisher said. "We can be on the plane headed back to Chicago, and Mac and Delilah can switch out the plates on this bad boy"—he patted the top of the seat in front of him—"before anyone here thinks to start askin' questions."

"It could work." Eliza nodded.

"Afterward," Sam added, "we'll call your pops, fill him in on what's happened and *why* we had come down here and did what we did. He can pull all his strings to cover any tracks we left behind."

Sam didn't catch Eliza's grimace. He was too busy watching Hannah's eyebrows pull down over her nose as she glanced over at Eliza. "Who's your pops?"

Fuck. He hadn't meant to let that slip.

Hannah picked up on the silence that permeated the inside of the vehicle and her frown deepened. She looked from Eliza to Fisher to Sam. "Who's her dad?"

"The chief of staff to the president of the United States," Eliza admitted hoarsely.

Hannah's mouth fell open. "So *that's* how you guys were able to get on a conference call with the FBI director when we were proving Grace..." She trailed off and shook her head. "I'd been *wondering* how it was you made that happen. Guess it helps to have family in high places, huh?"

Before Eliza could answer, Hannah turned in her seat and pinned Sam with a look. Her mouth was flat, her eyes troubled when she asked, "Do I actually know *anything* about you anymore?"

It was a rhetorical question. Which was why he didn't bother answering it.

But if he *had* answered he would've told her... *You know everything about me that matters, sweetheart. Except for maybe the part where I've gone and fallen in love with you.*

CHAPTER 28

Dell Seton Hospital

Vinny came awake at the sound of a door closing in the distance.

Er…maybe *came awake* was too strong a phrase. At best he was *fuzzily conscious*. His mind felt like it was wrapped in cotton.

What day is it?

Where am I?

He couldn't remember much except his name was Vincent Romano. He lived with his grandmother in New York City. And…

The cotton isn't only in my head. It's in my mouth too.

He tried to swallow and couldn't. Tried to lick his lips but his tongue got stuck to the roof of his mouth.

"Water," he said—or, rather, *rasped*—frowning in confusion when he heard his voice echo around the room.

He screwed his closed eyes tighter. Trying to concentrate. Trying to make sense of time and space and *himself*.

He wasn't in the back room of his nanna's walkup. That much was clear. There was no familiar *hum* and *honk* of traffic outside. No comforting scent of his grandmother's favorite lemon Pledge. No soft yellow glow from her prized Tiffany lamp pressing against his eyelids.

Unfamiliar voices sounded from somewhere nearby. They competed with the distant ringing of a telephone and the closer sounds of mysterious machines humming and beeping. The harsh smell of cleaning products mixed with the unforgettable stench of Betadine. And the light beating against his lids was severe enough to make him frown.

Something told him to keep his eyes shut. An ominous feeling that assured him he should cling to the last vestiges of oblivion for as long as possible. But curiosity, and a sense of desperation, won out in the end.

Blinking open his eyes was more difficult than it should have been. Each lid felt like it weighed ten pounds. But once his eyes adjusted, he instantly realized where he was.

A hospital.

But why?

Had he gotten into an accident? Had he been nailed by a yellow cab while jaywalking and—

It was like someone flipped a switch inside his head. Everything came rushing back with sickening clarity.

Yang. The plan to plant the malware. The months in Texas. Getting *shot*.

It was as if the pain had held off until he could remember its source. Suddenly, he was racked by a dull agony that began at his shoulder and radiated down the length of his arm.

Breathing through his nose because breathing through his mouth only dried it further, he glanced down and noted his shoulder was wrapped in a large, white bandage. There was an IV needle shoved into the back of his hand, administering a clear liquid. And the blue hospital blanket someone—probably some kind nurse—had pulled up to his chest was thin and faded from having been washed a thousand times in industrial strength detergent.

He racked his brain, searching for a memory of what'd happened to him after the car ride to the hospital. But blankness—deep, abiding blackness—was all he could recall.

Where are the people who brought me here? he wondered anxiously, his breaths coming hard and fast as he looked around the room. He half expected them to hop out of the shadows to pepper him with more questions and tell him again what an idiot he'd been.

But he was alone. His only companion was the bag of IV fluid hanging from a silver pole beside his hospital bed. Which was a relief.

Of course, that relief was short-lived when he realized that because he'd come into the emergency department with a bullet wound, the cops would soon show up and start asking questions. Questions he wasn't ready to answer. Questions he wasn't even sure he had the answers to.

And the answers he *did* have? Well, they were going to be *such* a disappointment to his grandmother.

He'd been able to hide his criminal activity from her over the years. But there was no way to hide this. No way to pretend he hadn't been *shot* and—

His thoughts came to a screeching halt when the door to his room opened. He blinked in disbelief when he saw it was Yang who'd come to visit him. Yang with that eerily soft smile that was incongruous when paired with his hard, flinty eyes.

Vinny tried to push up in his hospital bed. But movement caused the pain in his shoulder to grow fangs that ripped and slashed. So he remained flat on his back and watched as Yang slowly made his way around to the side of the bed.

"What are you—" Vinny's voice was little more than a dry rasp. He worked up what saliva he could and tried again. "What are you doing here?"

Yang cocked his head.

For some reason, Vinny was reminded of a snake that was about to strike. Apprehension prickled over his skin.

"I have been here all along." Yang's eerily soft smile widened. "Keeping an eye on you, Vincent."

It was odd to hear his real name spoken aloud. He'd been *Vick* for so long he'd kind of gotten used to the name. What was odder still, was the ominous note in Yang's voice.

Vinny felt icy fingernails drag up his spine.

"What happened?" he asked Yang, trying to tamp down the terror growing inside him. If Yang was a snake about to strike, then Vinny was the rabbit backed into a corner. "How did that D.O.D woman—"

His words died in his throat when Yang pulled a syringe from his pocket. Before he could utter a word, Yang injected whatever was in the syringe straight into his IV bag.

Horror and self-preservation mixed together and took over. Vinny reached for the IV in his hand, prepared to rip it out. But Yang stopped him by grabbing his wrist in a grip as hard and as unforgiving as iron.

For such a small man, Yang was unimaginably strong.

Vinny opened his mouth to scream, to alert the doctors and nurses to his plight, but Yang slapped a warm, dry palm over his mouth, stopping the sound from traveling more than a few feet. Even still, the muffled yell flayed Vinny's parched throat raw.

He tried shaking his head. But Yang's hand stayed over his mouth. He tried flopping like a fish—adrenaline had dulled his pain—but Yang threw his body over the top of him, keeping him pinned to the bed. And then...

He felt it.

Felt that first warm rush hit his veins. Felt his limbs grow heavy. Felt his breaths grow shallow at the same time the pounding of his heart slowed to a dull *thud*.

Within moments, he was paralyzed. Unable to move. Unable to look away from Yang's face as the man stood over him, smiling that terrible smile.

What he had mistaken as hardness in Yang's eyes was actually coldness. Deadness. *Evil.*

Vincent Romano's last thought before he left this world was...

The mysterious people in the car were right. I was a fool.

CHAPTER 29

Black Knights Inc.

Sam was tired.

No. Not tired. Tired was what he felt at the end of a hard day's work, a two-a-day baseball practice, or a fully geared-up training exercise.

What he felt now went *beyond* tired. It was a fatigue that reached all the way down to his blood and bones.

Which was probably partially to blame for the impatience in his voice when he barked, "Sir, it wasn't Eliza's fault."

They'd hopped on a call with the chief of staff five minutes after walking through BKI's front door. And for the last thirty minutes, he'd listened with gritted teeth as the old fart raked his daughter over the coals.

The poor woman had been gripping the locket around her neck so hard, Sam worried she'd bend the thing.

"Hannah is *my* friend," he continued. "*I'm* the one who made the decision to help her. Eliza was simply being a good teammate by keeping her cards close to her vest until I knew for sure what hand we were playing."

They were seated around the conference table in the war room. Ozzie had placed laptops in front of them for their video conference call. And it was the middle of the day, but Becky had laid off the heavy machinery so as not to disturb them. Which meant the only sounds to break the silence that followed Sam's declaration were the gentle hum of a drill being used down in the shop and Boss's muffled voice as he took a call in his office.

"I still should have been informed." Leonard Meadows's jaw was hard on the screen. But not as hard as his eyes.

Yeah, well, wish in one hand and shit in the other, and just see which one fills up faster, Sam thought coldly.

He'd never been a big fan of Eliza's old man. The dude was a politician through and through. Always out to save his own ass or advance his own career.

"You'd have told us to hand Hannah over to the FBI and let the feds deal with the threat to Texas," he countered.

Meadows opened his mouth, no doubt to do more grouching and grandstanding, but Hannah was wilting beside Sam. She sank lower in her chair the longer the video call lasted. And her expression had changed from tired to downright *haggard*. He stopped Meadows by lifting his hand, palm-out.

"Sir"—he worked hard to keep his growing exasperation from coming across in his tone, but he wasn't sure he succeeded—"I understand I overstepped some bounds on this one and that I dragged my coworkers with me, your daughter included. And I understand in order to keep your daughter's job here with us a secret from the various alphabet agencies who'll no doubt be investigating this matter, you're gonna have a bit of a mess to clean up. But the simple truth is, if we'd waited to pass along the information we had, if we'd hesitated even a couple more hours to act, Texas would be going dark as we speak."

His own jaw hardened as he added, "The mole the Chinese put inside the plant was going to upload the malware today. *This morning*." He pulled out the thumb drive they'd taken off the custodian and brandished it in front of the laptop's camera. "Ozzie has confirmed this carries the malicious code."

He took a deep breath and the smells of home, ground metal and bitter coffee, tunneled up his nose. He usually took comfort in them. But right then, they only reminded him how tired he was, and how much he wanted to *end* this conversation.

"Now," he finished, "instead of having a national emergency on your hands, you have a suspect whom you can interrogate to your heart's content." He made a face. "Not that I think the sorry S.O.B will be able to give you much. From what I got outta him, he was nothing but a patsy. Still, it doesn't hurt to try."

"Unfortunately"—Meadows shuffled papers on his desk—"if Mr. Romano knew more than he was able to tell you, we'll never hear it. The man is dead."

"Dead?" Sam blinked uncomprehendingly. "No." He shook his head, horror filling his chest at the thought of his misplaced bullet ending the man's life. As a precision shooter, he prided himself in knowing that each and every one of his kills had been intentional and that he'd never taken down anyone he hadn't meant to. "That can't be right. We stopped his bleeding. He was *unconscious* when we dropped him at the ER, but he was still very much *alive*."

Meadows glanced up and his mouth tightened into a thin line. "He's not now. I called the local FBI office down in Austin as soon as Eliza let me know what happened, right before you all jumped on the plane back to Chicago. I asked them to guard Mr. Romano until he regained consciousness and then—" he made a rolling motion with his hand "—interrogate him accordingly. Vincent died before they could get there."

"Vincent?" Fisher chimed in. "I thought his name was Vick."

More shuffling of papers. More frowning from the chief of staff. Finally, he said, "Apparently, he was using an alias. His fingerprints revealed he was actually Vincent Romano, arrested a few years ago on some sort of credit card scheme. Paid a fine. Did some community service hours."

Something about Vick's…uh…*Vincent's* death didn't sit right with Sam. And not just because he'd been the one to pull the trigger.

"What did he die of?" he asked. "Blood loss?"

Meadows shook his head. "Not according to the attending physician. She's guessing it was a heart attack or stroke. But we'll know more after the autopsy results come back."

"Shit." Sam ran a hand over his beard…uh…his stubble. It was odd to reach up and find himself void of facial hair. Setting aside his feelings regarding the part he potentially played in Romano's death, he focused on the more important matter at hand. "So we've hit a dead end when it comes to finding out if he knew anything more about Bishop."

"Bishop?" Meadows barked, his face contorting into a scowl so fierce it gave him jowls like a bulldog.

"Oh." Eliza nodded, still gripping her locket. "Right. In all the hubbub I forgot to tell you about that part. Vick…uh…*Vincent* mentioned his Chinese contact, Yang, was working with an American counterpart. A man Vincent said was named Bishop. We have it all on video. I'll send it over to you now." She hit a few keys on her laptop, ostensibly emailing to her father the video Fish had taken of the custodian's confession.

"B-but Bishop is dead," Meadows sputtered. "He couldn't handle the thought of being labeled a traitor and offed himself before he could stand trial."

"Exactly," Fisher nodded. "Which means Yang had to have been feedin' Vincent a line of dog doo. Because the alternative is that the man we fingered in the Grace Jackson plot wasn't the real mastermind but simply a pawn. Which would mean the *real* Bishop, the *real* threat to this country, is still out there somewhere pullin' strings."

"Christ." Meadows ran a hand through his thick thatch of salt-and-pepper hair. "This entire situation keeps getting worse."

"You'll need to inform the FBI about Vincent's mention of Bishop," Eliza said. "Send them the video we took. They're going to need to look into it."

Besides the death grip on her locket, Eliza was doing a bang-up job of keeping her composure in the face of her father's displeasure. Sam was proud of her.

"I'll add it to the list of chores I have to do to cover your tracks down in Texas," Meadows gritted through clenched teeth. "There's the security footage at the plant and the hospital that needs to be wiped. Is there anything else I should know about? Any *other* little tidbit you've left out, dear daughter of mine?"

The venom in the man's voice made Sam wince. But Eliza only shook her head. "That's it. You know all of it from top to bottom."

"Except for there still remains the question of Hannah's innocence," Sam interjected. "Or rather, it's not a question anymore. It's a fact. You have Vincent's video confession to prove it."

When Meadows took a sip from his coffee, it prompted Sam to do the same. But the brew was bitter on his tongue and burned in his belly.

Mostly because, from the corner of his eye, he saw Hannah wilt further.

Peanut, ever sensitive to the needs of any woman in his vicinity, hopped into her lap and started making biscuits on her thighs. His purr sounded particularly soft and content, as if he was trying to counteract the harshness of Meadows's tone.

Half the time I wanna kill that cat, Sam thought as Hannah buried her face in the feline's scruff. *The other half I wanna kiss his furry face.*

"I'll make sure the FBI gets the video of Romano admitting to framing Miss Blue, along with my assurances that the information there should be considered vetted and factual," Meadows promised gruffly.

This had Hannah straightening in her chair. But she kept scratching the base of Peanut's tail, making the cat up his biscuit production. The nervous hope in her voice nearly broke Sam's heart. "Does that mean I can go home?"

Meadows nodded, and if Sam hadn't been sitting right beside her, he'd have missed the little hiccupping sound of happiness Hannah made. He tried not to take it personally that she couldn't wait to get hell and gone away from Black Knights Inc.

"What about Red Square and the Dominion Pipeline?" Ozzie asked. "Have you heard anything more on that front?"

Meadows's scowl turned him into a bulldog again. "You can thank Miss Blue for foiling that plot as well. Or rather, you can thank her vigilante friends."

Hannah's confused expression matched the faces of those around her. "Wait." She sat up straighter. "What?"

"Seems the same people who gave you the backdoor into the FBI servers all those months ago when you were looking for evidence to clear Grace Beacham's name also had a backdoor into Dominion's system. They were able to squash the incursion and wrestle control of the pipeline back from Red Square."

"Kerberos…" Hannah breathed the name of the online white-hat hacker group with the reverence most people reserved for a deity.

"That'd be them," Meadows said with a snarl.

"If the oil supply to the East Coast is safe," Ozzie piped up, "why are you still wearing a face like someone shit in your sundae?"

"Because we don't know who these Kerberos folks are." Meadows gave his head a forceful shake. "And they seem able to access information and closed systems with impunity. Which means they're privy to classified intel that *no* one outside those within the government who've been vetted should be privy to. It's *beyond* dangerous; it's downright *terrifying*."

"But they do good work," Hannah insisted.

"For *now*," Meadows came back immediately, not trying to hide his political nature which undoubtedly saw conspiracies and enemies around every corner.

"And the country is safe," she insisted.

"This country is *never* safe, Miss Blue," Meadows scoffed. "Texas may have power and the East Coast may have fuel today, but that could all change tomorrow. Our enemies are vast and grow smarter by the day."

For a while after that, everyone was silent. Then the chief of staff began giving further instructions to Ozzie and Eliza. But Sam stopped listening. Instead, he squeezed Hannah's hand, hoping to lend her a little of his strength because it was clear—to him anyway—that the last thread that'd been holding her together frayed now that the double threats to the country had been dealt with and now that her good name had been restored.

In the last twenty-four hours, the poor woman had been arrested, had survived a harrowing escape from FBI custody, had nearly frozen to death, had raced to Texas to save the state from would-be destruction, and had been held hostage and stabbed.

Or more like *cut*. On the flight home he'd cleaned her up and placed a butterfly bandage over the inch-long gash on her flank. It didn't need stitches, but it might leave a little scar to mark the occasion.

Oh! He snapped imaginary fingers. *And she also watched a man get shot and nearly bleed out.*

If anyone deserved a good, old-fashioned emotional breakdown, it was Hurricane Hannah.

As if on cue, the moment Ozzie cut the secure connection on the video call and all their screens went dark, she collapsed back in her chair. Her face screwed up as a little whimper seeped out of her.

"Shoo. My turn." Sam swiped at Peanut, who hissed his disgruntlement but hopped off her lap all the same.

Acting on instinct, he lifted her out of her chair and into his lap. Her arms went around his neck. She buried her face in the crook of his shoulder.

And then she really let loose, her whole body shaking with the force of the sobs she tried to hold in.

The others were quick to discreetly adios themselves. Eliza and Fisher headed up to their rooms and Ozzie made for the stairs leading to the first floor.

Once they were alone, Sam ran his hands up and down Hannah's narrow back in a soothing motion. "It's okay, sweetheart," he whispered. "Get it all out."

The horror of the past day rolled through her in waves. Rolled *out* of her with the force of a tsunami. And all he could think as his heart was squeezed by a painfully tight fist was...

She's right. Who would choose *to live this kind of life?*

CHAPTER 30

I *should be dancing naked in the streets. Shouting from the rooftops. Eating an entire deep-dish pizza to celebrate the end of all this. But all I can seem to do is cry!*

The tears just kept coming. Cups of them. *Buckets* of them.

Why? Hannah wondered hysterically. *What the hell is wrong with me?*

But she knew the answer even as she asked the question.

Despite the relief she felt that her long nightmare had come to an end, despite the pride she felt that she'd managed to *mostly* keep her shit together through it all, she couldn't ignore the indisputable fact that along with her nightmare being over, so was her brief—all too brief—stint as Sam's lover.

Would he continue to see her, *sleep* with her for a while if she gave him the chance? Probably. They enjoyed each other's company, and the chemistry was freakin' phenomenal. But she had no doubt eventually he'd move on from her, in search of that tall, blond, buxom woman of his dreams.

And the longer she allowed herself to be with him, truly *be* with him, the deeper she'd fall in love. And the more the eventual ending would hurt.

Best just to stop this now, she told herself. *It's cleaner. Less complicated. Less likely to absolutely decimate me.*

Of course, the first step to doing that was to dry her damn eyes and get the hell off his lap.

It took a minute and two tries before she could kill the waterworks. But eventually she was able to sit up and scrub the wetness from her cheeks.

The instant her eyes focused on his face, however, his handsome, dear, *wonderful* face, she nearly broke down again.

She meant to thank him for everything. Meant to tell him she'd never be able to repay him for all he'd done for her. But when she opened her mouth, the words that spilled out on a strangled cry were, "C-can I call Cesar and t-tell him I'm okay?"

"Of course, sweetheart."

He tucked a strand of hair behind her ear, his gentleness and care pulverizing her already shattered heart. Reaching into the suit pants he still wore, he pulled out his cell phone.

The Jolly Rancher she'd secreted into his pocket came out with the device. And he bent to retrieve it off the floor.

"I'm going to be three-hundred pounds if you keep doing this," he teased, already untwisting the wrapper.

She could've told him he needn't worry. She could've told him that would be the *last* piece of candy she ever put in his pocket. Instead, she forced a wobbly smile and reached for his cell phone. "May I?" After he handed it to her, she nodded her thanks and finally managed to push up from his lap.

Her fingers shook as she keyed in Cesar's number. But that was nothing compared to how badly her knees trembled when he answered on the first ring and she heard his low, lovely, familiar voice. It hit her ears like a salve and, suddenly, all she cared about was falling into his arms and pouring her heartache into to his sympathetic ear.

"Cesar!" His name came out on a hiccupping sob.

She didn't register Sam steering her toward a chair and gently pressing her into it. She didn't register the myriad questions her roommate peppered her with or that she actually answered them. And she didn't register the slightly sad, slightly resigned look that crossed Sam's face when she told Cesar, "I just want to come home." Glancing up at Sam, she experienced a brief flash of anxiety. "I *can* go home, right? I don't have to stay here until Eliza's dad—"

"Of course you can go home," he cut her off. "You're free to leave anytime."

She was too caught up in her own emotions to hear the disappointment in his voice.

True to his word, ten minutes later he stood with her on the curb in front BKI's massive iron gates. Her borrowed dress and coat had been *more* than enough in Texas, but they weren't cutting it when it came to fending off the icy breath of a Chicago winter.

The sun might be out, and the day was still and windless. But the bitterness of the frigid air had her shoving her hands deep into the coat's pockets and hunching her shoulders forward in a useless effort to ward off the cold as they waited for her cab to arrive.

"Here." Sam pulled his stocking cap off his own head and transferred it to hers, shoving it down over her ears.

She knew her smile was wan and miserable, but she gifted it to him anyway. It was all she had. That, and the heartfelt words… "Thank you, Sam."

"Can't have you losing an ear to frostbite at this point in the game."

"No." She shook her head. "I mean *thank you*. For everything. I don't know what I would've done if you hadn't come racing to my rescue."

He pulled at his ear, the ear she'd licked and nibbled. It was already turning red from the cold. "Seems to me, you mostly rescued yourself. I just provided a few resources to help you along the way and—"

"No, Sam." It hurt to pull her hand from her pocket and expose it to the cold, but she did it to curl her fingers around his forearm and squeeze. "Thank you."

For a long time, she forced herself to hold his gaze. To say with her eyes what she couldn't say with her mouth. Which was that she owed him everything. Her very *life*.

His blue eyes glinted in the sun. "If memory serves, you saved my bacon about six months back. So how's about we call it even?"

The hacking and coding she'd done for him didn't come close to matching all he'd just done for her, all he'd just *risked* for her. But she knew arguing was pointless.

Instead, she nodded and said, "Deal."

He grew quiet then as he looked across the way to the bagel store and coffee shop. It was mid-afternoon. A quiet time in the caffeine trade. Even still, a man in a long coat and a furry trapper hat pushed inside and the bell on the door let out a *tinkle*.

The cheerful sound only highlighted Hannah's torment.

She took the opportunity to study Sam's profile. His straight nose. His razor-edged jaw. She was struck again by how much he reminded her of the *old* Sam now that his beard was gone.

Again, the pang of longing and nostalgia was razor-sharp.

Of course, she was careful to keep her thoughts from her face when he swung back to her, his hot breath creating clouds of condensation in the air.

His serious expression told her he was going to ask something personal, something about their relationship and where it was headed.

Since she wasn't ready to *have* that conversation, she preempted him with, "So what's the real deal with this place anyway?" She flung her hand back to indicate the factory building looming behind them.

A line appeared between his slashing eyebrows. "What do you mean?"

"I mean you have a"—she glanced around to make sure they were alone—"supersecret Bat Cave entrance and the ability to lay your hands on just about anything you want. Oh, and you have a direct line to the chief of staff."

When he opened his mouth, she lifted a hand. "And *yes*, I get that Leonard Meadows is Eliza's father. But there's more to it than that, isn't there?"

A muscle in his jaw ticked. Another began to twitch beneath his eye.

Sighing heavily, she relented. "Never mind. I'm D.O.D, so I know a *that's classified*"—she made air quotes—"face when I see one. Fine. Keep your secrets."

She canted her head and regarded his shuttered expression. Her heart softened at the look in his eyes. It told her he'd happily share all his secrets if he could. And there was peace in that. Happiness, even.

She couldn't have *all* of him. Not in the way she wanted. But he still cared for her. Still liked her and respected her.

She'd hold onto that. Keep that knowledge close to her heart.

"Just...be careful, okay?" She resisted the urge to reach up and smooth the line that'd formed between his dark eyebrows. "Because something tells me you were probably safer on the job when you were a Marine Raider and had a whole platoon to back you up."

She wasn't surprised when he didn't say anything to naysay her, simply smiled and nodded.

For a while after that, they were quiet, listening to the sounds of the city. A distant siren. The honk of a disgruntled driver. The general hum of millions of people going about their lives.

She went to stomp some sensation back into her frozen feet, then immediately regretted the move when her injured pinky toe reminded her of its presence. And *that* reminded her of her knife wound. The thing still throbbed and burned, even all these hours later.

She must've winced because Sam's expression turned worried, his tone even more so when he asked, "You okay?"

No! she wanted to scream. *I went and fell all the way in love with you, you big, wonderful dummy!*

Instead, she blew out another breath. "Nothing a hot shower and twenty-four to forty-eight hours in bed won't solve."

He nodded his understanding. "How 'bout after you're ready to crawl out, I take you for that steak dinner I still owe you."

Tears pricked behind her eyes. There was no more avoiding it. It was time to do what had to be done.

"Let's chalk all this up to what it was and not try to make it more, Sam." When he frowned, she clarified. "I mean, we *like* each other, right? We have history together. Throw in fear and danger and adrenaline, and it's no wonder we fell into bed."

She was surprised at how steady her voice sounded when her kneecaps were Jell-O.

"But let's not try to make this more than it was, okay?" she continued. Taking her hand from her pocket, she waved it between them. "You and me? We're not cut out for the long haul... Are we?"

She hadn't realized she'd been hanging on to a sliver of hope until he shook his head. His voice was rusty-sounding when he admitted, "I don't guess so."

She'd expected that response. Even still, she nearly crumpled into a heap upon hearing it.

"So let's stop it before it really starts," she told him, unable to keep the slight quiver from her voice. "While we can still be friends. And before either of us has the chance to hurt the other."

He opened his mouth to respond, but her taxi zipped next to the curb at that exact moment.

Saved by the cab.

Going up on tiptoe, she pressed a hasty kiss to Sam's cold cheek and whispered, "Thank you again."

For the span of a few heartbeats, he searched her eyes, looking like he wanted to argue with her. But, eventually, he only smiled sadly. "Anything for you, Hurricane Hannah."

If only that were true, she thought wretchedly.

After handing his stocking cap back to him, she turned toward the taxi. Like her dad always said, *there's nothing left but the leaving.*

CHAPTER 31

Kit Kat Lounge
Two months later...

"I'm really not in the mood to be out tonight," Sam grumbled as he stepped from the cab onto the sidewalk in front of the club where Cesar performed.

Two more cabs pulled up behind the one that'd carried him, Fisher, and Eliza to the venue. They disgorged the rest of the BKI crew.

"Come on." Fisher clapped a hand on his shoulder. "We've been doin' back-to-back assignments for weeks now. We *need* a little fun. I'm thinkin' a drag show is just what the doctor ordered."

For weeks after Hannah's ordeal, Sam had wracked his brain for ways they could potentially make a life together.

He could welch on his contract with Madam President—although there were stiff financial consequences associated with that plan. Or they could date casually until such a time as his contract was up. That way she wouldn't have to be truly *invested* in his dangerous life. More like a bystander. Although, *that* plan didn't hold up under scrutiny because he wasn't sure that when it came to Hannah he could *do* casual. Or, alternatively, he could ask her to wait for him, promise to stay friends with the knowledge that, as soon as his days of being a hired gun for the Leader of the Free World were over, they'd begin their lives together.

Or any variation of all the above, he'd desperately thought, more than happy to let *her* choose the path he'd take. Because, the truth was, he was miserable without her.

He'd found the soul that matched his own and living without her felt like someone had reached down his throat and ripped out his insides.

He'd tried texting her, tried calling her, but she'd always had an excuse to cut short the conversation before he could lay out his ideas, lay out his *heart*. And when he'd gotten fed up playing phone tag, he'd even gone to her apartment, determined to make her listen to him. Determined to make her at least *consider* what he had to say.

Unfortunately, Cesar had been the only one home.

"She's been really busy with work and trying to beef up the security inside her department so that what happened to her doesn't happen to anyone else," Cesar had told him as he stood outside their apartment door. *"But I'll tell her you stopped by. I'm sure she'll be sorry she missed you and the opportunity to thank you again for all you did for her."*

It was then Sam had known there was no solution that would work. No solution that would get him Hannah. Because she'd meant it when she said, *"We're not cut out for the long haul together."*

He'd done the only thing he could then. He'd respected her position and hadn't tried to contact her since.

Instead, he'd thrown himself into work, desperately searching for anything to fill the gaping hole inside him. He'd even tried to date. He'd let Fisher set him up with some woman he'd met on a dating app. But it'd turned out to be a colossal mistake.

Not that the woman hadn't been warm and charming. She *had* been. But Sam hadn't been able to drum up even an ounce of interest in her.

By the end of the meal, she'd dabbed her lips with her napkin, skewered him with a sharp look, and asked, *"So, who is she?"*

When he'd asked her to clarify, she'd said, *"The woman you've been thinking about all night."*

It was then he'd realized there *was* no way to fill the emptiness inside. That he'd simply have to resign himself to its presence and be grateful that for a short time, he'd known what it was to be made whole. To have met his match. His other half.

My better *half.*

"What are we waiting for?" Grace's voice dragged him from his thoughts. He glanced over to see her rubbing her hands together in excited glee. "Let's go grab some drinks and have some fun!"

The group turned toward the door where a *huge* bouncer with a smile that was nearly as big as his shoulders waited to usher them inside.

Sam remained rooted to the curb, however, looking over the buildings across the way at a sky that held the last lingering shades of sunset.

April in Chicago was a capricious thing. There were days when a man would swear spring was there to stay. The skies would be blue. The breeze would be sweet. And the lake would look placid and perfect. And then… *boom!* Another snowstorm would move in, blanketing the city in white that would quickly turn to gray slush.

At the moment, they were experiencing the former.

He closed his eyes and breathed in the familiar scents of warm concrete, fresh air straight off the lake, and the earthier aromas of the planter boxes that lined the sidewalk at the café next door.

"So…" Sam blinked open his eyes when Fisher nudged him with an elbow. "We doin' this or what?"

"What do I even say to her?" he asked, unable to hide the misery in his voice.

When Fisher had told the group about Cesar's invitation—apparently Fisher and Cesar had exchanged numbers because Cesar was thinking of learning the harmonica for his act—Sam had jumped at the chance, the *excuse*, to see Hannah again.

He'd missed her more than he'd ever missed anyone or any*thing* in his whole sorry life. But now that he was actually about to face her, especially knowing he couldn't have her, the decision to come felt like a huge mistake.

"Who?" Fisher frowned. "Cesarine?"

"No." Sam shook his head impatiently. "*Hannah.*"

"Oh." Fisher blinked. "Did Hannah decide to come? I thought Cesar said she only ever comes on the weekdays because she hates the crush of the weekend crowds."

Sam lifted his eyebrows, feeling simultaneously relieved and wretched. He'd just assumed…

Or maybe I hoped.

Yeah, that was it. Despite everything, he continued to live with the pathetic hope that someday, in some way, they'd run into each other and he'd be able to convince her there had to be a way to make it work.

How pathetic am I?

The bouncer gave each of them a jolly, heavy-handed slap on the back as they entered the club. The bartender, a skinny woman with impossible red hair that matched her lipstick, made them drinks stiff enough to have them coughing on the first sip. And the three tables Cesar had reserved for their group were right up close to the stage.

The bar smelled like sugary drinks, wig powder, and fried foods. And by the time Sam grabbed his seat, Eliza and Fisher were already up to their old antics, squabbling like a couple of kids.

He was about to lay into them when the house lights dimmed. The stage lights came up. And a hush fell over the crowd.

It *was* a crowd. Every table was full and it was standing room only at the back.

"Good evening ladies and gentlemen, all the gays and the theys." The announcer's voice sounded from the speakers. "Please put your hands together for…*Cesarine!*"

The bar exploded with applause as the opening bars of The Weather Girls's "It's Raining Men" filled the space. The curtains slammed wide and suddenly, there was Cesarine in six-inch heels and a yellow raincoat studded with a thousand rhinestones that caught the stage lights and glinted.

For the next forty-five minutes, Sam and the others enjoyed an amazing variety show. There was song. There was dance. And, of course, there was side-splitting comedy.

The drinks kept coming. The appetizers were tasty and fattening. And by the time the first intermission rolled around, Sam was feeling decidedly better about his decision to come out.

Instead of thinking of Hannah every second, he'd only thought of her every other second.

Maybe every third *second.*

It wasn't much. But it was progress. And he'd take it.

"Are you Sam Harwood?" The waitress who'd been quick to refill their drinks placed a hand on his shoulder to get his attention.

"Yes?" He blinked up at her in surprise.

"Cesarine has invited you backstage." The server's grin was genuine and friendly. "If you'll follow me?"

Sam glanced around at his teammates. To a man—and a woman—they made shooing motions with their hands.

Curiosity, and maybe a niggle of apprehension, had him pushing from his seat and following the waitress to the black, soundproof door next to the stage. She opened it and ushered him through with the instructions, "Down the hall and then first door to your right."

When the door closed behind him, the noise from the bar—the house music, laughter, and sounds of *clinking* glasses—was replaced by the gentle notes coming from a nearby radio. After staring dumbly at the closed door for a few seconds, he shrugged and made his way down the hall, stopping at the indicated door. He could hear voices and laughter on the other side.

He knocked, perhaps too quietly, because no one bade him *enter*. Cautiously, he opened the door and poked his head inside.

It was a scene straight out of *The Birdcage*.

A row of vanity tables with bright Hollywood-style lights surrounding their mirrors were arranged along one wall. Wig stands with elaborately styled hair pieces stood on just about every flat surface. There were overflowing makeup bags, feathery boas, and so much sequins, Sam had to squint.

Cesar was at one of the vanities. He'd removed his long, black wig and costume and sat in a wig cap and a silk kimono. At the next vanity over was the Little Edie impersonator who looked so much like Little Edie that Sam had initially done a double take when they'd come on stage.

What made him do a double take *now*, however, was seeing Candy sitting on a fuzzy footstool over in the corner. Her eyes sparkled as she listened to Little Edie regale Cesar with a raucous tale filled with dramatic flourishes and sound effects.

"Candy?" The surprise Sam felt at seeing Hannah's sister was reflected in his voice.

Every head in the room turned his way.

"Sam!" Cesar rushed toward him with hands outstretched in welcome. "I'm so glad you came and brought all your friends!"

"When Fisher passed along the invite, I jumped at the chance to see you perform." Sam allowed Cesar to drag him into the room. And he cautiously accepted the empty vanity chair beside Candy. "Hannah always said I should. And she was right. You were amazing." He turned to include Little Edie. "Both of you. I haven't had this much fun in a long time."

"Thank you, darling," Little Edie cooed. Then Cesar made the introduction and Sam marveled at the surreality of shaking hands with someone who *looked* like Little Edie but whose name, as it turned out, was Dan.

"What in the world are you doing here?" Sam asked Candy, catching her hand between both of his palms and feeling the giant rock on her third finger.

"I came to see Cesar's newest routine. Same as you." She gave his hand a friendly squeeze.

He tried to remember what it had been about her that'd fascinated him as an eighteen-year-old kid, and couldn't quite pinpoint it.

Sure, she was tall and tan and blond, built like the proverbial brick shithouse. But she was also…bland. A cookie cutter cutout of every other tall, tan, buxom blond who made a living as a brand ambassador or as an internet influencer.

Where was the sparkle? The pizzazz?

Where's the purple hair and the devilishly dancing eyes filled with intelligence and biting sarcasm?

"I also came to talk to you," she added and he blinked his confusion.

"We *both* want to talk to you." This from Cesar.

It immediately occurred to him there was only one reason for Cesar and Candy to tag-team him.

"Hannah?" he sat up as his heart tried to beat right out of his chest. "Is she okay? Did something happen?"

Cesar cocked his head in consideration and a terrible dread fell over Sam. "Physically, she's fine," Cesar assured him.

"She won't be fine for long if she keeps hoovering down a pint of ice cream every night," Candy muttered.

Cesar shot Sam's old high school girlfriend a disparaging look.

"What?" Candy lifted her hands. "It's true. Every time I video chat with her, she's face-first in a tub of Ben & Jerry's."

Ignoring her, Cesar grabbed Sam's hand. "But emotionally? Well, *emotionally* our dear, sweet girl is a mess."

"What do you mean?" Sam barely recognized his own voice. It was so hoarse. "Like, PTSD from her ordeal or—"

"More like PTSD from a broken heart," Candy interrupted.

Confusion was the first thing he felt at that pronouncement. Had Hannah met someone in the last two months? The second thing he felt was fury. What sorry sonofabitch would be dumb enough to break her heart?

Then understanding dawned, and the third thing he felt was hope. That damned perpetual hope was back.

Except…he had to be sure he wasn't misunderstanding.

"What do you mean her broken heart?" he cautiously asked. "Who broke her heart?"

"*You*, you big idiot." Candy punched him in the shoulder. "Who do you think?"

"No." He shook his head. "For me to break her heart, she'd have to love me."

"Sam." The look Cesar pinned on him said he thought he might be looking at the densest human ever to walk the planet. "Hannah has been in love with you since she was thirteen."

"No." He shook his head again. His breaths were coming hard and fast because the hope inside him kept trying to grow. He didn't dare let it. Not yet. "She had a crush. It was puppy love."

"Well, it isn't puppy love *now*." Cesar crossed his arms and narrowed his eyes as he regarded Sam. "So the question becomes, what are you going to do about it?"

"But…but…" Sam sputtered, not daring to believe. But *wanting* to. Desperately. "But she said we're not cut out for the long haul together."

Candy punched him in the shoulder again. He really wished she'd stop doing that. Her engagement ring was a weapon. "She only said that to save face. She thinks she's not your type. Not what you're looking for. And so she ended things before you could."

Not my type?

The notion was so absurd, he almost laughed.

His mind went back to those stolen moments down in the Bat Cave and then raced forward to the love they'd made together in his bed. The most delicious, most sensuous love making he'd ever experienced.

"How the hell could she think she's not my type?" His temper flared right along with his nostrils. "I showed her, *more than once*"—he emphasized—"just how *much* my type she is."

He remembered who he was talking to, her best friend and her sister, and lifted a hand. "But that's beside the point. She doesn't want to be with me because of what I do for a living. She mentioned more than once that she hated the thought of living life on the knife's edge."

"Any sane person would say that after being accused of being a criminal conspirator," Cesar scoffed. "After being arrested, after escaping the authorities, after racing down to Texas, and after being taken hostage and stabbed." He cocked his head before adding, "Don't you think?"

Well, yeah. When it was put *that* way.

"At any point did she tell you she didn't love you?" Candy asked. "That she wouldn't be over the moon if you were to say you love her too?"

"Well, *no*. But…but…"

"No buts." Candy punched him in the arm yet *again*. This time he caught her wrist before she could pull back and warned, "I swear, woman, if you do that one more time, I can't promise you'll get to keep this hand."

"Well *someone* needs to smack some sense into you." She sniffed, yanking her hand out of his grip.

"I don't understand," he shook his head, his thoughts a jumble. "*Why* would she think she's not my type?"

"Oh, I don't know. Maybe because she's always felt like the ugly duckling. Maybe because you dated *me*"—Candy pointed to her own chest—"in high school and when it came time to choose a wife, by the sound of things, you picked my twin."

"But that was coincidence," he scoffed. "That doesn't mean—" He stopped and shook his head. "You know what? None of that matters. Because what I'm hearing is that Hannah loves me. Like *loves* me loves me and wants to build a life with me."

Candy nodded. "And wants to have babies with you and watch Coen brothers movies and White Sox baseball with you until you're both old and fat and wrinkled. The question is, do *you* love *her*?"

"Of *course* I do!"

"Told you." Candy punched Cesar this time. "You owe me a winged eye makeup tutorial."

Sam stood so suddenly, his chair toppled over. He didn't notice. His entire existence was focused on one thing and one thing only.

"Where's Hannah?"

CHAPTER 32

728 West Addison Street, Apartment 2B

Hannah was on her second Coen brothers movie marathon in as many weeks when she heard Cesar's keys jiggle in the front door.

What in the world? Did I fall into a time vortex? He shouldn't be home already.

Setting aside her pint of Chubby Hubby, she lifted her cell phone from the end table and checked the time.

No. Not a time vortex. It *was* too early for Cesar to be home.

Something bad must've happened, she thought with alarm, her breaths quickening. Given the hatred leveled against drag queens from certain extremist sectors of the population, she lived in constant fear that the Lounge would be the site of something awful and violent.

Her fear turned to jaw-dropping surprise, however, when the door burst open and it wasn't Cesar standing on the threshold.

It was Sam.

All six-plus feet of worn jeans, leather jacket, and blue eyes that cut through the distance between them like a laser light.

"Sam?" His name squeaked from her as she pushed her sloppy bun, which had fallen behind her ear, back on top of her head. Unsurprisingly, it just fell down behind her ear as soon as she let go of it. "Wh-what are you doing here?"

Her eyes widened as he kicked the door closed behind him and started stomping in her direction. His big, biker boots thudded in rhythm to her heart. The look on his face was…

Mad? Annoyed?

She couldn't quite place it. Then she snapped imaginary fingers as it came to her.

Determined.

Sam was *very* determined.

But determined to do what? she wondered with no small amount of trepidation.

Before she could answer her first question, a second one popped out of her mouth. "How did you get in? Who gave you a key?"

"Cesar." His voice was so deep and delicious. Oh, how she'd missed the sound of it.

He stopped when his shins bumped the edge of the sofa. His breaths were deep and regular, making the front of his biker jacket expand along with his chest. And his eyes had those pinpoint pupils he got when he really focused on something.

Right then, he was focused on her.

She wished her T-shirt—which read: Chickens, the pet that poops breakfast—didn't have a spaghetti stain on it and that she hadn't pulled her comfiest, most raggedy pair of pajama bottoms out of the drawer earlier.

"Why?" she blinked up at him uncomprehendingly, her mind unable to grasp that he was truly *there*. Right *there* in front of her.

Was she dreaming? Or was she dead and this was her version of heaven? Had she fallen asleep and suffocated in her own ice cream?

"Because I need to talk to you, woman."

Good gracious, he looked good. His cheeks were darkened by a tan, proof he'd recently been somewhere sunny. And his beard had grown back. Once again, his square jaw was covered by a thick pelt of crinkly black hair that had felt *amazing* when it'd been brushing the tops of her thighs.

She was pulled from her salacious thoughts when he added, "Because there are some things we need to clear up."

The way he towered above her, hands on hips and looking so big and broad, had her fingers tingling along with…*other* parts of her.

She tried to ignore all of that. "What things?" Unfortunately, her voice was so quiet, he didn't hear her above the sound of Marge's character in *Fargo* saying, *"Oh, you betcha."*

Grabbing the remote, she muted the television, cleared her throat, and tried again. "What things, Sam?"

His expression was unreadable. So she wasn't sure if it was annoyance or impatience she heard in his voice. "Things like whether or not you're in love with me."

Damn you, Cesar!

No doubt she had her illustrious roommate to thank for this late-night visit. Because now that he'd stopped fighting his love for Pete, he thought himself the world's greatest authority on all things romance.

The prideful part of her wanted to lie and say, *No. Whatever gave you that idea?* And cue the innocent eyelash fluttering. But her honest side won out.

Still, she didn't think anyone would blame her for prevaricating. Just a little. "So what if I am?" She stuck out her chin. "It's not like it changes anything."

Something came over his face then. A sort of calmness or…*peace.*

Although, his jaw was still clenched tight when he declared, "Yeah? Well, that's where you're wrong."

Before she had time to figure out what he meant by that, he scooped her off the sofa and into his arms.

"Sam!" Her hands automatically twined behind his neck to steady herself. And when she breathed deep, the smell of sugary cocktails, a cool Chicago night, and *Sam* tunneled up her nose.

"Where's your bedroom?" His words were clipped. He was already stalking down her dimly lit hallway toward the back half of the apartment.

"Why?" she croaked, her fingers instinctively tangling in the hair at his nape. It was longer than when last she'd seen him. So thick and silky soft.

"Because I'm gonna make love to you like I've been dreaming of making love to you for the last two months. And I don't want to mistakenly do that in Cesar's bed. I don't think he'd appreciate it."

Her heart was already pounding, but now it skipped a beat.

He'd spent the last two months thinking of her? Fantasizing about her? *Loving* her?

Okay, that last part she'd thrown in herself. Because, you know, it was the missing piece. The most *important* piece.

But when his mouth sought hers, his lips so warm and hungry, she decided she didn't care. And when he found her room without her giving him any instructions, immediately tossing her onto her unmade bed, she welcomed him on top of her because she decided she'd take him any way she could get him, for as *long* as she could get him.

"You taste like peanut butter and vanilla," he growled approvingly between deep, thorough kisses.

"Chubby Hubby," she told him, closing her eyes and luxuriating while he showed her precisely what he'd been dreaming of doing with her, of doing *to* her.

Ninety minutes and three orgasms later, she lay beside him, dazed and spent.

"This has healed up well." He dragged a finger along the faint white line that was the only souvenir she had from Texas, tickling her in the process.

She giggled and wiggled away from his teasing fingertip. "You did a good job patching me up on the plane."

"Not according to your roommate and sister."

Her eyes had been closed, but at mention of Candy, she blinked them open. She had to work hard not to get distracted by his gloriously muscled, gloriously *male* body stretched out naked beside her. "When did you talk to my sister?"

"Same time I talked with Cesar. Tonight at the club."

He then proceeded to tell her about Cesar's unbeknownst-to-her invitation to the Black Knights to attend a performance, and how her best friend and her big sister had spilled the beans about her being in love with him.

Groaning her humiliation, she pulled the covers over her head. "I'm just going to smother myself with my own shame now. Don't mind me." Then she reconsidered. "No. First I'm going to kill them, *then* I'm going to smother myself."

Sam hooked a finger over the top of the coverlet, pulling it down. "Why kill them? If it weren't for them, I wouldn't be here now. And I think you *want* me here now, or..." He softly cupped her breast, thumbing her nipple and making her gasp. "Am I reading things wrong?"

Her body answered for her. Her nipple instantly hardening. Regardless, she went ahead and added the words, "I want you here. I've *always* wanted you here."

What was the use of playing coy? The jig was up. Might as well shove *all* her chips into the middle of the table.

"Good." There was no mistaking the satisfaction in his voice. "'Cause I don't wanna be anywhere else."

They were the sweetest words. And in other circumstances, they'd have made her heart sing. Under the *current* circumstances? They just made her want to cry.

"But for how long, Sam?" She searched his eyes, those blue eyes she couldn't help but get lost in. "How long before you pack up and leave me for someone else? Someone taller, booby-er, *blonder*?"

"Oh, Hurricane Hannah." He pushed her hair away from her brow, his expression softening. She used to hate that nickname. Now, she wanted to hear him say it a million times over. "There's not a woman on the planet with breasts prettier than yours." He gave her nipple another pass of his thumb as if to prove his words. "And I happen to *like* that you're a short-stack. Easier to throw you on the bed." He cocked a provocative brow. "And why would anyone choose to have blond hair when purple is an option?"

Pretty words again. But she couldn't help noticing... "You didn't answer my question."

"Haven't you guessed the answer?" His eyebrows lifted slightly.

In contrast, her eyebrows slammed together. "No." She shook her head. "Guessed what?"

"That I'm hoping to *never* pack up and leave. That I'm hoping for forever with you. If you'll have me."

His smile was warm. But not as warm as the expression in his eyes.

"What?" The word broke in the middle, getting caught up on her disbelief.

"My sweet girl." He cupped her face in his hands. His callused palms were so warm and wonderful against her cheeks. "Can't you see how much I love you?"

"But I-I'm not your type," she sputtered, blinking her incredulity.

"I beg to differ." He shook his head. "You're warm and witty and wonderful. Beautiful and brave and you have the *best* collection of T-shirts.

Not to mention you have really interesting taste in reading material." He hitched his chin toward the paperback novel lying on her nightstand. The cover showcased a buff blue alien holding a blond-haired woman whose eyes were closed in ecstasy. "I'd be a fool not to want to snap you up and keep you for my own."

She'd stopped breathing. So her words came out wheezy-sounding. "Y-you think I'm beautiful?"

"The most beautiful woman in the world."

Because she was her, her sarcasm and self-deprecation leapt to the forefront. "They say love is blind."

And because he was him, because he'd always had the ability to read her mind, he said again, "I adored you when you were thirteen, Hannah. You always made me laugh, kept me on my toes, and *got* me in a way no one else ever did or ever has since. But the minute you walked back into my life and I saw who the thirteen-year-old girl had grown into, the *amazing* woman she'd become, I was toast. Just…*bam!*" He clapped his hand. "Head over heels. Game over."

And…there it was.

That look she'd been waiting to see her whole life.

The look of happiness and adoration and hope. The look Pete always wore when he gazed at Cesar. The look she'd promised would make her go down on one knee and propose should she ever find it directed at her.

The only thing that kept her from making good on that vow was her fear that if she moved, the spell might be broken. Or she might wake up from her dream.

Truly, she still wasn't totally convinced she wasn't face-first in the Ben & Jerry's.

"Hannah?" She realized she was just lying there, staring at him without blinking, when he said her name. "Do you have anything you want to say about that? About me loving you to pieces?"

Her heart was so full, she could barely breathe. Which was why, despite her mischievous smile, her words were raspy when she recited one of his favorite Coen brothers quotes. "In today's cynical world, it's so hard to take that great leap of faith aboard the ship of love and caring."

His smile grew wide and her heart tripped over itself knowing she'd get to see that smile for the rest of her life.

"*Intolerable Cruelty.*" He correctly named the movie. "One of my faves."

"I know." She grabbed his cheeks and pulled him down so she could whisper against his lips. "I want to take that great leap of faith with you, Sam. You're the only man on the planet I've ever wanted to leap with."

A relieved breath trickled out of him and tickled her lips. And she thought it a wonder he ever could've had doubts about what she felt for him.

"Now." She licked her lips, loving the way his eagle-eyes focused on the movement. "If we're done talking, it's my turn to show *you* all the things *I've* been fantasizing about for the last two months."

When he grunted his approval, she hungrily reclaimed his lips and did just that.

EPILOGUE

Washington D.C.

"This is how I'll be contacting you from here on out," Bishop said to the man who settled beside him on the steps of the Lincoln Memorial. "If Miss Blue stumbling across our correspondence proves anything, it's that we're no longer safe communicating on the dark web."

"I will look for the mark on the bench." The diminutive, hard-eyed bastard that Bishop knew as Yang—although he assumed, like his own, that was a codename—indicated the park bench in the distance where a faint chalk mark marred the end of the seat. "And when I see it, I will wait here to meet you."

Bishop laughed, but there was no humor in it. "Old school. This is how the spies did it before the internet and cell phones."

"Sometimes the old ways are the best ways."

"Mmm," he hummed noncommittally, his eyes taking in the beauty of the early spring day. The world-famous cherry blossoms were in full bloom. And the tourists ambling around the National Mall in jeans and light jackets looked so content and carefree.

It was a lie, of course. Democracy was on the decline. Fascism was on the rise. Archaic laws were being passed, greedy despots were taking office, and books were being banned and burned.

Which means it's all going according to plan, he reassured himself.

The truth was, after Black Knights Inc. foiled the plot in Texas and after Kerberos circumvented Red Square, he'd lost a little faith in himself. Not in the *cause,* but in himself. He'd begun to think he wasn't strong enough, connected enough, *wily* enough to bring about the destruction he so desperately sought.

Because it is only from the ashes that a new nation, a stronger *nation, can rise.*

But looking around, there were signs to give him hope. The graffiti that the campus cops hadn't managed to clean off highlighted the political divide within the country. The way people from opposing sides eyed each other with disgust. The general *hum* of derision in the air.

Rome wasn't built in a day, he told himself. *And America won't be destroyed in a day, either.*

"Any luck identifying who is behind Kerberos?" Yang inquired softly, drawing Bishop's attention back to the moment.

"Unfortunately, no." He shook his head. "Whoever they are, they're good. Too goddamned good."

"And what about Black Knights Inc.?"

"They're more easily dealt with." Bishop ran a hand under his chin. "They think they're safe hiding behind Madam President's skirts. But the truth is, that just makes them more vulnerable. I mean, they assume no one knows about them. But *I* know their secrets and so do you."

"Maybe it is time the world knows too?" Yang slid him a considering look. "Expose them, expose the president and her staff who condone the work they do, and clear off the board with one swipe of your arm?"

"We're not there yet." Bishop narrowed his eyes as two little boys barreled up the steps toward him, both covered in drips of something sticky—ice cream would be his guess—and both sporting grass stains on their knees from where they'd rolled on the lawn like dogs.

He'd always despised children. Had never understood why anyone would choose to have them.

"I still think they can be taken down *without* going for the nuclear option."

"You said they would be finished during that operation in Colombia. You said there was no way for them to escape as outnumbered as they were.

And yet, they did escape in time to fuck up our plans for Texas."

"Patience, Yang." He offered the man a smile that contained zero affection. "Each day this country divides itself more and more. The cracks are growing."

"And you think yourself the wedge?" A dark eyebrow tracked up Yang's forehead.

"For now." Bishop shrugged. "But, when the time is right, I plan to be the hammer."

AUTHOR'S NOTE

As time and society progress, we become aware certain words and phrases that are part of our everyday lexicon actually have problematic origins or can be used to further marginalize already vulnerable readers.

As a writer and a lover of language, I strive every day to educate myself on out-dated, offensive terms and stereotypes, and work to eliminate them from my novels. (We're not talking swear words here, people.) But I'm still learning. And if I screw up, I'd love to be educated and allowed the opportunity to correct any mistakes. Because I truly believe the pen is mightier than the sword.

Or, in simpler terms, *words matter*.

ACKNOWLEDGMENTS

Major thanks to "The Asheville Crew" for keeping me hiking, laughing, and karaokeing. You all save me from atrophying behind the keyboard by forcing me (sometimes unwillingly) out of my pajamas and into the real world. Glad to be on this part of the journey with all of you.

Big hugs to Joyce Lamb for your editorial eye. You told me I didn't need you for this one. But the truth is, all your contributions (the ones you didn't think mattered) made all the difference. The devil is in the details, after all.

As always, props to the people who do the unsung work of getting a book into readers' hands: Marlene Roberts, proofer extraordinaire, Jennifer Johnson, formatter for the stars, and Erin Dameron-Hill for the beautiful cover.

And last but certainly not least, thank YOU, dear readers, for coming back for more Black Knights Inc. I hope you all had as much fun jumping back into the world of motorcycles and mayhem as I did.

OTHER BOOKS BY JULIE ANN WALKER

Made in the USA
Columbia, SC
29 November 2023

27395734R00157